Staccato Publishing
Zimmerman, MN

First US Edition: March 2012
Second Edition: September 2012

Author: HK Savage
Editor: Sara Johnson
Cover: Paragraphic Designs

ISBN: 978-0-9835742-5-5

Printed in the USA

The Path

by HK Savage

Prologue

He knew it wasn't good when the police came to pick him up from Mike's in the middle of the night. Brandon was waiting in the back of the squad car as he was escorted from his buddy's house, still wearing his flannel pants and gray tshirt.

"Hey." Brandon's white chalky skin and sweat-damp hair lent him the air of a man in the throes of a deep and prolonged illness, so different from the proud, athletic near-man he'd been until he'd changed a few months ago.

At first the brooding withdrawal had only been visible in glimpses, masked by the otherwise good nature of a brother well liked by the majority of those in his class as well as on his hockey team. Steadily, the sullen darkness had gained momentum until it became Brandon's prominent disposition.

Faced with this shadow of the brother he'd regarded as a nearly invincible demi-god, Drew was more frightened by the shrunken shoulders and smell of fear marking him than the presence of the officers.

"Hey." He snuck a few guarded glances at the shaking figure beside him, terrified to ask and childishly hoping that by not saying anything he could somehow undo whatever awfulness had been done.

The popcorn in Drew's stomach churned and he tasted the syrupy sweetness of the Slushie he and Mike had so gladly ridden their bikes two miles to buy, thrilled by the lack of parental guidance only a few hours ago. The remnants of its blue raspberry flavor, sour in his throat, threatened to climb back up.

"It's Mom and Dad." Brandon was staring straight ahead. His eyes were unfocused, the words halting and flat.

"Why don't we hold off on this conversation for now?" the officer in the passenger seat, far too young for his paternal tone, intervened, twisting around to give them both a stern appraisal. He nodded to himself after Drew murmured that he would, and Brandon seemed to fold silently in on himself.

The other officer came around the back of the car to the driver's seat. Drew caught the spooked look that passed between the two in the brief flash of the dome light before the door closed. "We're taking you boys to the station, we can talk about it there. Your Mom's sister is on her way from Tampa. She'll be here by morning," the driver told them without turning around.

Drew scooted himself farther back into his seat, sparing a sideways glance at his brother. Forgetting the weakness he saw now, he reached into his memory to find the one of his brother that he sought. Drew mimicked the self-assured fold of Brandon's hands and the cocky set of his jaw. He could be strong like Brandon. Not *this* Brandon, but the one he'd seen break an arm without a tear while taking his bike over a jump. Biting his lip, Drew managed to keep his eyes dry and the fear knotting his insides from running rampant for the remainder of the ride.

At the Peoria Police Department a salt and pepper woman in a plain gray suit and over the top sympathy that put Drew on edge sat them down and bought them sodas. Neither boy drank from his can, both cradled them instead as props. When she began to speak Drew tried to tune her out, listening instead to the determined fizzing of the carbonation against the thin aluminum sides. She spoke up, demanding his attention.

Sighing, Drew forced his gray eyes up to meet hers. The tortoiseshell frames and lenses of her glasses caught the light, washing out the eyes themselves. Drew thought of Peppermint Pattty's sidekick Marcy from the old Peanuts cartoons. His family had never missed an annual showing of the Charles Shulz characters' holiday specials. The knowledge of that ritual now feared lost brought tears prickling back to his eyes and Drew took a deep, shaking breath, holding it until he felt dizzy.

Her eyes flicked over to Brandon who had yet to acknowledge her. Frowning, she saw him as a lost cause and concentrated her attention on the younger brother.

"There's been an incident, Andrew. At your house this evening there was a break-in. As far as we can tell, the burglars didn't know anyone was home, your parents surprised them. I'm sorry, they were killed." She reached a hand across the distance between their chairs to rest her fingertips on Drew's knee.

He had to force himself not to push her hand away. Her touch was more real than her words and he focused on the anger her trespass induced.

Again he studied his brother, deciding how to take the news he'd intuited the second he'd seen the look in his friend's dad's eyes when he'd come to get him from the rec room where they'd been playing video games, blissfully unaware. He'd known from the second he'd seen the officers' pale faces and their refusal to meet his curious gray eyes that this was what they had come to tell him.

Brandon was still staring blankly at a spot over the woman's head. His dark hair had begun to dry in straggly clumps on his forehead, framing his thin, pale face in dark contrast and parted over his ears like an elf from the Tolkien novel Drew read last year in AP English. For the life of him Drew couldn't think of this woman's name. Ignoring the eyeless woman's obvious desire to engage him, Drew sought answers from his brother instead.

"Did you see what happened?" Gray eyes sought his brother's blue ones, the same blue as their father's.

Blinking as if waking from a dream, Brandon turned his head a few inches before he caught himself and went back to staring at his spot on the wall. "I was sleeping. They were quiet."

The social worker in charge of managing this little conference sat up a little taller, withdrawing her bony hand from Drew's knee. Her tight lips told him she did not believe the seventeen year old's explanation. At twelve years old and under the blind worship a kid brother has for his elder sibling, Drew bristled instinctively at her, wishing she would leave and give them some privacy.

"What'd they do?"

At first Brandon didn't seem to hear and the judgmental woman granted them at least a pseudo private exchange. Waiting, Drew began picking at a string on his flannel pants wanting the painful wait to continue as long as possible, not wanting to hear what he needed to about the night that would change everything.

When Brandon's hoarse voice broke the silence, Drew didn't look up or even flinch for fear he would cause Brandon to break off. "They took some of Mom's jewelry from upstairs. Dad never heard them, at least I didn't hear him fighting and there weren't any gunshots or anything. They must've had knives or something. There was so much blood." During his telling Brandon had begun rocking himself. Drew had gone cold.

***

For the next year, while they waited for Brandon to turn eighteen so he could petition for custody of his brother, they lived with their Aunt Christine in Tampa. During that entire time the boys held to an unspoken agreement never to mention their parents or what had happened that night. Brandon said he didn't know anything and Drew believed him, though the police were never fully convinced and brought him in on more than one occasion. The lack of evidence linking their older son to Mr. and Mrs. Carter's deaths precluded law enforcement from pursuing charges and the case remained unsolved. There was no way one person could have inflicted so much damage they said, not with that little evidence of a struggle and there was never an accomplice tied to Brandon as a suspect.

Drew didn't see his parents' bodies, they were cremated before the funerals. Nor did he ever step foot in the house again. To think of them or the home where he'd grown up sullied in such a way was something he couldn't handle. It was enough to know they were gone and curiosity could not outweigh his need for a pure memory of his childhood, now gone with their loss. It was a long while before he felt the need to know the details of what had happened. And with that knowledge came the soul-crushing realization that he could never succeed in erasing those images from his brain, try as he might, from that moment on.

Chapter 1

"Cassie, the Directors and I have spoken and we are concerned by your continued inability to perform competently in the field." Anna Saraferas came around her desk to lean on it, crossing her arms and looking every bit a model for conservative women's clothing as opposed to the less glamorous position she maintained. Her Greek roots were allowing the woman to age gracefully. The long dark hair pulled back into a sleek chignon held no traces of gray and her olive skin remained smooth and unwrinkled, the cut of the charcoal suit she wore accentuated her still enviable figure with the heels pushing her close to a goddess-like six feet.

Anna was a powerful woman and she carried the burden of her office well. For the last four years she had been the Supervisor in Charge of Investigators working for the organization solely responsible for keeping practitioners of magick free from mass persecution and policing their society to prevent the use of dark magick. In other words, she was responsible for the whole of the witches' police force if one were to translate it into layman's terms.

Tutela ab Veritas was the name the original three Directors came up with for the organization after the Crusades. It was during the first wave of holy wars, later to be dubbed The Crusades, in which practitioners were abused mightily. The losses they suffered finally pushed the society to hide the practice of everyday magick from the whole of the non-magickal world.

Veritas, as it was commonly known, sent out triads of investigators whenever and wherever they received reports or saw mention in the media of "unexplainable occurrences" worldwide. Occurrences that might threaten to expose their world, opening them up once again to the fearful wrath of non-magickal folk known in magickal circles as "regulars."

In the face of Anna's doubt of her abilities Cassie sat silently, staring at the plaques and awards from Anna's days as an Agent. Numerous, they lined the far wall behind the desk and gave Cassie something to pretend to study while keeping a mask of cool indifference firmly in place. There was nothing for her to say.

They both knew the only reason she'd been passed out of the Academy after three years of failed academics was because the professors didn't want to admit what *she* already knew, that the only known mixed blood witch to get this far in a century was a dud. They'd essentially given up on her in the classroom, thrown her out into the field, and left her under the tutelage of two understandably reticent partners to either sink or swim. And now, six months later, Cassie had shown no improvement after more than twenty cases. Not only was she dead weight, she had nearly gotten herself and her partner Quan killed when she'd failed in the simple task of getting out of the way while her partners apprehended a dark practitioner just last week. Honestly, she had been expecting this meeting with Anna long before this most recent mishap.

Watching Anna's unlined face twist in consternation, Cassie felt compelled to answer. Though she was at a loss for what to say, muttering an inadequate, "I'm sorry."

Anna's lips pressed tightly together, she had been expecting more. "The Directors were under the impression that we should be seeing something from you by now." She shook her head, the light above shining brightly on the glossy black tresses. Anna was not one to willingly put her Agents in danger by pairing them with a "maybe." The elegant supervisor had not hidden her concerns for the safety of Cassie's partners from the day of the initial assignment. Only the absolute power of the Directors and their search for greater and more powerful witches had gotten Cassie this far. "They have left it up to my discretion to determine whether there will continue to be a place for you with Veritas."

Cassie felt her stomach tighten and frowned to keep from breaking the stoic facade. She did not want to have to tell her father she'd failed, not like this. Her getting off the reservation was important to him, it had been important to her mother. He'd gone against his mother's and the tribe's wishes at great personal cost for this. "Yes Ma'am."

Gliding back to her tall black leather chair behind the sleek custom desk rumored to have set her back her entire first paycheck, Anna folded her hands in her lap and sat back, the queen surveying one of her drones and none too happy with what she was seeing. "I am sorry Cassie." The wide mouth split into a cool smile. "As you know, witches with your unique blend of gifts can be a challenge to bring along."

Cassie nodded because she was supposed to.

"The Directors and I feel six months has been ample time to prove yourself capable as an investigator. But from what I've seen, unless you can bring something more to the table, I'm afraid we are going to have to face the fact that field work is not a good fit for you." Anna's firm countenance softened, as did her tone. "Consider yourself on probation, your next assignment will be your last chance."

"Of course." Swallowing hard, Cassie put her hands down on the arms of the chair and heaved her body up. No words were available for disagreeing with her boss' honest dressing down, although that didn't mean she had to let her disappointment show. "I appreciate the opportunity you've given me here and I'm sorry if I've been a burden for Quan and Julia." Her two partners were some of the best in the field. Surely their careers would survive the hiccup of being tangled up with hers for this brief snippet.

"I'm sure you haven't been a burden, Cassie. Julia and Quan have never said a bad word about you."

There was no way that was true.

"I hope this next mission will be a success for you." Anna gave her a tight smile and turned to face her computer, signaling the end of their chat.

"Thank you Ma'am." Cassie bobbed her head, feeling her newly shortened black ponytail bounce gaily with the gesture. Automatically, she ran a hand across her brow to push back the bangs that once swept across her forehead, though they currently rested above her black brows after a minor accident involving a spell gone awry. Her new layers required significant numbers of bobby pins to craft the ponytail she always wore, and her bangs had yet to learn that they needed to do something other than hang straight down or part in the middle of her forehead.

"Oh, Cassie." Anna looked up, a pen poised over the thick stack of parchment papers the Directors insisted upon using, saying they gave the company credibility. Like there was another organization out there managing witch affairs that they needed to compete with. "Keep your phone on, your team moves when we get confirmation on final details."

With one more cursory head bob and nearly inaudible "ma'am." Cassie ducked out of the office, closing the frosted glass door behind her. The commercial gray carpet muffled her steps as she made her way to the silver doored elevator for what was likely the last time. With the last assignment on deck, the clock was ticking on Cassie's short and disastrous career with Veritas.

The lack of wood anywhere except in the individual offices was intentional. A large number of the witches in Veritas' employ were elemental, drawing power from nature. In an effort to keep the building neutral territory, all the materials used were synthetic with the exception of the Supervisors' offices. Even the materials that looked like metal were actually specially reinforced polymers and space age materials no known witch could draw power from, thereby giving her or him an unfair advantage.

Only inside the privacy of their offices were the Supervisors, with the long hours and energy-sucking work they often had to conduct, allowed to bolster their reserves with whatever power supplies they needed to manage their performance. Fortunately, Anna was an earth witch and the basswood her desk had been carved from provided that extra jolt for her. Cassie had heard of a supervisor who had been Hindu and worshipped Kali, the most fierce form of the Goddess. She allegedly kept an aquarium full of rats for the occasional "pick me up" sacrifice whether she had someone in her office or not.

Not shy of blood, Cassie did have the strong respect for life her Grandmother and Mother had instilled from birth. It had been the only commonality of the teachings from both branches of her family tree and the one that had ingrained itself the deepest. Life was to be protected and held dear above all else. It was also the main reason Grandmother had broken with her son and Cassie when he had announced Cassie's acceptance to the Academy. Grandmother did not believe that a career with Veritas would allow her granddaughter to keep her soul clean and her path to the ancestors clear.

"Without the ability to speak to our ancestors, we soon lose our way, Little Sparrow." Grandmother always used her tribal name. "You cannot follow your own path if someone else is choosing it for you."

Dreading having to face her Grandmother, more even than her father, when she returned home with her career gone flat, Cassie cast off the image of their faces in favor of mentally working through what she had left in her bank account while she exited through the high glass-domed atrium.

In minutes she was sitting behind the wheel of her sunfaded yellow beetle feeling four decades older than her twenty-four years. Sighing, she turned the key and waited. It took its usual mixture of repeat efforts with the key, gas pedal and prayer before the small engine shuddered to life.

Her concern for finances had nothing to do with the state of her transportation. Most of the money she earned went home to help her family with the house that always seemed to be leaking from somewhere or was settling and cracking in new and unusual ways. In a perfect world she'd be able to buy them a new house altogether, but this world was far from perfect and all she could manage was to keep propping up the old one on her junior investigator salary. It would have been her promotion to fully licensed field investigator that would have brought with it the money to finally lift her family out of the poverty her father wore as a sign of personal disgrace and the one he'd sworn to her mother on her deathbed not to let their only child fall into. It had been that promise that had shored up her father's will when he'd held his ground against his raging mother, confirming that Cassie would not be assuming the role of Shaman as the women of their bloodline usually did, but would follow a different path with those from her mother's world.

Chapter 2

At home, Cassie gathered the things she needed and put them in a small pile in the middle of the room before she lit some sweetgrass and tried to still her thoughts. It was an undertaking given the chaos of her mind and whirling emotions, they kept taking her thoughts and running with them in an endless game of "what if." Her mother Veronica and Cassie's teachers had called it Grounding and Centering, saying it was essential to any spell. Her grandmother had called it hooey.

As Medicine Woman for her tribe, Barbara Porter, also known as Singing Bird had taken over Cassie's magickal education after her mother passed away. She'd been relentless in trying to eradicate all of her daughter in law's teachings to instill her own in their place. The school had gone in yet a third direction, attempting to make rigid the more flowing teachings of her family members. Cassie struggled with both, resulting in a confused mess of rules and "feel" that had her doubting herself at every turn.

School and her mother had agreed on the necessity of this first step so Cassie figured there had to be some validity to it. Hoping to find some success at some point, Cassie began each spell by feeling herself first root to the physical place, then let her consciousness become clear.

She closed her physical eyes to see only from the one in her mind. Envisioning the same peaceful waters her mother had taught her to use as her focus, she could feel her body becoming light as she let go to float adrift, losing the sense of her physical body until only thought remained. Then she cast her circle of protection, feeling a pop when it closed around her. That done she slowly, cautiously, opened her eyes to see that the sweetgrass had burned down only an inch. She was getting faster; that was good, though she still moved carefully in fear any sudden move would break her painstakingly laid barrier, which protected her from any outside influences. Out of habit her fingers brushed past the new bangs, needlessly sweeping them aside.

Holding her movements to the barest minimum, Cassie struggled to keep her mind from returning to its physical senses. The tedium of ritual and ceremony was not her strength; none of this was. The energy of the circle wavered and Cassie took a breath to clear her mind.

The fingers she watched light the candles were as unfamiliar to her conscious thoughts as those of a stranger. Seeking clarity and control of her powers, she'd selected white and orange candles with those properties and had set them around herself in a circle.

Just as Veronica had taught her as a young girl, Cassie began to mutter the words, guiding the energy she was pulling from the elements. The Fire of the flame and the Water from the cup she'd brought as well as her nature, the Air around her and the Earth beneath; she drew it all into her being as the center point in a wheel of energy flowing around her. It was essential for her to acknowledge the elements, but she specifically remained tied to the water like her mother had shown her, feeling the presence of the others while keeping them at the edges of her circle, guarding yet not entering. Only Water was welcomed inside, which was why she brought the cup.

It was how her mother and her mother's mother down the matriarchal line as far as the stories went, had all controlled their power. To ground and pull through the element tied to their energy. There had never been a question of how Cassie would control hers because she was a woman from her mother's family and it was as much a part of them as their magick itself.

The air around her moved in waves, the energy gathering within her circle pricked at her skin, the air itself becoming cool and damp with faint drops of dew forming on the thin dark hairs of her arms. The feeling was not quite right, not the warm, comfortable feeling her mother said she would feel, the feeling of homecoming. No, Cassie had the distinct impression she was being allowed a grudging use only and, at the slightest misstep, the power she struggled to find would evaporate back into the air itself. Her tongue flicked over her lips nervously.

Frowning unconsciously in concentration, Cassie reached out. She stretched her energy, opening a door psychically by speaking the words of a prayer to the oak tree, a tree sacred to her father's people. It was strong, and with its roots running above the ground and below it tied together the elements of both sides of her bloodlines. Cassie had been attempting to use it these past few months to bridge the gap keeping her from her birthright that was her magick and the stability her career would give to her and her family. Failure was not an option.

The new energy of the Earth felt wild and uncontrolled; a hot wind blew over her flesh, heating it with a shiver. Cassie's nerves vibrated as she tried to contain the opposing forces and she felt the all too familiar pull as the new energy beat against the confines of the circle and pushed to force out the Water. It was as much an intruder here as she was only it was wise enough to know it didn't belong. The muscles in her shoulders pinched and Cassie shrugged them back down, breathing in her nose and out her mouth to let go of the tension, stubbornly refusing to give up.

Keeping her tenuous hold on the warring energies raging through her, barely able to keep it all in check, Cassie held out her hand over the mug of bottled water she'd brought in for this purpose. It was a simple elemental spell and one she should be able to cast in the field with minimal trouble. However, it was the very same one that had gone wrong and altered her hairline last week.

Her murmurings were low, it was doubtful anyone more than a few feet away could have heard. The tips of her fingers and palms of her hands began to warm. Without pause, Cassie shifted to place a hand over the ceramic mug and for several hopeful seconds while her hand hovered just above the rim, nothing happened. Steam rose, the outside of the mug grew warm, and Cassie let a smile play at her lips as the heat reached her nearby fingertips.

Then, as soon as her flesh touched the ceramic, the air around her stopped swirling and pressed in on her in an instant, trapping her breath inside her. It bucked her command to go into the contained liquid, the liquid pushing back, refusing the entrance of the Earth's energy she only tenuously controlled. Neither would follow her will and the container cracked audibly, a casualty of the war between them. Feeling the energy surging within, threatening to turn on her, the vibrations heating her skin and oxygen depriving her until she felt faint, Cassie rushed to send it out of her before it consumed her, burning her alive.

Placing both hands on the ground to either side of her, she let all of it rush out into the ground where it belonged, feeling the humming in her body go from maddeningly chaotic to utterly still within seconds. The cup split in two, the handle sliding onto the floor with a tinny crunch as it settled in the small puddle forming around it.

Breathing heavily, Cassie let her head hang down and watched a drop of sweat gather on the tip of her nose before she flicked it away with a growl. "I'm sorry, Mom. I can't do it."

It was an effort to release the circle and blow out the candles. Frustrated, she rose, stretching her stiff legs and gathered the broken pieces that bore evidence of her failure, to discard them in the kitchen garbage. Cassie was getting low on mugs. This was the third one this week.

Feeling the time to admit to her family that she was one of the mixed witches who couldn't even muster enough control to make a cup of tea was rapidly approaching, she took a long look around at her small apartment's living room. It would be a shame to leave and go back to the home her father shared with her grandmother in North Dakota. Grandmother had moved in after the death of Cassie's mother. It wasn't that she was ashamed of the meager quarters on the reservation, it was just that this was the first place she'd been able to call her own. It had been a relief to be out from under her grandmother's intense scrutiny and criticism, which had become unbearable in the months between her acceptance to the Academy and her departure.

The garden level Chicago apartment had a calming presence, an attribute Cassie credited to the underground tributary running from a subterranean stream into the nearby lake. In all, the unit was less than six hundred square feet and had little more than a galley kitchen and the world's smallest tub but the open living room allowed her the right amount of space for practicing her craft.

The paint job she'd gotten permission to do last year had made it feel cozy and warm. The living room and kitchen were a light creamy color, like coffee with too much milk; while her bedroom was a rich chocolate, setting off her butter-colored bedding, making it look sumptuous instead of bland, framed as it was by the dark of the walls and the rich gold flecked in the beige carpet. Only the bathroom remained in its original off white state. Try as she might, Cassie could not bring herself to paint it blue. Even the *color* of water didn't feel like it belonged anywhere near her. It made her feel oddly swollen, as though she'd consumed a bucket's worth in the past hour and it bogged her down with its sloshing weight. Yet more evidence that she had failed to honor her mother's memory and lineage.

Shuffling her feet wearily, Cassie took a self-pitying trudge over to the little half wall separating her narrow kitchen from the living room. She laughingly called the area her dining room though she rarely ate there. Cassie slogged past the small table to the aquarium in the corner. The adjoining space behind her, when not in use as a magickal battleground, was used as a living room and housed a humble greenish brown couch at an angle to a small television on a cart that could be swiveled to face the kitchen when she decided to spend the day cooking up holy water or a big batch of soup. In place of a coffee table, Cassie had stacked two wine boxes with their burned in logos facing out and a matched piece of pine laid across them. A swatch of burgundy silk lay decoratively atop the plank to dress it up; just barely protecting the wood. She'd found pine to be relatively unobtrusive to her energy fields and it was a lot easier to carry and rearrange when she needed more space than the metal or heavy stones some of her fellow agents found strength in.

The aquarium in the corner was lit both by the kitchen and living room lights so she'd never bought one for it specifically, and there was no need for a lid. Its occupant was not one to perform acrobatic feats.

"Hey Bunny," Cassie sang out, feeling her mood lighten. The soft tone of her words soothed her as well as the multicolored creature inside. Sometimes she thought she heard the memory of her mother in her cadence now that she was grown; her father had remarked on how similar her voice was to that of her mother's. Sometimes when she wanted to pretend she wasn't alone, Cassie would talk to her pet and pretend it was her mother lending her advice or comfort.

Reaching a hand into the glass cage, Cassie scooped up the floppy haired peach and white guinea pig chirring happily at her. Pig cradled in the crook of her arm, she moved back around the wall to the fridge where she retrieved a carrot from the bag she'd bought for both herself and her furry roommate.

Fuzzy friend nibbling and chattering happily, Cassie took a seat on the couch letting the overstuffed cushion wrap around her. Her eyes stung, whether from defeat or exhaustion, it mattered not. The result was the same and Cassie let her lids go down, closing the curtain on her day. At some point, the repeated strains of Beethoven's Ode to Joy pulled her out of her slumber and woke Bunny from where she'd nodded off curled up on Cassie's shoulder. Carefully she eased Bunny down onto a cushion and trotted to the table where she grabbed her phone before the last Ode wrapped up its cycle.

"Hello?" There was no hiding the groggy sound of sleep from her voice.

"Did I wake you?" It was Anna and she didn't sound the least bit repentant.

"No," Cassie said what was expected, even if it was nowhere close to believable. "I was just reading."

"Good." Her boss never wasted time with personal trifles. "We've gotten confirmation that the reports of disturbances in the Tampa area are intensifying and we've heard through our Watcher that the source is using a local club to draw energy from the unsuspecting masses. Your triad is expected on the eleven a.m. flight into Tampa tomorrow. Your files will be on the plane, you can familiarize yourselves on the way."

"Thank you Anna." She hung up her phone, returning it softly to the light wood tabletop, stomach clenching in dread at the thought of facing off against another witch so soon. Hopefully she could complete her last mission without getting either of her partners killed. She'd been trying to stay out of the way, minimizing her exposure as a flop as well as avoiding endangering either of them, with some reasonable amount of success. Still, in the end they knew she didn't have what it took to be an investigator. For the first time, Cassie was almost thankful her mother wasn't there to see her fall on her face.

"What do you think, Bunny?" she asked her little friend as she swept her up from the couch, turning the little animal in her hands to face her. Amber eyes regarded small black bulging ones. "Are you going to be lonely while I'm gone?"

Bunny gave a gutteral squeak and wiggled her whiskers, delighting in the attention. She was often left alone for a day or two; if it was going to be longer Cassie's neighbor, an eleven year old girl, came in and took care of her. That meant when she left Cassie would have to put all of her magickal paraphernalia into the hall closet where she'd installed a lock.

If she could do proper magick she could have set it all on a shelf and spelled it to be unappealing, it would have been so much less work. God knows what the neighbor thought she kept in the obvious hiding place, but it couldn't be helped. And when she got home, the unit would need a thorough cleansing to clear out the child's energy. The girl left less than an adult though, which was why Cassie had encouraged her and not her mother to come in.

With a kiss to the top of her peach head and a rub to the ears, Cassie replaced the pig in her glass home. A few extra shakes of food and another cube of hay and Bunny was ready to "batch it" for a few days.

"Good night," she wished the little furball already burrowing into her hut for the night. Cassie envied the simple creature's ability to sleep so easily, she knew that she would not be so lucky.

Chapter 3

"Hey Drew, you done yet?"

"Yeah, be up in a sec." Drew hung up the phone in the downstairs bar and finished counting out the till for the night. The bartender had come up short again. "Damn." He mumbled, shaking his head at the woman's dumb move. Satisfied he had counted it right three times in a row, Drew closed and locked the till. He took the extra cash out to go in the safe; they did their deposits in the mornings given their late hours and large cash amounts. They were less likely to be jacked in the daylight than three a.m. doing a night deposit.

Tired and strung out from a night of schmoozing and keeping things running smoothly on the floor of the club he and his brother ran in downtown Tampa, Drew poured himself a glass of scotch before making his way to the office. It was a ritual, one they'd kept since opening two years ago. Brandon took care of everything behind the scenes including making the all-important investors happy and Drew handled the floor and the staff.

Despite having no real education beyond high school to fall back on, Brandon had proven resourceful in ways to support himself and his brother. In the last few years he'd been on fire, venturing into several different business deals and making decent money with Drew at his elbow doing whatever his brother asked of him. Then, three years ago Brandon announced he wanted to put down roots. He was going to open a restaurant and nightclub in the heart of the city.

Drew had been nervous. The wheeling and dealing they'd done up to then had been low risk. Restaurants and clubs were notoriously bad business deals and neither of them had any experience running something on that scale. The public was fickle and the hours were terrible. Plus, with the economy turning, people were going out and spending less on entertainment. It was a bad time to roll the dice, he'd argued. Yet Brandon had been able to convince the bank and several investors that Carter's was going to be a success. He had the prime waterside site chosen, renovated, and doors opened for business within a year of his initial announcement that he was making a go of it; a record by all accounts.

And it had proven to be their most lucrative venture yet. Every night the club did a good business and from Thursday through Saturday it was packed with two hour waits for tables.

Drink in hand, Drew walked from the downstairs bar into the main entry that divided bar from restaurant, and up the stairs. At the top of the stairs was a short catwalk style landing with a polished chrome railing and large cube of frosted soundproof glass. The chrome handle was the only sign of a door. Drew's worn brown Pumas made barely a sound as he strode across the high gloss wood of the dance floor, taking in a view of the city muted by the effect of the tinted glass from the far outside wall and backlighting of the dance club. He made a right to go down the hall to the office. The black insulated steel door was open but the back of his knuckles rapped on the doorframe anyway.

"Come on in." Brandon didn't look up. He was typing something on his laptop, which sat on his glass-topped desk with the streamlined black phone and a lunchbox-sized silver square that was the monitor for their security system. Drew locked the money from downstairs away before he was officially off duty. Then, he slouched into the black leather chair turned to put his back to the wall instead of the door.

Brandon loved modern touches. Glass, metal, anything with a chrome finish; he bought it. "It calls to me," he'd told his brother when he'd asked. The steel girders that made up the bars had been his choice; Drew had been leaning toward oak. Even the bar tops were steel girders welded together. The bar set the tone for the entire establishment.

Warehouse chic Brandon called it. Drew found it cold but this was his brother's show. He was just there to help, as usual. Brandon was the more aggressive of the two, going after whatever he wanted whether it was a place on the hockey team, a job or a girl. And much like in business, he usually got it. The deaths of their parents had only served to intensify his drive.

Drew was more of an easygoing personality, though equally charismatic, making him the perfect choice for manager and face man for their operation. His designated role suited him and he kind of enjoyed not having to think too hard, allowing Brandon to call all the shots and direct him where to go.

Right now he wished he could take some of the stress off his brother. Brandon didn't look good lately. His long, lanky frame was leaner than usual and there were new shadows under his eyes, matching the hollows under his prominent cheekbones. Long fingered hands shook with a near constant tremor and his left eye had developed a nervous tic. Bearing their mother's angular features, Brandon was in direct contrast to his brother. Drew had stayed more boyish and softer featured like their father. It accentuated the age difference between the two men as did the dimple that refused to leave Drew's left cheek no matter how old he got.

At just under six feet with an athletic frame and striking gray eyes Drew could keep a crowd happy. He was attractive enough to flirt with the women and good-natured enough to fit in with the men. There was something about him that had the peculiar but incredibly useful ability to keep the peace.

Brandon had told him it was his unflappable nature, crediting his ability to "cool" a room to his inner peace. The two laughed about it a little too hard, knowing that until only a few years ago that hadn't been Drew's way at all. Brandon however, ran too hot to be good when things got ugly. It was the same intensity that allowed him to run the object of his desire to the ground without fail, whereas his brother would wade in with near lethargy and, within minutes, have the crowd turned around.

The scotch tasted good. Drew took another pull and let it sit in his mouth, feeling its warm burn on his tongue before allowing it roll down his throat. For a few minutes he stared at the back of the silver box showing Brandon views of both front and back entrances. When they started to burn he closed his eyes and rested his glass on his denim clad leg, waiting patiently for Brandon to finish his report. It was probably for the investors, they were always asking for updates on the bottom line and growth, things that held no interest for Drew.

Finally Brandon spoke, his tight voice sharp in the quiet of the near abandoned club. "Looks like tonight was another good night, Drew."

Drew could hear the tic starting above his brother's cheek without needing to confirm it by sight and, honestly, preferred not to. Free hand running through sandy waves, ruffling them into a thick mess before scratching it back again, Drew answered with his eyes still closed. Sleep was beginning to sound good and it was making him dull. "Yeah, we've got a thief though."

"Dana in the lower bar?" They'd discussed Drew's suspicions before.

It was an effort to raise his heavy lids. "Yeah, she's short again tonight. That's three times in the last two weeks. I checked it after I covered the lunch shift and it was dead on. I counted it three times after she closed tonight and I'm coming up forty short. She's the only one who was on it all night, Jaime left it alone."

"Do you want to tell her or do you want me to do it?"

"I got it. She's off tomorrow, I'll call her when I get up and give her the news." Even if the woman was a thief, Drew knew she had a kid at home and his dad wasn't in the picture. She was skimming but that didn't mean she had to have Brandon ream her out in front of everybody. Getting fired was going to be hard enough. He felt badly for the kid though; it wasn't his fault his parents were dumb.

Grunting was Brandon's only reply. His mind was already moving on, taking Drew's with it. "Think you can handle things for a few days without me?"

Sleep was temporarily pushed off; Drew's mind sharpened. "Where are you going?" Brandon was taking a number of short overnights lately. He was elusive about them and more than once

Drew had wondered at his honesty about his destination. Last month he'd said he was going to Massachusetts and Drew had seen a receipt sitting on top of his trashcan for a coffee in Atlanta. At first Drew thought it was a woman. Unfortunately, it wasn't.

"Terry wants me to go to North Carolina with him. He's got a business opportunity for me, for *us,* and wants me to meet with some of his people." Brandon stared boldly at his brother, daring him to disagree. The tic undermined his challenge.

Drew felt that familiar gnawing in the pit of his stomach; Terry Pritchard was bad news. He had come into their lives about the time Brandon had decided to open the club and slowly but surely, he'd been insinuating himself in their lives ever since. Brandon used to make the decisions about what he wanted, not anyone else. Call him selfish, sure, but you always knew what Brandon wanted. It was one of the things that drew people to him; his surety of purpose, his drive.

Now, nothing was decided without Terry having a say. Sometimes Drew thought the guy had some sort of hold on Brandon. He'd asked once if Terry was blackmailing his brother. All he'd gotten was chewed out and a glass thrown at him. Fortunately Brandon didn't have the arm Drew did or he'd have been in the hospital getting stitches. And when Terry started sidling up to Drew harder than ever a few months ago, he'd shut the man down cold telling him to go to hell. Pritchard had just laughed. Twice he'd sent some of his girls over and Drew had politely declined. He didn't want anything that guy was selling. Brandon had asked him not to offend him, he was one of their biggest investors. It was only out of respect for his brother he didn't pull the guy out back and beat him senseless. Drew hoped to buy him out some day and be clear of him for good; maybe then his brother would be able to relax.

Terry Pritchard was the only thing in this world that had succeeded in getting a rise out of Drew for more than five minutes. Even then once the initial rage was past, Drew had a hard time summoning enough anger at the man to seek him out. He would have seen it as a character flaw on his part, laziness or simple mindedness, if he had spent more time thinking about it. But he didn't. Something always seemed to come along to distract him.

"Oh. Sure." It was pointless to argue. Where Terry was concerned Brandon couldn't be reasoned with.

Brandon stared at the monitor, avoiding his brother's gaze. The tic made it look like he was winking. "I know I'm leaving you on a Thursday night but I should be back before things get busy for the weekend."

"It's cool, Bran. Don't worry about it. I've run the club before."

"Yeah, I know you can do it. I just hate to leave you with everything. I'll be back as soon as I can wrap things up there." Guilty eyes flicked over before being drawn back to the monitor's face.

He suddenly didn't feel like sitting and having their usual nightly powwow after close. Standing up, Drew stretched and downed the rest of his drink. With a rub to the front of the white dress shirt he wore under his black sport coat he announced, "I'm whipped. I'll see you when you get back, all right?"

Brandon gave him a queer look but other than some new wrinkles between his brows, gave no indication he was displeased. "Okay. Hey, be careful while I'm gone."

The genuine warning in Brandon's casual dismissal left Drew with an ominous feeling. "Always do." Taking care not to exit too hastily, Drew left his glass on the bar and walked out into the muggy night air at last beginning to give up a few precious degrees.

In a few weeks the humidity would be unbearable but it was a mild spring so far and he was not complaining. The sweltering heat was something he'd never been able to get used to and Florida left him feeling like something was missing. Someday he wanted to hand the reins of the club over to a manager and go back to the Midwest or even the West Coast, anywhere Terry Pritchard didn't exist was fine.

That was the thing about losing your family, nowhere ever really felt like home. Drew thought it for the millionth time.

Hitting the button, he heard the locks pop and climbed into his new toy. The silver 370Z had been a Christmas present to himself. He'd been socking away all of his profits, not a hard task when you spend every minute at work. It was actually hard for him to find the time to spend money so he'd had a good amount laying around when his old Blazer had finally died on him. The new car had been a luxury he'd thanked himself for every day since. Today was no exception. Drew found himself settling into the seat, the tension already easing off his shoulders as the engine growled to life and he pulled out into Tampa's perpetually thick traffic, heading up Dale Mabry Highway toward his condo on the outer fringes of the city.

Chapter 4

The jet touched down in Tampa at a little after three in the afternoon. It had been a relatively uncomplicated flight from Midway where Veritas kept their small fleet of private planes. The need for their own modes of air travel had become essential after the heightened scrutiny given bags with unexplained weaponry, powders and liquids essential in their line of work post 9/11. None of the triads of investigators were complaining; the new arrangement beat traveling coach by a mile.

Quan and Julia were both quiet on the flight over. All three spent the majority of the time in the air reviewing their files on a man named Terry Pritchard. According to the Watcher in the area, he was the leader of a church called the "Ray of Light." Really it appeared to be flock of less than twenty people, mostly women in their late thirties and into their fifties with money, then of course the handful of young impressionable girls who all claimed to be true believers worshipping Terry as their "spiritual guide."

A charlatan like Pritchard and his mindless devotees was not usually the type of group Veritas concerned itself with; lost souls and women on spiritual quests after their husbands left them were plenty. But Pritchard's little cult had been raising no small amount of power or money and was getting noticed.

A Diviner who happened to be in the area working on another case about a year ago had felt an unusual stirring of magick when passing by a restaurant one night. Diverting to check it out, he found a man accompanied by several oddly grouped women of varying age and appearance raising what felt like sex magick in the middle of the dance floor. Unable to come off his case at the time, he'd reported it when he got back.

Anna promptly put eyes on him. Since then several incidences of disappearances reported by concerned families had ended with wide eyed women, swearing to family and reporters that they were happy, and wanted to remain with Mr. Terry and their new "sisters." It was time to bring in a team to find out if Pritchard knew what he was doing when he was drawing these women to him and irresponsibly raising energy as volatile as sex magick in public. Provided he wasn't doing it on purpose and didn't know that it was dark magick, someone would to explain to him how to live under the radar. He would also be given the choice of working with a trainer based in the area to educate him on how to wield his talents, or he would be brought back to Veritas to face his punishment for using magick for dark purposes as well as risking exposure to the regulars.

Quan Long was the second son of a river family originally from China, near the headwaters of the Yangtze River. Water had dominated their lives for generations. He had joined Veritas a decade before when he was Cassie's age. Being the second son meant Quan had to make his fortune on his own, his father would look to the eldest son when he grew too old to maintain the cargo ferry he had taken over from *his* father.

Getting an invitation had not been much of a challenge for the normally subdued young man according to the rumors. Quan wasn't one to talk about much of anything, but Cassie had heard the story at the Academy. A triad had been sent out after several boats were found fifty yards from the banks of the river with no reports of high waters, storms or any other natural phenomenon to explain the relocation of the vessels. Pulling power from the water gave him a strength not often seen in a witch so young and he was welcomed eagerly into the program.

His father had been proud to receive the invitation and he'd accepted on the spot. If his father's decision had been disagreeable to Quan no one could tell, and he was one of the best now working in the field. Rumor also had it he could have his pick of management positions when he retired from active duty in a few years.

The same could be said for Julia Departes, the fifty-something Creole woman who completed the triad. The sacred number three so central to all of Veritas' operations dictated the setup of their partnerships expanding them from the traditional set of two seen in "regular" organizations. Julia's Haitian grandfather had taught her the often misunderstood way of their people.

Vodou was a spiritual and magickal belief system that stemmed from their blended culture of French, African and Spanish peoples who came together on their island home. Her grandfather had come from a divided Haiti when the nation was without leadership and the church and Vodou practitioners had gone to war. Sadly for Julia she'd inherited her father's strong ability yet not his dark skin. Being of a lighter complexion, she was not readily accepted by the Creole population in Louisiana where her family had finally settled after fleeing their war torn home.

The arresting caramel colored beauty had been shunned as one of the elitist class and ostracized by the community. Vital to the practice of Vodou one must be part of a community worshipping the same gods and invoking the same spirits or Loa. It had been because of her search for an accepting "community" Julia had left her backwater hometown in the swampy lowlands. Being from a magickal family, she had been aware of Veritas' existence since childhood and sought a place in the Academy to train for a position as an agent.

It was because of the immense talent of her two partners that Cassie had been teamed up with them. The assumption being that with their guidance Cassie would learn to untangle her powers with minimal risk to all parties involved. Mixed bloods like her didn't come along very often. However, when they did, and if they were able to master their powers without being driven insane in the attempt, they were without exception the best of the lot. Having no living contemporaries to guide her, Cassie found herself alone among her fellow practitioners. There was no one who could help her to weave her magicks together, no one to help her figure out what she was doing wrong or if she too would eventually have to leave her post in shame.

As things were, she was too proud to admit the extent of her difficulties beyond what everyone was already guessing, that she was having trouble blending the energies. She couldn't bring herself to reveal to anyone outside her family the way the magick rebelled against her. It didn't just refuse to work with her, it was repulsed by her. And with her mother gone and her grandmother turned away from her in anger that left only her father as a possible confidant. The same father who hated himself for how much he counted on his daughter's livelihood to keep a roof over their heads.

Cassie felt crushed under the pressure to find a way to perform and prove herself to Anna without placing her partners in danger with her ineptitude in the meantime. The complexity of the operation alone exhausted her.

The trio collected their assorted bags and climbed into the waiting vehicle parked inside the hangar, an ordinary looking maroon sedan of American design. Being the junior member, Cassie ended up as the driver. Quan hadn't learned how and preferred to observe from the backseat.

The GPS guided them to the home of Jim Salter, Pritchard's designated Watcher. Cassie listened in mute disdain during the interview process, glancing around the company owned home cluttered to the point of absurdity. Everywhere she looked, on every flat surface, there were small ceramic figurines of birds. Fighting to keep her lip from curling, Cassie wrote the fat, wheezing informant off as being one of those hangers on with barely enough talent to earn a place on the Witch's Registry. Watchers were considered by some to be bottom feeders, jealously wielding information about those with real talent for a monthly stipend.

"Pritchard is the real thing," Salter rasped around a silicone mask, attached by a thin tube to an oxygen tank sitting beside him on the aged gold and green floral couch. "He's got a house in St. Pete but comes here all the time to this club up the street called Carter's." He gasped in a few shaky breaths, his yellow waxy pallor going pale with the effort. "I've gone in there to eat a few times when I've seen the guy or one of his groupies go in." He shook his head, frustrated. "I can't get close enough to get more than a vague sense of their energy. It's been sex magick for sure, but only sometimes. It changes. It's hard to pin down. I'm not so sure he knows what he's doing out there." His forehead creased. "The energy levels and type are erratic, they change. Either he's green, which would explain the inconsistency, or it's not just him. That's all I can tell you because whatever they're doing it's on the club level upstairs." He laughed harshly patting his soft stomach. "Obviously I'm not what they're looking to let in up there."

"We appreciate the information, Mr. Salter. You've given us a place to start." Julia smiled kindly at him.

The older man's shoulders came back as he sat up a little straighter and looked her in the eye. "Anything I can do for the cause Ms. Departes. I only wish it was more."

Quan disappeared from the room without a sound, the clicking latch of the front door marking his exit before Julia or Cassie had even begun to stand.

"Not a big talker, eh?"

"No," Julia gave a soft, throaty chuckle. "Good thing we didn't bring him for his conversational skills." The last vestiges of her accent softened her words.

"Yeah, he's a Water. They're never the ones who will tell you what they're up to, they'd rather operate below the surface." He gave an awkward, choking snort. "Typical. It always looks calm on top so you walk in just to have your legs swept out from under you, then it holds you down while everyone else looks out at it and tells you how pretty it all is."

Surprised at his insight into Quan's elemental ties, Cassie looked over the man again. She still didn't see much in the paunchy senior who appeared better suited to a career of ice cream tasting than monitoring for the organization. Cassie decided Salter must have heard about Quan through the grapevine. That would be easy enough, the man had a reputation.

Julia avoided touching the seated man, a common tendency among magick users. Instead of shaking his hand she tipped her head and touched her forehead in a sign of respect and thanks before striding out the door. As Cassie straightened her tan pant leg over the top of her brown runners she gave him a tight half smile and turned to leave.

Catching her eye, Salter smiled coolly. "Don't discount people so readily, young lady. Veritas doesn't keep *anyone* around if they can't pull their weight." Staring evenly at her, his expression grew more vague and his expression went slack. He spoke in a monotone. "You're going to get someone killed if you don't sort yourself out."

Taken aback, Cassie felt her face flush. "What? You don't know what you're talking about." She stuttered, hurrying to back out of the tiny room, in her rush knocking over several figurines. Anxious, she bent down and plucked them out of the carpet to replace the ceramic garbage back on the table beside her.

If Salter was offended by her abruptness, he gave no sign. He ticked up the corner of his mouth at her and reached over, hand finding the mask for his tank without a need to break eye contact or blink. After several breath cycles, his eyes reclaimed their former life and released her from their hold that had unnerved her nearly as much as his astute observation.

Salter cocked his head, studying her. "You can't possibly be safe in the field. Your energy is almost completely blocked." He frowned. "Why?"

Without knowing where the honesty came from, maybe Anna's warning yesterday that she was on borrowed time, maybe the fact that she was feeling overwhelmed at bearing the responsibility for keeping her father and grandmother afloat; she couldn't be sure. Regardless, Cassie sagged, leaning with a hip against the doorframe. "I'm a mixed blood." To one in her world, that said it all.

Understanding dawned in the man's pale features and he nodded slowly, jowls shifting as his waddle pressed up and down on his chest. "Of course. I knew a witch like you once." His head, sadly shifting side to side, quickly quelled the hope that had begun to flutter in Cassie's chest.

Angry and frustrated she blurted out rudely, "How can you see what I am?" Normally a witch had to use her magick to be sensed by another witch. Even Quan couldn't find someone unless they pulled enough power to leave a "trail," and he was one of the best.

Round shoulders rose then dropped, noncommittal. "Why do you think Veritas keeps me around?" He raised the mask hanging limply in his hand and gave her a knowing smile. "It isn't for how fast I run the mile."

Fear began to creep in after the initial shock had worn off. "Are there many more like you?"

"No. It's a sort of mutation of Divination. Not many like me but when they find us, they snatch us up. It's a handy thing to have someone who can see through smokescreens to better know the strengths of one's enemy before he strikes." He lowered his voice, for a moment devoid of its rasp. "Or his weaknesses."

"I don't suppose you can see how to unblock me?" Cassie braced herself for the inevitable disappointment.

"I can't do that. You're too… confused. I can't tell exactly what you are. There's a little of everything in there, like you're pulling in too much and it's all clogging up in there." He studied her hard, eyes narrowing in suspicion. "Do you know how to let go of stored energy?"

Cassie stuck out her chin stubbornly. "Yes, we learned it in the first year at school."

A big hand waved, the mask's plastic tubing dinged against the steel canister. "Then there's no need for me to tell you what you already know." Thinking better of letting her off completely, Jim Salter leaned forward. "You must know that if you're going to use more than one magick, you have to release them all separately. You know, open a circle, close a circle, take energy, release energy. Otherwise, the one you don't release builds up and constipates your flow." He twisted the knob for his canister and the hiss of oxygen filled the room. "You need to get yourself figured out. I'm going to check on you in a month. If you're not dead yet, I'll expect to see your problem solved. This job's too dangerous to be dragging useless weight around."

Tight lipped, Cassie nodded and walked out. She couldn't bring herself to tell the man she would be glad to have one more month. If she didn't get herself straightened away Anna would cut her loose when they got home in less than a week. Heavy hearted, Cassie trudged out to the car.

"What took you? Was Mr. Salter telling you about his days as an investigator?" Julia looked back at the house, sad understanding in her coffee colored eyes. "I feel bad for him; he must be lonely in there. I heard all of his people are gone, his wife died last year."

Cassie eyed the house framing her partner's profile. "*He* was an Agent?"

Quan spoke up from the back seat. "It is said he was a great one before he was hurt."

Twisting in her seat to see if he was kidding, Cassie gaped at him.

Sensing Quan was done speaking, Julia took over. "He and his partners were looking into some bad business in Houston. Dark magic, disappearances, human sacrifice, that kind of thing. They were in a tight alley. The triad had their witch cornered and then, right as she was throwing a ball of fire at one of his partners, he stepped in the way to take the hit. He saved his team but suffered severe burns in the process. As I understood it they did a lot with grafts but his lungs were burned beyond repair." Julia's voice trailed off leaving an echoing silence in the car.

Salter's implied accusation that she would bring that same fate down on one of her partners took on a whole new warning. Cassie turned the key hard enough to crack the plastic holding it on the metal ring. "To Carter's then?"

It wasn't necessary to read minds to know that Julia and Quan were thinking the same thing as Salter. She was a risk and having her with them put them in danger. That was probably another reason the Directors placed her with the best, even if it did pose a different sort of danger. With them she was less likely to cause collateral damage, but if she did, the loss would be all the greater.

Chapter 5

Carter's was a modern rectangular block of smoked glass and steel shining in the late afternoon sun, converting the glass into a gigantic network of mirrors. Cassie drove the half mile up the block to the club and parked on the street with a clean line of sight to the main doors a few storefronts away. By the lack of traffic coming and going they could assume Carter's was a "nights only" kind of establishment.

Cassie pulled out her phone and looked up the number. A quick call and she spoke to a polite albeit aloof young man who confirmed the bar would open in a few minutes at four. The restaurant, however, would not be seating until five. They settled back to wait and Cassie's hair went up on her arms as Quan opened himself up to follow the hint of any significant energy trails. No one said anything, allowing him better focus, though Cassie had seen Quan perform this same task unshaken when he was under direct attack. She doubted a rock concert would break through when he was "under." Cassie envied him his focus.

"There is nothing there now," he announced quietly after a few seconds.

"Is there a trace of anything recent?" Cassie asked his reflection in the mirror before looking over to see Julia worrying at her lower lip. Magick typically left a trace that someone as good as Quan could pick up even a few days after it was used. Someone less adept could sense it for maybe a few hours tops.

"There has not been anything of significance there for some time." Quan stopped in his report, voice cutting off abruptly bringing both women's heads around. His eyes closed and Cassie felt her hair go up again. Quan had gotten a whiff of something.

When he opened his eyes, he spoke distractedly, his thoughts turned inward. "There is another energy there, although it is faint. It is much less powerful than what Mr. Salter reports and it is not sex magick." A wrinkle appeared between his jet black brows. "I don't think." Black eyes opened and he stared straight ahead at the club's quiet entrance. "I am thinking there is someone in there who is unaware of his own power."

"Leaking" was what it was called when someone was using energy without his or her knowledge. It was low grade and therefore next to impossible to find unless one was looking for it.

Julia tapped the digital clock on the dash showing it was two minutes after four and clacked her tongue on the roof of her mouth. "I'm feeling a little dry about now. You?"

Inside, the building already dimmed for the evening crowd yet to come. Cassie felt her body humming at Quan's steady output of energy. Even using a low grade like he was to search the occupants, he was so powerful it was hard not to feel insignificant next to him, or their third partner for that matter. The calm façade was in no way indicative of what the woman was capable of. Having witnessed it on numerous occasions, Cassie couldn't help but see Julia's gentle demeanor as an illusion. Cassie wasn't even on the same planet as far as talent and control went

She sighed and took up the rear, letting the other two lead the way through the giant glass doors to the large scale rust and black painted metal bar, staffed by a nicely built man who stood with his back to them. Whatever he was doing with his hands was making the muscles in his torso shift and pull at the deep blue fabric stretched across his frame. One of his hands went to his temple as they drew near. He absently rubbed at it before returning to his chore; she was still unable to see anything from her rear view. Cassie felt a pang and thought of the guy she'd left behind on the reservation for this.

She and Todd would probably have gotten married if she'd stayed. Their first kiss had been in grade school behind the portable classroom. He'd asked her to go walking out on the river when they were fifteen and he'd borrowed his uncle's truck where they'd spent the night on a pile of blankets in its bed, watching the stars. They'd figured out even greater mysteries in the same place when they were seventeen. Theirs had been a comfortable sort of love, the kind that fits and she had easily seen it lasting for a long time. It wasn't full of fireworks like the movies, but it had been good and it had suited them. He was the only one who hadn't cared about her mixed blood.

"It could be this one." Quan was eyeing the only other soul in the building straight ahead of them.

"Let's grab a chair." Julia's voice broke into her reverie and Cassie refocused, letting her eyes scan the dark, modern interior for anything amiss on a physical level leaving the other two freedom to operate without concern. At least as far as scouting went Cassie served a purpose.

They each took a high backed bar stool; its red cushioned seat she'd first thought was vinyl revealed itself to be the real thing. The smell of leather hit her nostrils seconds before her hand ran over its slightly irregular surface. There was some serious money here.
"Hello there. Is it too early for a drink?" Julia took the initiative in gaining the man's attention and let her drawl roll forth.

Startled, the man spun and Cassie saw the bar glass and rag in his hands. His face was open and honest. Sandy hair with natural streaks of honey carried a heavy wave that suited his boyish looks well. The gray eyes, at first wide in shock, acclimated quickly and had a softness about them that spoke volumes of the gentle character within. This could not be someone working with a dark practitioner like Terry Pritchard.

Faced with three thirsty customers, the bartender finished wiping the low ball in his hand, set it on the bar top and slung the white towel lightly over his shoulder. Leaning on his hands now resting on the lip of the bar, the generous mouth curved up into a playful smile as he put on a face clearly intended to draw more tips. Winking at the woman who'd asked the question, he let out a low chuckle. "If the doors are open, it isn't too early. What can I get for you?"

Julia's return grin was genuine. The man had real charm, Cassie had to give him that. "I'll have a vodka tonic with a twist of lime, please."

"Sure thing, Ma'am. Can I see your id?" He flashed an even set of white teeth as he played with her.

Cassie couldn't be sure, but she thought she saw a little flush creep up the woman's neck, which was only just showing the signs of her age. Watching Quan to see his take, Cassie was not surprised to feel her hair tingle as his energy surged. What was interesting was the falter in the bartender's confidence. His face fell and for a split second Cassie saw a glimmer of fear, the smallest view of the boy within the man, before he put his bravado back in place and turned to face Quan.

"You, sir? Pick your poison." His left hand twitched on the bar as Quan continued to reach, sniffing him out.

"Vodka cranberry."

The bartender gave a brief nod, making no effort to joke or make small talk with the small Chinese man, all in black from shirt to trousers. His shorn head and dark clothes gave him a severe mien, as did the unfeeling stare he was leveling at his quarry. Quan was great as an investigator, though admittedly lacking in his interpersonal skills.

Their subject visibly relaxed when his nervous eyes rested on Cassie. Younger and smaller than him with her delicate frame and what she would argue were mild good looks, she instantly put men at ease. They never saw her as an object worthy of more than a cursory flirt nor as a threat, though in present company she was the least dangerous. He seemed to sense that subconsciously.

Leaning on an elbow he let the smile creep back into his features. "And you, miss? What's your pleasure?"

That he was used to flirting was clear. That he was expecting it to work on her rubbed Cassie the wrong way almost instantly. What little warmth she'd felt for him dried up at once. Glaring down her straight nose at his confident swagger, she sat up straighter and folded her hands on the cool metal surface of the bar top.

"I'll have a ginger ale."

Seemingly amused and by no means offended by her snub, he flashed another smile and turned to make drinks.

The hair on her arms went down and Cassie glanced over at Quan. He was serenely eyeing the man bustling around behind the bar, which looked a lot like a steel prison, cast as it was with an eerily purple glow by the running lights under the bar as well as the upper hood.

Julia was watching their subject move efficiently to fill their orders, her chin resting lightly on her palm. Twitching her neck unconsciously, she tossed her shoulder length wavy hair back out of her way. The movement sent a shot of light dancing along the few gray hairs smattered amongst the dark majority. Another of the few indicators of her age, the vague crow's feet by the corners of her eyes, deepened momentarily in her concentration. The total picture was one of warmth. Mixed with a little magickally enhanced charisma and years of experience, and Julia could inspire trust in anyone. She could get people to tell her just about anything.

Carefully casting her spell to draw the unwitting man in, Julia developed a flirtation that started to get personal. Lowering her voice and moving over a stool to give them privacy she hinted at being recently divorced and trying different things to "find herself." If he were their man or associated with him, she would be the perfect addition to his "family."

Good natured and a willing listener, the bartender gave them nothing other than his name, Andrew. His friends called him Drew, and as far as trying new things went, he recommended dancing. He would be upstairs himself in the nightclub bar after seven. They should come back later. It didn't get going until after about ten or so, he winked at Julia. He'd given Quan a dubious glance, Cassie a longer one. Cassie kept her eyes from rolling as she turned away from his overconfidence.

Irked by his imperviousness to her usually successful charms, Julia turned to Cassie when Drew excused himself to serve the newly arrived bachelorette party sidling up to the far side of the bar. As soon as he saw the veiled blonde leading the charge, Drew's demeanor altered. He swaggered over, the mild flirtiness he'd been maintaining turned to raw sexuality in an instant. His target's shoulders stiffened, her features oozing into a dreamy pleasant mask. Tongue running over her lower lip, the bride-to-be leaned on the bar to better show her precariously harnessed cleavage.

Quan reacted without hesitation. Cassie felt her skin tingle at the same time she watched Drew stumble. Quan was trying to feel what sort of energy the man was raising. His effect on the opposite sex was too strong to be credited solely to a handsome exterior. Wiping a hand across his brow, Drew gave a small shake of his head and resumed his approach.

Grumbling under his breath, an unsatisfied Quan pushed off of the stool. Julia and Cassie followed suit, trailing him out to the car. A short farewell was called from behind them before another one of the girls pulled his attention back to her with a simpering giggle. Cassie rolled her eyes at the girl's simplicity. A good bartender knew how to work a customer for tips and this guy was no different; magickally enhanced maybe, but still just a guy working a girl for kicks. Cassie felt her hackles go up reflexively.

Only after the three were gathered inside the privacy of the car did they all relax. Quan muttered a soft curse.

"I know," Julia concurred. "What is it about that guy? I couldn't get anything out of him. He's completely blocked and unless I miss my guess, he has no idea." She rubbed a hand across the front of her neck, worrying at her lower lip. "He was using a charm spell or something like that to avoid detection."

"His energy is not one I can easily recognize. He smells of earth magick and also something else, maybe air I think. It is hard to know for certain."

Both grew quiet and Cassie could almost hear what they were thinking. She swallowed hard and stared out the windshield.

When she spoke, her words were sticky in her throat. "He could be a mix, like me."

Quan grunted his agreement. Julia's lips were tight. It was true most couldn't sense the mixes. Even Salter, the great Diviner, hadn't been able to figure her out right away. She wondered for a moment if Salter had ever met the bartender then decided it was unlikely or he would have mentioned it. Surely the curiosity of another mixed blood would have commanded his attention.

She'd thought this bartender, Drew, was only a leaker and not powerful enough to have been the source of the reports. Cassie hoped that once they had a talk with him and set him up with a trainer to teach him control, they wouldn't have to worry about him anymore. But someone had given him that charm. Cassie gritted her teeth.

"There's more than one witch at work here," Julia said quietly, her fingers tracing the side of her neck distractedly. "Drew's allure is undeniable, although he's using it for petty stuff. He's not working with Pritchard to collect followers or he'd have nibbled on me."

Cassie thought she heard a hint of bitterness at her partner's rejection. That didn't happen often.

"Still," she continued, "I think they're more than likely in cahoots. They're both using a different form of sex magick; that can't be a coincidence." Her fingers paused in their stroking and her tone grew wistful. "And it was *awful* hard to say no to that draw of his."

All three were silent until finally Quan spoke up. "Cassie did."

The mood in the car shifted.

"You've got something there, Quan." Julia was grinning. Her eyes locked on Cassie and her fingers fell to her lap. "And he didn't sense anything strange about her. He relaxed with her. I saw it."

46

Another grunt from the backseat marked Quan's assent.

Cassie didn't like the idea of being on the front lines. Should a magick fight break out because of her inevitable misstep she might put one of her partners or the occupants of the club in danger. "Why don't we just follow him, or bug the place or something?" she suggested, hoping to sideline the recommendation she felt coming.

"You know a listening device won't pick up somebody using magick. We need to have you in there to see how many more of these folks are coming in here and if they're using any other clubs. You can resist being pulled in and no magick is even necessary. Come on, you can manage *that*, Cassie." Julia's jab gave a rare glimpse into her harder side.

No help was coming from the backseat.

Arguing was pointless. When Julia made up her mind there was no winning and Cassie, being on such thin ice, gave her little sway. She'd been lucky up to now with her partners asking her to do very little. Anna had been lying when she said they weren't getting fed up with her; Cassie could feel their disillusionment. Trying to keep her dread under wraps, Cassie offered a tight smile. "I'll go in when it gets busy and try to blend."

"We don't want you to blend. You have to inspire him to tell you everything and that," she wagged a finger at Cassie's conservative garb, "is not inspiring anything."

"You have something in mind I take it?" she asked between clenched teeth, not liking where this was going.

Julia's generous mouth curled into a slow smile only a true southern woman could pull off, equal parts sugar and wildcat.

Cassie didn't mess with it fearing she would draw the claws.

"Of course I do, honey."

Chapter 6

Quan checked them into their hotel while Julia took Cassie shopping. By the time they got back several things had changed. The club and restaurant were hopping with valets on duty and people were streaming inside, dressed to the nines. That, and Cassie no longer looked like a mild mannered office drone.

The dark purple organic designs in her lilac sheath dress perfectly complimented her dark hair, tanned skin, and light golden eyes accented dramatically for a night out by Julia's knowledge of makeup. Even Cassie, normally hypercritical of her appearance, could find no fault in the reflection she saw staring back at her in the mirror. She would never admit it to her makeover artist but Cassie felt glamorous.

A few minutes before ten, when the noise from the club was becoming audible from the street, Cassie put her hand on the car door's handle and gave her straight hair hanging loose to her shoulders a nervous smoothing. "I think it's busy enough now. I'm heading in." Actually, she was so apprehensive about what she was about to do, Cassie was eager to begin. It was better to have something to do than sit here and fidget.

"If you have any trouble in there, call us. We're right out here."

"Will do." She leaned down to look back inside the car and gave a brief twitch of her mouth, noticing neither of her partners smiled back. Cassie leaned back and patted the door in a wordless farewell, listening to the clack of her heels on the pavement like a death knell. "No magick necessary, what could go wrong?" she muttered to herself, not sharing in Julia's confidence.

Cassie had a momentary urge to change course and flee as she crossed the street. She heard a whistle from somewhere behind her and hoped it was aimed at someone else. All too quickly, Cassie was stepping up the sidewalk by the valet station. A short Hispanic fellow hustled to open the door for her. Cassie gave him a gracious smile and was rewarded with a thorough visual inspection.

Her partners watched her disappear from the car.

"I hope Anna knows what she's doing," Julia muttered, her teeth scraping over her lip.

Quan sniffed.

Cutting her eyes at him, Julia waved a hand at Cassie's figure disappearing behind the door. "She's not like other recruits, Quan. We're talking about more than a job working out here." Julia frowned. "If she's pushed too hard too fast she could fall apart."

"Madness has always been a possibility for her. Anna is aware of the risks and we have all taken great care to avoid it. Maybe too much." He shrugged. "We can protect her from herself no longer, she must eventually test herself. It is time for her to go to her destiny."

Julia blinked and said nothing. She wasn't so sure.

Cassie stood in the entryway, blinking in the darkness and taking in the atmosphere. In the few hours since they'd left, the place had been transformed. People were everywhere. The sounds coming from both sides were deafening.

To her right was the restaurant. Like the bar, a mixture of dark steel and red leather was sparsely lit by overhanging disks creating intimate pockets of dim light only at the tables. To the left lay the bar, still lit by the purple running lights in addition to a central overhead beam turned on since they'd left that gave the woman tending bar an ethereal glow. Straight ahead of her was the stairway to the club lit by the same purple running lights and guarded at its base by a dark podium. The sound of conversation mingled with silverware and glasses clinking; somewhere a man guffawed loudly.

Scanning the crowd in the restaurant and the bar on the lower level Cassie failed to see Drew. The absence of tingling on her flesh evidenced the lack of magickal activity on the premises. She started for the stairs.

The host stepped out from behind his podium to head off Cassie's approach. By the way he lifted his chin she could tell he was going to give her trouble.

"May I help you, miss?" His light inflection at the respectful title held a hint of mockery.

Cassie's fingertips fluttered against her thigh. His disapproval was clear, though unexpected. Surely she looked good enough to gain entrance; this wasn't one of those clubs where they only let the beautiful people in. The heavy backside of a man resuming his seat in the restaurant was evidence of that fact.

She pointed and gave him the same smile she'd given the man at the door. "I'd like to go upstairs, please."

"Were you meeting someone?" He arched one finely plucked brow and the light reflected on the shine of his lip gloss.

Cassie's smile faltered. "Uh, sort of."

"Wait here please, I'll check the numbers." He stared pointedly at her. "Fire codes." The thin black man lifted a cord lying against his black tshirt, which sported the club's name in blue to match the neon out front. The cord ran up to a device hooked to his ear. Turning his face, his words were lost to her.

Cassie kept her face impassive while she waited. It took all she had not to fidget. So much rode on her success tonight it was impossible not to be anxious. She didn't want to leave Veritas having never lifted a finger to help on an assignment without botching it. Even if she were unable to use her magick, she wanted to be at least as good as a "regular" agent would be on the job.

Chin held high, she could give the appearance of confidence, even if inside, she was wilting, Cassie tossed her hair back behind her shoulders and a throat cleared behind her.

Wheeling almost fast enough to lose her balance in the unfamiliar footwear, Cassie barely managed not to trip. She was glad she didn't. Not two feet behind her stood the bartender and her target, Drew. Where had he come from?

"Uh hey, you're the bartender, right?" she said lamely, wishing she could hit rewind and pause until she could come up with something better.

Confusion temporarily clouded his gray eyes, darker now that he wore a black Cuban shirt with the same pair of jeans that fit him so well from earlier. His hand ran through the sandy waves in what she was willing to wager was a nervous habit meant to buy time while he smiled blankly at her, trying valiantly to place her face. Her question seemed to have stopped him from trying to charm her.

Cassie felt the stirrings of attraction at this glimmer of a real person and was quick to remind herself of the nauseating way he played with the female clientele using his good looks for either profit or amusement. She blinked long and slow, head tipped down coyly to look up through her thick black lashes. Two could play at this game.

"Drew, isn't it?" She spoke softly, mimicking Julia's exaggerated manner of speech minus the accent. "I was in earlier with some friends of mine," recognition flickered behind his eyes, "and I wanted to come back by myself so I could get a better look around." Head still tipped away from him, Cassie gave him a half smile meant to be mysterious.

"You sure didn't give the impression you were interested in anything when you were here before." A small wrinkle formed between his brows.

Embarrassed she hadn't considered the effect of how cold she'd been, Cassie thought quickly. "That guy was my boss. I couldn't say anything in front of him." She touched her bangs.

Mention of Quan produced a grin. "Yeah, he didn't really seem like the kind of guy who encourages much of a personal life."

"So, what do I have to do to get up there?" She flicked her dramatic lids up, letting her eyes linger on the darkened dance floor upstairs. The glass walls served to block most of the sound but not sight. Silhouettes of bodies merged, blurring the lines between individual dancers until it was one large multicolored writhing mass; its own hydra lit from below by lavender lighting, washing out the legs into a white-blue dream. The crimson ceiling tiles cast the top of the creature's heads in a devilish glow while the middle twisted and swayed, black and hidden.

That Cassie might have to become a willing participant in the orgy above would have had her as red as the ceiling had she let herself think about it. She didn't. Her persona for the night could handle the flirtation she told herself, giving her permission to nearly throw herself at this man to get what she needed from him. If it worked she only had to do this once.

So slowly did he consider her implied offer, she didn't think he was going to go for it. A furtive glance at the sneering lips of the uppity host seemed to confirm her suspicion she would soon be turned down.

Drew's glance skimmed automatically and without thinking over the crowds, subconsciously ticking off the numbers, running through how many he'd seen upstairs a few minutes ago. By his estimation they had to be running close to maximum capacity up there. About to suggest she get a drink in the bar while she waited, Drew opened his mouth to speak and noticed the host's barely contained animosity toward the woman. He'd never liked the man much.

"Tavaris, I'd like a bottle of champagne sent up to my private table." His serene profile remained non-reactive at the host's blatant shock, yet Cassie thought she saw the fading remains of a challenge as his eyes swung back to her. Lifting a corner of his mouth into that same playful smile he'd tried on her earlier, Drew held a hand out and waved her past the gatekeeper currently unhooking the red velvet rope to allow her passage.

Cassie strode steadily up the black carpeted steps, flushing uncomfortably at the thought of him walking only a few steps behind her, eye level with her rear. When finally they reached the summit and stood on the landing, Drew moved up beside her to open the door.

Cassie took an involuntary step back from the tooth rattling music that poured out and glanced over at her host. He was not just a bartender, of that she was certain. She was guessing he was at least management, potentially an owner by the way he'd handled the guy downstairs. Drew became more interesting in her eyes. Why he would flirt shamelessly and yet hide his clout from women was contradictory to what she'd assumed of him.

"Are you sure you want to go in?" He raised his voice to be heard above the dance beat.

"It looks great." She shouted back as loud as she could without looking like she was in pain. "You're not a bartender, are you?"

Only a moment's hesitation and Drew answered with a wink, waving her inside the ear crushing terrarium. He led her back along the outer edge of the dance floor, past a bar lit by red lights and surrounded by thirsty dancers taking a break. They moved toward a table on the farthest side of the floor from the speakers. The sound was still loud but it was possible for Cassie to hear him when Drew asked her if she would like to take a seat. There was already a bucket of champagne chilling at the table. She hadn't seen it come past them.

Drew grinned at Cassie's puzzled expression. "We have an elevator at the far end of the hall. It's easier to run things between the bars."

Cassie had noticed a dark hallway behind them she assumed led only to the restrooms.

"Have a seat," he motioned her into the high backed "c" shaped black leather booth. The other booths and upholstery upstairs were a mixture of the two colors, black and red, adding to the insane energy and chaos of the place. With an exaggerated sway to her hips Cassie slid into the booth only to abandon the attempt at seduction in favor of speed and distance when she saw Drew coming in after her. Both sat facing the crowd and Drew poured. "Drink?" He slid a flute of bubbling golden wine across the foot or so of table between them matching the distance of their bodies on the seat.

Cassie's skin remained tingle free. For whatever reason, Drew was not trying to manipulate her. Her vanity took a small hit. "Thank you." She smiled and held up the glass, lifting her chin to look him full in the face before taking an experimental sip. Cassie's first taste of champagne was good. Her brows rose at the unexpectedly pleasant taste, taking another quick sip before replacing her glass on the dark table.

Drew peaked his brows raising his glass expectantly with her. When he saw her surprised expression at the taste, his return grin was easy. "So, why did you really come back?"

Cassie hadn't counted on him being so direct. She tossed her hair and put a shoulder forward, posing for him. "I told you, I wanted to get a better look around."

In her mind she was already discounting her chances of getting anything out of this guy. If Quan's sweeps revealed nothing of his power source and Julia hadn't been able to get him to confide anything, how was Cassie going to get anything off the guy? Her eyes swept across the open throat of his shirt, searching for cording or a chain leading to an amulet or talisman. His wrists were also bare, as was the left hand with its lengthy fingers absently stroking the stem of his glass, though the right was resting on the chair out of view.

Cassie could see her father's face when he heard of her dismissal from Veritas and she considered her options. One way to find out someone's power was to draw it. Taking in energy was something she could do competently enough, provided she wasn't called on to do anything with it. Closing her eyes for a moment, she ignored the elevated temperature coming from the dance floor nearly making her sweat and the man beside her whose clean, lightly musky scent wafted on the heat to her nostrils. Pushing all of that into her periphery, she cast a small spell she knew she had practiced in school as well as under Julia's expert tutelage.

Protection spells on such a small scale would not even raise Quan's attention outside. This would merely provide her mind some cover should Drew prove able to sift through it, once she opened herself to him. Anything more complicated was doubtful with this crowd of possible witnesses and casualties.

No sooner had she muttered the last words of the spell than she felt an arm snake behind her, sliding her across the leather and slamming her into his side. Bone ground painfully against her and he twisted his shoulders until his face was within inches of hers when her eyes flew open. Cloudy gray eyes filled her vision and she felt his fingers tighten around her other arm, locking her into place.

Her eyes went wide as her heart raced and she leaned back as far as her captor would let her. She silently chastised herself for being sloppy. He might not know what she was doing, but she'd seen him react when others used magick. He obviously knew enough to guess the source of what he was sensing.

Drew's eyes narrowed, he was on the verge of violence. "What's the matter? Isn't this what you wanted?" Drew's gentle features were twisted in anger.

He leaned in and Cassie shrunk back to keep their bodies from touching any more than they already were. Instinctively, Cassie firmed up her protections.

Feeling her pull even that small amount of energy, Drew's expression switched from fury to confusion and held a hint of the same fear she'd seen downstairs at their first meeting. She felt a tweak of sympathy for him.

"What are you doing?" He pushed himself away from her and took his arm from around her back. "Who are you?" He ran his right hand across his forehead and Cassie saw proof of what she's suspected. Set in a silver ring on his first finger was a chunk of opaque stone marred by light green flecks.

Cassie ignored his questions. "What kind of stone is that?" She pointed with her eyes while she searched the databanks of her memory for the name of that particular stone. Far back somewhere, she knew she had learned about it. It was a special stone. She recalled that much at least.

Drew was visibly off balance. "I don't know." He answered uncertainly. "My brother gave it to me a few years ago, he said it was good luck." He ran a shaking hand through his hair. "I think you should go."

Figuring to cut her losses for the night and try again tomorrow, Cassie accepted the dismissal. Without arguing she slid out the way she'd come. A backward glance revealed a man distressed, his head resting on a hand, elbow on the table. The other hand shook as he picked up his glass to down the rest of his champagne, and for a second she felt bad for him. When she got out to the car she was going to see about arranging a trainer for him right away. They could find Pritchard without him.

Backing away, she failed to see the woman cutting across the dance floor with three drinks balanced precariously in her hands until it was too late. When the cold sticky liquid had made its way down Cassie's back and the ice cubes were still sliding around at her feet with what remained of the shattered glasses, Cassie turned to the owner of the furious voice behind her.

"What the hell!" The drink holder was fortunately not much bigger than her in heels though she looked daunting, glowering in Cassie's face with alcohol clouded eyes. She glanced sideways toward a table on the edge of the dance floor where several friends looked on laughing, and cut her narrowed eyes back to Cassie.

Great, she thought. The Latina woman wasn't going to let this go easily. She was going to make this about pride. Fortunately for Cassie, her training had included the non-magickal sort as well and she'd proven herself effective in that realm. She didn't want to linger here and held out hope she could beat feet before Drew caught on to her causing trouble in his bar.

"I'm sorry, I didn't see you." She was a regular, Cassie had felt that when they'd collided. That meant as an investigator she couldn't use magick against her unless her life was in danger. In her case that was good; she might accidentally set one or both of them on fire if she tried. "Let me buy you another round." She tried to placate the woman, though she didn't need any more alcohol if her eyes were any indicator. They were having trouble focusing.

As she'd suspected, the woman was not so easily soothed. "You think a drink is going to fix this? What about my clothes?" Pointing at the few tiny specks of liquid, barely visible through the dark pattern on her shirt, and one shining wet blop on her skirt, she continued, "I should tell the management about this. Somebody's gotta pay for my clothes." Her neck went up and she started scanning for someone in a club tshirt.

Money, it always came down to money. Cassie only had twenty dollars in her purse and that would barely cover the drinks in this place. "Look, I don't have much cash. I can buy you drinks and that's about it." She smiled and waved at her outfit. "You can't even see the marks on the shirt and you'll be dry before the next dance."

They were drawing more stares from the dancers around them; several ice cubes were being crunched on the floor as people moved toward them to listen. Cassie thought about calling Julia but that would definitely get Drew's attention and arguably get her banned from the club.

Cassie backed away, not wanting to make a scene.

The drunk girl lumbered unsteadily forward, driving Cassie back again. A male spectator announced, "Cat fight," and the people around them turned to watch. One high heel slipped on an ice cube and Cassie's ankle twisted, bringing her to her knees. She felt a piece of glass drive itself into her leg and her hand went to it instinctively. A hand came down and grabbed a chunk of hair, pulling her painfully to her feet. Cassie hopped up on one foot, the other ankle not wanting to cooperate just yet.

"Don't you crawl away from me. I'm not done yet." Her hand tightened its grip when Cassie tried to smack it away.

Not normally one to have a temper, Cassie was also not going be pushed around. On the reservation she'd been picked on for being only half Sioux and had learned how to stand up for herself. This girl had crossed the line and Cassie gritted her teeth.

Twisting on one foot Cassie grab the woman's wrist in her hands, pressing a thumb into the tender underside to free her hair and brought the offending limb up behind her attacker, raising it painfully. Her bad ankle objected to its enlistment and she stepped up close to the shoulders, using her attacker's body to balance. It also allowed Cassie to speak to her so no one else could hear.

"I don't owe you anything. It was an accident and I apologized. This is not worth a fight and both of us getting kicked out of here just so you can show your friends you're tough." The shoulders remained tight for less than a count of ten before she relaxed to alleviate the pressure. Seeing her moment to make her escape, Cassie released the woman, pushing her forward and took two hopping steps before the drunk's hand flashed out and grabbed her arm. In a barrage of pushing and hustling that couldn't have passed for any form of recognizable dancing, Cassie ended up with her back pressed against the smoked glass of the outer wall with the foul breath of a very drunk and pissed off woman right in her face. Several catcalls reached her ears as Cassie gauged the likelihood of taking this woman out and getting lost in the crowd before Drew saw her.

The woman mistook Cassie not fighting back as giving up and gloated. "You think you can disrespect me?" Her eyes glowed black. This far out of the direct light, the red from above lent them an eerie otherworldly cast.

"All I have is $20 and you can have it." She realized in that moment that her hands were empty. Heart sinking, she realized she'd dropped her purse in the fall on the dance floor and couldn't hope to get out without being seen. She would have to go right back in front of his booth to look for it. "Uh, I dropped my purse out there and I don't have anything on me. If you want to give me a minute, I'll go grab it for you." Playing weak ate at her but she had to remember her mission.

A self-satisfied smirk twisted the woman's thin lips. "Why don't you crawl out there and get it for me and then I'll decide if that's good enough."

Cassie's stomach dropped. This woman was pushing her too far. Mission or not she wasn't going to crawl. As she felt her temper flare, Cassie could sense her energy swelling inside her, threatening to overwhelm her protections. If she didn't control it she was going to hurt somebody. Closing her eyes, she took a deep breath to steady herself.

Chapter 7

Cassie's skin tightened sending the hairs on her arms straight up.

"Can I help?" Drew's voice held no trace of the confusion or suspicion it had when she'd left him moments ago.

She opened her eyes letting her gaze fall on the set of his jaw before wandering up, surprised by what she saw there. Or rather what she didn't. Drew was entirely unaffected by the budding violence in his club. His smile was no different from when he was drawing women in. Underneath that however, she felt another stirring of something, a disruption in the energy around her. She felt it's pull.

A twitch of his hand drew her eye and the light caught the silver on his finger. It was the ring. It shared the same Earth element as Cassie and it's energy called to her, the scent of damp dirt and fresh grass played at the periphery of her senses.

Cassie felt her attentions shift as she recognized the power in the way that the element called to her and, at the same time, the way it repelled a part of her. It was a battle she would normally have attributed to her dual nature only this time, Salter's words popped into her mind. The timing or situation, whatever it was, gave her clarity and she heard him, "you know how to clear stored energy, don't you?"

Sudden understanding exploded in her mind and Cassie felt the burning heaviness of stored energy in her body and mind, this time breaking it down and feeling it for what it was. Almost tearfully she reached for it, knowing even as she did so that she'd identified the primary source of her problem at long last.

Whereas previously she had been grasping blindly in the shadows for the energy inside her, not seeking or calling it by element, her attempts to cleanse herself had left her frustrated and empty. Perpetually seeking release with no promise of real satisfaction, this time was different. She felt the burning inside her ease as she guided the newly identified offending masses of separate energies through her arms, on fire with the sheer volume, into the palms of her hands facing the floor. Taking a steadying breath to be sure she didn't lose control of it, Cassie sent the roiling energy in one solid push from her body, returning it to the Earth. The water filtered through it's cousin to find its home as well.

At once lighter and less conflicted, Cassie felt she'd lost a burden she hadn't known she'd been carrying for longer than she could remember and saw that she was closer than ever to figuring out her magick. Buoyant both in mind and body, cleared of the subversive energy, Cassie longed to be nearer to the ring and the source of her tranquility. Cautious, she held herself in check fearing the sudden draw she felt to the powerful object. The strength of its power disturbed her.

Meanwhile, the woman was left blinking as Drew's simple words began to influence her and she fell under the spell of his allure. Her grip loosened and she took a step back, returning Cassie's ability to breathe.

The shadow of suspicion had passed from his features and, grinning benignly, Drew nodded at Cassie before shifting his attention back to her attacker. "I saw the unfortunate little run in you two had back there on the floor. Why don't you head on over there to my bartender and tell her your drinks are on me the rest of the night. We'll give you and your party the real VIP treatment. I'm sure we can turn your evening around," he finished with a genial smile.

"Thanks." She winked hazily. "Would you like to join us?"

"Unfortunately, I have work to do. Maybe next time," he flirted back.

Suddenly amicable, she made her way over to the bar without argument or a sideways glance at her party who Cassie could see was watching their interaction with great interest. They would think she was getting the apology from the management she thought she deserved and she got to be the hero that upgraded their night. Crisis averted.

With drunk chick no longer in her face, Cassie tried to stand up off of the glass wall and faltered. The ankle was not yet ready to bear her weight and even in the dim light she could tell it was getting puffy. The remnants of Drew's exuded charm dropped from his face and she watched him study her curiously.

Calmly, he held out a bent arm for her to take hold of. Cassie stared at it, biting her lip as she considered her options. She doubted she could walk well without him, but with as much pain as she was in, her protection spell had faded and she couldn't bolster it. Her ability to block any leaking from him through her defenses would be severely limited. And then there was the call of the ring. She could only guess at how long she could resist a call of that magnitude should she get too close.

An image of Quan having to come in after her made the decision clear. Taking a deep breath she held out a hand and gingerly threaded it through the crook of his arm.

At the first touch, Cassie felt her shoulders ease. The ring not only blocked him psychically it blocked him physically as well. She didn't need her protections spells. If he had any magick of his own, it was well masked as long as the ring was on his finger. Its power was all she could feel and it made her dizzy.

Her human cane, Drew guided her back in the direction of their table then turned right to go down the dark hall. At her hesitation to go into the darkness with him he explained.

"I have an office down here with a first aid kit. We can't have an obviously injured woman hopping out of here. It's bad for business."

Cassie bristled at his unfeeling explanation for what she's assumed was compassion. "Thank you. That's very kind," she replied crisply before she caught herself. Whether she was liked or not by him didn't matter, being in his office gave her a chance to get the closer look she needed. Maybe even find the reason Pritchard was drawn to this place, see if there was a connection linking the two men. That would be important should Pritchard come to trial for his actions.

They moved at a slow but steady pace. Cassie gave up being proud in favor of relief, leaning gratefully into his solidness. The entire time she was touching him she felt the pull of the ring, its elemental energy calling to the similar element within her.

The hall was dark, the only break in the blackness coming from the purple running lights along the floor and the exit sign above. In the middle of the wall on the right side her guide stopped, his hand pushing open a door she hadn't noticed in the dimness. Drew flicked on the light and released her arm to let her through first.

The office was simple. Straight ahead sat a large glass desk with a phone and what looked like a small television set offset by two black leather chairs, their backs to the door. Along the walls she saw several framed prints that must have been the original designs for the club; she recognized the layout in the black and white etchings easily.

"I share the office with my brother," Drew informed her, ushering her to the chair nearest them and swinging the door partway shut. "Have a seat." When Cassie was off his arm, he disappeared into a small alcove previously hidden behind the door and she heard some rustling. Reappearing momentarily, he held a small red tackle box in his hand.

Plopping it down on the desk, he reached across and picked up the phone. That it was only a few buttons told Cassie the call was internal.

"Yeah, hey Jaime. I've got a mess and some broken glass out on the dance floor. Can you get someone out there to clean it up?" He waited for the other party to answer. "Great. I figured you'd already be on it." Another pause and he turned his head to eye Cassie. "I know who it belongs to. Just have it brought back to the office when you can spare somebody."

He hung up and went to work digging in the bag. "They've got your purse at the bar."

"I heard."

Her flat tone brought his eyes around. "What, not interested in playing anymore?"

"Injury kind of takes it out of a girl, you know?" Cassie pointed at her legs. A good amount of blood, dried and fresh, marked her leg from an inch long puncture below her left knee continuing to drip onto an already purple and swollen ankle.

"Hmm." Drew removed her shoe and touched the puffy joint, making Cassie jump. "Sorry." He flicked his eyes up and grimaced in sympathy before resuming his tentative examination. "It looks like you twisted it pretty good. We can wrap it up and get you on your way as soon as I get this blood cleaned up but you should see a doctor." His hands were sure as he finished his exam and opened the tackle box to extract what he needed.

"What are those for?" Cassie eyeballed the tweezers he wielded over her knee.

"There's still a little piece of glass in there." Drew pointed and Cassie's eyes followed, seeing the small clear shard protruding from the blood source.

Cassie held her breath and clenched her fists on her thighs. When the piece slid out, she let out her breath with a small noise.

He regarded her through a clump of hair that had fallen over his eye.

"It hurt," she fumed defensively.

He snorted and put a folded gauze pad on her knee. "Here hold this with some pressure." He unwrapped an alcohol wipe he'd extracted and went to work efficiently cleaning up her lower leg, then grabbing a flesh colored plastic bandage large enough to cover the wound. Next, out came an ace bandage and he propped her leg on his thigh, the better part of his back to her so that he could have free access to the ankle and foot.

As Drew moved her foot to wrap it, it tweaked the injured area and Cassie let out another sound before she could bite down on her lip to silence it. Amused, he turned with his mouth slightly open and she glowered at him to stop him from earning himself an elbow to the eye.

A knock at the door halted any further snide comments or impetuous actions.

"Come on in, Jaime."

Jaime, a leggy blonde, strode in. Her snug black tank top, a female version of the host's, hung loose barely brushing the top of her short black shorts. In her hand was Cassie's little black clutch purse containing nothing more than an id, lipstick, a cell phone, and her aforementioned twenty dollars in cash.

"Yours?" She held it out pleasantly.

Nodding, Cassie reached for it only to be halted by Drew's tightened grip on her calf to keep her from moving her leg.

Catching the look she gave him, Jaime laid it atop the small black metal file cabinet beside the door. "I'll just set it here while Drew plays doctor." She winked at Cassie and nodded to the tackle box laying open on the desk. "We don't have much need for that here, not like my last job." She smiled admiringly at Drew, making a conscious effort to keep his head down. Cassie watched a hint of color climb over his shirt collar. "This guy can mellow anybody out. He's our good luck charm."

"Yeah, I saw him in action. It was impressive." She agreed, studying Drew and wondering again what the stone was in that ring.

"What happened out there? Did she fall?" She took a step in to get a better view. Catching sight, she pursed her lips and sucked in. "Ooh, that looks painful. I saw a scuffle but who can hear anything out there?" She laughed and rolled her eyes. "Did you trip or something?" Her big blue eyes were open and friendly.

"I'm clumsy. I ran into a gal with some drinks and then slipped in the mess," Cassie answered her honestly.

Drew dismissed Jaime who was not appearing to want to leave any time soon. "Thanks for bringing her bag, Jaime. Can you mind the store while I take care of this?"

Happy mood intact, Jaime dipped her head. "Sure thing Boss." She turned to leave and paused in the doorway. "Hey, any idea when Brandon's coming back? I got a call today from one of Pritchard's girls asking if you or Brandon were here. It sounded like he wanted to come by." She frowned. "I don't like the idea of having him here. I don't want to have to deal with the guy or his zombies."

"What are you talking about? He's *with* Pritchard." Drew stopped himself short, shooting Cassie a quick glance. "Was it you? Were you waiting to catch me alone?" His eyes once more turned accusatory.

"What are you talking about?" Cassie could sense that things were about to turn and she had to find a way to stick around. Mention of Pritchard and his "girls" had her full attention.

"Are you another gift?" He snorted, disbelieving her shock. "Come on, it's not like he hasn't sent girls in before. You're obviously one of his," he gave her a once over and shrugged, "a little classier this time, but let's face it. You came on a little strong out there and then there was that older lady, classic Pritchard material."

"I have never met this guy Pritchard and neither has Julia." She caught herself before she said partner. "Nobody sent me; I came of my own free will." Okay, that was a lie.

He watched her through narrowed eyes while Cassie worked hard to keep her cool. She was not leaving here without hearing more about Terry Pritchard and how Drew and his ring fit into all of this. Finally Drew spoke to Jaime over his shoulder, "I'll be back on the floor as soon as I take care of this situation."

Jaime laughed nervously. "Don't take too long, Drew. You know how Thursdays are, worse than Saturdays if you ask me. Anything can happen."

"Almost done." His eyes stayed with Cassie, not blinking until after the door clicked shut and then he was on her. "Who are you and why did Pritchard send you?"

"Cassie Porter, and you?" She managed to not sound sarcastic. There was no harm in giving her real name. They did it all the time. Agents gave their real names because Veritas supplied post office boxes and answering services, relaying any information along to protect their identities. All agents of Veritas lived in corporate owned condos and apartments all over the world. It was a carefully crafted method by which employees were kept safe and somewhat isolated.

"Drew Carter, my brother and I own this place but then, you already knew that." He cocked his head, brow creasing again. "Why did Pritchard send you?" His hands had stopped working and her foot lay forgotten on his thigh.

"I told you already…" She began and he jerked his hand up to cut her off.

"Stop it. We both know you're no good at this." He actually smiled when he saw her offense. "Seriously, you're too obvious. It doesn't suit you."

"Is that supposed to be a compliment or an insult?"

"I'm not sure exactly." His good nature was peeking through and Cassie watched the heat fade from his expression. Being serious almost seemed a challenge for Drew. He pressed on, minus the intensity. "You're good but you're not getting out of here without answering my question. Are you going to tell me or not?"

Cassie rested her hands on either side of her on the chair, looked him in the eye and sighed before shaking her head deliberately. "I'm just a girl trying to live a life I'm clearly not cut out for."

It was a true statement. Something that Drew seemed to recognize as well because he recommenced wrapping her leg without any further questions, giving it a final smoothing over before lowering it to the floor. Standing, he stretched his back, lifting both arms before reaching to get her shoe from the floor and hand it to her. Moving toward the door, he let a hand fall on the knob. Plucking the purse off of the file cabinet with the other, he looked back at her.

"Do you have a car or should I call you a cab?" He aimed his chin at her bandaged limb. "You're not walking anywhere."

"If you hand me my phone I can call a friend to come get me." She reached out to take her purse from him. His stopping just as her hand closed on it. Cassie looked up expectantly.

"Have a drink with me. It'll take a while for your friends to get here." He proposed impulsively, seeming as surprised by the request as she was.

Cassie blanked, uncertain of his intentions or of her safety with him. Injured, she would have a limited capacity to defend herself. Regardless, he was offering her exactly what she needed. An opportunity to get face time with him that carried with it an opportunity to go fact finding.

"Sure, one drink wouldn't hurt." Her hand found her phone no problem and she dialed Julia. When she answered, Cassie steered the conversation. "Hey." She gave Julia only a second to give a one word answer. "I twisted my ankle dancing so I was wondering if you could pick me up here at Carter's. What would it take maybe fifteen minutes do you think?"

"Are you in danger?"

"No, I'm okay with waiting if it isn't too long." She flashed a friendly smile at Drew. "I don't want to wear out my welcome with the management."

"Fifteen minutes exactly, Cassie."

"Thanks, I'll meet you in the bar downstairs." She hung up and slid the phone back into her clutch.

"We have fifteen minutes, huh? Well, I'd better hurry and get those drinks."

Chapter 8

Drew excused himself to get more champagne, she'd seemed to like it before. As the office door closed behind him he ran his hand through his hair.

"What am I doing?"

If she wasn't with Pritchard then who was she? There was no way he believed her story that she'd come back for him. That was a line and a bad one at that. He meant what he'd said that she wasn't believable as a party girl. Though what told him that, he couldn't say. It could have been the way she'd handled the fool on the dance floor. That was more than self-defense at the Y.

Drew fished his phone out of his pocket and dialed his brother. No answer. He didn't leave a message. If he wasn't with Pritchard then where was he? Drew knew Brandon had secrets. A man barely into his thirties, with virtually no resume, barely in his thirties doesn't inspire the kind of financial generosity it took to build the club without making some questionable deals, but at what personal cost? And why had Pritchard chosen to invest with him?

Brandon and Drew talked about almost every aspect of the business except for how the whole thing started. Drew had the feeling his brother was hiding something, keeping him away from something like he'd done since the deaths of their parents. Since that night Brandon had been overly protective of his little brother, getting custody and taking him from their aunt as soon as possible. Together they'd bounced around, living in hovels at times and yet there had never been a doubt in Drew's mind that Brandon would keep him safe.

Then Drew had gone off the deep end at eighteen, not to return until only a few years ago. Brandon had taken him in and helped him get his life back together, at the same time developing an uncanny streak of good fortune. In recent years it seemed every deal Brandon touched turned to gold. They should both be settling back and enjoying their success, except Brandon was getting fidgety. Drew could sense it. He was itching to move on to his next venture. Doing the deal, the acquisition, was where Brandon's true excitement lay. Drew just wanted to settle, to feel like he was tied to something instead of drifting through life. He craved an anchor.

Unfortunately he also couldn't be without Brandon and when Brandon left Carter's, so would Drew. He would follow his brother into a school of sharks, steaks in each hand if he asked, though it didn't mean he wanted or liked it. What other choice did he have? Brandon was all he had left in this world.

***

While Drew was gone Cassie didn't have much time. She spun in her chair, scanning the room. There was nothing lying out in sight, everything was off the desk but the phone and monitor showing views of the front and rear entrances. From the cords sticking up through a hole in the glass, she could tell the computer that usually sat there was missing. Damn.

Next to the door sat the black file cabinet. Cassie hobbled over and found it unlocked. Inside were a number of files on employees, no names Cassie recognized until she reached Jaime Trask. Curious if that was the woman who had brought her purse, she flipped open the file and groaned.

Jaime was a perfect employee. Hell she was the perfect woman by most standards. Bartending nights to pay for college, she was a senior at the University of Tampa studying law. It was doubtful she was tied up in any sort of sex magick circle with Pritchard. Besides she seemed to genuinely dislike the guy.

A few more cursory scans of random files revealed nothing suspicious. Defeated, she replaced the files and shut the drawer. Leaning on the cabinet to take the weight off her leg, she took in the rest of the office, considering what she might be missing. It was as she stared at the sparseness of the room that she realized what she *wasn't* seeing was what told her the most.

It was the brother. Brandon was the witch associated with Pritchard, Jaime'd hinted at as much. The choice in materials in the club and the office spoke volumes. All metals and glass, all organic in nature and nothing else. Brandon was a practitioner too and it was more likely he was the one working with Pritchard, not Drew. Drew was too blocked to be using his power for much more than a few tips and maybe some action.

She'd caught Drew's reaction when Jaime mentioned Pritchard. Whether he worked for him or not, Drew didn't like Pritchard, though it sounded like a one-sided dislike. Why was Pritchard sending unwanted gifts to Drew? What did he want from him, did he know about Drew's magickal talent and want to recruit him?

Cassie was back sitting in her chair when Drew returned with two glasses of champagne and some ice.

"For you." He handed her one glass and raised the ice pack aloft before handing it to her. "Also for you."

Somewhat awkwardly, Cassie tried to find somewhere to put her foot up except there was little for elevated surface space in the office aside from the desk and chairs. Both chairs were soon to be occupied and to put her feet on the desk gave him a very good view up her skirt.

Having handed Cassie her items, Drew stepped back and scooped up her feet in his free hand. He swept them both smoothly with him to set them on the desk, and in another moment, he had the ice pack resting on the bare ankle. Clumsily, Cassie started to shift her hands underneath herself in preparation of sitting up and hiding the backside of her thighs and more but Drew picked up his chair and angled it to take himself out of the line of sight.

A little surprised by his unexpected chivalry, Cassie sighed and relaxed, letting her joint cool under the ice pack. Relief was almost instantaneous as the blood began to flow back out of her foot. The throbbing in her purpling toes ebbed. Letting her head fall back she "hmmm'd" contentedly.

"Better?"

"Mmm hmm."

"I think that's the happiest I've seen you yet," Drew teased. "Every time I see you either you're mad or someone's mad at you. It's good to see you have another side."

Cassie opened her eyes and turned her head. She was temporarily at ease, having both repaired things somewhat with Drew and confirmed that he did in fact know Pritchard who would be returning at some point in the near future. She was definitely going to have to tell her partners about Brandon. They should spend some time checking into the connections between those two. "Speaking of which, what is up with your host? Don't you usually want someone friendly doing that job?"

Drew shrugged and took a drink. "He hates Cubans."

Cassie snorted, taking a drink. "I'm not Cuban."

"Then what are you? Puerto Rican? I see something exotic in there." He slouched in his seat stretching his legs to cross his ankles out in front.

"Part Sioux. Sihasapa, if you want to get technical."

Drew's brows rose. "What else is in there?" He was thinking of her unique eye color, that couldn't be Native American.

"Mom was Welsh. I'm mixed." Cassie stopped talking abruptly, wishing she hadn't shared even that little bit. She hadn't given him much, considering he couldn't possibly understand the underlying meaning of what she'd told him. Mouth pinched, she twisted her neck to check the clock over the door. Ten more minutes. She was going to have to stop drinking or she'd tell him everything.

"Why does that bother you, that you're mixed?" Drew was watching her curiously. He could see her walling herself off the

73

way she'd been when he'd first seen her this afternoon. "This is America, everybody's mixed."

"Yeah, but I was mixed growing up on a reservation. That's different." There she'd gone and done it again. Cassie smoothed her skirt before raising her glass to her lips. Maybe she did want it after all.

"There's a story there." He tapped a finger on his glass and waited.

"Everybody's got a story," she shrugged, "mine's not all that interesting. Tell me about *your* family."

The smile slid from his eyes leaving only a shadow of itself lingering on his lips. "My parents are dead. All I have is a brother."

"I'm sorry." Cassie sensed the strength of his reaction, but it was fuzzy. Her eyes slid down to his right hand and the ring that rested there on the first finger. The ring was an amulet, it was blocking him from inside as well as outside energies. She could feel it now that her senses had been cleared. That explained his pains when people used their magick near him. He could still feel the energy surge as the stone took it in. "Was it recent?"

Tracing the path of the bubbles rising in his glass on the other side, Drew answered flatly, "No, we were kids."

They both felt the change in the conversation, discomfort creeping in to fill each heartbeat of silence yet neither could do anything about it. Each of them was caught up in their own thoughts. When the phone in Drew's pocket buzzed, both jumped and Cassie flinched as her heel dropped off the edge of the glass.

"Yeah?" He answered without looking to see who it was. Drew sat up, his rigid posture at odds with the casual tone he maintained. "Hey, how's North Carolina?" He only glanced at Cassie before rising to get up and face the wall, lowering his voice.

Cassie strained to hear.

"So everything's going okay out there? He's there with you?"

She watched the muscles in his jaw working. Piecing together what she'd heard and his reaction, she could surmise that Brandon was lying about being with Pritchard and Drew wasn't happy.

"Are you still planning on coming back tomorrow?" He paused for his response. "Great, I'll see you then. Nope, everything's fine here. Busy but there's nothing wrong with that." The laugh was forced. "Hey, I've got someone in the office, I'll talk to you later?"

The tops of his ears went red for only an instant. "No, it's not like that. You take care of yourself out there and I'll see you later."

He didn't turn around right away. When he did, there was no evidence of upset remaining from his conversation with his brother. It was as if he'd hit a reset button, like upstairs after their argument. It wasn't normal.

"Your friends will be here soon. Let's get you downstairs; you might take a while." He set down his drink to help her.

Somewhat grudgingly, Cassie took her shoe and allowed him to help her to stand and walk. The high nap of the carpet in the office, she assumed was for sound deadening, combined with the lack of any real light to speak of caused her to raise her foot much higher than she wanted and increase the flexion of her injured limb. After a few halting steps Cassie's hand was guided onto Drew's forearm again and she leaned heavily on him.

Instead of turning left to go back the way they'd come, they went right and down into the blackness of the hall. Absently, Cassie wondered if this darkness was legal though she'd been in clubs even darker than this in New York. Briefly, her thoughts ran to nights when Pritchard was here raising energy and she thought of what acts might transpire here away from the lights. She was glad she didn't have to touch the walls.

"We can't have you going down the stairs," he said, yet this time Cassie didn't automatically assume the worst for his secreting her past the dancers. She had seen glimpses of another man behind the business-only, charming-for-money façade. Drew was essentially two different people. "There are tons of stairs there, I thought you'd do better in the elevator." A button glowed on the wall when he pressed it.

"You're probably right." She glanced up at him, genuinely appreciative.

The black doors opened to reveal a polished chrome interior almost blinding by contrast to the darkness all around them.

"Does your designer have a problem with light?" she asked, half kidding.

Grinning, Drew turned with her to face the doors as they closed. "Brandon read up on it and apparently the darker the better when it comes to restaurants and clubs. People like the anonymity. It makes them feel daring, they do things they normally wouldn't, and they like it. It brings them back."

Cassie waved a hand at their shiny surroundings. "Yeah, taking your clothes off in here would feel too much like being at the doctor's office." Embarrassed to have mentioned nudity because of where her thoughts went, Cassie directed her attention to her feet.

Drew was quiet for the long, painful ride down.

The doors opened on the far side of the purple bar and Cassie immediately let her focus shift to what was outside the glass in front, falling on the sedan parked out front. Patting his arm, she somewhat reluctantly extracted her hand. Walking was a lot easier with a crutch even if the crutch thought she was a fool or a prostitute. She wasn't sure which was worse.

"My ride's here. Thank you for your medical services and the drink. They both helped." She turned to leave and wobbled.

"Where? Let me help you." Replacing her hand on his arm he searched the crowd, craning his neck over her head for signs of movement in their direction.

Not wanting her partners to see her so dependent upon their target, Cassie wanted to be shut of him before they came in. "No really, I can make it." She slid her hand more assertively from his arm and he caught her elbow.

"Seriously Cassie, how stubborn are you? There's no way you're making it anywhere on your own and you can't fall in here, it's too crowded. You'll get stepped on." He was still scanning the crowd.

At the same time she opened her mouth to argue, Drew's arm tightened and he hissed a curse. Following his sightline to the bar and expecting to see Quan, Cassie saw someone else staring coolly at the man beside her. A woman not much younger than Julia hung on his arm with a vacant expression in her eyes. The dark hair fell away from his prominent widow's peak in stark contrast to his pale face and brilliant green eyes. As they both watched, he shoved himself away from the bar and strode directly toward them, the woman dragging along on his arm a mere afterthought.

Chapter 9

Cassie did not need an introduction to know that this was Terry Pritchard. The picture in her file had been taken from a distance but there was no mistaking that cocky twist to his thin lips. His picture hadn't done justice to the polluted aura that surrounded the man. It was no wonder Drew hated him.

Pritchard was obviously used to being in control, and from the way he practically strutted through the crowded bar, he had a certain expectation that things would remain the same here. Taking in the whole package, Cassie blinked in surprise. The tan polo shirt was acceptable enough, but the olive green cargo pants and were not only out of place in this upscale club, but also on the leader of a cult known to fleece its members out of near fortunes. She guessed that his allure came from within. Deep within.

The forty something woman on his arm looked like she'd just come from a grade school classroom in matched knit blue pants and top adorned with a ladybug pin sparkling from her chest. The empty look in her bloodshot eyes and slack jaw turned Cassie's stomach. She wished her ankle could hold her while she pounded the ass who'd done this to somebody's sweet little mom.

Given the thickness and volume of the crowd, Pritchard had to come far too close to be heard. "Drew Carter, just the man I was hoping to see." His voice was as slimy as his aura.

When Drew let go of her long enough to take the outstretched hand, Cassie felt the soothing comfort she'd accredited to the champagne fall away and was hit with a wash of rising energy. Her eyes went at once to the sedan out front with two shadows sitting unmoving inside. Quan must be wondering what she was doing in here; she knew he could feel this. He would even know that it wasn't her energy, that made it doubly dangerous. Shouldn't he be in here by now?

Juggling her shoe and purse made a quick grab at her phone unwieldy at best, and any sudden moves on her part would most likely land her on the floor. A circle to protect them both until help arrived was the best she could hope for, but there were an awful lot of witnesses and potential for casualties if things went bad. She deliberated the wisdom of screaming "fire."

The crowd made her nervous. Control hadn't been a strong point to now and she feared harming them as much as herself if she tried to perform a spell. She might also provoke a reaction from the witch raising power at that very moment. Her skin danced with the level of energy he was commanding. It wasn't sex magick, but this was definitely their witch.

Drew was grimacing when he picked up her hand again and she felt the calm come flooding back. Glancing down, she saw the ring on the hand she was holding. It could have been the effects of the ring or the dispelling of the pent up energy from earlier, regardless, something in her pushed her to act. Without removing her hand from her support, she turned her sight inward and muttered the words she knew by heart. In seconds she felt the warmth of the circle surround her and Drew as well.

The second it closed Cassie watched the cocky smirk fade from Pritchard's face. His glare switched from one to the other, settling on Drew as the perceived obstacle and his pinched expression slid down to Drew's amulet. He recognized the stone for what it was.

Drew's hand flew to his head, palm pressing his temple. Cassie felt a passing qualm knowing she was causing him further pain though it was tempered by the knowledge that she was also keeping him safe from worse.

"Pritchard what are you doing here?" Drew blinked and rubbed his hand over his forehead. "Brandon isn't here." He failed to mention that he had no idea of his brother's whereabouts given his alleged traveling companion was standing right here and he was nowhere in sight.

"I'm well aware of your brother's whereabouts. No, I am interested in seeing you without your big brother's interference for once." Sensing the circle blocked both of them, Pritchard let his eyes fall to Cassie. "And who is your new friend?"

"Just a guest who's suffered a minor mishap. I'm escorting her out." He hitched her hand up, pinching it tighter between his forearm and rib cage. She could feel every muscle rigid against the back of her hand. "We're busy tonight and I don't have time for this so if you don't mind, I'll have to excuse myself." Drew started to step around him and Pritchard held out a hand to stay him.

"I'm not asking, Carter."

Cassie felt his energy surge as Pritchard tried to break through her circle. Instinctively she pushed back and felt the skin on her arms begin to tingle and itch as their energies went back and forth, countering and testing each other. Too long supporting her, Cassie's ankle twitched and she wobbled losing her hold on Drew's arm.

Eyes wide, Drew stared at her. He felt the difference when he released her and her circle wavered. "What is that?" One hand went to his head as the power around him grew more erratic.

Without her crutch and the confidence boosting stone, Cassie stumbled literally and figuratively. When her circle broke, it sent energy spinning into the air and the volume of the voices around them grew louder, even the regulars could feel the increased vibrancy in the room. Without hesitation Pritchard attacked, sending a searing hot pulse into her brain; the psychic equivalent of a flash bang grenade. Beside him, the forgotten woman only watched vacantly.

Reeling, Cassie saw Drew shaking his head, gray eyes gone wide and felt the need to protect him. Narrowing her eyes, she glared at Pritchard. There was not even a moment's pause in her actions as she held out a hand and felt the gathering of her energy through the floors, alleviating the tingling on her skin's surface as she willed it into her palm. Without thought of the effects or how horribly wrong this could go, she readied herself for the release. Pritchard stared at her for only a second before she turned her palm out and pushed the ball toward him with a single command.

"Stop." She'd spoken only in a conversational tone yet the strike had been strong.

Pritchard hadn't anticipated her strength, and the defensive counterspell he attempted to block with was too late. It veered off, striking an overhead light, blowing the bulb in a flash. Someone in the crowd screamed as several people were struck by flying glass.

Unmoving amidst the ensuing chaos, Terry Pritchard gaped at Cassie. "You're like us."

Floored by what she'd done, Cassie only barely registered the man's voice. "What? No, I'm not like *you*," she stuttered.

Panicked clubbers were pushing back and forth, banging into them and Cassie was nearly shoved to the ground. Drew caught her and righted her, then let go as if he'd been burned.

When she looked again, Pritchard and his drone had disappeared. Cassie busily scanned the crowd for him to no avail. The combination of dark and proximity to the door would have aided any escape attempt.

The immediate crisis averted, the staff busily worked to calm the remaining few, continuing to comfort the scared and offer care to those wounded. Cassie turned her focus back to Drew, finding him leaning on an elbow against an iron table in the bar. He did nothing to help his employees. He merely watched them bustle about, shell shocked by what he'd witnessed.

Making her way to him, painfully and unsteadily through the shifting throng, Cassie laid a hand on his arm.

Refusing eye contact, he kept his glare over her head and aimed at the door. "Enough screwing around. You're going to tell me who you," his jaw clenched and Cassie turned to see Julia and Quan stride through the door on full alert, "and your friends are."

When he did lower his eyes to hers, they were dark and furious. "And what the hell is going on here."

An explanation with someone as close to the edge as him and in mixed company was inadvisable. Her partners had gathered that Drew was upset and fell in, letting him lead the way to the elevator. Catching sight of Cassie's hobble, Quan put an arm around her waist and dragged her along.

Quan made use of the opening to question Cassie, hopping and panting to keep up. "What happened in here? I felt a powerful witch, and then I felt another. Was either one *you*?" Quan was not one to sugar coat things.

Cassie filled him in quietly and Julia walking beside them listened while she kept watch for any further threats. There were none. The regulars settled down and order was restored. Any other practitioners had left with Pritchard. Her skin was decidedly non-tingly.

Dropping back she informed them of Pritchard's interest in Drew, her discovery of his amulet, and the possibility that his brother was working with Pritchard. Remembering what she'd overheard, she added the fact that Brandon was lying to Drew about something he was doing for Pritchard.

Cassie left Drew's possible involvement out of the equation for the time being, telling herself it was superfluous at this point. She would tell her partners should she see any evidence of wrongdoing down the road.

"And what of the discovery of *your* magick Cassie?" Quan prodded. "There is a new scent to you and at last some control, perhaps." He afforded the room behind them a backward glance, checking perhaps for signs of fire or mayhem.

Automatically defensive, Cassie's voice shrilled. "The light bulb blew up when Pritchard hit it, not me." Catching the hitch in Drew's step at her mention of the magick fight, she lowered her voice. "As far as my breakthrough goes, I don't know." Cassie watched Drew's back, the shadows playing tricks and making him appear only partially of this world, disappearing and reappearing as he walked from one light's glow to another. "At first I thought I was getting it from the ring when I was touching him." She pointed to the ankle in response to Quan's perked brow. "It was necessary. But then my circle broke and he tried to blast us and I just, I don't know, I just reacted. There was no time to throw up another circle or anything, it was so fast. There was no time to think."

The chrome doors opened and the four were bathed in pale light. They entered the elevator and rode in uncomfortable silence, not to be broken until they had filed in past Drew holding the door, and he clicked it shut behind them. When it did, Drew whirled on them.

"Talk." Arms crossed, Cassie thought he made for a rather intimidating bouncer. Drew wasn't overly musclebound; it was the look in his eyes, calm with an undercurrent of proposed violence, that was more worrisome to her than gigantic biceps and a shaved head. She was willing to bet he could handle himself in a fight should it come to that. He had that air of quiet confidence that men who had proven themselves carried as opposed to the toughs who felt a constant and irritating urge to show everyone what they could do.

"My name is Julia Departes, this is my partner Quan Long and you've already met our youngest partner Cassie Porter. We are here investigating Terry Pritchard, nothing more." Julia took the lead, her calming persona specifically tailored to this sort of situation. She spoke without moving a muscle, encouraging him to match her relaxed stance and tone. "We aren't here for you, Drew."

"Are you guys cops or something?" His eyes roved over each one assessing them suspiciously, barely giving Cassie any more pause than her partners. There was something they were holding back. Drew could sense it. He could sense it in the same way he could tell the older woman was attempting to handle him again. For a moment he felt his temper rising.

"Yes, we are," she replied with certainty. "We were advised that Mr. Pritchard was a frequent customer as well as a business associate?"

Features going loose, Drew waved a hand dismissively. His demeanor no longer prickly, he had returned to cool indifference.

Again Cassie noted the curious shift. "We don't have anything to do with that guy's business. He's slime but he's a customer; that's it. You can't arrest me because I let a dirt bag drink here."

"You're right, we can't. But we can ask you what your brother's affiliation with Pritchard might be." Cassie was done messing around too. Standing on her ankle hurt and she wanted to go back to the hotel where a hot shower and warm bed awaited her.

The muscles in his cheek twitched, the only sign of his vexation as Drew pulled his emotions back and let his face shut down going stony. "I think I want my lawyer."

"A lawyer can't save your brother's life. We can," Quan said softly.

"Is he in danger?" Speeding back to full alert, panic in his eyes, Cassie saw they were merely confirming for Drew what he already knew. "Pritchard's dragged him into his crap."

Glancing at her partners to make sure she wasn't overstepping first, Cassie saw that they were fine with her taking the lead. It was hard not to wonder if Anna had ordered them to step back and let her sink or swim on this last mission. She would do her damndest to show them she could make it in the field. Sticking out her chin, Cassie met his eyes coolly. "Drew, you're right not to trust him. We think Terry Pritchard is using your brother." She wanted him to see them as allies, as people he could trust and confide in. "And I'm guessing he wants something from you too. Do you have any idea what that might be?"

Shoulders sagging in defeat, Drew shook his head. "I don't know. What do you people suggest I do?"

Cassie wasn't sure what to tell him. She looked expectantly over at Julia.

"Pritchard is getting desperate to get his hands on you judging from the scene he made tonight. I think we wait for him to approach you again except this time we let him think he's got you. We'll keep an eye on you and step in if things get ugly." It sounded so simple coming from Julia, it always did. That was why people believed her and trusted her. Cassie wondered if Julia could teach her that. If they had more time that is.

"But if he's dangerous how are you going to help? Where are your guns? Are you going to do whatever it was she did downstairs?" He pointed at Cassie, rolling his eyes when she looked like she was going to argue. "What, like I didn't just see you throw a man without touching him? And am I supposed to pretend there isn't something that happens whenever I'm around any of you that makes me feel like my head's going to explode?" His left hand absently found the ring on his right.

Cassie gawked, unsure how much they were intending to tell him. If they overwhelmed him he might not be able to function properly when they needed him to.

"That's an unusual ring you have there. May I?" Julie held out her hand and offered him a warm smile.

Hesitant to part with it Drew began to slide the thick silver band down his finger. When it was nearly off Cassie felt her skin tighten. Quan was not going to let this chance to "smell" Drew unprotected go by without taking advantage.

"Stop it!" Drew mistakenly accused Cassie, glaring at her and the ring was cast loose as his hand flew. "I said stop." He pointed a finger in her face and she felt something sting her skin.

Touching the spot on her cheek she felt something wet and her fingers came away red. He'd actually cut her. Equally shocked, he left his offending hand hanging in midair while the other three stared.

"It looks like Brandon isn't the only one in the family with teeth," Julia drawled in the stunned silence.

Chapter 10

"Oh my God, what did I do?" Drew gawked, his pallor gone ghostly. He looked as though he might be sick.

"Hmm," Julia found the ring where it had landed behind the desk, examining it before handing it back. "You'd better put this back on. For safety."

He did as he was told, not taking his gaze from Cassie's cheek where a faint trace of blood was beginning to seep a through her fingers as she held it against the sting.

Cassie, on the other hand, was seeing Drew in an entirely new light. He didn't need protecting, he needed training.

"Has that ever happened before?" Quan tipped his head and squinted up at him.

"No, never. Well, I never made anyone bleed." His voice was hollow. "After our parents died we lived with our aunt here in Tampa. Brandon and I both came even though he was old enough he could have stayed behind. He wanted to stay with me; he's protective." Drew gave a little snort and a wry smile. "Aunt Christine didn't want him; it never sat well with her that he was home when they were killed. She blamed him, I suppose. Mom was her only sibling and their parents were both gone so they were all they had left. Like Brandon and me." His gaze was distant. He was with his thoughts, years away.

Drew's story gave their triad way more than he thought. After they left here, Cassie and her partners would be looking into the parents' deaths, that much was certain.

He continued, calm and emotionless. "After a few weeks the police were really leaning hard on Brandon. They thought he was involved or something. Christine told him he had to leave, she didn't want him in her house. They started yelling, really having it out. Christine telling him to get out and he was being seventeen, daring her to call the cops and make him leave. I was only twelve and I didn't want him to go. When she picked up the phone I kind of freaked out." Drew squinted at his hands and Cassie caught their tremor. "I don't remember everything that happened, just that I wanted her to stop yelling and put down the phone. I yelled and grabbed it out of her hands, and then…she fell." His voice cracked.

Cassie saw the frightened boy there in him again. No one could explain to him what had happened and he'd lived with the fear that he was dangerous for fourteen years. Even an amulet couldn't take all of that away.

Julia pressed him gently. "What happened to her, honey?"

Shrugging, Drew looked up. The moment was passed and he was coming back to himself, standing with a fixed gaze on the back wall over their heads. "She fell. The paramedics said it was a seizure from the shock and the excitement. She pretty much avoided us both after that. We lived on one side of the house and she lived on the other. The day Brandon turned eighteen he sued for legal custody and we left the day it came through. I haven't seen her since."

The sound of the air conditioner blowing through the ducts was the only noise in the office. Cassie felt compelled to comfort him. She had heard similar stories from clients on other cases, although she'd remained relatively untouched by their sentiments. It wasn't an intentional coldness. Cassie had been too busy trying to figure out how they had come to discover their power and in almost every case she had gone home and tried to replicate it for similar results. Clearly none of those situations had worked. This time was different. And she was oddly grateful to him.

Not knowing really how to be comforting, she wobbled as best she could on her good foot and the toes of the other to reach him. She half expected him to stop her, but he didn't. "I'm sorry, Drew. We're here to help you." For a brief instant she forgot that they were going to use him as bait to catch his brother and Pritchard. Right at that moment she meant it.

"What, you've got some magical way for all of this to go away? For this nut job to leave us alone and weird stuff to stop happening to us?"

His guess was frighteningly close to accurate, giving Cassie hope that he would be receptive to what she was about to say. This was always a tricky conversation, even though the clients knew something was different about themselves by the time they were having it. She'd seen people overjoyed to learn they had special powers, seeing themselves as a sort of superhero. Some were relatively indifferent and others wanted to know how to make it go away.

There had been one young woman, heartbroken to learn that it had been her uncontrolled magick that had set her house on fire. Her parents and baby sister had gotten out but her grandmother had not. It hadn't been a week after they'd met with her and arranged for her to meet with a "personal trainer" when news reached Veritas that she'd taken her own life.

The price of magick in Drew's family had already been great. It was a safe bet Brandon was responsible for the deaths of their parents. She could only hope that it had been accidental. Brandon might take the news hard as well if he didn't already know.

Drew's eyes searched hers and she saw his apprehension though he tried to keep it hidden. She recognized inquisitiveness in his look. He had it in him to believe. However, the question remained: What would he do with the knowledge once he had it? Could he live with it? Taking a breath and shifting her weight on her feet, Cassie laid it out for him.

"Drew I'm sure you've guessed by now there are things in this world that we can't always see. Ways to manipulate energy that don't always make scientific sense." She paused, letting it sink in. He showed no signs of interrupting. Gambling on his level head, she let the other shoe drop. "Magick is real. And you show signs of having some talent. It tends to run in families, so it's likely your brother is the same." Better not to let him know their guesses at his brother's ability level just yet. "With some guidance we would be happy to arrange, you could both lead relatively normal lives providing you're careful. Working here, it actually sounds like you may be using some of it already."

All three watched him. Waiting.

At first, they saw his impulse to deny it and his mouth opened, lips twisting to make some sort of comment or discount her declaration, then his mouth snapped shut. His inner struggle was visible. Cassie thought he was going to be understanding until the words he finally chose took her by surprise.

"Get out." He took a menacing step, forcing Cassie to hop hurriedly back to avoid bumping into his advancing chest. "Whatever game you're playing, I don't want any part of it. And if Pritchard put you up to it to scare me, tell him I'm not afraid of his little show downstairs. If he wants something from me he can come talk to me like a man, alone." Raising his finger, he pointed at Julia. "You leave Brandon alone, he's got enough on his mind without your nonsense."

"How do you explain what you saw downstairs?" Cassie pressed, willing him to listen to reason. "What about how you feel when people use their magick around you? You said it yourself, it feels like your head's going to explode." He couldn't refute his own words.

"I get migraines," he snapped, chopping a hand through the air before any of them could argue. "And I don't know *what* that was down there. I'm sure it was some sort of stunt you two worked out to try to get me rattled. Well it won't work. Now get out of here. If I see you in my club again I'll have you thrown out."

Julia spoke softly, forcing him to listen. "The effect you have on people, have you always had that? Have you ever had a woman say no to you?" Julia asked, arms folded and making it clear she was not afraid of him. "Or were you even better before you got that ring?"

Drew blanched though he jerked the door open. His decision stood. "I'm good with people. That's why I do what I do." The door remained open, his arm held out impatiently waiting for them to leave.

"Can you stand there and tell me there's no such thing as magick and yet you see the difference in yourself with that amulet you wear." She took a slow step into his space. "I'm curious if you wear it to block out others or is it to keep yourself locked up." Only that strange effect of a drawl on a northerner kept the words from pushing him over the edge she was sure, yet Cassie watched him bristle as Julia struck the nerve she'd been aiming for.

"I told you three to get out and I meant it. Now leave or I'll be forced to help you out."

Typically closed mouthed, Quan stepped silently around where Drew stood trembling, his rage at the intruders barely contained. Cassie could see his pulse throbbing rapidly in his neck. It matched the pounding she could feel in her entire lower leg above her swollen ankle as she made her unwieldy way past next to where Quan waited, again taking her under his wing. Julia was the last with some parting words for Drew.

"Here's my card, honey. Call when you're ready to talk about it. Hopefully it's before anyone else gets hurt."

To a point, they would let him choose the timetable on his initiation into their world. Having gotten a taste of his ability, his place there was certain as was his brother's. However, Brandon's entrance would be more urgent if he was hurting people. Drew, thus far, was relatively harmless.

His answer was the sound of the door slamming shut behind them.

Ch. 11

Quan ordered Cassie to pull over when they'd cleared the busier part of town.

"Turn in there." He pointed to a dark street marked with a subdivision sign yet no residential lights behind it.

They wound through the curving streets, past the few occupied homes, stopping when they reached the end where several yet unpurchased homes backed up to another street, still mid-construction. Victims of the housing market glut, these partially built skeletons stood forgotten, already weathering in the extreme Florida climate, their fates uncertain.

"Show me what happened with Pritchard." Quan opened his door and stepped out of the vehicle, his body breaking the beams and casting a long shadow on the frame of the home beyond. The timing of his exit removed any hope of disagreement. Not that the odd man would humor one anyway.

Cassie put her hands on the wheel, the adrenaline rushing through her making it hard to hear outside her own head. "Be right there," she mumbled. The thread of confidence that had begun to weave itself into her consciousness after tonight's incident had passed, leaving her usual doubt in its place.

The dome light stayed on, illuminating the remaining occupants. Julia paused with her hand on the door, eyes following Quan as he moved past the scope of the headlights and into the darkness beyond. "There are two fronts for us to cover now, Pritchard and the Carters. Quan loves a challenge; you know he'll want Pritchard. That leaves you with Drew to wait here for Brandon's return. He's scared but he trusts you." She waved off her partner's dubious frown. "I see it in him and so do you. Don't be afraid, Cassie." The experienced woman attempted to encourage her. "This could be the breakthrough Anna's been waiting for, that we've all been waiting for. We need to know if you can handle it."

Julia's reminder that her career rested on her functionality didn't help the lead balloon in her chest. It wasn't enough that she'd made a connection with her magick, now she had to show she could command it. The incident in the club might be a fluke and Cassie feared she wouldn't be able to reproduce it at will.

Again she called up the image of her father's pride on the day she was accepted into the Academy. It had been a given granted her lineage but it had given her father a rush nonetheless. It was the need to see that pride in his eyes again that drove her, the need to make good and to show her grandmother that her mother's blood had not made her weak.

It was vital that she prove her merit by honoring both of her parents' contributions to her powers and be able to provide for her family. To be able to quash the rumors at Veritas and on the reservation, as well as in her own father's house, that her mixed blood made her weak and confused the spirits so that they could not hear her prayers. With a juvenile stubbornness, Cassie wanted to show them all she was one of the good ones while it was the flip side of that very coin, the one that was far easier to believe, giving her the crippling doubt in herself that she never would.

Sighing, she turned off the car and opened her door to join Julia, now waiting by the front of the car to help her trudge over the uncertain terrain. "Please don't let me screw this up." She muttered to whatever spirits or gods might be listening. Quite frankly, she would be loyal to any of them right now if they would claim her and help her to keep her job.

"Over here," Quan called out, moving to make himself visible in the partial moonlight.

They closed the distance, stopping a few strides away. Julia made certain Cassie was stable and stepped out of the line of fire.

"How far apart were you in the club?" He wasted no time in getting started.

Eyeing the distance, Cassie teetered two hop steps forward. "This is about right."

"Tell me exactly what happened."

This time making certain to hit on all the details, Cassie relived the potentially life-changing moment, "I stumbled and when my hand came off Drew's arm, that's when my circle broke." Letting her thoughts be spoken aloud, "I lost my confidence but then when he caught me again I could tell the ring was transferring some of its influence over to me. I felt like I could do anything."

"Is that why you chose to attack instead of cast another circle?"

Cassie took Quan's remark to be accusatory. "There wasn't enough time and I could feel the energy building in my hand. It never felt like that before. It felt right." Cassie realized she was giving them more insight into the depth of her problem than she'd intended. Quickly adding, "Then, I pushed." She wished she could see his expression. Julia was nibbling on her lip, she was nervous.

"Show me," Quan ordered.

Cassie was going to argue then she saw his stance shift and his hands go up, palms facing one another yet not quite touching like he was praying. Quan was pulling power. The bright blue light flared in the space between his palms and hung there, waiting to do his will. Cassie began muttering an incantation, the instinct to cast a circle ingrained from her earliest years.

The shock when he hit her was relatively minor considering she'd seen him knock three rogue witches down with one blast. This one blew her back about four feet landing her squarely on her backside. Julia hurried in to help her struggle to her feet. Meanwhile, the ankle was screaming at her, fresh blood leaked from the reopened cheek laceration and she was fairly certain she was going to have a huge bruise on her butt from a rock that had surely torn her skirt.

"I'm not really dressed for this exercise," she muttered crossly, brushing herself off with Julia's help to stabilize.

Her older partner snorted in amusement.

There was no sympathy from Quan either. "What did you do differently?" She could hear his smart tone and picture the raised eyebrow. He knew full well what she'd done.

Feeling vastly less glamorous than she had at the start of the evening, Cassie groaned. "I couldn't help it, it's a habit to cast a circle first. Protection's good you know."

"And were you in a protective circle at Carter's?"

"No, I..." Cassie hadn't earned the right to argue, not with *her* track record. Biting her tongue, she swallowed her sarcastic comments.

Quan moved into the light. "Then you should not be in one now."

"I know, but it's a habit..." Cassie repeated, wincing at the whine she heard in her tone.

"Your habits do not work." The clouds shifted and the moonlight framed his face in half shadow, casting his features in a ghoulish mien. "It is time for new ones."

A response was neither necessary nor expected. Quan waited barely long enough for Julia to get out of the way before his palms came together again. This time, Cassie was ready and made a conscious effort not to cast a protective spell.

What struck her was the intentional lack of preparedness she had to maintain. In her training with her mother and then at the Academy she had been taught to first cast a circle to protect herself before opening herself up to any external power sources such as she did to cast a spell. Grandmother didn't agree with Veronica's different spells, yet hers was a magick built upon ceremony as well and both women had drawn their power from the elements.

Though they were different elements, Water and Earth, they used a similar caste system which was why Cassie had attempted to merge them. It was also that blur between the different elements she was inviting into her body's energy balance that made it hard to differentiate enough to know what was stuck. With that clog unstuck, her mind and energy balance were easily able to restore themselves and automatically seemed to draw the energy she needed from either of the elements available.

Cassie's new style diverged from both of her parents' ritualistic types, favoring a free form she was having trouble reconciling after such a long time practicing and drilling complex and simple spells.

Taking a deep breath, Cassie held her hands palms out toward the ground and relaxed. The water was not far below the ground here, she could feel it coursing beneath her feet, at the same time feeling the roots of trees and plants long dead and decomposing in the ground. She could feel it flood her body. The skin from her feet all the way up her sides tingled and raised goose flesh as the energy raced up and down, igniting her nerves until her entire body seemed to hum.

Directing it to her hand, she gathered and wound it into a writhing, swirling ball of blues and browns eager for release. When it had grown to the size of a softball, and Cassie felt the colorful mass fighting to flow back into her or unravel and fling out in a chaotic wave, she saw Quan's hands spreading apart from their prayer position. As they spread, beginning to fan out, the bright blue ball of power sparked from within, ready for its own unleashing. He was a breath away from launching his attack as Cassie let hers fly to strike first.

A bright burst of light marked where her attack hit Quan squarely in the chest followed by a surprised cry as he was thrown backward, arms wheeling to land in a heap against a pile of construction debris behind him.

"Crap. Quan, are you okay?" Cassie stumbled and hopped her way over to him. Julia left her to manage on her own to check that she hadn't in fact incinerated their male counterpart.

By the time they reached him, he was already sitting up and patting the smoldering fabric on his shirt. As experienced as he was, Quan wouldn't have let her hit him on purpose. Would he? Cassie could see that he had blocked most of the force but some had definitely gotten through his defenses.

She'd actually scored on him! She couldn't believe it. Forcing herself to breathe through her nose while holding her lips firmly in her teeth Cassie was able to keep herself from grinning and laughing like an idiot.

The smell of burnt cotton and residual goose flesh were evidence of victory. Something had changed in her magick. That fact was now indisputable. Twice, not just the one fluke, but twice she had successfully used this less organized method of manipulating her elements. Elements, not element she noted with an "aha."

Two had to be balanced and maintained within her for her magick to work. Mixed blood didn't mean choosing one, it meant making them work side by side and avoiding either one from building up to outweigh the other. Cassie struggled to maintain her composure. She couldn't tell if she wanted to cry for how stupid she'd been or if she wanted to pump her fists in the air and dance. It was so simple! How had she not seen it before now? Jim Salter was going to get the best ceramic kitty money could buy.

"What was that? It looks and feels completely different from what she's been doing." It could have been her imagination but Cassie thought she heard something akin to fear in Julia's voice.

Head canted to the side curiously, Quan studied his young partner. "I believe you have found the key to your power, Cassie."

She took a few breaths to slow her racing heart. "Really?" What it meant was sinking in. Cassie's emotions threatened to overwhelm her.

He allowed himself to be helped up, brushing dust off his pants while he answered. "Your channels were blocked and your magick could not find its balance within you. You've learned to open yourself up and let your powers flow through you in harmony. They will no longer be at war inside you."

Eyes pricking with happiness turned incredulous as Cassie blinked rapidly. "You knew what the problem was? You knew this whole time I just had to 'clear my channels'?" Sarcasm dripped from her words. Salter's mention had been the first she'd even heard of such a thing. "Why didn't anybody say anything?"

"Magick is individual, as unique to the witch as her thoughts. The teachings can only go so far. When the student has her knowledge, she must apply what she knows to what she feels in her powers. No one can do it for her." Quan shook his head mildly. "Being mixed merely complicates things. If you would have tried to force your power to copy another's, it would have driven you mad."

Embarrassed that she'd been such a heavy burden to so many who had watched her, waiting for her to go nuts or blow herself up, angry that it had taken this long for her to figure things out Cassie snapped her mouth shut and covered her face. Yelling at her partners wouldn't do anybody any good. Instead she let the hot wave roll over her and felt it pass, taking with it the last of her strength leaving her exhausted and drained.

Speaking in her low voice, lilting hauntingly in the darkness, Julia put a hand on Cassie's shoulder, "Now that we have you figured, we can finally teach you some things."

The three ran through a few more exercises before headlights twisting through the streets told them it was time to move on. Cassie leaned heavily on Julia's arm on the way back to the car, sweating and completely spent.

"You've done well, Cassie." The older woman patted her arm. "Anna will be pleased."

Exhausted and simultaneously elated, Cassie sniffed. "I hope she hasn't already made up her mind that I'm beyond hope."

"*We* haven't." Julia's teeth flashed in the moonlight. "We aren't your partners if we aren't willing to help you, Cassie."

All three were quiet on the ride back to the hotel. Quan assisted Cassie into the building while Julia hung back to have an employee help her with the bags. The last three rooms on the top floor were theirs. Julia and Cassie were on the same side with an adjoining door, Quan's room lay across the hall.

Julia knocked on the door adjoining their rooms with Cassie's bag. They'd left it open and she came through to leave the bag on the side chair. Cassie sat on the edge of the bed, her eyes beginning to droop.

"Quan's called Anna to update her." She eyed the dirty, once tan wrap and the overall disheveled appearance. Cassie looked like she'd been in a bar fight and hadn't necessarily done all that well. "We'll have a healer here by breakfast for that ankle." She frowned and leaned in to examine Cassie's cheek. "They ought to be able to keep the scarring down to a minimum. I'm going to wash up and then if you'd like to join me I was going to get myself some food downstairs." Her deep brown eyes sparkled. "I heard they have a real Creole chef here. What I would give for good etouffee." Her voice trailed off.

Her stomach fluttered at the thought that Quan had already reported the good news to Anna. Excitement won out over the nerves that came with knowing if she was a full fledged investigator a lot more would be expected of her. It was still a very real possibility that she could get her partners in trouble or let everyone down. "Thanks Julia, but I'm probably just going to get some room service after a really, really long, hot shower. I'm beat."

"All right. I'll be downstairs if you change your mind." With a wave, Julia walked back through their shared door closing it with a click after her.

Cassie turned the lock for privacy and hopped to the bathroom, her head reeling from the day's events. A hot shower, a light dinner and maybe some ice on the side for her ankle were about all she could imagine wanting tonight. She was almost right. She barely ate her dinner and got her foot resting under a bag of ice before she fell asleep. Cassie didn't move until the alarm went off at eight.

Chapter 12

After he slammed the door on the three charlatans, Drew watched the monitor to make sure they left the club. What they'd tried to sell him about the reality of magick was irritating, and yet, on some baser level it struck a chord. Then too there was his annoyance at himself for having lost control again and hurting the girl. He'd thought he had that part of himself under control.

"Magick tends to run in families," she'd said. Try as he might to guide it away from that place, Drew's thoughts refused to be deterred. Eventually he relented, giving up on diverting and following them down where they wanted to go.

Brandon had been a kid when their parents died, both of them had. Sure he'd fought with their parents like any normal teen. But there'd never been any threats made or acts of violence or anything. Brandon had never acted out or done anything hurtful like Drew had to cause their aunt's "seizure." No way Brandon was like Pritchard, or even Drew for that matter. All too readily Drew was willing to believe that if there was a weak link in the family it was him.

Rethinking his original impressions, Drew decided the older lady was a crackpot and that guy with them gave him the creeps. And yet deep down, lurking in a place he didn't want to acknowledge existed, a little voice had agreed with everything they'd said.

Then there was Cassie. He wasn't sure what to make of her. For one thing she didn't fall all over him. That was a first for him from a woman, or a man for that matter. Then when she'd come back looking so good and practically throwing herself at him, if he hadn't thought she'd been from Pritchard he might have taken her up on it and seen how far it would go. She'd nearly had him convinced she was there on her own until the man himself had shown up in the club. What happened when he did?

Regardless of what he'd said to get them out of his office, Drew wasn't so sure it had been a trick. And yet, what else could it have been? He hadn't seen what Cassie had done after she'd stepped in front of him and started mumbling. That was when he got one of those headaches again. Regardless of what he'd said to get them out of his office, Drew wasn't so sure it had been a trick. And yet, what else could it have been? He hadn't seen what Cassie had done after she'd stepped in front of him and started mumbling, but then the headache had disappeared. Just poof, like that, everything had gotten all warm and comfortable. Drew was able to see Pritchard looking like he was thinking really hard about something. That was when Cassie lost her balance and his headache had come screaming back. Eyes closed, he hadn't seen what happened but when he opened them again Pritchard was gone. It didn't make sense. If it was a stunt what was it supposed to prove? Was he supposed to feel some sort of gratitude toward Cassie for what, protecting him? From what? Magick?

He wondered what the hell Pritchard had dragged Brandon, and now him, into. His curiosity now driving him, the anger having dissipated within minutes of its initial fiery surge.

Drew dialed the bar, spinning his ring out of habit while he waited for her to pick up. "Jaime, can I get a scotch in here?"

"Sure thing, boss."

Two minutes later Jaime knocked twice and entered. "Here you go, boss." She set it on the desk in front of where Drew leaned back in his brother's chair. Technically they shared the office even if everything was pretty much Brandon's. Drew said he didn't need his own, his duties were on the floor. In truth, it had more to do with the end of the night wrap up meetings they had here. It had become a routine he looked forward to after a long night breaking up fights and playing to the female patrons who threw themselves figuratively, and sometimes bodily, at him.

The novelty of the barrage of ready flesh no longer had the effect it once did. This apparent Midas touch he had with women had grown tedious and he'd gone the complete opposite direction. Drew hadn't brought anyone to his bed for nearly a year.

"Is everything okay Drew?" Jaime rested a hip on the edge of the glass, a long tan leg dangling over its edge. She meant nothing by her familiar pose.

Jaime was entirely devoted to her academic career and Drew had made their professional relationship clear from the very beginning just to be sure. She was too good of an employee to lose over a fling.

"What was up with the tussle downstairs? Somebody said they saw Pritchard starting something with someone downstairs. Is that true? Was he here?"

Like Drew, no one on staff really liked Pritchard and Brandon's continued acceptance of the man, investor or not, was a stain upon his character. Drew frequently had to enlist his charismatic charm to smooth over the irritation and downright disgust of employees after they saw Pritchard and his zombie like groupies in the club dancing and doing God knows what upstairs. Most of the time the other patrons cleared out, although on occasion they stayed and things really got out of control. Several times now they'd had to seal off the upstairs and tell people it was a private party. The old Brandon never would have let that kind of thing happen in the club no matter how much money this guy had dumped into the place.

Jaime's arrival broke up the gloom he'd been nursing. Drew gave her a quick flash of a smile. "They were just guests, that's all. Pritchard wanted to get into it and the girl happened to be there when he had a tantrum. You know Pritchard when someone tells him no."

That was true enough. Typical of any cult leader, the man was little more than a needy child, and took rejection about as well as one. Several of the women on staff had given him reason to have a fit when he'd tried to indoctrinate them to his cause. In those cases, when it involved Pritchard, Brandon insisted that *he*, not Drew, act as soothsayer.

Brandon never let Drew spend more than a few seconds with Terry Pritchard if he could help it. Most of the time he sent Drew out to pick up some supply he needed right at that moment, purposefully keeping the two from being in the same room. Drew figured his brother was trying to avoid a fight between them knowing how Drew felt about him. Even with his level temperment, Pritchard got under his skin.

"Oh. Well, I hope nobody got hurt." Jaime hid any personal feelings she might have on the subject of Pritchard, choosing to pursue something more interesting. "Speaking of which, what did you do with the girl who was in here earlier, the one with the sprained ankle?" Jaime fluttered her eyes. "I saw the way she was looking at you."

Drew frowned and spun his glass on the table, studying the pure amber liquid inside undiluted by ice or water and it occurred to him her eyes were the same warm caramel color when she wasn't glaring. He shook his head and laughed it off. "She was nobody. Just a dancer who got hurt and I was trying to help so she didn't sue us."

"A nobody who was sitting at your private table?" She gave him a knowing look. "I haven't seen that in a while."

He said nothing.

Jaime watched him swirl his glass and take a mouthful, holding it for a moment before swallowing. Whether he admitted it or not, something was eating at him and she wanted to help. That was hard to do if he didn't want to open up. Leaning forward, she eased herself off the desk and swatted his leg. "Suit yourself, Silent Bob. You know where to find me if you need an ear."

He raised his glass in salute and she touched her fingers to her brow in return. Jaime closed the door behind her, leaving him to his thoughts.

Cassie Porter. That's who was in his thoughts. There was something about her that stuck with him. Maybe it had been the clumsy efforts to be something she wasn't. He was sure the only true thing she'd said to him had been that she was "trying to live a life she wasn't meant for." Oddly that struck a chord with him even if he couldn't be clear why, and that troubled him as well.

Irrationally, he been outraged when she effectively hid herself behind the distant cop façade she'd affected when they'd confronted him. Although why that mattered was a mystery. It had to be because she had come to harm here in his club not once, but twice. Drew could see the cut on her face in his mind's eye and felt a melancholy sort of guilt over it wondering how he'd managed to hit her face with the ring without seeing it. That was what he'd decided *had* to have happened and his attachment to her was a need to apologize for it.

Fleeting, the emotions tied up with his interest in her were already beginning to fade as well as the anger at the trio's attempted scam. What did remain was the fact that he wanted to talk to her again without those two around.

Taking another big swallow, Drew fished the woman's business card out of his pocket and stared at it. The scotch was beginning to take effect and he could feel the warm fuzziness enveloping his brain.

Julia Departes
Veritas
Client Relations

Downing the last of his drink he picked up the phone and dialed the number, sure at this hour he would reach her voicemail. He was just going to check on the girl, try to talk to her and find out if she was okay, he told himself. He could use the excuse he was following up after her fall at the club. He could offer to pay any medical expenses.

"Veritas, how may I help you?" A woman's voice answered after the second ring.

The front legs of the chair came down with a thud and he sat up straight, startled to have reached a live person. According to his watch it was nearly midnight here on the East coast. He'd assumed they were local. "Um, yes, I was trying to reach Julia Departes?" It came out as a question.

"This is her service. Is this an emergency?"

"No, no it isn't."

The woman wasn't the least bit perturbed by his difficulty. "May I take a message?" she prompted.

"Yeah, please. Um, here's the thing... I'm actually trying to reach a coworker of hers, Cassie Porter. Could I leave the message for her?" He held his breath feeling like a teenager hoping to impress a girl's mother.

"Yes sir, you can leave a message for Ms. Porter if you would prefer."

"Great, uh, could you tell her Drew Carter called? From the club tonight. I was calling to check back and see that she was okay." He left his number and hung up, feeling like a total ass. "Good thing that wasn't a machine." He reassured himself. At least Cassie wouldn't hear him stumbling like a buffoon. Nervously he fidgeted with his ring, welcoming the peace that little habit gave him.

He was just about to get up when a movement on the monitor fed by the camera at the rear entrance caught his eye. The lanky limbs and awkward gait gave him away before the widows peak came into sight. Pritchard was back, but why was he skulking around the back door? Welcome or not, he'd always used the front door. Why should now be any different? Unless he was trying to avoid the same three people who had been dominating Drew's thoughts for the last hour.

Another movement and Drew refocused. What was Brandon doing here? Wasn't he supposed to be gone until tomorrow at the earliest? Drew sat up and stared, curious to see what the two were going to do in a dark alley with little to no foot traffic except for the occasional club patron who might try using the space for a little privacy whether it was to go to the bathroom, have a quickie or buy party drugs. They'd certainly had enough trouble with the latter recently.

Brandon didn't look good. The black and white of the video accentuated the shadows under his eyes and hollows in his cheeks, which had been becoming steadily more prominent since last fall. He looked like an animated skeleton staggering around behind the building. Faced with such a stark picture, Drew couldn't believe how he was wasting away, mentally kicking himself for not having noticed it had gotten to this point. Tomorrow he was going to tell him he had to go to the doctor and get checked out. Hopefully he wasn't really sick or something that was too far advanced by now to be helped. He couldn't fathom what he would do if something happened to his brother.

Two more figures stepped into the alley making Drew sit up. They were obviously male given their height and the aggressive way they moved as they crossed into the halo of light cast by the halogen over the door. Brandon and Pritchard had their backs to the camera to face the strangers approaching. Drew had never seen either of them before but could guess by the hour and the lurking that this was an illegal operation. The main guy was watching them coolly, his second man was jumpy, twitching too much not to be on something and swiveled his head enough to make Drew dizzy watching him.

Pritchard's hands gestured broadly as he spoke. It looked like the leader from the opposing team didn't like Terry Pritchard any more than Drew did. Drew could assume whatever business they were conducting was not going well. He was considering heading down to try to keep the situation from getting out of hand when it became clear it was too late. Something in the way Pritchard's hands moved was eerily familiar.

Pritchard flung his hands up like a referee in the end zone at a football game and Brandon attempted to jump sideways. Pritchard was faster and caught his arm yanking him into his side. Captivated, he watched the drama spinning wildly out of control on the tiny screen.

The main guy stepped back and pointed, clearly pissed off while his second pulled a gun from his waistband and thankfully held it on Pritchard. He failed to see Brandon as a threat and rightly so. It looked like Brandon was near collapse, his limbs flopping about like a ragdoll as Pritchard tugged and held him in place.

Drew wished he could see his face to see if he'd fainted. He sat, unable to move, riveted to the screen.

Something in Pritchard's posture changed when he touched Brandon, he stood taller and his hands ceased their commotion. The one not on Brandon reached out to the leader across from him. Brandon's shoulders at the bottom of the screen jerked upright and he suddenly threw his arms out wide, mirroring Pritchard's gesture only with both hands. The expressions of both men facing the camera changed from anger to terror and then agony in seconds.

The twitchy one dropped his gun and put his hands to his chest following his leader, already pressing at his shirtfront, to his knees. For what couldn't have been more than a few heartbeats, both men wavered, staring frozen in horror at whatever it was Pritchard and Brandon were doing. Drew could see no weapons but for the gun on the ground by Twitchy. Pritchard's hands were still accounted for and appeared empty. Brandon's came up over his head slapping shut with his palms together.

It was at that point Drew remembered what was bothering him about Pritchard's hand. It was the same thing he'd seen him do inside the club when he'd had his "thing" with Cassie.

What did Brandon have to do with any of this stuff? Unable to move if he'd wanted to, Drew watched the figures, waiting to see what would happen next. Wondering if Pritchard would knock them back like Cassie'd done to him.

He didn't. What actually *did* happen was lost to the scope of the viewing device. All Drew saw was the two kneeling men go rigid and fall to their sides, still holding their chests. Then the cameras all went to static.

"What the hell!" Trance broken, Drew jumped up and shouted at the monitor banging it with his hand. He'd forgotten the glass he held until it broke and dug into his palm in the same instant he heard the heavy base of the tumbler clatter on the desktop. "Damn." He spat a curse, jumped to his feet and rushed from the office.

The elevator would take too long. Drew streaked across the crowded dance floor, nearly knocking several dancers off their feet in the process and not bothering to offer apologies in his wake. Drew took the steps three at a time and hurdled the velvet rope, scaring the glitter right off the host as he grabbed the corner of the handrail and swung himself with the assistance of his own centrifugal force around to head out the back and through the kitchen. When he burst out the rear door, blinking in the sudden bright glow of the bare halogen bulb, Drew stood swaying and panting as his brain tried to make sense of what he was looking at.

Unsteady, he dragged his feet toward what had been the leader of the two men. The soles of his slick dress shoes slipped on the wet ground. Twisting his neck and forcing his eyes to look beyond the immediate area, Drew saw only dry pavement and felt no hint of rain on his upturned face. Nor was there a drainpipe or hose that would explain why the ground and walls were soaked and dark. He slipped again and went down to one knee. There was a wet slapping sound when he hit the ground with an open palm to catch himself.

The light from behind him cast his hand in shadow. Standing, he brought his hand up to the light and saw the dark red stain on it matched the lower leg of his pants. Three more staggering steps brought him to the fallen leader now lying in a twisted heap. Drew blinked a few more times before his brain caught up with his eyes and he felt his stomach heave. Stumbling and sliding, he made it back to dry ground and leaned against the side of the building. He barely felt the concrete that made up the less artistically constructed back wall as he puked his guts out.

"Hey Drew, everything okay out here." Tavaris' voice trailed off as the host who'd followed him out, wondering if they were being robbed, took in the carnage. "Oh my God, oh my God, I'll call the police."

Drew didn't object as he heard the metal door clang shut behind Tavaris' retreating figure. All he could think about was that he hoped Brandon was far away from here by now so that the police couldn't find him. That they wouldn't make the connection he had.

The image of this scene superimposed itself on the one in his memory. The one he'd seen in the police file he'd bullied out of an officer when he'd finally been able to confront his parents' deaths. The weakness in his legs was only partially due to the gore and death he found himself surrounded by at present.

"Run Brandon," he gasped between retches. "Just run."

Chapter 13

By nine o'clock the next morning Cassie was a new woman. The healer had gotten her ankle down to only mild bruising, a faint red line marked her leg where she'd fallen on the dance floor, and the one on her face was barely visible. Between that and the best beignets she'd ever had with her coffee that morning, she was over the moon. Oh and of course there was the matter of no longer living in fear of discovery for being a magickal flop. If the healer hadn't told her to take it easy she would have done cartwheels.

Cassie was stopping back in her room after breakfast when her phone rang and she hustled to catch it. It was her service.

"Good morning, Ms. Porter. Drew Carter called last night. He wanted to see if you were okay. Did something happen, ma'am?"

Cassie's lips curved involuntarily and she felt a bubble of excitement in her chest. "No, nothing big. Thanks Karly." She hung up, holding her phone absently to her chest thinking about the man she'd met last night.

He'd been an intriguing combination of kindness, indifference, and anger. Sometimes in the same instant. It was undeniably linked to the amulet he wore. Though he clearly didn't consciously understand that he or his brother had anything to do with the deaths of their parents, there had been hints that deep down he knew there was something different about him, like that story about the aunt. That sort of thing told her he was suspicious of his ability on some level. His partial belief in the existence of magick was not unusual nor was his reaction. There was really nothing about him that set him apart from any of the other uninitiated and untrained witches and practitioners from various sects and walks of life, and yet she'd found her thoughts drifting back to him since they'd left the club. That he'd called and checked up on her meant more than it should.

Cassie chastised herself for allowing the distraction. Last night's progress didn't undo three and a half years of botching things. It was only a step in the right direction. It was going to take some serious buckling down to completely convince Anna that she should be allowed to keep her job. *That* was what Cassie should be worrying about, she reminded herself.

"Cassie." Julia knocked on their adjoining door. "Cassie, we have a situation." Her typically easy voice was high and urgent. That usually meant someone was on fire. Literally.

Snapping out of her daydream, Cassie tossed the phone on her bed and hurried to unlock the door. Julia promptly rushed past her. Almost simultaneously, there was a knock on the main door and Julia opened it to allow Quan entrance.

"We don't have much time to lock this thing down." Julia's accent was thick enough to challenge Cassie's ear until it adjusted. "Local police are holding Drew Carter for questioning in a double homicide that happened at the club last night." Seeing Cassie's eyes bug out and mouth fall open, she held up a hand. "Now don't jump to any conclusions. He's not a suspect, yet." She gave them both a meaningful look and Quan stared at her, maddeningly dull.

"When did that happen? Did Pritchard come back after we left?" Cassie's fists were clenched at her sides. She forced them open and took a breath, feeling the beginnings of energy tingling on her skin. Another deep breath and the tingle disappeared. Drew had been pretty upset at the man, but Cassie wouldn't have put it on the level of a killing rage, although sometimes people surprised her. Had that been why he'd called her? Hopefully their visit hadn't pushed him to take off his ring, the kind of surge that could come from that would easily explain a spree of violence. Her hand found her cheek absently.

Julia shook her head. "No, it wasn't Pritchard. The police are saying it was a drug deal gone south in the alley behind the club. Plenty of witnesses saw Drew running down from the office like his ass was on fire. An employee was out right on his heels and said he was just standing there throwing up on the crime scene."

"Pritchard." Cassie forced herself to be calm, chaos danced just below the surface.

"I don't think so, Cassie." The crease in Julia's brow deepened. "Research sent a copy of the police report from the parents' deaths this morning. The two last night were killed exactly the same way as Mr. and Mrs. Carter were fourteen years ago." A slight tremor ruffled the pages as she held out the file. "It's bad."

It had to be if Julia was shaken. A glance told her Quan had already seen the file; he wasn't even looking at it. Taking the offered folder, Cassie flipped through its bright white pages, not letting her eyes linger on the photographs. Again, finding action better suited to her mood than sitting around. Cassie's eyes went to Julia.

"Do we have anyone at the station where they're holding him? Anyone in Research with access to their network who can take down the file so they don't find it?" Cassie was scrambling, telling herself it was for the protection of the regulars and for the sake of public safety. If the police would make the family connection and put pressure on Drew he could lash out and hurt more people. If he could kill from a distance, he was far more powerful than she'd thought. Guilt wracked at her insides. It was irresponsible for them to have left him like that last night. "We can have someone go to," she looked at the insignia on the front of the file, "Peoria to get a hold of the actual physical file. That's not far from headquarters."

Closing her eyes, Julia gave a grim nod. "We have someone working on losing the file both in the system and the hardcopy. We have a friend in the station here in Tampa working on moving things along to get him released except Drew isn't cooperating. He doesn't want to give his statement or talk to anybody and the police are getting a touch anxious. They're holding him right now saying it's just a matter of procedure, although it could turn into something else if he keeps needling him like he is. Anna wants us to get over there and get him out before he stresses out and does something. We're hoping he's wearing that amulet and it's keeping him reined in for the time being." She exchanged a look with Quan. "Anna wants Quan at the crime scene to see if he can pick anything up. There's a chance it was the brother. If it was, we're definitely going to have to bring him in for trial. That'd be four bodies on his head.

Either way, Anna wants both boys under our watch right quick. It's a good thing you're up and running Cassie. She wants you heavily involved in this one, she says we have the Directors' full attention."

Cassie's stomach plummeted. They all knew what that meant. If the Directors were involved there could be no mistakes. Cassie gulped. The possible scope of damage, should this go badly at the police station, was extensive. Memories could be confused if need be but it was never total nor was it without its risks. "Okay."

"I will go now before the police ruin the trail." Quan turned and left to hail a cab without delay. The clock was running. The more people who went to the scene, the harder it would be for him to sniff out the trail and potentially track the witch.

"Are you ready for this?" As usual, Julia sensed her junior's trepidation. "We not only have the very daunting task of keeping that young man calm, we also have the greater challenge of getting him to lie convincingly to the police and tell them he doesn't know anything about anything. I'm going to need you for that; he doesn't much like me yet." Her eyes crinkled in the corners, her mirth went no farther.

Cassie was picturing the look on Drew's face when he'd ordered them out last night. That and the bodies of his parents in the pictures from the police report flashed front and center in her mind. Cassie lifted her chin and nodded. "I can do that."

Their standard business casual dress would do for their purposes. All they had to do was be respectable and try not to raise any suspicions. Their friend at the station, also known as a sympathizer in some circles, would be able to get them in to see Drew without having to rely on false pretenses. Julia could easily pull off the role of a lawyer, but Cassie would be hard pressed to play anything but concerned girlfriend, and that one would most likely push the precariously balanced client over the edge.

Cassie drove while the GPS directed them to the station where Drew was being held. Being the ranking agent and her age giving her credibility, Julia walked in first and took the lead. She asked for Wendy Schumacher.

They were told to have a seat and Officer Schumacher would be with them shortly. It was nearly ten minutes before Julia's name was called and both women turned toward the voice to see the officer bustling their direction at an efficient clip.

If she wasn't actively using her magick there was no way of telling if she was a witch or not without Quan. What Cassie *could* see was that the "friendly" officer was an average height, probably a good three inches taller than Cassie, and at least twenty pounds heavier. Julia rose and Cassie followed suit. Officer Schumacher greeted them with a nod to each. Her mildly hooked nose, wide hazel eyes, and chestnut hair cut short and swept to the side gave her the outward appearance a cute, if not handsome, young man at first blush. It took a second to see that her breasts were bound and hidden among the extra pounds along with the womanly curve of her hips. She wore no makeup nor did she wax or tweeze any of the light hair that most women concerned with femininity would eradicate with a tenacity usually reserved for guerilla warfare.

"Officer Schumacher, thank you for seeing us," Julia greeted her warmly, keeping her hands at her sides, which told Cassie the woman was a witch.

Smiling back, the officer backed up to give them space to stand and follow. "Of course, I'm always willing to help out a friend of the family. If you could come with me, I'll bring you to him." She turned and took a few steps back the direction from which she'd come. "We should hurry, the lead detective doesn't like being stonewalled. It's making him want to go hard on Mr. Carter. He's thinking of slapping him with obstructing justice if he doesn't talk soon. The guy's got a sheet too." Her face twisted even with her shoulder to keep her voice down. "Nothing major, but with the tie to drugs here *and* in his past, it could give the detective all the ammo he needs to paint a picture, if you know what I mean."

Newly motivated to get him out as fast as possible, they sped through the tile corridor, the long narrow windows giving them quick flashes of the white stucco building close beside them until they reached the elevator. When the doors opened on the lower floor, gone were the minimal touches of comfort from the upstairs level. This was the floor devoted to the less welcome and yet more common element that spent time here.

The overhead fluorescents hummed and one flickered partway down the hall to cast the grey painted walls in a sickly green light. Industrial gray and white tiles marked their passing, sending each footfall echoing through the dungeonlike chamber like a warning.

The hall came to a "T" with a desk sergeant to their right behind a cage and a bank of desks as well as a few small offices on the other side. Their escort pointed to the offices.

"He's down here. For now he's still just a witness." She led them past several rows of desks sparsely occupied by a few officers working at computers. One was in the process of taking a man in cuffs into one of the offices.

Officer Schumacher pointed to a closed door three down from the end on the far wall. Cassie's pulse picked up; she was nervous to see him after how things ended last night. Squaring her shoulders, she prepared herself for the anticipated attack. What she found was far more unsettling.

Peering through a small narrow window in the door they saw their client staring blank faced at the surface of the plain metal table in front of where he sat. There was no sign of yesterday's swagger in the curved shoulders and drooping head of Drew Carter. Last night had aged him ten years. He failed to look up at the sound of their shoes marking their arrival.

"I can only buy you about twenty minutes. They've got him isolated hoping he'll break." Officer Shumacher gave him a pitying glance and added. "They're probably right." With a brief nod in their direction, she left and closed the door.

In the ensuing silence, Julia touched Cassie's arm and pulled her back to the door where she spoke in a hushed whisper. "I'm going to let you speak with him alone." Raising her brows, Julia's eyes held hers. "Remember, he is to give them a statement that he saw nothing of the act, only that he went to investigate something he'd seen on his security camera. After they get that they have to let him go, they don't have enough to hold him. The only reason they're holding him now is because this is one of those cases that gets under their skin and him keeping quiet is pissing them off."

Cassie's eyes darted to Drew and back. She wondered if it was too late for Julia to play lawyer and argue to get him out without having to rely on Cassie.

"I'll be outside seeing what I can get out of the locals. Cassie," she regarded her young partner down her thin, straight nose, "keep your cool and don't get him riled."

Chapter 13

The door shut softly, leaving Cassie alone with Drew who had yet to acknowledge her presence. She was beginning to wonder if he was in some form of shock or if his silence was intentional. She pulled the chair across from him out from the table, unable to stop the grinding noise that screeched through the small space. He flinched but did not look up.

"Drew?" she tried his name softly. "Drew, I know you can hear me. I got your message." She caught the slight tip of his head at the sound of her voice. He was intentionally ignoring her. Her lips tightened. "I know you hear me so you can quit pretending right now."

His eyes flicked up at that, alarming her with the little life reflected in them, and even less in his monotone response. "I heard your boss. I'm not telling anybody anything."

"I know you didn't hurt anybody, Drew." As she said it Cassie felt the honesty behind her words. This man was not a killer. His hands being under the table hid the status of his amulet but she was willing to bet he had it on. He'd never taken it off and he hadn't hurt anybody. "Did Pritchard come back after we left?" She guessed at the real killer's identity based on what she knew of the players involved. Brandon. This was Pritchard's and his brother's handiwork. Drew wasn't talking to protect his brother.

Drew showed a glimmer of life and Cassie knew she had guessed right about Pritchard. Relief ran through her that he wasn't their killer. "We can handle Pritchard if you tell us where he is."

There was no response.

"If you help us find your brother we can use his statement and yours to bring Pritchard to justice. I'm thinking Brandon knows some things that could really hurt Terry Pritchard's chances of staying a free man." Inwardly she cringed at the crucial omission. What she'd told him had been truthful. The only part she'd left out was that most likely his brother was also facing the death penalty from Veritas for what he'd done.

"What are you going to do with him when you find him?" Of course he meant his brother, Drew didn't care a bit about what happened to Pritchard.

"We want to speak with him about his magick and get him the help he needs to get a handle on life with powers. His fate depends entirely on him." Cassie told Drew the same thing she'd told parents and spouses for the past six months. "What we would do is arrange for a trainer posted in the area to work with you both. If he is especially talented he might be invited to the Academy where all agents go for training. Or you could too." She remembered to look him in the eye and smile. Julia said that was the best thing to do when telling families or clients something difficult.

"Is that where *you* went?" Gray eyes bored into her, his intensity arresting. Drew was eager for something else to talk about than his brother or the gore in the alley. It pleased Cassie that he was disturbed by it. That was a good sign.

"Yes, I did."

"So when did they find you?"

Shame finally allowed her to blink and look away. "They knew about me from the beginning."

Drew's brows pulled together. "What do you mean?"

"I'm mixed, remember?" she reminded him pointlessly, forgetting he wouldn't understand.

"Are they racist?"

"Not exactly." She swept a hand across her forehead and sighed thinking of how much had changed in the past twelve hours. "It's not the blood, well, not how it affects my *skin* anyway. It's my magick. Mixed magick is never a for sure thing and they watch the people who have it very carefully."

"Does that make you a special case or something?" That he didn't so much as bristle at her casual mention of magick spoke volumes of his anxiety level. Cassie had to get him out of here. Even if he hadn't hurt anyone yet he still could.

She humored his question, liking the idea that someone didn't look at her like she was a freak. "Special is a kind word for it." Cassie was amazed again at what so easily rolled out of her mouth around him. As a rule she hadn't talked to anyone about her feelings on the subject, not since her father had put all his faith in her to stand in as their provider. Those and other potential worrisome feelings about life and magick were kept locked tightly away with her other shames.

Like the fact that she could never please her grandmother and she feared her mother had died thinking her daughter was a failure. Swallowing, she forced a smile and told him something that would encourage him to trust her, thinking they were swapping secrets. "Mixed bloods like me usually wash out in their first year. That's why they put me with Julia and Quan, they're the best and they're supposed to keep me from doing anything stupid. Last night was kind of a first for me, I hadn't worked magick in the field before."

Drew leaned back with his hands nearly in his lap, considering her. "Do you know why I called you last night?"

Blinking, she hid her surprise at the abrupt subject change. "You were being polite and checking up on me after I fell in your club."

Averting his eyes Drew picked at something on his pants under the table. "I was checking up on you because there was something that bothered me about you." He noticed the way she touched her hair when she was nervous. "I thought your partners were being unfair, using you like they did."

120

"Why, because they sent me in to talk to you? Would you have preferred Quan?" Cassie laughed at the picture of how that would have gone.

"I thought they wanted you to do more than talk to me." He looked up at her through his long brown lashes.

Humiliation raced through her. Cassie felt her face and neck color. "Oh, uh, hmm."

He shifted in his seat and she caught a flash of silver peeking out from under the edge of the table. He was wearing his ring and a fresh white bandage on his right hand. Drew flushed at what he'd just intimated to the woman here to help him. "So, I guess we need to get out of here, huh?"

Relieved to hear him talking sense, Cassie stood up. "I'll have Julia get someone to take your witness statement and we'll go."

Drew was pale but gritted his teeth and nodded. "I saw nothing, got it."

When she reached the door his voice brought her around.

"Was it sprained?"

"What?" She saw his eyes on her ankle. He'd noticed her lack of a limp. "Oh that. We had a healer come this morning for a little help. You can barely tell anything happened." She lifted her black trouser leg to show him her green bruise above a normal sized foot tucked neatly into a black ballet slipper.

"Maybe it wouldn't be so bad being one of you." He touched the bandage on his hand moving under the table.

Cassie offered him a smile before going to find Julia.

Chapter 14

An hour later the three of them were back in the sedan.

"Where do you think your brother would go?" Julia asked Drew when he'd settled into the passenger seat, preferring Cassie's immediacy to the back. Julia didn't object, wanting him to feel comfortable. Whether it was due to her efforts to foster trust or because he'd had a hell of a night Cassie couldn't guess, nor did it matter. Either way, it seemed to be working. At present Drew had his head resting against the door, alternating his attention within and without the car but also answering questions willingly. Julia conducted her interview with the back of his head.

"It depends if he's with *him* or not." Drew let a little venom creep into his words. His dislike for Terry Pritchard was clear.

"Have you tried to call him?"

"He's never carried a phone, he says he can't get them to work."

"Hmm. That's a side effect of too much energy running around in his body. It happens with the strong ones sometimes before they learn how to contain it all." She spoke gently to soften the shock of what would be beyond bizarre for a newbie.

Cassie felt Julia's hesitation at further insinuating herself in what she hoped was developing between Cassie and Drew. She was waiting for Cassie to delve into the more unpleasant subjects. Cassie was the one he trusted. Manipulating him at such a vulnerable time bothered Cassie.

Sure, she knew field agents had to manipulate clients and sometimes regulars for missions. She'd had classes on it at the Academy and studied case files. But this client had a face, and a history, and it was his family they were going after. It felt wrong. Then again, the alternative was to let Brandon and Pritchard go and end up with more dead bodies. Or she could fail and lose her job, costing her family dearly.

Swallowing her qualms for the greater good, Cassie kept her eyes forward. "Drew, what did you see last night?"

He was quiet for a long time and Cassie slid her gaze sideways to catch him staring blindly out the windshield. At last, when she'd nearly given up on getting an answer, Drew's haunted words came out halting at first, before picking up a flow.

"We have cameras. They're on both entrances," he began slowly.

Cassie had gathered as much from the monitor she'd seen on the desk. Pretty standard for an operation like theirs. It was easy to picture him sitting there with his feet up and a drink in hand, that easy way about him. Her heart pained her. Had he thought of his parents?

"I saw the dealers come. One of them was jumpy. I'm pretty sure he was on something." His mentioning of the tiny details was good. He might have seen more than he realized. "I was planning on going out there if Brandon needed help. Then, I couldn't move when I saw the jumpy guy pull a gun. I was afraid if I moved he'd pull the trigger, like I could keep him from pulling the trigger by staying still." He drummed the backs of his fingers on the side window, his nails beating out a popular tune on the glass she couldn't quite place. Cassie recognized the sound of self-defeat; it was all too familiar.

"Brandon tried to leave and Pritchard grabbed his arm. He couldn't fight back, he's been sick lately. He looked so weak I thought he was going to pass out." His voice, though more forceful at mention of his brother's ill treatment, was still faint and hard to hear. Neither woman spoke.

"That was when Pritchard put Brandon right next to him and threw his hands up. Like he did in the club." His voice and fingers stopped.

"He was casting a spell." Cassie confirmed what he was piecing together.

Drew nodded, turning back to the windshield. "But then something must have happened, I couldn't see. Brandon went totally stiff like he was in pain or something. He threw his hands out just like Pritchard and all I could see were the faces of the dealers and they were scared, I mean really scared. They went down and then the monitor cut out." He ran a hand through his hair, mussing his waves already out of place from the long night. "I ran but by the time I got there." He cleared his throat, struggling with the memory. "It was over and Brandon and Pritchard were both gone. I don't know if they left together or if Brandon got away or what." He turned, his worry for his brother unguarded and exposed.

Feeling his eyes on her, Cassie met his gaze and wanted in that moment to spare him the pain he was feeling as well as what he was in store for when they executed his brother. His statement had cemented it in her mind. Still, as a human being Cassie felt for him.

Drew was strong and capable, yet there was a vulnerability in him that reached out to her; she understood it. It didn't make him weak, it made him stronger that he could function despite having lost his parents; that he had kept from confronting the possibility that his brother was a murderer and ostracizing him as well spoke of a loyalty she could only imagine. He loved his brother no matter what he'd done and wanted to protect him and he suffered greatly for it. Cassie felt the protectiveness she had for Drew twisting into loathing for Brandon, his selfish, undisciplined brother who had chosen his associates so poorly. It was because of Brandon's actions that Drew was in the position he was in.

She offered him a gentle smile, hiding the iron behind her assertion. "We'll find him Drew. Don't worry."

They pulled up at the club and all was quiet. It was not yet eleven o'clock in the morning, far too early for anyone to be inside. They didn't bother going in, walking around the side of the building instead to find the alley cordoned off with yellow police tape, like that would keep anyone out. The repulsion spell, however, did the trick, making regulars and witches alike not want to be anywhere near the perimeter Quan had set.

Julia and Cassie shrugged off the discomfort prickling at their backs telling them to leave to meet their partner. Drew trailed behind, stopping short of the tape. Quan was standing with his back to them, the toes of his shoes barely outside the reddish brown spill the size of two small cars parked side by side. No one had hosed off the sidewalk yet, Cassie knew that was up to the property owners. Once the police gave the "all clear" that they were done with their on scene investigation the building owner would be able to clean up. Most likely it would be gone by business open.

Julia moved ahead, ducking under the yellow tape to join Quan. Cassie kept to her primary job, that of keeping Drew close and continuing to inspire trust and possibly getting further insight into their quarry in the process. Dutifully she stayed with him. When Drew pressed closer to hear Quan's report, the hair went up on her arms. Catching a glimpse of Drew squinting, she called out, "We're going to step inside."

Julia took one look at Drew and bobbed her head. Quan did not respond, he was intent upon his process. The nearness of the ocean and the causeway that passed not two miles from the club let him draw on his element, Water, making his magick overwhelmingly strong here. Drew could feel it too.

Drew had his hand to his temple. When Cassie touched his arm she was ready for the impact of the ring, working hard to ignore its seductive whispers. "Come on, it won't be as strong with the brick between you two." She pointed at the side of the building. "Thicker materials like this are insulating."

He closed his eyes briefly in visible pain and fished the keys out of his pocket. Cassie followed him under the tape and into the back door. As soon as it shut there was instant relief. "Thank you." He aimed a quick flash of teeth at her before heading across the floor to the bar where he grabbed a glass and a bottle from high up on a shelf. He held up a second lowball in askance and Cassie shook her head.

"You're not much of a drinker are you?" he asked curiously as he poured half a glass, then splashed one more glug on top, no ice.

"Not really. Plus at the Academy they explained how alcohol affects your control. Nobody wants a witch getting wasted and testing out her latest spells on the populace." She chuckled, remembering just such an instance. The poor witch had been nearly expelled over the fiasco and her victim had taken the rest of the term off to recover from the shock of being partially liquified.

Drew was gaping at her his drink hovered in the air.

"What?"

"You talk like it's all so normal, this witchcraft and voodoo stuff." He waved his glass toward the hall leading to the back door.

"Did Julia tell you she practices vodou?" Cassie didn't remember hearing them discussing the subject.

Three shades fell from his lightly tanned complexion and he took a drink. "That lady does voodoo?" He stared at the dark hall, half expecting some sort of monster to come rushing out.

"Whatever you think you know about vodou," she enunciated the word to point out the difference, "or even magick for that matter, isn't accurate. Julia is really a very sweet woman and I've never known her to do black magick." Though she'd seen her come close a couple of times. Something told her now was not the time to tell Drew that. "Most everybody has some sort of magickal ability and they don't even know it." Cassie fell back on an old script she'd used on many a client to try to normalize their situation. "Maybe they can guess what time someone will be home or they have a gift with animals or knowing what someone else is thinking before they say a word. Maybe somebody dreams things that come true or has a knack for playing music without ever having a lesson. All of those things are forms of magick. It's far more rare for people to have something like you and your brother where other people can see it or it can physically affect someone else." Her hand unconsciously touched her cheek where he'd left evidence of exactly her point. She watched his eyes follow her hand and he took another swallow, he'd already drunk half of his heavy pour.

"What did you mean when you said last night was a first for you? Have you never been in a wizard's duel or whatever you call it before?" He leaned an elbow on the bar. Talking kept him relaxed, and the alcohol would also help matters soon enough at the rate he was pounding it.

Cassie fingered an imperfection in the metal of the bar top, letting the pad of her finger rest in the divot. "I told you, mixed bloods usually wash out." She shrugged offhandedly, downplaying the seriousness of her situation. "Well, I was about there and then something changed last night. It was the first time I've been able to defend myself without screwing it up." Her hand brushed her bangs before she could stop it and she flushed.

"What changed?" He was staring at her again. Cassie felt warm and gave him a nervous smile.

"I don't know." She pointed a finger at his ring. "When I touched you I felt the amulet influence me like it does you; it took the edge off my nerves, I guess. It was like it was all clear. I knew I could do it, then he broke my protection and I couldn't get it back in time. I had to react on the fly. That was it. That was my breakthrough."

"I didn't understand most of that." He gulped again. The glass was nearly empty.

She laughed in spite of herself and Drew laughed with her. Cassie liked his laugh, it was warm and real. She didn't doubt his claim from the night before that his luck with women had little to do with his ring. Heat crept up her neck at the thought of his love life. He was out of bounds for her and she had to remind herself of that. Nothing could jeopardize her place with Veritas again.

"Some forms of magick are dependant upon spells and some aren't. I was using the wrong format so to speak. I was trying to use the wrong parts of my parents' magicks. It never felt right. And then last night it finally felt like it fit, like it was mine." It felt good to say it and to realize that she was, at last, her own person and had her own power. For the first time Cassie felt like she had an identity that had nothing to do with being from two worlds. She was just her.

"You talk about your mother like she's gone. Can I ask?"

"She died when I was twelve, cancer." She waited, expecting the turn of the conversation and knowing she needed to pursue it and at the same time feeling like something slimy you might find under a toadstool doing it. Using her loss to further tie him to her was cheap.

"I was twelve when my parents died too but I suppose you know that."

"I saw the police report," she said quietly.

"Then you know they died the same way as those two." He drained his glass and reached for the bottle still on the bar. "Brandon was home. The police always tried to tie it to him but there was no trace of drugs in their systems that would have allowed one person to do," his voice got thick and he coughed, "to do that to two healthy adults. Brandon didn't have a mark on him and there weren't any signs of a struggle. It was like they just dropped in place. Police never solved it." Drew was watching the liquid in his glass, swirling it on the bar and watching the lazy vortex it created.

"You were at a friend's house that night; did you go back to your house?" She couldn't imagine a twelve year old seeing carnage like that when it was his parents.

"No." Drew's hand shook and he put it flat on the bar. "That night I swore I'd never ask what happened. The cops and Brandon were so spooked I guess I knew it had to be bad. When I was eighteen I thought I could handle it and convinced a cop I knew to let me read the report. I thought it would help to know everything, that I could finally put it to bed. It didn't." He fast-forwarded, editing the years in between and the fallout that had nearly destroyed him, not wanting her to know how weak he'd been.

Unwittingly Drew was driving the final nails into his brother's coffin. When they found him, they would bring him before the Directors, there was now no question. The Directors were the only members in Veritas allowed to conduct executions. There was no doubt in her mind that that would be the recommendation of all three members of her triad. The thought of condemning Drew's brother sickened her. The job she so needed and wanted all of a sudden made her feel like a phony, something she found hard to stomach.

There was a bang as the back door slammed shut causing Cassie to jump. Drew clammed up upon seeing who was approaching.

Quan moved not a muscle, giving Drew a long appraising look then turned to Cassie. "It is chaos."

She shot a wide eyed look over at Julia who nodded slowly, her feelings locked behind a serene mask. "Are you sure?" she asked needlessly. Of course he was sure. He was Quan and he had been here for an hour. She was sure he'd been thorough.

Quan's talent was great and his ability to figure out others' magickal types and follow them over land unflaggingly was well reknowned. It was most likely one of the big reasons they'd been brought together in the same triad. Who better to figure her out and head off any catastrophes before they became too great?

"What does he mean?" Drew broke in, his voice rising. He knew they were discussing his brother even if he failed to understand what exactly it all meant.

Cassie waited, watching Quan who gave a small nod. Sighing at how useless it was to try to glean anything from the infuriatingly opaque man, she filled Drew in. "Chaos magick, it's the hardest to train and the most unpredictable. It all depends on the witch and his mind, whether it can be considered reliable." She left out that it usually drove the user insane what with being faced with the absence of a higher power or limits beyond one's own desires. If they didn't destroy themselves they were typically put to death for some crime stemming from their limitless ability.

Drew said nothing, he tossed back the rest of his drink and poured yet another. Cassie could see him fighting to divorce himself from the conversation as well as his own thoughts. He'd taken in a lot today and now this. The constricting of his pupils told her he was beginning to find his escape. Briefly she wondered if it was a good idea for him to drink considering his past drug history. His file had been full of petty crimes all related to drugs and the lifestyle until an assault charge a few years ago. After that it stopped. She would hate to see him go back to it.

"Drew, where do you think Brandon would have gone?" Time was ticking away and Drew was sitting here getting wasted while they all sat around watching him. A glance around the room showed her partners to be in a similar state of agitation. Julia's fingers were tapping anxiously against the side of her thigh and Quan might have been frowning.

"I don't know. I hope he ran, but maybe he's at Pritchard's little church. Who knows? Obviously I don't know my brother very well." He waved a hand dismissively.

"Cassie, why don't you take Mr. Carter home and stay with him for the time being?" Julia offered, seeing his declining state. Sensing Drew's objection, she headed it off. "Quan and I will follow all leads. We'll call you if we find him."

His mouth shut. The alcohol induced fog he'd so enthusiastically sought now cut him off from any sort of lucid thoughts. Cassie said that she would. In a way she was glad not to be chauffeuring another one of Quan's frustratingly silent tracking trips.

***

Julia wasn't so lucky. They left with her driving while Quan sat mutely beside her.

"For the record I think this is a lot for her. She's only starting to figure out her power." The older woman wanted to see her young partner succeed and was less certain of the wisdom of this first solo mission than her Supervisor and partner sitting beside her. Leaving her with a client who had little self-control was a questionable call considering Cassie's own control issues. "It's easy for Anna to say it's time from behind that desk, she won't have to pick up the pieces if it turns out it's too soon."

Shrugging, Quan replied noncommittal, no indication of how he felt one way or another. "At some point she must do this. It is how we all prove ourselves." Twisting in his seat beside her to offer her a view of his black eyes, Quan gave her a vague smile. "I am reasonably convinced they both will survive the next twenty-four hours." He then followed with the odd little symphony of tittering and snorting that concocted his laugh. Julia rolled her eyes, glad it was a rare occurrence.

***

At the club Cassie called a cab, failing to get a straight answer from Drew as to where his car might be and not being in the mood to go searching. Drew had one more drink he didn't need while they waited. He was well on his way to passing out by the time the cabbie came. Cassie locked up the club with the keys he sloppily fished out of his pocket and, by the time they reached his condo fifteen minutes later, it took both her and the driver to get him out and up to his sixth floor unit. She'd kept his keys and let them in, one of Drew's arms over her shoulder, the other over Esteban the cab driver.

"Down here." She guessed the short hallway at the far end of the unit led to the bedroom. She was right and they let him fall onto his bed so that she could pay Esteban for services above and beyond his fare. Cassie tipped heavily figuring Veritas wouldn't object.

After the door was locked Cassie looked around. It was simple, modern and clean. She was guessing a cleaning woman was responsible for the latter. Typical for Florida, all the floors were tile to prevent termite damage and to keep it cool. The large, open unit was painted in a sterile cream color with stainless appliances and natural brown colored stone countertops to match the floors. A center island had two coffee colored bar stools tucked underneath to function as what appeared to be the only eating surface in the place.

The living room had the same neutral flooring with minimal furniture; all of it matched and looking like something someone else would buy for a bachelor to furnish a condo he would never be in. The sofa was tan leather, angular and too stiff to be his choice. Only the television mounted on the wall and the dark brown club chair across from it seemed like they suited the man now sleeping in the other room. A cherry wood coffee table sat in front of the sofa, its smaller mate was beside the club chair topped by a cork coaster marked by the sweat from countless drinks. Yes, this was where Drew relaxed when he was finished worrying about everyone else for the day.

Cassie sat down in the chair letting the butter soft leather envelop her. The back was too tall for her. It would be perfect for someone his height. She flicked on the television. It was on sports, of course. Glancing around, she saw a small bookshelf and got up to peruse its contents.

Good old Oxford had its dictionary there on the top shelf with a few books on automotive repair and general fixes. He was a man who didn't mind getting his hands dirty. Cassie could respect that, her father had always been handy with a toolbox.

The second shelf was more revealing with a few bestsellers about military men doing the right thing even if it meant going against the establishment; typical and uneventful. There were also a few older titles, one by her favorite Russian author.

"He's got depth too." She nodded in approval.

Being in his home, Cassie didn't miss the chance to search for hints as to where Brandon might be in case Drew hadn't been entirely truthful about knowing his brother's whereabouts. Though that type of thing happened often when loved ones felt they were protecting each other, Cassie didn't think that was the case here. Drew had not been anything except honest with her, which was more than she could say for herself. Regardless, no matter what Drew chose to share, they had the number one thing that would bring Brandon back to them. He was just beginning to snore softly from the other room.

Pushing herself out of the chair, she got up to see if she could find a blanket to put over him since he was lying on top of his dark gray bedding. A long thin linen closet in the hall across from the bedroom afforded several choices. Cassie picked out a blue plaid blanket that wasn't too heavy and closed the cream painted cabinet door, slowing when she reached the bedroom.

Drew had rolled over onto his side, one arm under his head and the other thrown over his stomach. Both feet hung over the edge of his queen sized bed with his shoes on. Cassie crept in, not wanting to wake him, and set the blanket down beside her so that she could unlace and remove his shoes. That close, she noticed the brown stains on the bottoms and on his pant leg.

Her heart wrenched, it had to have been a nightmare. She wondered again if he had seen the faces of their parents as he looked down at them in the blood and the gore, and if he was still denying who had killed them all.

He moaned faintly, speeding Cassie in her actions, hastening to slide his now sock-clad feet up onto the mattress and spread the blanket over him. Just as she leaned over him, tossing the far corner over his back, Drew's eyes popped open. They were the lightest gray, a few flecks of blue in them she hadn't noticed before. She froze.

"Cassie what are you doing?" He sounded perfectly sober, never mind the fact that he'd downed nearly half a bottle of booze in less than an hour.

"I'm putting a blanket on you." She gave him a small smile.

"You're a nice girl, Cassie. Don't get mixed up in all this. You'll end up like those other two."

She wanted to ask which two he meant, figuring he probably meant her partners given the fact he wasn't too keen on them, but, with a shudder, she considered he might have meant the two dead men in the alley. She shut that thought down. It never helped to think about what could happen in the line of duty. His eyes closed again and she stepped away.

She'd nearly reached the doorway when he called out after her, apparently not asleep after all.

"Do you think it hurt? It looked like it hurt."

"I hope not. It was fast so if it did, it wasn't for long." She gave him the best answer she could and it seemed to satisfy him or the alcohol reclaimed him because his soft, even breathing sounds once again filled the room.

Chapter 15

It was nearly dinnertime when Cassie heard rustling sounds coming from the bedroom. He shuffled into the bathroom where she heard splashing and gargling noises before the door opened.

He emerged from the hallway running a hand through his light brown waves. He'd changed his clothes to faded black jeans and a fitted gray tshirt that had Cassie looking hard at a commercial for pudding on the television.

"I thought I heard you out here." He too watched the commercial, finding it easier to talk to the screen than the woman in his chair. "Sorry, I don't usually go too far with booze." He grimaced at the memory of her and the cab driver pouring him into bed. "Too many guys fall into bad habits working where we do." He said nothing about his history.

She was getting up, her eyes wide and nervous. That she couldn't look at him bothered him. "Are you hungry? It's almost dinner, have you eaten at all today?" She finally directed her gaze at him, concern lined her brow and her eyes were warm.

Drew was attracted to her, a new feeling for him since it wasn't purely sexual. Not that he hadn't thought of that too. She was nicely built, not too frail like a lot of girls he saw at the club. And after the way he'd seen her handle herself with the drunk on the dance floor he could imagine where she'd gotten that body. Hard work, not some crazy diet. His stomach growled and she smiled, dissipating the tension in the room with that one casual gesture.

"Let me see what you've got around here."

"Don't bother. I'm never home, I don't have any groceries."

She moved toward the kitchen anyway, intent upon making her own inspection. A few jars he knew to be pickles and olives slid around, and the door shut. She stood back up and put her hands on her hips. "All you have are garnishes and beer."

Nervous, his hand found its way to his hair, a habit he hated. Self-conscious, he put his hand in his pocket. "I told you, I'm never home."

"Well what do you propose we do about dinner?"

"I have menus." He pointed and walked into the kitchen to open the drawer next to the coffee mugs. Drew took them down and set them on the counter.

Cassie began flipping through them. "What are you in the mood for?" She made a move he'd seen her do a few times now that didn't make sense. She brushed her hand across her bangs like she was sweeping them aside although they barely reached her brows.

"Did you get a haircut recently?" He pointed at her hand falling to her side.

Her cheeks flushed and his interest peaked. "Until last week I haven't had bangs since I was a kid. I suppose it looks silly now."

"What happened last week?"

"Oh, I almost set myself on fire doing a spell," she said flippantly and pointing at her hair, though he heard more behind the offhanded delivery. "This started before Julia was able to stop it, hence the new haircut."

Drew stared at the side of her face as she went back to perusing the food choices. How could someone be so easygoing about all of this magick stuff? Sure, the last few years he'd known something was different about his brother and he'd even suspected it about himself since that time with Aunt Tina, but magick? Real freaking magick? And here she was talking about it like it was normal, like he would talk about a football game.

"How about Indian?" She pointed to one. "I love curry."

136

"Me too." He liked the way she looked up at him and smiled. She had a nice natural look, not like she did last night with all the makeup or the way the girls who came to the club painted themselves. No, this one was different all right. He cringed to think how different. Leaning back against the counter he pulled the phone from his pocket. "Do you know what you want?"

She nodded and he dialed from memory.

While they waited for their food Drew wandered into the living room, settling for a spot on the stiff couch he'd paid too much for but the saleswoman had told him was the epitome of Italian style. He'd seen Cassie on his chair and let her keep it. When she followed him out she pointed at it.

"Don't you want your chair?"

He shrugged. "I sit wherever, it doesn't matter."

"You sit here all the time, don't lie to me." She crossed her arms in mock severity.

"How do you know?"

"It's the only thing in the room that says you." He watched her cheeks pink again.

Drew watched her shift uncomfortably on her feet for a minute before he reached over for the remote and used it to point at the chair. "Have a seat." He couldn't stop his mind from considering what would happen if he invited her to sit with him. She plopped down a safe distance away in his chair.

They watched the better part of a show on penguins in Antarctica though the details escaped him. Thoughts swirled through his head about his brother and whatever chaos magick was, their dead parents, and again whether Brandon had caused it, even if by accident. Then there were thoughts of this woman and her coworkers, one of whom practiced vodou while the other scared him in a way he couldn't put his finger on.

Despite his better judgment, Drew felt like he could trust Cassie, if not her odd partners. It wasn't just the fact that he was interested in her, he felt an inexplicable kinship with her. It could have been the hint of sadness he caught sometimes when she didn't think anyone was looking. It was a feeling he knew from personal experience came from deep wounds in the soul. Drew felt a renewal in his draw to her when he'd seen her at the police station. The real her, not some show she was putting on. She'd walked in and he knew he was going to walk out with her regardless of what he'd said at the club. Her partners were something else, but she stood apart from the others he'd known through the years. He wanted to know her, bizarre stories and all.

She jumped when the door buzzer echoed through the room.

"Dinner." He pushed himself up off the couch.

Cassie was quicker and pulled a few bills from her back pocket. "You stay put, I got it."

He thought about arguing except, honestly, his head was killing him since the aspirin he'd taken in the bathroom hadn't had a chance to kick in. Drew figured if he heard any more about magick his head was literally going to blow up. The thought brought back images he would rather forget. "Okay."

She eyed him for a minute then turned and walked out. When Cassie returned, bag in hand, Drew had pulled two plates out as well as silverware and set their places on the counter.

"What can I get you to drink?" He had two glasses in his hands. "All I've got is water and beer." He looked sheepish. "Sorry," he raised the glasses in a shrug, "I haven't entertained in a while."

"Is it tap water?" She swallowed her pleasure at hearing he hadn't had company here recently, scolding herself for her foolishness.

"Yeah."

She shook her head. "Sorry, too many minerals and chemicals in this area. I'd have to boil it first." She watched him thinking about that and wished they could somehow stop talking about how different things were when one lived a magick friendly lifestyle.

It did permeate all they did, true. It took some minor precautions and adjustments and then it was perfectly normal and easy to live that way. Like keeping kosher. She'd been raised in it so it was the only way she'd ever known. "I'll take a beer." She set the bag on the counter. "The heating process cleans it."

Removing the containers, Cassie lined them up and paused to inhale the fantastic smells emanating from the steaming contents. Even the rice was making her mouth water.

"What did you get again?" She popped the lids off of the plastic bottoms, far less leaky than the old cardboard containers and less fun.

"It's called Paneer Bagh-E-Bahar." He laughed at her perplexed look. "Take some, there's more than enough to share."

Drew was pleasantly surprised to see her take a healthy scoop of each dish and put them on not just hers but on his plate as well, adding a scoop of rice down the middle. Something about sharing food was intimate for him, surely due to the times when food had been scarce and he and Brandon barely had enough to get by. The thought of sharing with her was easy. She was helping Brandon, maybe even him. It was her job yet it felt like she really cared. That automatically got her a lot of credit in his book. It had been a long time since anyone else had believed in Brandon as a person.

They sat at the barstools on the other side of the island eating in comfortable silence with the television blathering on in the background.

"What do you think they're doing right now, your partners?" Drew asked, taking a swig of his beer. He leaned back against the metal back of his stool having eaten enough to take the edge off his hunger.

Cassie finished chewing her chicken curry, also grabbing her beer bottle to take a drink and wash down the cacophony of flavors coating her mouth. "They'll be following the scent the witch left at the scene."

Drew frowned at her, clearly confused.

"It's something Quan does," she explained. "He's one of the best at differentiating us by the 'scent' of the energies we use. If he gets a scent, he can follow it anywhere."

"So does everybody have different kinds of magick? I thought there were only like four or five different types."

Cassie's brow flicked up in surprise. Drew *was* a believer.

Self-conscious, he shrugged. "What, I hung out with a girl into the new age thing a while back. Some of it rubbed off."

She halted her lip from curling at the reminder of his "way with women." She considered briefly teaching him a little about blocking. It wasn't her place but he and the women around him could use it. "There are lots of basic types and then you've got the personal spin everyone puts on theirs depending on their culture and family influences." Cassie pushed her plate away, her stomach sufficiently packed. If Drew was ready to discuss this, she would. After all, the better he understood what they were dealing with the better he could understand when the time came for difficult decisions to be made. She could only hope that he wouldn't hold her personally responsible when things ended badly for Brandon.

"What if he gets the 'scent' of the combined magick Brandon and Pritchard used and can't find them if they're not together anymore?"

Surprised at his comprehension, Cassie spun her chair to face him and he did the same, their knees nearly touching. "Good

140

question. Think of it like cooking. You can identify the different ingredients within a recipe by smell if you're familiar with them, and Quan is familiar with lots of different types of magick. He'll be able to track them together or apart." She was sure of her answer having seen Quan track a self-proclaimed Wiccan high priest across two states eventually finding him holed up with one of his followers, a young girl barely over seventeen who had about as much magickal ability as a rodent but was willing to kill for him.

Drew's hand held a faint tremor as he raised his bottle to his mouth for a long pull. For someone who proclaimed not to hit it hard he was certainly pouring it down today. He must be pretty stressed, who wouldn't be.

Having the same thought, Drew set down his beer and pushed it away from himself on the counter. "I'm gonna have to get some soda or bottled water or something. That's just going to get me in trouble." He swung down from his seat bringing him a hand span from Cassie's face. Her pulse jumped.

She ducked her head, trying to hide the effect he had on her, she was like a teenager around him. Even Todd, her old boyfriend, hadn't made her dizzy like this. She couldn't deny that some of her interest in him at the club hadn't been feigned. He was easy on the eyes and what she'd seen of what she *wanted* to believe was the real him was intriguing. Cassie reminded herself that none of that mattered. Drew was a client now and the rules on that were clear. No touching. That, and the fact that he was going to hate her very soon made the right choice obvious.

Drew's eyes had darkened to the color of slate as he looked down at her, frozen on the edge of her chair. She couldn't keep her gaze from returning to his in spite of herself. When he reduced the space between them to virtually nothing Cassie was compelled to look up or have her nose pushed into his shirt. What she saw in his expression warmed her body, her breath came faster. She was painfully aware of every beat of his heart, the heat his body was pushing out at her, fanning her own temperature until she was uncomfortable in so much clothing. His entire being seemed to call out to her.

"How far were you willing to go last night? In the line of duty?" His voice had gone husky.

She stared at the thrumming pulse in his neck. "I'm an investigator, not a prostitute. There is only so far I'll go for a job." It had been a long time since she'd been with anyone and her body had made up its mind.

"Are there any rules about this?" His fingertips reached out to her chin, sliding backward along the curve of her jaw, holding her perfectly still with only his touch.

She could tell Julia she did it to inspire his loyalty, never mind that made her exactly what she denied being. It wouldn't be the first time an investigator had crossed the line for good cause. She punched another hole in her resilience. Swallowing, Cassie took a moment to find her voice. "You aren't a part of our investigation so there are no rules on what I'm allowed to do if I want." The lie rolled out easily.

"Do you?" He leaned in, lips mere inches from hers.

She was losing the battle between mind and body. "Do I what?"

"Do you want?" As he spoke, the air moved against her lips.

"Yes." She closed her eyes and whispered the word, barely getting it out before his lips closed on hard on hers. Her brain gave up the fight and fell back to let her body take over. Cassie felt her skin alternate between burning and freezing where his flesh touched hers and then fell away.

They moved to the couch, the bedroom too far for the need overtaking them both. When his legs bumped against the edge Drew stumbled and Cassie took advantage, pushing him down with both hands on his shoulders drawing no objection from him. She'd only ever been with one other man but her hands held no traces of timidity as she pulled off her top and then reached out to do the same to him. Pleased she saw excitement ignite in his eyes at having her take control, she let herself go taking the initiative to find out what gave him pleasure. The woman she became under his touch unlike the one so crippled by a lifetime of self-doubt.

Chapter 16

They ended up in Drew's bed, having eventually made it there for another less frantic second round. Cassie lay with her head on his chest and his arm wrapped around her back.

"How long do you think this hunt might take?" Drew's chest rumbled against her ear.

Her fingers traced the curves of his chest drowsily. "It depends. It could take hours and I've seen it take days." The guilt over what she'd done had yet to set in and she wanted to luxuriate in the pleasure before waking up to that reality.

He kissed the top of her head. "Days, huh?"

She chuckled. "It might take that long to get my strength up."

"It'd better not." He laughed with her.

Cassie felt his arms shift and glanced down to see the fingers of his left hand run over the stone on his other hand. A warm ripple ran through her body.

Drew caught the direction of her gaze. "What do you think would happen if I took off this ring, I mean, amulet?" He used the word uncertainly.

"I'm not sure without knowing more about what kind of protections are on it or how long you've had it." Cassie told him honestly. "You've never worked with your magick before and you might hurt someone or yourself without meaning to if you didn't have someone looking out for you."

"Brandon gave it to me after a trip he took a few years ago." His hand traced the faint red line on her cheek. "How exactly does this thing work?"

"I've been thinking about that. It looks like Green Aventurine, which is a form of quartz. That would make sense considering your brother gave it to you and he feels a need to protect you from outside influences. He wanted to keep you safe from Pritchard and maybe even himself." Her feelings for Drew were already clouding her judgment. She wanted to believe Brandon was an unwilling participant in Terry Pritchard's plans. Dangerous was dangerous regardless of intention, she had to remind herself.

Drew listened rapt while Cassie went on to tell him what Julia had shared after handling the amulet last night.

"Quartz is a pretty major stone because it's so common and multifunctional. It can take the place of several stones so the user only needs to carry a few." She held out a hand. "May I?"

"Sure." He gave her his hand to let her examine it.

Cassie flinched as her finger grazed the stone's face, its influence far stronger with direct contact. Its siren song flooded her senses, dulling the sharpness of her fears. It told her she need not worry and Cassie felt herself being drawn in. Desperately she wanted to give herself over to it, give up her life's concerns as irrelevant.

Sense returned with a sharp phantom pain as the tissues in her cheek continued to repair themselves, ripping her back to reality. Immediately she responded, removing her finger and cutting herself off from its powerful seduction. The strength of its power over her faded back to the dull buzz she'd enjoyed through the contact she had with Drew's body. The hum keeping her in a contented bubble from which she did not yet wish to withdraw. "Do you feel anything from it?"

"Yes," she said simply, not letting him in on the extent of its sway over the earth side of her nature. Her water, fortunately, allowed her some modicum of control. "Do you?"

He looked down at the stone again. When he spoke he was thoughtful. "It made a huge difference for me at first. Hardly anything bothered me after I put it on but I think it's worn off now. I barely notice it anymore."

Cassie told him what she knew of his amulet's powers, keeping her eyes on his, watching for sensory overload though the stone itself most likely protected him from such a thing. "Julia recognized it as a special class of quartz. It's called the 'Stone of Heaven' because it's such a strong stone with overwhelmingly positive properties. It's said to lend happiness and confidence to its wearer. People have reportedly been more charismatic under its influence as well. And," she added the real reason she suspected Brandon had given it to his brother, "it's also the best one for psychic healing."

Drew pursed lips and exhaled slowly. "It all comes back to that doesn't it?" It wasn't really a question. "What happened when we were kids. Now that it's happened again, he's in trouble, isn't he? Even if the police don't find the old report or make a connection. He's in trouble with *your* people."

Faced with Drew's unsettling insight, Cassie blanched. To tell him now, like this, felt like she'd only been with him to distract him. Hadn't she? she asked herself accusingly. She'd gone to bed with him knowing his brother's life was forfeit when her partners found him, or she did.

"Cassie?" He shifted to see her face. "Is Brandon going to be okay?"

She looked him in the eye. "I don't know." She hated herself for lying to him. It was going to hurt him deeply when he discovered the truth.

Drew said nothing, his arm fell away from her leaving her colder still than her deception. "I should take a shower. They might call soon."

Offering no resistance, Cassie let him slide out from underneath her leaving her alone, all at once feeling the kind of unclean soap cannot take away.

When he returned to the bedroom to replace the towel around his waist with clothes, Cassie ducked in to the bathroom to clean up as best she could without a change of clothing. She finger combed her hair and let it hang dry. Drew had taken back his chair and turned on a sporting event, which type exactly escaped her, preoccupied as she was. Friendly again, he raised his hand to her when she emerged from the hallway, his face curiously distracted yet pleasant.

Cassie's duty was to stay with Drew and she would. Even though she felt stir crazy with nothing to do and not at all comfortable sitting on the overly firm couch where, little more than an hour ago, things had been so different.

Sliding her phone from her pocket and stepping into the bedroom, Cassie made a call to father. He was the one person who had always stood up for her and given her comfort when she most desperately needed it. Without him she never would have survived the disappointment of her grandmother or taunting of the kids on the reservation. His comfort was what she craved now.

"Hey Dad." Her voice cracked and she cleared her throat. She wouldn't have called if she'd realized how close her emotions were to the surface.

"Cassie, hi. Are you okay?" Her dad, William Porter, picked up on her mood, although whether it was because of something in her voice or the fact that she was calling on a weekday, she couldn't be sure.

She forced a shaky laugh. "Yeah it's fine. I wanted to talk to you and I have some free time that's all."

Unconvinced, he let it go. "Your grandmother was just talking about you. She had another vision about you last night."

"Another one?" Inwardly she groaned. The last time they'd seen each other, things hadn't ended well. Grandmother had told her that if she went to the Academy with "those people" she would darken her soul until there was nothing of light left in her. She had condemned her granddaughter to walk a path apart from the spirit world, adrift from their help and guidance. It was the same as being damned in her father's world.

147

He cleared his throat and she heard the hesitation in his voice at bringing up such a volatile subject. "She said she saw a little bird." Cassie's name within the tribe, Little Sparrow, referred to how small she'd always been, like her mother's people, not tall and leggy like her father's kinsmen. "The bird was dancing with a dog when a flood came and washed them both away. The sparrow was too wet to fly."

The elemental ties in the vision did not escape Cassie's notice.

"The bird washed up on one shore, the dog on the other, and there were unable to get to each other. Then a man came and he was wearing a mask. He offered to help the bird to reach her friend only she had to climb inside his pocket to go with him. Once she was inside she could not get out."

Grandmother's argument that as long as Cassie walked two paths she could not be seen by the spirits, nor could they speak to her to guide her, was a familiar one. She wanted her granddaughter to choose one and then she said her future would be bright because her heart was good and the spirits respected that. Grandmother was not a cruel woman, even if she had little patience for those who opposed her will.

"Thank Grandmother for telling me. I'll be careful." Cassie paid proper respect, knowing it was expected.

"I will."

Cassie heard the bathroom door close next door. "Hey Dad, sorry to cut it short but I have to go."

"Duty calls," he joked, pride audible in his tone.

"Yeah, duty calls," she repeated half-heartedly. "Maybe after this one I can come for a visit." She offered, temporarily homesick.

"That would be nice Cassie." He paused awkwardly and Cassie felt her stomach tighten in anticipation.

"Todd's getting married on the next full moon." It was good luck to marry with the waxing of the moon. Marriages and even births to some extent were planned accordingly.

"Tell him congratulations for me," she said hollowly, all of a sudden wanting to be done with the call and thoughts of home. "I love you Dad."

"Love you too, honey. Be careful out there," he added soberly, pride not canceling out the real risks his daughter took to support their family.

Cassie sank down on the floor, leaning her back against the wall, and let her head fall forward onto her knees. The phone still in her hand rested on top of her head.

Lost in her thoughts, Cassie startled when Drew's voice cropped up from only a few feet away.

"I need to go to the club to check on things; we opened an hour ago." He was eyeing her curiously. "Is everything okay?" Gray eyes flicked to her phone.

She saw his tension at her defeated posture and the phone and guessed the direction of his thoughts. "It's just home."

"Did something happen?" The genuine nature of his concern pained her.

She sniffed, her emotions once again threatening to erupt. "My boyfriend's getting married."

"Boyfriend?" Brows rose.

Cassie laughed harshly, wiping at her eyes. "Sorry, habit. He's an ex-boyfriend."

For a moment he seemed uncertain what to do then squatted down beside her. "Was it serious?" He rested his forearms on his raised knees and stared interestedly at his thumbs, posed side by side as if to compare them for symmetry.

The question caught her off guard and Cassie wasn't sure how to answer it. "I don't know if 'serious' is the right word. He was my best friend and then we ended up together. He's been part of my life as far back as I can remember." She wiped her eyes again. "Now he's not."

"Does it bother you that he's getting married or are you upset that he's moved on?"

Cassie blinked at him. She was getting the feeling his magick was tied to emotions, he was too intuitive about people he didn't even know. Her neck heated at the memory of how he'd known what she wanted in bed without so much as a hint. That usually took time and experience with each other, it was not a first time kind of thing no matter what the romance novels say.

She shrugged, considering his question. "I guess I'm a little jealous that he gets to choose what to do with his life." She admitted. "My whole life I've been in this tug of war between my mother and grandmother about where I would end up and how I would practice. That's probably why I could never figure out how to handle my magick, I was always trying to force it and never took the time to listen."

Sharing her innermost guarded thoughts with him was effortless, not at all like they were being wheedled out of her without much choice on her part. Cassie wouldn't stand a chance when he removed the amulet and got some training on how to really use that power of his. He could be better than Julia, unless Cassie missed her guess.

"Until last night I was worthless. They were getting ready to kick me out of the company. My father would have been crushed. He and my mom wanted me off the reservation more than anything, which was why he got between Todd and me in the end and sent me to the Academy." Cassie stared at the phone, seeing her father and grandmother's faces in her mind's eye and wishing there was a way to satisfy them both.

She waved a hand. "So here I am, doing what I have to, while life goes marching on for everyone else."

"What would you do if it was up to you?"

"I don't know. I've never let myself think too hard about it before."

He sank down on his rear and put an arm around her to draw her close. Cassie let him, liking the warmth he provided. There was an unexpected release in sharing what she had with him. She'd been worrying for a long time with no one she could share her private thoughts with. Not since she'd gone off to the Academy. This felt good. With opening up came the rush of emotion those carefully hidden thoughts carried. As they broke loose, so did she. Cassie choked and the tears ran over while Drew stroked her hair and made her feel safe.

When her eyes had run dry, her head lying on his shoulder, Cassie sniffed and gave voice to her earlier observation. "I can't believe I told you all that. I'd hate to see how strong you are without that thing."

"Do you think that's my deal? Getting people to talk?" he half-kidded.

"I've known you how long and you've gotten me to tell you things I've never told a soul." She twisted her neck to look him in the eye. "Seriously, if you're looking for a new line of work you could easily have a place with Veritas."

"Is that what your magick police force is called?"

Sniffing, Cassie giggled. "It used to be called Tutela ab Veritas, Guardians of the Truth but they've shortened it to just Truth. The original Directors formed it during the Middle Ages when things were bad for us. Magick was being manipulated to serve non-practitioners. We call them regulars," she explained. "They were killing us off; using us up and frying our brains for personal gain or destroying us out of fear. Kings, the Church, anyone looking for an edge over his enemies."

"It's that old and no one knows about it?"

"Veritas is well known in magickal circles, in families who have attended or been touched by Veritas. We keep our presence a secret only from regulars. That's what we do. It's the ones like you and Brandon who occupy most of our time. You're born with these abilities or they come on in puberty depending on the witch, and you have no idea what to do with them because no one's ever told you. It's not as uncommon as you might think. Maybe your parents had minor abilities and they got stronger with your generation, it happens. Either way, once we find you we have a duty to teach you control and how to operate within the law, and under the radar.

"You're thinking Brandon won't be able to live within the laws, aren't you?"

Cassie scooted over, putting some air between them and the numbing effects of the ring. She hoped to maintain some amount of professional privacy. She was partially successful. "Chaos magick tends to give the user no boundaries. Brandon might object to the limitations." She watched that sink in. Drew went pale and looked ill. "It can consume the witch if he isn't careful."

"Something has been wearing him down," he confessed, his concerns for his brother now taking on a whole new dimension. "He hasn't looked good in months. I was going to make him see a doctor when he got back." Tucking his worries behind a masculine grimace, Drew stared at his hands. "It's the strain, isn't it? Pritchard's making him use his magick and it's wearing him out. What if it isn't his fault?" Drew's loyalty to his brother was blind.

If Drew was correct, that would put Pritchard up with other enemies of Veritas such as Julius Caesar, Hitler and Napoleon. Even the Papacy had not been above using up witches in the name of personal gain saying they were "fighting the devil with his own." Explaining that would be too much of a history lesson to go into at present and it might do more harm than good for Drew to see how much damage could be done under the thumb of one powerful ruler. This was fast becoming a complicated mission, more than she was equipped to handle. She wished, not for the first time, that her partners were here with her to take the reins. Cassie leaned her head back against his shoulder and rested her hand on his arm, letting the amulet's comforting glow quell both their fears for what might be coming. Right or wrong, she welcomed the bliss the stone afforded.

Chapter 17

"Come on." Cassie grudgingly shook off the fuzzy feeling after a few minutes. She stood, smoothed out her pants and offered Drew her hand. "Didn't you say you needed to check on things at Carter's?"

Drew reached up to take her hand, climbing gracefully to his feet. "I should, plus it'll feel good to have something to think about other than my brother."

"Let me call Julia and let her know we're moving." She picked up her phone where it lay on the floor. "Do you want to call a cab?"

He cocked a bewildered eyebrow at her before it hit him. "Right, my car's at the club. I forgot about that." He ran his hand through his hair, doing his best to look contrite at the reminder of his overindulgence. "How do you feel about bikes?"

Cassie's eyes went wide just as Julia picked up. "Uh, Julia, hey. Have you found them yet?"

"No. Is everything all right?" She caught Cassie's weird tone and turned away from the stretch of road behind them. The formerly maroon sedan, now brown with dust, sat parked on the roadside. Quan, dressed entirely in black and walking on the balls of his feet, paced up and down the edge of the dried grass and newly greening cypress grove.

"Um yeah, fine," Cassie replied awkwardly. "We're going to head to the club; Drew has to check on things since Brandon's out." She continued before Julia could object. "We might as well have someone on the club since Pritchard's people could come and we don't want anyone to think anything unusual is going on."

Julia "hmm'd" and Cassie moved on quickly again. "How is Quan doing?"

There was a long pause while Julia nervously eyeballed Quan, suddenly gone still. His hands shifted and came together. Her skin twitched for only a nanosecond as his temporarily weak pull afforded him only a fraction of the power he wanted and needed to tie into his prey. "Quan's getting too far inland, he's having a hard time figuring something out. It's like…" Her voice trailed off as she watched her partner stop pacing.

In a rare display of emotion, he kicked a rock and balled his fists stalking back to the car.

"It's like what?" Cassie prompted. Julia was not often at a loss for words and her distraction had Cassie worried, she could hear it in her voice.

"The scent is splittin' and comin' together. With Quan… limited like he is…He can't rightly tell which trail he's followin' for sure. It's like Pritchard's switchin' colognes on him. He's *him* under it but he keeps throwin' smells on top to shake us. It doesn't make sense." She lowered her voice, "It ain't pretty." Her accent was getting thicker.

Julia was worried. She could see that Quan was in one of his moods. He didn't often get upset. When he did he was scary, like a gathering storm you saw coming and had no hope of outrunning.

"Cassie, I've been thinkin' about it and I want you to check out this church of Pritchard's. Go tonight after hours if you could. We don't need a full scale war on our hands." Irritation crept into her orders. Quan was waiting in the car and she didn't want to go in there with him emanating frustration like he was. It was going to be a long trip. "We're gonna be a little while longer and we should check out Pritchard's home base. I'm guessin' his ladies will have heard something from him by now."

"Will do." Cassie was watching for Drew who had disappeared down the hall. The sound of keys jingling reached her ears. "Be careful Julia."

"You too, honey."

Cassie felt a warm bubble in her chest at her mentor's term of endearment.

She put the phone in her pocket as Drew came around the corner, a faded black leather jacket hugging his shoulders.

Drew's expression was guarded. "Have they found anything yet?"

"No, not yet." Cassie hadn't been sure he would want his brother found knowing about the risks he was facing, but his disappointment was easily discerned. "Don't worry, Quan will find him," she offered.

Distracted, Drew fidgeted with the keys in his right hand. Movement caught her eye and Cassie glanced down to see Drew absentmindedly stroke a finger over the top of his ring. The change was dramatic. Almost instantly, the lines in his forehead disappeared and his frown relaxed into a vague smile. A vague smile she was beginning to form a theory about.

Cassie was fascinated at the speed of the process and by the fact that she doubted Drew even knew he did it. For now she kept her observation private. It made her curious how much of him was him and how much was his amulet. There was a possibility she wouldn't recognize him without it. It was also possible that he might not feel the same way he did now about her. Or she about him, she realized with a pang. What if she had underestimated what it was about Drew that attracted her?

"A motorcycle, huh?" She changed the subject and forced a smile.

Grinning, Drew jiggled the keys. "Trust me?"

Not certain how either of them could really answer that question, Cassie grinned back. "Absolutely."

Growing up on the res Cassie had ridden dirt bikes with Todd and some of the other kids. It wasn't something she craved like a lot of kids did, but it was a way to fit in and that she did crave.

She hadn't had much opportunity to drive one herself being one of the youngest and a girl, two huge marks against her according to the boys who owned said bikes. So what she'd learned rapidly was that your ride depended wholly on the abilities and kindness of the driver. If he wanted to scare you he would and crybabies weren't invited back. Todd had only scared her once and she'd pinched him so hard he'd been nothing but a gentleman thereafter.

Drew was a little bit of both. When they first got on he was careful, gauging her level of comfort. After he figured out she wasn't afraid, he added speed and sent the Ducati weaving through traffic. Cassie could feel his skill in the way he handled it and knew that they wouldn't get into any real trouble. She let him play, enjoying the liberation and temporary distraction of the ride.

All too soon the ride was over and Cassie felt the wind on her face dying as Drew pulled up to park in a lot along the far side of the building. He maneuvered it in behind a little silver coupe, its sleek curves illuminated by the light above.

"Know the owner?" Cassie pointed to the car he was blocking in.

He unzipped his jacket and hit the locks on the 370Z. "I spent a long time with nothing." Drew gave her an easy smile, one she didn't believe came from him but from the stone his finger brushed again in passing. Her eyes were catching it more often now that she was watching for it. It was like a drug and he couldn't stop himself from seeking it's euphoric glow.

Eye to eye with his ignorant dependence on the amulet, Cassie felt her heart sinking. The warmth she felt for Drew was based on a partial picture of who he was. For as long as he wore that stone, she wouldn't know him nor could she trust either of their feelings as being real. His earlier kindness was just as likely to have come from the stone as from him. The epiphany stung and she had to hurry to put a false smile in place as Drew turned back to her.

"Shall we?" He winked, offering her his arm.

Taking it, Cassie felt the edge of her disenchantment fade in the stone's glow, ignoring what her craving of euphoria said about her growing dependence.

Tavaris was on the scene, once again acting as gatekeeper. He was busily putting the list of specials in the silver holders to sit on each tabletop before the restaurant got fully underway. Cassie felt no small satisfaction when his eyes fell on her and he noticed her familiarity with his boss. Wanting to tweak him, Cassie leaned her head on Drew's bicep and watched the host's shining lips tighten. Cassie debated saying something in Spanish while she opened herself up to sense any magickal activity in house.

"Hey Tavaris, everything cool here?" Drew hid his grin at Cassie's move to needle the guy. He deserved it.

To his credit, the host was respectful. His disdain for his boss' companion didn't carry over to the man himself. Tavaris raised his voice to be heard over the din coming from across the way at the bar. "The reservations are down. It's going to be little slow on this side. It can't be helped."

The men exchanged a look. Cassie assumed there was some sort of expectation for respectable patronage the night after a double murder in your back alley. Bar attendance, on the other hand, was through the roof already. Letting out her breath slowly she gave a silent "all clear" on the magick front.

"It's wild over there already." Tavaris confirmed Cassie's guess that this was an unusual turnout for your typical Friday happy hour. "Jaime's been here since noon and she's had the cops out twice to kick people out of the alley and upstairs is already almost full. We're glad you're here." He sighed and looked up through glittery eyelashes.

Drew gave her arm a quick pat and laughed. "Let me do a walk through and see if we can get things a little more orderly."

The tendons in the arm Cassie held tightened as his fingers once again found the stone. She felt a renewal in the peace flowing

158

through her. Before she too could lose herself to it, Cassie forced her hands free and put a few inches of separation between them.

"I'll wait in the bar down here where it's quieter." She looked up doe-eyed at him and blinked rapidly.

Snorting, he let his hands drop. "I won't be long." He assured her, already mounting the darkly carpeted stairs working with the glass and insulation to neutralize the thumping of the dance music above.

The bar wasn't just full, it was packed. Cassie couldn't see any free seats much less one where she wanted to be. Somewhere she could have a good view of the door and the hall. Hopeful she could manage to find someone willing to bump over for a party of one, she weaved her way up to the side of the bar nearest the front windows. Cassie was stuck behind the front line of people when the bartender flagged her.

It was Jaime from the night before. She waved Cassie up and put her head down to speak to the two men sitting on the red topped stools nearest her. With a few good-natured grumbles washed away with one of Jaime's girl-next-door smiles, two seats were suddenly free. She gestured for Cassie to take one.

"Saw you come in with the boss." She brought her head close so she wouldn't have to yell. "What's up with that?" She reared back to give Cassie a speculative look. So genuine was the woman's inquiry, Cassie couldn't feel offended by its intrusiveness.

"I don't know, I think he's a nice guy." Cassie shrugged and let her eyes skim the stairs where he'd disappeared.

Far from satisfied with the limited response but too busy to pursue it, Jaime frowned and held up a finger to someone calling out an order across the bar. "What can I get you?"

"A hot tea." Cassie smiled at Jaime's strange look. That was probably the only one of those she would sell tonight.

"I'll get one sent over from the kitchen." She went to the phone below the mirror, ordering Cassie's unusual request before moving on to manage the alcoholic needs of easily three dozen patrons and the steady back and forth traffic of the other serving staff managing appetizer and drink delivery to the outlying tables.

When a server at long last brought her tea, Cassie could tell right away from the lack of steam that it was tepid at best. A finger inside the pot confirmed it was stone cold. She was staring at it, debating whether it was worth even pouring when she was struck with an idea.

Browsing the other occupants, Cassie could see that no one was paying any attention to her, she was essentially alone in the crowd. Casting her eyes back at her mug, she decided. As a precaution she filled her cup only halfway and put a hand over the rim.

Sending another look around to be sure she was still uninteresting to the masses, Cassie hung her other arm down by her side and opened her palm to the floorboards. Using the same amount of effort as she'd used in her previous attempts, Cassie felt the tingles race up her skin eagerly answering her call. In another breath, she sent it into the cup and steam began rising from the liquid inside. She pulled her hand away at once to prevent herself from sending too much in and blowing up the cup. Mesmerized, she sat, watching the steam, pride surging in her breast.

The success of the basic spell was cathartic. The boost it gave her eclipsed the one she'd gotten from last night's exercises with Quan. Tonight was better because she was alone and had chosen to call her power, not forced it with fear. She'd really worked it out! Cassie was no longer a witch in name only, she was really and truly a witch. It was hard to keep from jumping up and dancing right there on the bar but she refrained to maintain her low profile.

Elated, Cassie considered how difficult it would be able to put her years of training into practical use or if she could even start doing it by herself. Here and now.

Scanning her surroundings Cassie took in the activities and conversations of the regulars oblivious to her idea of turning the bar into her classroom. Cassie searched for another opportunity to try out another minor bit of magick, one that no one would notice. Her gaze landed on the silver shaker, frost from the last drink still hazing its metal sides. It was the same spell she'd just conducted except on a larger scale, and with the addition of distance it presented a challenge for control. Cassie glanced sideways out of the corners of her eyes and began to pull.

She blissfully lost herself in her small victories and successfully got rid of every trace of ice above the bar. Jaime was running like crazy, selling twice the booze of an hour ago because everyone drank their rapidly warming beverages faster. To her great amusement, Cassie had also unwittingly convinced Tavaris they had an electrical problem. She'd flickered and shut off every light in her general vicinity in alternating patterns, a light show for her own personal pleasure. Her fellow customers found the whole thing amusing, shouting when the light above each of their seats would go off. More than one group had turned it into a drinking game.

Bored with the lights, Cassie debated whether she could get away with tying the shoelaces of the guy next to her. His pick up lines were terrible and the woman he was hitting on was actually giving him the green light, which Cassie was sure was due more to the fourth rum and coke she'd ordered than the man's underwhelming prowess. She decided to go for it.

As her downturned hand began pulling energy, feeling that newly familiar tingling dance along her skin Cassie caught sight of a movement on the stairs beyond Mr. Swinging Single. In a heartbeat, her joy turned to remorse. Drew was coming her way, his face ashen and clearly in pain. She'd forgotten about his sensitivity in her exuberance, the buildup from her festivities must have been agonizing for him.

A quick push down, making sure to clear the residual from both elements from her system, and Cassie released the energy back into the ground. Energy not "put back" could be damaging and she'd gotten lucky last night when her broken circle had been dissipated among so many. She wouldn't risk that again. Cassie had to remember she was using potent magick even if it was on minor spells.

The earth element that was tied to her nature gained its energy from the creatures existing in it, living and dead, and the trees tied into the network of life-giving roots extending the world over. It was one of the richest sources of power giving earth witches a slight advantage over their other elemental cousins. Her second element, water, was all around her. Water was under her feet, in the air and in heavy concentrations on the coasts. Water witches on islands and even in the tropics were exceptionally powerful because of the heavy density of their element in such close proximity. Cassie, with the good fortune of having both, would surely never be far from a power source.

Cassie had gone on her bender, neglecting the comfort of those around her, much to her mortification. It was a rookie mistake and she was lucky none of the regulars had picked up on it, a fact owed directly to the high volume of alcohol sales, not Cassie's discretion.

The direct line of his approach told Cassie Drew knew exactly where his headache was coming from. Sitting up straight and spinning to face him, she didn't have to fake the sincerity of her apology when he got close enough to hear it.

Drew stalked right up, stopping only when he had interposed himself between her legs, sending a rush of blood up the side of her neck. The move surprised her, putting him intimately close before she could think to object. He placed his cheek directly beside hers and ground out between clenched teeth.

"What the hell are you doing down here? I can hardly see straight." His voice was strained and he was holding the edge of the bar so tight his knuckles were white. Violence or vomit, one or both, were not far for him at this point.

The thought of pending violence from him brought Cassie up short. "Drew, are you mad right now?"

He turned his head to stare at her, incredulous. "Yes, Cassie. I am mad right now. At you for making my head hurt." He spelled it out slow and sarcastic, his teeth flashing as he bared them.

Chapter 18

On a hunch, Cassie put her hands on his arm. She felt nothing; the stone was silent. Her hand caught his and the fingers on her opposite hand traced over the face of the stone. Nothing. She turned her excited eyes up to find him staring coldly at her.

"Is that shocking to you?" He let her hold his hand in both of hers, feeling too ill to bother removing it. Drew waited out Cassie's manic phase not understanding at all what she was getting so jacked about. That he was mad shouldn't surprise her. The thing that was plucking at his nerves was the fact that she was excited about it. And now she was way too interested in the stone out here in front of everyone. She was the one who'd told him how important it was that no one else find out about the existence of witches or their "powers." Now she was down here turning his bar into a circus, risking exposure for her own amusement. Jaime was watching them from the other side of the bar. He sniffed, trying to ascertain if she'd been drinking.

Cassie's warm golden eyes sparkled in the overhead light undaunted. "I've figured it out." She held his long fingered hand in one of her small tan ones. With her other hand she grasped his amulet in her fingers, eyeing him meaningfully. "Do you trust me?"

It was easy to figure out what she wanted to do and he stood bolt upright. The thought of losing the effects of the amulet gave him no qualms; he had recovered from his childhood tragedy and Pritchard was miles from here. Drew needed no protection at the moment. And yet fear sent its cold barbs into his skin raising a chilled perspiration immediately under his arms. Drew's fear was not from outside but from within. He was terrified of his actions without the mitigation of his brother's gift. His eyes darted to her cheek, evidence of his lack of control the one time he'd removed the stone. It would be far too easy to hurt someone here without knowing what he was doing. Drew's thoughts flashed to the bodies in the alley and he shuddered. What if he was as deadly as his brother?

That Brandon had played a part in last night's deaths as well as his parents' was no longer in question, Drew could deny the evidence no longer. However, he continued to hold out hope that it had been an accident. If he could get Brandon alone and talk to him, find out what had happened that night and even last night, Drew knew they could argue their case. Together, he hoped they could explain to Cassie's people at Veritas that Brandon didn't mean any harm; he could learn to follow the rules. Drew would help him. They would learn together.

"Isn't that dangerous?" He made a point of sending his eyes to roam the room taking in the crowd. "What if something happens?"

She shook her head. "I won't let you hurt anyone. If it looks bad, I'll give it back."Antsy, Cassie's knees bobbed up and down on the edge of the stool. "We don't have much time before it recovers. I want to see if this works."

Drew was hesitant but in answer to her question of trust he nodded, watching her pull the ring from his hand and drop it unceremoniously into the teacup behind her with a plop as it hit the water. For two blinks nothing happened. Then, the pain in his head began to flow out of him leaving him feeling like he'd taken too much cold medicine, all balloon headed and fuzzy.

"Is anything different?" Cassie asked him, her eyes searching his face for any outward signs of change.

He started to say no and stopped. A strange sensation, far back in his mind, began to mumble to his consciousness. At first it was so faint he had to struggle to hear it, like a conversation in another room he could hear the rumblings though not the details. He strained to hear and then it began to get louder.

"Drew, maybe we should go to your office." Cassie started to worry the ramifications of leaving him open and unprotected in such crowded quarters. He was beginning to look a little vacant. The possibilities of what could come of her impulsive move outside of any protections began to sink in and automatically her eyes scanned the crowd for dark hair and a widow's peak. Cassie firmly believed Drew was not a threat to anyone here given that he wasn't being provoked, yet she hadn't considered the impact on him of being unguarded for the first time in years.

That her experiment would be exposing him to emotions and moods he hadn't honestly experienced fully in years pulled at her need to protect the wounded soul she knew lay beneath. She adjusted her grip on his hand, her fingers wrapping around his and she grabbed the mug from the bar. "Come on," she urged him, slipping off her bar stool and returning Jaime's curious stare with a curt wave. Let her think they were heading off for some alone time. That was sort of true, just not in the way Jaime might think.

Allowing his body to be pulled along to the elevator, Drew barely registered what was happening around him in favor of listening to the things floating to the surface in his mind. Thoughts he had long considered gone and forgotten, save for passing superficial remembrances, turned up for him to consider in full force. The wild parade of years of emotional memories kept distant by the ring he'd thought no longer affected him turned to agitation as last night's events crashed into him. When the doors opened on the upstairs hall, Drew gasped as he was pulled under.

Cassie's hand flashed out and hit the door close button just before she threw the stop switch. The shiny box went black for a count of three before the backup lights flickered to life, casting their faint blue-white glow over the two occupants. The thrum of dance music became an impatient clock, counting out their seconds from outside the reinforced doors.

Drew's conscious mind succumbed to the overstimulation and caved. He went under and his legs failed him. Already disconnected from his physical body, he felt the carpeted floor rush up, barely cushioning the severity of the impact with the steel floor beneath it. Images of the bodies in the alley filled his senses, bringing back the burnt metallic scent of blood and vomit, mingling in his memory with the details of the police report from another similar murder confusing the two in his mind. For the first time since he'd slipped the amulet on his finger Drew saw his parents bodies as they'd been that night. The images of their deaths clear as the day he'd demanded that he had the right to see the report; the report he'd made himself read believing it would give him peace. It did not. Instead it had filled him with a fierce rage he'd been unable to control. That his parents would be struck down randomly and with such violence in their own home and the fact that the killers had barely even taken anything to justify the intrusion had inflamed his sense of injustice. He'd gone what could only be referred to as temporarily insane. Lying there in the metal box Drew's nose was filled with the stink of death and blood, sharp as if he was standing there staring down at any of their lifeless eyes, frozen in terror at the pitiless torment that marked their last moments.

For almost five years after learning of the horrific details of his parents' deaths, Drew had turned his fury on himself. He drove too fast, took too many drugs, drank too much, and slept with anything he could get to say yes, which was a lot. Brandon, busy trying to make a fast buck and get them into a decent living situation, could only watch helplessly as his brother destroyed himself. They couldn't afford detox or therapy even if Drew would agree to go, which he wouldn't. Desperate, Brandon had called Aunt Christine, pleading for help when Drew almost died from a lethal combination of alcohol and pharmaceuticals.

Christine had been too frightened at the prospect of seeing Drew out of his head to come. The memory of what he'd done the last time he'd lost control forever tainted her mind against him, but she'd sent a check in a show of support. Brandon had taken that money, and with the calm that comes with a sure thing, had invested it on a small time real estate deal. That was when their luck had changed. Drew had later referred to it as Brandon swallowing a silver spoon. That hadn't been quite accurate, he now realized.

It was more likely Brandon's implausible and meteoric rise to overnight success had been due to magick and his meeting Terry Pritchard. After Pritchard's arrival two things happened: Brandon could do no wrong with investments and Drew was given his amulet and told it was good luck, not to take it off.

167

With its help, Drew had been able to bring himself back from the brink with relative ease. With it on, the complexities of his life suddenly seemed trivial.

Clear minded, Drew was certain Pritchard was blackmailing his brother. The man must have figured out Brandon's ability. Satisfaction mingled with culpability and he nearly choked. He had been right and he had done nothing. No, worse than nothing. Drew had let his brother pay the price for saving him from his weaknesses while he'd gone bobbing along in a general state of apathy. There could no longer be any doubt about Terry Pritchard's hand in his brother's success and current physical decline. Not with this final piece of the puzzle falling into place. Terry Pritchard was forcing Brandon to use his magick, and it was killing him. And that Brandon had done all of this to save *him* tore him apart.

Laying in the near dark with his mind fully exposed to all of its darkest corners all at once, Drew felt himself drowning. His eyes were open though unseeing, staring vacantly at the ceiling shining in the dim blue light. The sound of his ragged breathing filled his ears and he could feel his pulse race as his chest tightened until he saw spots. Part of him hoped that he would die and Brandon would be released of his obligation to Pritchard while another part of him wanted to live to watch Terry Pritchard die a slow, painful death.

A warm "tug" in his head brought his attention back to his body, away from the memories and guilt. He blinked. Another "tug" and Drew was back in the present. Blinking again, his eyes focused on the underside of Cassie's chin as she hovered over him, her soft voice sounding in an even cadence although the words or their meaning were unclear. The tight clamp on his chest loosed its grip and his breathing grew steadier. The guilt and anger filling him faded, becoming more tolerable and easier to bear. He stared at Cassie and as she finished her spell and looked down at him. What he saw there made him blanch.

The lack of proper lighting could not hide the shine from the tears in her eyes, nor the worry etched plainly on her face. Her concern for him was more than professional. He could feel tenderness in her touch and it scared him. Drew had taken great care in keeping his encounters superficial. Memories of earlier that afternoon replayed in his mind and he saw the same gentle expression on her face when they had been alone together.

The removal of the amulet that had so effectively shielded him showed him why everything over the past few years had been easy to keep at arms length. Drew understood by its absence how he had been capable of avoiding deep emotional thoughts, good or bad, for any duration. With the return of his normal human emotional range, his guarded views of relationships remained as they had been before the stone altered him, back to when it had been the fear of loss that had driven him, whether consciously or not, to avoid caring for anyone other than his brother.

Cassie's affection for him was visible and, faced with it, Drew panicked. Hurrying to tear himself away from her, he felt the need to hide himself from the fear of being hurt.

"Drew, can you hear me?" Her voice faltered when she saw him struggling to get to his knees.

He cleared his throat. "I'm fine, let me up. We should get out of here before someone notices the elevator is out of commission."

Turning her face aside, Cassie backed up to let Drew stand. Running a hand over the front he smoothed his shirt, used his fingers to brush back his hair and glanced down at her. "Come on, get up." His voice was harsh even to his ears and he saw a flash of hurt before she closed down, her face going blank as she grabbed the ring and tossed it in her pocket. Rising to her feet, Cassie backed up to lean on the farthest wall of the claustrophobic metal box. She pulled her phone out and cursed.

"Let's go to your office. I need to make a call and I can't get a signal in here." Her distance was not solely physical. Cassie had read between the lines and heard his message loud and clear.

Inside his office, Drew waited in his brother's chair, keeping the desk between them as he listened openly to her conversation.

Leaning the backs of her legs against the file cabinet by the door she dialed and shifted from one foot to the other until she realized how nervous she looked. She forced herself to be still. Julia took forever to answer and sounded annoyed when she finally did. Cassie filled her in without bothering with polite small talk. "The amulet acts as a cache absorbing the magick it feels around it. That's what gave him the headaches, it was the buildup. He doesn't know how to get rid of it and the energy beats him up. I took it off of him." Her gaze flicked up repeatedly though she caught it each time, never letting her eyes reach him. Her awareness of him was painful to them both. "Yeah, I'm guessing he's back to normal."

Unconsciously, she went back to shifting from foot to foot. "Uh, I don't know if that's wise. Should I leave him here? Alone?" Her lips tightened and she nodded her head stiffly. "Okay." As she was about to hang up, adding in a rush, "Hurry back."

That last part he could guess at relatively easily, Cassie didn't want to be alone with him. Drew gritted his teeth against the impulse to explain himself to her. This was the only way for them. She lived who knew where, traveling all over the world seeking out murderers and other dangerous folks. Like Pritchard.

Even if he had the guts to try, Cassie was the worst possible choice for someone like him. The chance of losing her was even more so than if she were a normal girl without a life threatening career path.

Cassie's throat clearing brought his attention back to her. "Julia says they're going to be a while longer. Quan's got them up in Georgia outside a town called Swainsboro. Ever heard of it? They're pretty far inland now. Quan's having trouble and it's going really slow. He's not as strong that far away from water." She spoke faster in her heightened anxiety.

For his part, Drew tried to think what could draw Brandon to that area and came up blank. "Brandon doesn't have anything up that way. It has to be Pritchard." He stared at the desk, wiping at imaginary debris on the opaque surface. "Does Quan know if they're together?"

Lips tight she shook her head. "No, she said his trail's blurry and keeps shifting. They keep having to circle back and it's going really slow. I don't think Julia could get him off the trail now if she tried. He's never quit on a chase." Her amber eyes were half wild. Cassie ramped up until she was pretty much voicing a stream of consciousness. "When Quan is on something he doesn't let up. Like when he was tracking down this real black magick type in Detroit. This guy we were after, he was taking kids off the street. Sometimes he'd take them right off the playground. He'd figured out how to absorb their energy and when he was done, he just dumped them. They were alive but they were fried and the regulars couldn't figure it out. They were like zombies. He had snatched seven kids by the time Quan caught up to him. He was so strong."

It was unclear who she meant was strong, Quan or their quarry.

Cassie's artificially wide eyes turned inward at some scene playing out in her head. "Quan wouldn't quit, even when Anna called us back. He said that kind of evil can't be allowed to walk the Earth; it throws everything out of balance. No amount of good can offset that. When we found him, he fought. I've never seen anything like it." Slowly her head wagged back and forth, her hair brushing over her shoulders. "We were in a warehouse by the water. Quan was at his most powerful there. He was in his element." She snorted at her macabre pun, and then the illusion of mirth disappeared. "This guy, the bad guy, he was a Representational witch. He used power he drew from an object. He used an amulet too, not the same kind of stone as yours though, and he stored the kids' energy in it. Quan used the water to pull enough power to separate the kid's souls from the amulet. He set them free and they turned on the man who'd held them hostage. He was sobbing, begging me to kill him." She looked down at her feet, seeing the man's ghost still pleading for mercy and she shook her head deliberately, exactly as she had when he'd asked her to save him. "We had to put him in the trunk on the way to the airport; we couldn't listen to it."

Drew stared, his blood frozen at her recollection of the capture of a man who'd done a crime arguably in the same class as his

171

brother. It was impossible not to see the similarity. Quan wasn't going to stop until he caught him. And what then?

He had to get rid of Cassie so that he could get Brandon away from here when he returned. And with a sinking feeling in the pit of his stomach, Drew knew that he would. Brandon would come back for his brother when he was able, making it most likely he would come to Drew's or go to the club.

As soon as the other two found Pritchard or tracked him back to Brandon, a fact Drew believed wholeheartedly was inevitable, they would take them into custody and from there he imagined the worst. Cassie had never been exactly forthcoming about what they did after they caught someone if they weren't "trainable."

"So what do they want you to do?" Drew rested his hands on his thighs to avoid fidgeting.

"We're supposed to go to Pritchard's church and see what we can find. They don't want us to go when no one's around. Our numbers would put us at a disadvantage." She emphasized the "we," avoiding eye contact by staring at a spot on the floor.

That was one way to get her out of the club. Drew looked at his watch. "When are we supposed to go?"

"Now."

Perfect, all he had to do was drop her off and leave her there. That would give him enough time to get back to his place and check if Brandon had been by. "Let me give Jaime some instructions for the night, I'll be right back." He could trust Jaime to hide him if Brandon showed up here in the meantime.

***

Julia hung up the phone and made a popping sound with her lips, a habit she had when she was debating something. It drove peace and quiet loving Quan nuts. They were sitting in the car outside a natural food store getting dinner.

"Yes?" he inquired sharply.

Used to his strict moral code, tight adherence to duty, and honestly piss poor sense of humor, Julia folded her arms and leveled a look at him meant to remind him that he was not her first partner nor was she willing to let him take anything out on her. Respectfully, Quan gave a slight nod of his head and forced a placid expression that went no further than skin.

Her reply was a sarcastic two-second smile, equally shallow. "Cassie's taken off his amulet." She raised her brows at his open mouth, using her dominant position to maintain control of the conversation. "The headaches he was getting were from the stone's receptivity. She thought the best bet was to remove it." Nodding deeply, eyes wide to purvey her own misgivings, she went on. "Right. So, now he's raw, emotional and with only a green broke agent keepin' him from going down the same dark road as his big brother. Killin' is killin' whether it's by accident or otherwise." Julia was pure Louisiana in her displeasure. "We need to go back."

Quan dug in his heels, passively resistant. He crossed his arms and settled himself squarely in his stance. "I will find him."

Squared off, they stared each other down, well matched in stubbornness as well as magickal ability. Yet another reason their superiors had paired them. Recognizing the folly of walking away from the investment in time and energy they'd put in thus far, Julia dropped her arms first.

"You have a day. After that, unless he's close enough you can count his pores, we're gone. Hear?"

Quan graciously accepted her extension. "Agreed."

"All right then. Lead on, water dog." Julia swept an arm broadly.

Aside from a slight narrowing of the eyes, Quan gave her no hint how deeply the barb stung. No one had ever eluded him. This one would not be the first. He vowed it, calling upon his ancestors, his element alone unable to give him the strength he now needed. Quan longed for their pursuit to take them nearer a water source.

Chapter 19

Cassie sat in the passenger seat of his car, too preoccupied to lean back and enjoy listening to the powerful V6 wind out on the long, sparsely populated highway and watch the lights of Tampa's nighttime sky fly past her window in a neon blur. Drew had offered to drive, saying he knew where he was going. That was good; had she been behind the wheel, she would have crashed for all the attention she would have given the road in front of her.

Cassie's conscious mind was currently tying itself in knots over the implications of what she'd done with, and to, this man beside her. In twenty-four hours he had gone from stranger to lover and abruptly back to stranger again. And now here she was readying to enter the lion's den with only him beside her, not at all convinced she could count on him if things got ugly. She considered giving back his ring. At least he would be protected, if not helpful.

What if his brother was there? The image of herself face first on the ground popped into mind. On top of all that twirled her apprehension over facing Drew when she took his brother into custody. For the first time, Cassie considered walking away from Veritas and her family. If she couldn't perform the duties expected of her, maybe it was time to face the fact that she wasn't Veritas material. All too soon the growling of the engine quieted to a low purr, drawing Cassie's mind back to the task at hand.

"It's that one, on the right." Drew pointed his chin at a low brick building, a whitewashed peeling expanse of stucco over concrete. The span was punctuated every few feet by a different generic storefront, worn and weathered to the point of gray exhaustion. A narrow strip of parched grass out front separated the building from the cracked sidewalk. They obviously didn't hold many church picnics here.

The neglected building was on the corner attached to sa stripmall and surrounded by several others just like it, all of them crying out for a facelift and general cleanup. Drew drove past the structure to pull into the lot behind it. Cassie cast him a questioning glance.

"It's darker around back." He drove into a space up against the building and shut the car off. Their field of illumination immediately reduced itself by half. They had to rely on the nearly nonexistent glow of the sole inadequate halogen perched on a pole in the center of the lot. "I'm assuming you don't have a key."

"I don't need one," Cassie snapped sharply. Her nerves were strung tight.

The darkness emanating from the chest height windows had her working to slow her speeding heart and rapid respiration. On the plus side, it was likely that no one inside meant an easy in and out, provided she didn't mess up. Taking a few moments to steady her nerves so she didn't lose control and burn the place down, Cassie considered the details involved in breaking into a building.

There weren't any posted security signs, although she had to assume Pritchard had a service, or at least the mall as a whole employed one. Her newfound magickal competency gave her limitless choices for entry strategies, and all of them acting alone. Right now, as much as she was trying to affect an air of confidence, Cassie would have given just about anything to have one of her partners there with her to make sure she didn't forget something and alert the entire local police force. As it was, she planned on going in alone and leaving Drew in the car. He would only serve to complicate things in the state he was in, and the state he put her in.

Cassie was looking out the windshield when she felt him stir beside her and held out a hand to stay him. Both of his hands came off the steering wheel, held up in mock surrender. She had her wish; he would stay behind.

"Keep an eye out for me?" She meant to say us; no matter. The stone face she could see out of the corner of her eye probably didn't hear her anyway. With a sigh, Cassie got out of the car.

Putting her mind back to the pressing task of her first solo breaking and entering attempt, Cassie opened herself up to sense for magick while she surveyed the vicinity. The mundane lot backed up on a cinder block retaining wall responsible for holding back a steep natural area with some sparse scrub brush and a few scraggly looking palms. The trees were planted in a pseudo artistic swirl in the hopes of dressing the area up, yet they only served to make its air of abandonment even more resonant. Revealing their neglect with drooping yellow and brown fronds, they cried out for the water they deserved.

Sympathetic, Cassie reached out and tapped into the warm swirling place in her body where she felt her tie to her mother's element. There was a relatively high water table here. It required only a minor amount of draw from her to bring it to the surface and direct the liquid toward the roots of the dehydrated trees. Releasing the energy she no longer needed, she felt empty without the comforting tingle of magick. That it had so seamlessly welcomed her once she'd cleared its path into her system moved Cassie. Alone again, Cassie opened her eyes to see the other visible signs of disuse.

Scattered about the ground below the trees was evidence that this place was long forgotten. The white cardboard of a fast food wrapper and paper bag lay in a half-crushed heap holding dirt and old rainwater, the bright waxy packaging nearly glowing in the dark against the light-sucking soil and dead Bermuda grass in which they sat. Whether they'd blown in or been discarded by a passing patron didn't matter. Either way, the overall vibe was easy to interpret, even for a novice.

This church was not well attended nor well regarded by the community. No proper sign hung on the awning advertising itself to the populace. There was only a small hand colored white posterboard placard in the window that decried this to be the "Ray of Light" Church. Terry Pritchard was listed as the "Spiritual Guide" instead of declaring an ordination. The whole thing seemed to be a slapped together afterthought in the hopes of lending credibility to a farce.

Coming to the door, Cassie paused and held out both hands palms down toward the sidewalk under her feet. Reaching this time for the cool black soil below, Cassie caught a whiff of dank earth, closed her eyes to gather herself, and pulled. The skin on her arms tingled and she felt the flesh on the back of her neck prickle in the night chilled air. Opening her eyes, she raised one palm and held it roughly a foot from the glass and metal door. Focusing her thoughts on the lock cylinder, she let one quick pulse of energy arc from her hand to the aluminum handle. One click and the lock spun, a thin tendril of smoke curling up from the keyhole and Cassie reached out to pull the door open. She took a firm hold of the handle, expecting some amount of resistance. There was none.

She opened the door, ears straining for sounds of an alarm system, assuming they had one. Sure enough, they did. Two "whoops" shrieked in the deafening quiet and Cassie scanned the front walls, willing her eyes to adjust faster. The red light marking the control panel guided her partial night vision to her goal. Another pulse of controlled energy silenced its call with a pop. Without a backward glance at her backup, she continued inside.

The sounds of her light leather soled footsteps were loud on the paper thin carpet. Worn and rumpled, it was barely enough to cover what sounded like a wooden stage, not an office floor. Cassie was glad to be alone; there would be no sneaking around in here. Her palm tingled as she carefully guided the energy to the surface, turning the flat of her hand a glowing golden brown. Frustratingly, it was only a tiny flame at first. Frowning, Cassie stared at it and fed it, concentrating more of the energy zinging through her body into a unified direction, the shift in its current making her skin tighten into tiny goose bumps under her thin clothing.

The flame grew into a small ball. Holding it out, she let the light shine outward, illuminating several feet in front of her and no more. Anything more powerful was risky and not just for fear of discovery, but also because since reconfiguring her magick, good luck didn't necessarily mean it was all going to go as planned.

She didn't want to have to explain extensive damage or blow herself up. Small was better for now.

Able to see properly, Cassie began her search. The "church" was really an office with a terribly ordinary looking entry leading straight into a front office area where Cassie could make out what had to be a receptionist's desk nearest her and a few more behind it. She stopped at the front desk first. Light orb held out, Cassie followed its glow and began opening drawers one handed.

There were no dead bodies or signs that read, "Cult leader on a power hungry binge works here." It was all terribly ordinary. By the lack of any personalization she was guessing no one actually filled the role or chair on a regular basis. There was a package of post it notes still in the plastic, two pens and a pencil in a black plastic holder on the fake wooden desk. Its surface was obscured only by a large blotter calendar, perfectly clean. That, in and of itself, spoke volumes. No blotter calendar in the history of offices could remain clean for more than five minutes if someone was within ten feet of it. All those blank squares just screamed out to be doodled on. Everyone knew that.

Moving on, she came to three more desks in a row on the left hand wall, all in the same pristine state of disuse. Cassie didn't waste her time. She turned to follow the curve of the back wall, in keeping with the rule of mazes, so she didn't miss any hallways or doors. It led her past an alcove with a fountain, the restrooms which received only a cursory glance and eventually spilled into the copy room slash kitchen. Here were actual signs of life. A half consumed carton of soymilk was in the door of the fridge, an open ketchup and one blue cooler bag sat forgotten on the top shelf of the dated biscuit colored appliance.

On a round table in the middle of the room were a few colored pencils and a stack of blank copy paper mussed up where someone had been working on a project or sign of some sort. Upon closer inspection all the pages were blank. Next was the copy machine, which had a recycling bin beside it. Cassie took the liberty of pilfering through it.

***

Cassie had been inside for a few minutes when Drew saw headlights slowing along the front side of the building with a turn signal flashing. Cursing softly, he shook his head wondering why he'd delayed. He should have been gone by now. He was going to leave when Cassie had gone in and he'd waited, figuring he would give her a minute to get further inside before starting the car. His hand had been on the key ready to start and then, when the alarm had gone off, he knew he couldn't.

Like it or not, she was relying on him as her backup. It was wrong to leave her exposed like that and he couldn't make himself do it. In his mind's eye he could see Pritchard standing over Cassie, clutching her chest in agony, and he knew he couldn't abandon her. Shuddering at the image, he cursed again and convinced himself he was staying only long enough to make sure she was free from danger. Drew was debating whether she'd caught the alarm in time when he saw the lights. Instinct from years when they had nothing and resorted to some minor theft jobs to eat, kicked in and Drew hopped out of the car to make a dash to the far side of the building. There he took up a position where he could observe unnoticed. He'd parked right in front of the door in case they needed the headlights but in hindsight it hadn't been the best choice.

The car that pulled in was not from a security company. The doors of the black sedan, too high priced to be a fleet vehicle, remained unmarred by loud logos and the roof held no light bar. The black Lexus parked right next to the Z and two women got out.

It was hard to see much in the mix of shadow and light. All he could make out was that the women were roughly the same height, about five and a half feet, and the driver was about fifty pounds overweight while the passenger was a waif unfamiliar with the sun. From what he knew of Pritchard's cult, it consisted entirely of women. The driver would have to be one of the wealthy older members he fleeced to finance his enterprise and the younger was one of the barely legals he kept around for other reasons. It was these young ones he'd sent to Carter's to curry favor with Drew, and he'd first confused Cassie for. He didn't know what the girls saw in the guy, but they were willing to do anything for him. It made Drew sick.

With his newly restored clarity of mind, on top of the whole magick thing, he wondered for the first time if Pritchard's control over his women went beyond your run of the mill brainwashing. A little magick could cement the women's loyalty far better than a little manipulation.

The older of the two women peered in the windows of the Z, Drew holding his breath until she moved away. Exhaling in relief, apparently prematurely, he forced himself to bite his tongue a second later when she leaned over the front end, swung her hand up, and metal glinted in the low light. A hissing sound reached him over the hum of passing traffic and Drew swore under his breath. She wasn't done. Around she came to slash his other front tire before folding and replacing the knife in her purse. Drew made a promise to Pritchard that he would beat exactly that dollar amount out of his hide.

Finished maiming the car, the abuser grasped the church's door handle and signaled to the waif standing by at the front of the sedan. Slack-faced, she followed the older woman who, handily enough, fished a small flashlight out of her purse before they went inside, the door closing softly behind them.

"Damn it," Drew cursed aloud. "He had to send MacGuyver?" What else did she have in that bag? The air leaving his tires was taking his escape plan with it. Thinking a cab could meet him on the street, his hand slipped into his pocket then halted as soon as his fingers touched the screen. That lady had been handy with a knife and now she was between Cassie and the door. His brother might be at his condo right now or at the club waiting for him, and he was stuck here. Torn, Drew paced, roughing his hair.

What was he thinking? Brandon needed him; he should be on his way. Let Cassie sort this out. She had magick. If she was able to defend herself against Terry Pritchard, certainly she could take care of one middle aged woman with a knife and a half-baked lightweight. He had to find Brandon before they did.

Cassie and her ilk were not going to be lenient on Brandon if they found him first. Drew told himself no one else mattered, that it was still the Carter brothers against the world. In his mind he saw her face as she hovered over him in the elevator, she hadn't left him when he'd been helpless. And he saw the look of her as she lay entwined with him, her dark features relaxed and unguarded. She didn't deserve to be abandoned.

"Damn it, damn it, damn it." One last double handed hair yank that left him looking half mad and he took off at a jog down the sidewalk, following the faint glow of light inside.

***

Cassie read the sheet she'd pulled off the top of the recycling twice before folding and pocketing it. The crackling page obscured the sounds of footsteps at first but after she'd smoothed it in her jeans pocket, she could hear them clearly. Two sets, both of which were too light and stealthy to be Drew. Grimacing, Cassie closed her hand and snuffed her light as she trotted across the room to tuck herself behind where the wall jogged back to make a doorway for a storage closet. It was barely enough to provide her cover, she would be hidden from a cursory glance only. Anything more was impossible given the simple, open floor plan of the room. When the intruders entered, all they had to do was turn to the side and they would see her. Cassie forced her breathing to steady and waited.

The flashlight's beam peeled back the shadows, gradually growing more visible and allowing Cassie to track their progress. They followed the back wall, echoing Cassie's movements perfectly. She knew at least one of her pursuers was a woman when a light voice whispered.

"Mary, should we call the police?" The fact that she whispered didn't hide the slur. Was she drunk? "What if it's more of those men from up north?"

"Hush, Caroline. Mr. Terry says he doesn't want the police here; we can handle this." The other woman had a voice that probably boomed when she wasn't working to keep it down. As it was, it was a stage whisper at best and anyone in the office would have been able to hear it.

The light preceded their echoing steps on the poorly insulated wooden floor and when it turned into the copy room, it was like someone flicked a switch. Reflecting on the white and gray faux marble floor and bouncing off the white painted cinderblock walls it was bright as day in there. Cassie's position was exposed before they took two steps in.

"Who are you?" Mary demanded, no longer bothering to keep her voice down now that her prey was sighted. Cassie had guessed right, a sea captain would have been proud to have her lungs. "Caroline, take the light." Head swiveling to catch sight of any more intruders, Mary approached.

The young woman, Caroline she was guessing, was sloth-like in her movements. Whether it was drugs or alcohol Cassie couldn't tell, either way she was out of it. Cassie had already figured Mary to be the greater threat given her sobriety and greater bulk, and that was before she heard the click of metal on metal. Her eyes jumped to Mary's hand seeing the four inch blade protruding from the ka-bar's graphite base. It appeared not all of Pritchard's women were helpless widows or empty headed fools. This one could manage just fine on her own.

Cassie held her hands out peacefully. As far as she knew, these two were regulars even if they were working for a witch. By law, magick was a last resort to be used against them only in the most dire of situations and so far this didn't qualify. That and Cassie didn't want to hurt someone unintentionally. Grandmother's warning that her soul would suffer in Veritas' employ came back to her. She shook it off. It wouldn't come to that if she handled things right. Making her body relax and her voice steady, Cassie hoped to keep things cool. "Look, I don't want any trouble. I didn't take anything yet, see?" Passing herself off as a common thief seemed like the right choice.

Mary was no fool. She grinned coldly and tipped her head back toward the door. "That's your car out front, right?" Her accent held no hint of the South. Mary was a transplant, although that was true for half of Florida; New York or Jersey sounded closer to her point of origin. "Anyone who can afford *that* car is not robbing a church with nothing in it unless they're a junkie." She took a step. "You're no junkie. Now tell me why you're here."

Training to be an investigator in the field had included handling an attacker with a weapon, but training for it and actually facing a woman with a knife and a steady hand were two different things.

Cassie sidestepped, angling out into the open box of a room, giving herself some space to maneuver. Mary lowered her knife to stomach level and took a step forward. Caroline slouched in place, content to hold the light while the other two faced off.

Drew watched the women square off, waiting. If he jumped in now he might only make things worse. He was losing faith in Cassie's ability to talk Mary down although she probably had a spell or whatever to disarm her opponent. The waif was no threat, she looked like she was ready to tip over any second. She earned only a few sideways glances.

Cassie thought fast, trying out a new angle that might put the knife-wielding Pritchard-ite at ease so that she could disarm her without getting disemboweled. "Listen, my sister disappeared after talking to this Pritchard guy. I heard he runs this place and I'm just trying to find out if she's with him."

"Why didn't you come around asking about her during normal business hours?"

"Things didn't go well at home when she left, I didn't want to spook her if she saw me."

"What's your sister's name?" The knife didn't budge.

Wavering her voice enough to incite sympathy, Cassie looked hopeful. "Becky, Becky Stordahl." Her hand went out palm down and she began to pull, preparing for the worst.

"I've never heard of her."

"I don't understand. We assumed she was coming here when she left." Her face fell she looked every bit the dejected sister. Drew had to admire Cassie's nerves; she wasn't easily rattled.

Mary's shoulders straightened, she eased out of her crouch and Drew breathed easier. The woman was buying Cassie's story. He exhaled and started to back away. He could leave Cassie now. She could manage her way out of this.

"She's one of them," the waif's thin reedy voice screeched, frantic. "I see it in her."

At the first shriek Mary's knife shot up and the tension level in the room shot to nuclear. "What? That's not possible!" The anxiety he heard brought Drew rushing back. Nervous and armed would not end well for Cassie. Once again, he made ready to jump in.

Caroline remained where she was, flashlight still held aloft. Above the beam of light her eyes had gone enormous and black in the shadows. She raised one hand to point. "The girl's like Mr. Terry, she has the light of the divine in her."

For a moment, Cassie was hopeful thinking this Seer's vision had given her a free pass comparing her to their leader. Eyes flicking back and forth between the two she waited.

"Remember what Mr. Terry said," Caroline reanimated building up steam, "beware false prophets. They don't share their strength and love with us like Mr. Terry. They are demons lying in wait to lead us astray." She waved the flashlight at Cassie. "We must destroy them."

Apparently Mary agreed and, in an instant, she sprang. Cassie's nerves were tight and she was ready when Mary leaped, sidestepping at the last minute. Mary stopped herself and spun with her prey. They circled and Mary feinted at her, leaving no doubt the weapon was not purely for show.

Drew could see that her attacks were not intended to wound, they were meant to kill. He could not hold himself back any longer. Seeng a use for what Cassie and her partners had said was his skill, Drew walked into the room planning to cool Pritchard's two women down.

"Hey ladies, what's going on here?" He made a conscious effort to will them calm, aiming one of his best crowd cooling smiles at them.

Mary brought herself up short and twisted toward the newcomer. The knife went down to her side, hidden behind her leg. Cassie kept her eyes on it. Caroline turned around and aimed the light at Drew. Squinting, he held up a hand to block the blinding beam.

"He's one of them too!" she shrieked. "Send them both back to Hell!"

Lips tight, Mary stepped back to face both Cassie and Drew. "Come on Demons! I'm ready for you." She hissed and lunged.

Cassie put her hands up defensively and blocked the blade from catching her face, feeling it slice into her forearm instead. She sucked in through her teeth as her other palm struck Mary's attacking arm and pushed it aside, allowing Cassie to step in and follow up with a palm heel to the nose.

Reeling backward, Mary held the knife up in one hand while her other flew to staunch the flow of blood pouring from her face. She blinked and shook her head, blinded by the automatic tears blurring her vision.

While Drew looked on, assessing the severity of the wound from the thin stream of blood running down Cassie's forearm, the beam from the flashlight tilted, making the room appear to shift with it and an ear-piercing banshee cry rent the air.

Caroline had moved, her speed a shock after her previous slugging about. The long willowy girl landed on Drew and clawed at his face. He threw up his arms instinctively to fend her off, feeling her nails dig into his arms and neck.

186

Working in the club, Drew did well to avoid most fights. That didn't mean it was always one hundred percent effective. Carter's was relatively peaceful under his influence although sometimes he would be a little late and find himself wading into the mix, which is where most of Drew's doctoring skills came from. As any club security or owner will attest, one of the biggest challenges for male bouncers is stopping a woman's attack without actually striking her. Fortunately Drew had some experience in that realm.

Fast so that he could knock her off balance, Drew jumped sideways and ducked at the same time. Predictably, the banshee riding his back teetered and he took advantage, spinning the other direction before she righted herself. As she came loose, scrambling to keep her hold, Drew reached out and caught her as she slid down, then clamped his arms down over her, efficiently trapping her. Frustrated, she shrieked again.

Flinching at the ear splitting sound, Drew shifted to keep her contained under one arm and put the other hand over her mouth, cupping her chin to keep her from biting. He'd learned that lesson the hard way in his first few weeks at Carter's and gotten six stitches for his oversight. "Cassie, behind you."

Dropping and spinning, Cassie swept a leg out and tripped Mary who went down like a stone with a dull thud. Regaining her feet, she put a hand over her bleeding arm and stepped into the light to better examine it.

"Is it bad?" He gave Caroline a firm jostle to stop her wiggling.

Cassie was twisting her arm to inspect her wound on the underside by the elbow. "I don't think so, it's hard to tell in this light. Hold on." She scooped up the flashlight and ducked back into the little alcove where she'd hidden earlier. Rustling sounds ensued and she emerged with a roll of packing tape, holding it high in victory.

Kneeling down to the prone form, Cassie picked up the knife from where it had fallen beside its owner and wiped it on her pants, closing and pocketing it. She took the woman's pulse and set about taping her hands and feet, keeping her on her side to prevent her choking on her own blood, before rising and pointing at the barely subdued Caroline. All she caught of the Seer's face were her eyes, glaring at her over Drew's hand, which covered nearly the entire lower half of her face. "Can you hold her still?"

"I think I can manage it."

A few more spins of tape and Caroline was restrained. Using the flashlight held like a torch, Cassie was able to look in her eyes. Seeing they were bloodshot and her pupils were pinpricks, Cassie exhaled harshly. "She's drugged out of her mind. She's no use to us like this." Disgusted, she tore off a final slap of tape and clapped it over her mouth. Drew laid his charge down beside Mary, who was breathing shallowly on her side. Wiping her arm on the underside of her shirt, Cassie put one more strip of tape over her cut and looked around to be sure she wasn't leaving anything behind.

Drew watched her methodical handling of the situation and considered what he knew of this woman. She was capable of handling herself, that was for sure. He found the knowledge oddly comforting. And yet her detachment chilled him. It spoke to a side of the compassionate woman he wasn't sure he wanted to know.

Glancing up, Cassie caught him staring at her, a curious expression on his face. "What?" Her expression was blank.

He shook his head. "You don't seem upset by any of this."

Cassie held out a hand, waving it at the bodies on the floor, thankful for the sake of her soul that they were both still breathing, and rolled her eyes. "This is my job. I may not have been too quick to pick up the one part." She avoided mentioning magick in front of the still conscious Caroline watching them from the ground. "But I've gotten used to," her eyes lingered on Mary's barely moving form, "the rest of it." She rubbed the smooth band of tape on her arm, embarrassed at the warm feeling enveloping her at his coming to her aid when he had seen these two coming in. "We should go," she mumbled and brushed past him, ready to leave this place.

Turning around to see if he was following, Cassie caught him staring after her. That he was working through something in his head was obvious. She had to assume he was discomfited by the discovery that her job was not always clean. At least he was speaking to her again, for now. That was sure to end soon.

The awkward silences that had dominated their dynamic since she'd removed his amulet had been filled with her mental war, the back and forth of telling herself she'd been reckless in her dalliance with a client while the hopeful voices told her how to justify it to her superiors.

On their way out, Drew's eyes caught a glimpse of yellow atop the refrigerator out of Cassie's sightline. "Let me see the flashlight." He held out his hand to her retreating form as he diverted to investigate in the fading light. The glow turned his way and he felt its weight in his hand.

The yellow legal pad had been tossed carelessly up there as someone retrieved their lunch most likely, and had been forgotten. The pages of scribbled notes made no sense to either of them but what did catch their eyes was that Swainsboro was written beside the name Toohey. Drew liberated the pad, tucking it under his arm, and after a brief sweep revealed nothing more, they made their way back up the stairs.

"What's in Swainsboro do you suppose and who's Toohey?" Drew asked as they retraced their steps, failing to notice the fact that Cassie did not answer.

Emerging from the building, Cassie saw the tires on the Z and sighed. "When were you going to tell me about this?" Her hand fell back, slapping her thigh in exasperation.

Drew's nerves were taut and he bridled at her condescending tone. "Sorry, there wasn't really a chance to talk about my car repair issues. I was busy saving your neck."

Cassie spared him a cutting glance, pulled her phone from her pocket and dialed. "Agent Porter calling in with a situation. I need a car towed." Stepping out, she peered around the building's corner to see the street sign and reported it. Phone slid back into her pocket, Cassie gave Drew a quick look, only to catch him eyeing her curiously. She found his scrutiny unnerving.

"Come on, I saw a gas station not far from here. We can call a cab to meet us there. We don't want anything else tying you to this place. It wouldn't be safe." She moved off, leaving him no choice but to follow, needing to be in control.

Drew jogged up, catching her as she turned the corner and hit the sidewalk heading back the direction from which they'd come. "What do you mean it wouldn't be safe for me? What about you? Don't you think Pritchard's already curious about you after what happened in the club?" It went against the grain for her to be trying to take care of him. He had his pride.

Staring straight ahead, Cassie watched the oncoming traffic for overtly curious onlookers, familiar faces, or law enforcement. Her training was much the same as any other officer in the regular ranks except hers included the use of magick and the apprehension of magick users. Being aware of her surroundings was key to being good at her job.

"They won't find me; I don't really exist." She sensed his hesitation at her foreboding declaration. "If you went looking for any of us outside of Veritas channels you would never find us. That's how Veritas keeps its agents and our families safe." She sneaked a look at him and saw him concentrating on traffic as well, his expression troubled.

Chapter 20

They walked on in silence, both pretending to watch everything else, yet so keyed in to one another when Cassie stumbled on a high spot in the concrete Drew caught her elbow.

"Thanks," she grumbled, unexpectedly flustered at his closeness, pulling away to keep her wits about her. It was none too soon that the neon green tower marking the gas station came into sight and they ducked inside behind a tall rack of snack cakes to wait for their ride.

The cab company directory assistance referred them to showed up ten minutes after they called. They rode mutely to Carter's where they were going to pick up the Ducati and, Drew didn't know it yet, but he was going to disappear for a while.

Drew kept his nail gouged neck out of the driver's sightline easily enough by turning his head and Cassie held her arm down at her side, covering the blood stain on her clothes. Blood was leaking out from under the nonabsorbent tape bandage in a light trickle, not severe but enough to be annoying.

She wondered if she had time to call the healer to meet them at the hotel. It would be safe to stay local for only a short time. Drew was in danger and, regardless of how mixed up as she was about him, her duty was to protect him and keep him close until his brother and Pritchard were recovered.

Brandon Carter and his motives remained a mystery. He cared for his brother, that was undeniable. The ring had been, without a doubt, an attempt by Brandon to protect his brother from Pritchard's influence. Yet that was years ago and Drew had said Brandon was changing lately. His physical changes could very well be because Pritchard's hold over him had grown more powerful and he might not be able to defy his master any longer. What had happened in the alley was damning in the extreme.

Cassie hoped Julia and Quan would return soon. She welcomed the break from Drew the reinforcements' arrival would offer. And the perspective she desperately needed.

Cassie needlessly reached for the slim wallet she carried in her pocket in place of a purse; Drew had already handed a twenty to the driver.

As the car pulled away he lifted his chin stubbornly. "I'm not a child, I don't need you to take care of me."

"This isn't a date, it's business." She tried to hand him twenty dollars and he refused, backing away from her.

"You told me last night I wasn't a client and there was no business between us, and now I *am*? You can't have it both ways."

Cassie latched onto the chance to reestablish some boundaries between them. "You're in danger now that they know you've come after them." She leaned in closer to keep their conversation private; standing on the curb had them nearly within earshot of the valets. "You have magickal abilities, are untrained, and you're exposed both physically and psychically to a number of things, including a very dangerous witch. I owe you protection."

That she wasn't touching him made no difference. She could feel the masculine charge her words shot through him, sending his back arching rigidly to put his chest in her face. "I don't need anyone's protection."

Cassie strained to meet his elevated gaze. "Whether you want to admit it or not, you do and you'll deal, or you're going to end up like those guys in the alley." At the sight of his haunted expression, Cassie regretted speaking so harshly.

Hating herself and her job, she watched him turn and continue past the valets, giving them a quick nod and acknowledging their friendly hails. What she'd done was being cruel to be kind. Drew needed to understand what he was up against if she was going to keep him safe. Even *with* her, it might not be enough if Brandon and Pritchard came at them together. Disturbed at the thought that she might not only lose his trust, but that she could also be responsible for his demise, Cassie said a quick prayer to her mother's patron goddess, whom she'd adopted when her mother passed. Asking Brigit to look out for her charge assuaged some of her trepidation.

Cassie walked in and Tavaris was at his post. Yay. Shooting him a severe look she saw him back down from whatever it was he'd been about to say. Catching sight of Drew's familiar figure disappearing in the shadowy interior, Cassie easily vaulted over the velvet rope to follow and caught him at the door. Though he never looked back, she knew he was aware of her. At the top of the stairs, he threw the door wide enough to allow her through without actually holding it open.

Jaime was in the upstairs bar tonight and gave a slow wave to them both. Her boss didn't bother to do more than dip his chin and Cassie managed a poor excuse for a smile. Dance music beat loud and fast, the blue and red lights following the frantic drumming with a crazed strobe effect that cast Drew's movement in a disjointed, macabre game of hide and seek. The sound faded when they reached the blackened hallway, the light from the office bringing Drew's outline flashing back into view as he opened the door.

With his profile so clearly illuminated it was impossible not to see his step falter and jaw drop. Instinct kicked in and Cassie rushed after him unthinking, pulling power through her palms as she ran. His hand had fallen limp from the handle, leaving the door to swing open and allowed Cassie a clear shot to leap in and throw herself into him, sending them both crashing to the floor.

Cassie was already bringing her hands up, sending a blast at the intruder when Drew took her by surprise and twisted underneath her. The muscles in his chest hardened and his arms encircled her, trapping hers at her sides and sending her attack flying off out of control and into the framed drawings on the wall. They came sliding down with a crash.

"No Cassie," he hissed in her ear. "It's Brandon."

She stiffened, eyes searching for a man sitting at the desk only to find him sitting directly opposite her on the floor, beneath the desk. The sickly face staring back at her was probably handsome when he wasn't seriously underweight and overstressed. Wild, haunted blue eyes looked straight through her and she felt that tug again, the same one she'd felt when she'd met the real Drew, the one under the superficial playboy facade. Here was another man who'd grown up afraid, one who needed her help.

Drew felt Cassie's acceptance that his brother was not an imminent threat as she stopped struggling. "It's Brandon," he repeated, quieter this time. "Brandon? It's cool Bran, Cassie can help you." As he reassured his brother, he pictured Brandon in dark robes and a pointed hat standing trial in front of a panel of similarly garbed wizards and snorted.

Cassie turned and raised a quizzical brow. She probably figured he was cracking up. It was a definite possibility, Drew himself couldn't be sure. It wasn't every day his brother faced being sent up for magickal misconduct. Cassie could tell Drew was struggling with his brother's sudden appearance and such a shocking one at that. She felt responsible for his poor handling of it; his nerves and emotions were most likely still raw from the removal of the amulet. Seeing him this way had to be hard.

Torn, she struggled with Brandon turning up as well. On one hand she wanted to comfort Drew, but on the other, she was facing a potential criminal who was arguably a threat to the greater population. There wasn't time to get Drew squared away; he was just going to have to manage and she would help where she could.

"Brandon," she used a gentle voice, treating him like a victim and not one of the offenders. "Brandon, can you look at me? My name is Cassie Porter. I'm an agent sent here to look into a man named Terry Pritchard."

He flinched at the mention of Pritchard's name though outwardly he was otherwise vacant. Drew remained motionless, watching intently. Cassie flushed, realizing their entrance and ensuing contortions had left her sitting on his lap with his arms around her, on the floor. To move might spook Brandon so she stayed where she was, refusing to concede how unauthoritative her position happened to be.

"Brandon, can you tell me about where you've been? Do you know where he is?" Experimenting, she avoided saying Pritchard's name, this time seeing Brandon only tighten his eyes, a less volatile reaction and one she considered an improvement.

Still he said nothing. Cassie was attempting to figure out a plan of action when her phone rang in her pocket. Trying to catch it before it upset him, she answered quickly.

"Cassie, we're comin' back." It was Julia and she didn't sound happy. It was windy where they were, the gusts were audible through the speaker.

Instantly, Cassie feared the worst. When a man is being hunted he's a lot like an animal, he goes home where he's most comfortable to hole up or make his stand. "He's turned back, hasn't he?"

"Yep." Julia's hand covered the phone and there was talking in the background. "He laid a false trail, we just figured it out." Julia sighed, frowning down at the much abused body of a well dressed young black man lying splayed on his stomach with his limbs at odds from his body, most likely from being dumped from a moving car. His body lay only a few feet from the road in a small stand of saplings. From the road he'd looked like garbage, it was easy to miss.

Quan was furious to have fallen for Pritchard's trick. He squatted with his hands hovering over the young corpse, trying to capture what traces he could of the elusive witch's power. An eelskin wallet lying open on the ground identified the man as Alfred Toohey. They had no idea who he was or why Pritchard would have used him, other than the fact that magick matching Pritchard's had been stored in the man planted here to draw them in after Pritchard laid the trail and abandoned it. It was a sick man's treasure map and they'd just found what was under the "X."

Julia closed her eyes and turned away. "How's it going there? Is Drew handlin' things without the amulet?"

"Uh, yeah. The amulet was definitely keeping everything from hitting him. He seems like he's doing okay on his own though."

Drew changed his position abruptly and Cassie nearly lost her balance. Her hand shot out to catch herself, wrapping around his neck to secure her position. He flinched when her fingers caught the fresh scrapes.

"That was the source of his charm."

Tipping his lap, Drew dumped her unceremoniously on the floor. Unaffected, Brandon continued to stare listlessly at their antics. Cassie clambered from all fours onto her feet and aimed a withering glare at Drew.

Cassie stepped out into the hall and proceeded to fill Julia in on their visit to the Ray of Light, what they'd found on the notepad, and the street fighting skills of the older woman in addition to the drugged Seer, Caroline. "We're having the car towed; our people should have it out of there by now but I can't be sure Pritchard's people didn't get enough to track it back to Drew. I'm keeping him with me from here out." Hearing the defeat in her partner's voice, Cassie worked to incite confidence that they didn't need to worry about things there.

"Good, sounds like you've got it all under control." Julia sounded tired. "What did you say the name you found in the church was?" When Cassie repeated the name, Julia craned her neck to get examine the wallet more closely. They had a match and she told her young partner as much. "I'll call it in to see what Research can find to connect the two." Continuing with the debriefing, Julia changed the subject. "Have you heard anything from Brandon?"

"Funny you should ask," Cassie replied dryly. "I'm looking right at him. He's not a threat in his current condition."

Annoyed, Julia shifted her phone to hear Cassie's muffled voice in one ear and a pitched, rapid-fire verbal assault on Pritchard in the other. Julia listened to both partners go on and wondered why she hadn't taken the offer of a teaching position at the Academy when Anna had offered it a few months ago.

Seeing how she'd stepped up on this mission, Julia was confident Cassie could handle Brandon, damaged as he was. Quan's pronouncement overshadowed anything Cassie was saying after she heard one word. Chameleon.

Chameleons were a rare sort of witch and almost always dangerous, more even than chaotics. A chameleon, like his reptilian namesake, had the unique ability to tie in to the magick of any witch he laid his hands on. That explained why the deaths of the drug dealers in the alley so closely resembled the deaths of the Carter's parents. It had been done with the same magick, only a different witch. Toohey must have had some semblance of magick as well, though it had been covered up by Pritchard's dummy charge.

Cassie went on, oblivious to the happenings on the other end of the line and grateful for the routine of giving her report. "He's pretty shaky, Julia." She finished. "I think Pritchard's done something to him, he's terrified and he looks half dead. I'd like to call a healer."

More mumbling before Julia came back. "Sounds good, honey. Get him a room at the hotel and lay low. Keep 'em both out of sight until we can get back." She paused, doing some math. "We should be able to get back by tomorrow evenin.' Keep an eye out, Pritchard might show up lookin' for his boy."

"Will do." The line went quiet and she replaced her phone in her pocket. Taking a deep breath, she let it out and put her game face back on.

Drew's backside was to the door, his front half had disappeared through a hole in the floor beside the desk amidst the shattered pictures. Brandon hadn't moved, it was possible he hadn't even blinked.

"Drew what are you doing?"

A muffled hum drifted up, his words undistinguishable until he came up holding several small stacks of green and white bundles. "If we're going to run, we need cash. I don't have a lot after the car. This was my emergency money in case I could get Brandon to break away from... him." He cast a nervous glance at his catatonic brother. "It's enough to get us out of the country or something until I can get us set up somewhere safe and get a job. Thanks for your help Cassie, but I've got it from here."

"You're not running anywhere." Outwardly unperturbed, Cassie leaned against the cabinet beside the door. "My partners are on their way back. They said we should head back to the hotel and I'll keep you two safe." Praying he wouldn't make her stop them, Cassie watched the outline of the shell of the man Drew would risk his life for. He was rocking back and forth. Brandon was completely broken, even a healer would have trouble bringing him back.

Drew got up and walked past her giving no heed to her words. He grabbed the first aid kit and dumped out its contents, returning to stack the bundled cash within and pausing only long enough to aim a frightening gaze at her. "I have my brother back. We're leaving before he comes for him. I'm not losing him again."

"Drew stop." Cassie was more unnerved by his break from reality than Brandon's catatonia.

"He's coming," he whispered harshly, forcing the words between clenched teeth.

Cassie swallowed the lump in her throat, keeping her expression placid. "You can't run from him. *He* can't run. I can keep you safe. Stay with me, Drew." The backs of her eyes pricked at the voicing of her true desire, probably the last time she could say it without inspiring hatred in him. It wouldn't be long now and he would detest her.

He listened. Sitting on his haunches with his hands on the money and a defeated slump in his spine, he looked up at her.

The trust she saw in his eyes inspired a greater self-loathing than any amount a magickal blockage ever had. Slowly, Cassie went over to put a hand on his arm. "We have healers who can help him. I can call and have one here in a few hours." She could do that for him at least.

"How can they help this?" He turned his face only partway, unable to look upon his brother so destroyed.

"Our healers can handle psychic damage."

Drew let his head fall into her chest and gave in. For as much as he feared what would come of Brandon once Veritas or Pritchard got a hold of him, Cassie was right. Brandon was in no state to make a run for it and there was no doctor *he* knew who could help him. No, he would have to throw in and trust Cassie again in order to save his brother. He would rather visit a sane Brandon in prison than a vegetable in a mental hospital.

"I'll get us a car." Laboriously he pushed himself up with his hands on his thighs and grabbed the house phone. "Jaime, yeah. Did you see him come in? Yeah, he's not feeling great that's why I'm calling. My car is out of commission, I was wondering if you could call one for us? Thanks. Let me know when it gets here."

Chapter 21

In spite of Cassie's assurances that he didn't need it, Drew tucked his bag under his arm and brought his small fortune along to the hotel. Getting Brandon the room next to Quan's and putting it on Veritas' account was a process. That Cassie paid, to keep it from being tied to either of the men, was the source of yet another argument between the two. All the while Brandon hung limp and suspended by Drew's arm, a ball cap from the office pulled down over his face to keep anyone from noticing the virtual corpse they had dragging along with them. Drew caved on the payment only because the strain from escorting Brandon was taking its toll on him, not all of it physical.

"Please let me help," Cassie whispered while they waited for the elevator as Drew stumbled, catching himself on the wall.

"No, there's no reason for us both to be tired. I can't defend us if he comes back. You can." They still weren't saying Pritchard's name out loud even though Brandon was far from hearing them. His eyes were closed, his head lolled forward with the swaying of Drew's stride. Cassie knew what it cost Drew to admit that he would have to rely on her if it came to a fight, he was a proud man.

By the time Cassie slid Brandon's key card in the lock, Drew's face was wet and flushed and he looked about ready to pass out. The healer she'd called from the cab, the same one who'd fixed her up the other morning, would be here within the hour. Given the shape he was in, Cassie would insist upon having Drew examined as well. While she was at it, it would be wise to use the opportunity to get a read on anything else the amulet might have left behind psychically.

Running on pure willpower, Drew let Brandon fall gently on the bed. Cassie had rushed ahead of him to pull the blankets down so he didn't have to wait. Freed of his burden, Drew stumbled back, his knees threatening to buckle. Cassie offered him an arm for the short shuffle over to the tan and red striped chair in the corner.

The second his hand touched her, a mind-numbing flash of weariness nearly took her knees out from under her. Finding it hard to breathe, Cassie blinked as a blanket of concern for Brandon covered her, smothering all of her other thoughts. Sending her eyes over to the man who lay unmoving in the cream and gold bedding, his skin barely distinguishable from the pale pillowcase, Cassie felt grief at his loss and feared for his death. Even more than death, she feared for the loss of his sanity, knowing that the independent spirited older brother would sooner lose his legs than his mind.

Gasping, Cassie ducked out from under his hand once Drew was seated, both of them shaking and spent. "Here, keep your distance from him for now," she cautioned, leaving the room to get the complimentary bottle of water from the small kitchenette counter. "Drink this, you'll feel better."

Drew took a long drink. Screwing the cap back on, he gave a short, tired laugh. "Still have that ring? I'm thinking feeling nothing was a hell of a lot easier than all this."

Cassie sank down to kneel in front of him, being careful not to touch him again. He was raw and she was tired, leaving her defenses patchy at best. Another dose of Drew's emotional upheaval might interfere with her already severely compromised ability to maintain a professional distance, not to mention draining her as it had Drew.

Her hands rested on her legs. "There's nothing wrong with using an amulet, lots of witches do it in certain situations. If you feel you need it, I have it." Her thumb stroked her pocket where it rode wrapped in an insulating rubber glove Drew had thrown on the office floor.

But he was shaking his head. "No, I don't want to use that thing again. I wasn't me while I wore it." He raised his face to hers, brown waves clinging to his head from sweat. "I'd rather be like this than a zombie without a care or thought deeper than what's for dinner." Gray eyes flashed resolute through the exhaustion dulling his expression.

Hearing him say it made Cassie's chest ache. Their encounter had been during that zombie phase and although it pained her to hear his confirmation that he hadn't felt anything more than the pleasures of the flesh, she was still pleased to hear that he sought deeper feelings. He was going to figure himself out and find a happy life. The joy she felt was bittersweet.

Drew's eyes closed and if he hadn't nodded off, he would soon. His head rolled against the cushioned top of the chair and Cassie leaned against the bedroom doorway to watch Brandon, lying still as death, his features were waxy. She'd nearly forgotten they were expecting company when a knock at the door made her jump. She hurried through the short hall and into the sitting area to answer before waking either of the men.

The healer, a forty something woman dressed in a light blue top hanging out over tan casual dress pants, showed Cassie her Veritas badge marking her a Doctor Martha Jones. Even though they'd already met, it was procedure to show id.

"They're in here." She aimed a thumb over her shoulder and started to turn.

Dr. Jones balked, taking her shoulder bag off to lay it on the table by the door. "They? I was informed it was only the one suffering severe psychic fatigue." A thin finger tucked a stray strand of ash blonde hair behind her ear.

"It is, but his brother carried him in from the parking lot."

"Oh." Dr. Jones understood with no further instruction and, needing only that, brushed past Cassie to first take a look at Brandon, then Drew. Initial triage complete, she straightened and her expression was grim. "He's been used up. It must have taken a huge effort for him to break away from the one controlling him, and to stay away. I'm assuming he is coming back?" Using a regular or fellow witch was strictly prohibited, according to law. Dr. Jones did not have to inquire as to the character of the man responsible for Brandon's current state.

"I'm pretty sure he's on his way."

Dr. Jones' thin lips were pressed firmly together, pushing the color out of them as she continued examining Brandon and frowning all the while. "Do you have any idea the type of magick that one practices, where his strength lies?"

Cassie wagged her head. "Not really." She tipped her head toward the sitting room and they moved out of Brandon's hearing range. "He's only just shown up. He's been missing for a few days and I don't know what either one's real strength is. Quan is saying Brandon's is chaos magick but whether it's pure or has been manipulated by the one who's using him, we can only guess at this point."

"Well, as awful as he is, we must be grateful for his master 's return." Dr. Jones went to her bag and began to unpack her supplies: stethoscope, arm cuff, bag of stones each individually wrapped in silk, bowl, glass bottle of holy water, etc.

"Why?"

She stopped unpacking to study Cassie's confused features with warm brown eyes. "What do you know about the borrowing of another's energy?"

Cassie shrugged. "Book stuff from school mostly, and some stories here and there."

"Using another's energy forms a tie that connects the two beings until the initiator chooses to sever that tie. It's not only his physical being that will suffer with the distance between the two. Their energies are essentially joined." Dr. Jones put her stethoscope in her ears. "If the other one doesn't return, then that which constitutes Brandon will cease to exist. She put the end of the scope to his chest. "This one will become nothing but a soulless husk until his physical body eventually gives up and dies too."

Cassie's hands needed something to do; there was little for her in a room that wasn't hers, but she couldn't bring herself to leave. She settled for making coffee. After bringing a cup to Dr. Jones, she poured one for herself and leaned against the wall to watch the healer work.

Dr. Jones set several pieces of rough cut quartz around Brandon's body and poured a container of holy water into her bowl. Cassie recognized the container as a cleansing station for when the stones were full of the dark energy overwhelming Brandon's system. They would be unable to save him as long as he was connected to Pritchard, but they could hold him back from the brink and buy time until her triad was able to arrive. Maybe one of them knew something that could sever the connection. Sympathetic to anyone suffering a fate worse than death, Cassie included Brandon in her prayer to Brigit, asking her to guard his soul. It was the best any could hope for at this point.

Next, because it was a nonsmoking room and they couldn't burn sage or sweetgrass for purifying, Dr. Jones pulled out several sage smudges and her eyes flicked up to where Cassie stood. "I need your help getting his clothes off."

Neither woman relished touching a man so full of dark energy. Cassie set down her cup and joined Dr. Jones at his bedside. It was a king sized bed which made undressing the patient awkward. Dr. Jones climbed up on the bed and loosened his belt, pant fastenings, and top few shirt buttons, making it simply a matter of pulling everything off. They both tried to limit their contact to his clothing but several times, when her hand brushed his skin, Cassie felt the darkness stick to her like cling wrap.

The darkness sucked at her, its fingers stretching and clawing to find purchase in her during their chance meetings. Its fingers scraped at the insides of her mind, leaving her feeling raw and abused. By the time they had Brandon down to his underwear both women were exhausted.

Dr. Jones wiped her brow with the back of a hand. "Let's give ourselves a little brush off before we go on with him, shall we?" She set about wiping Cassie down with a smudge stick in firm sweeping motions, starting at her center and flicking out. When she was done, she set the smudge bundle in a plastic bag and picked up another for herself.

"Here, let me help." Eager to keep busy, Cassie took the smudge and performed the same ritual cleansing on the doctor and placed the used bundle in the bag with the other. Their contact had only been incidental yet still Cassie could feel the absence of it when the darkness had been brushed away, she couldn't imagine what Brandon must be feeling or Drew for that matter.

"Thank you." Dr. Jones straightened her shirt and grabbed another smudge bundle. "There is some salt in my bag. Could you pour some so that I can cast a circle? I would like to close it just as I finish his cleansing. How are your defensive spells?"

Circles were second nature to Cassie. Although not always fast under pressure, she could cast an effective one and leave it while she stepped out. The nice bit about being the one who cast it is that she would be the one who would feel it if anyone tried to disrupt it, a sort of warning device for intruders. "I'll cast it."

"Good."

Ten minutes later they both stepped outside Brandon's protective magickal bubble and the doctor had turned her attentions to Drew. Her brows furrowed and her fingers slid down over his forehead. "What's this?" She closed her eyes. "Has he suffered a shock? His mind is patchy and overloaded in spots. It doesn't seem right."

Cassie bit her lip, fearing the full ramifications of her recklessness in removing the amulet the way she did. She told the doctor what she'd done.

"And you removed it only a few hours ago?" She stood up putting her hands behind her hips and stretching her back. Yawning, she bobbed her head in approval. "He's doing exceptionally well for having so much thrown at him and with such a raw emotional mind. He's strong."

Cassie made a relieved sound, drawing Dr. Jones' eye. "It was hurting him, the amulet," she explained, feeling questions in the brown eyes as they regarded her calmly. "Whenever someone would use any energy around him it gathered in the stone and shorted out the protections. While those were down he would be on his own, no protections, no idea what was happening." She felt tears welling up, speaking faster as the guilt she felt for bringing harm to a man she was rapidly growing fond of gave way to relief. "He's never had any training and he's so sensitive to others' emotions, I think his magick is sentimental but I didn't think of that at the time. It was foolish to have taken it off without thinking of the consequences. Especially with *him* being so interested in him. If I can't protect Drew, I've failed them both." Hearing herself running on, Cassie cut herself off with a choke and took a ragged breath, uncomfortably blinking back most of the tears welling there and wiping at her eyes for those that had escaped.

The doctor was watching Cassie, her thumb pressed up against her lips as she thought. "What exactly is the nature of your relationship with Drew? Is he a client?"

Cassie blanched. It was the question she'd been dreading for fear it would mean the end of her career. Then there was the simple fact that she really didn't have an answer.

"As I said, we met Drew during the course of our investigation only a few days ago. I was assigned to stay with him and wait for either Brandon or Pritchard to show up and be taken into custody. During that time he has proven himself a valuable asset and, given his status of untrained witch, I have a duty to protect him from harm until such time as he can be paired with a trainer for a thorough education."

"I'm not here as an investigator, Cassie. There is no need to be so formal." Dr. Jones gave her a kind smile. "I'm asking as a Healer. You are clearly under quite a strain being responsible for the lives and mental status of two unguarded men, one of whom you clearly care about." She lifted her chin at Cassie's intent to interrupt. "If you have feelings for the one, I fear you will not think clearly. This is a delicate situation and one that, if handled poorly, could result in the loss of both, if not all three of you."

"I *am* thinking clearly," Cassie rumbled obstinately, ignoring Dr. Jones' statement confirming exactly what Cassie feared.

The doctor's brows rose and she pushed back more firmly. "All I'm saying is that if you let your emotions for the one get in the way, you won't be able to protect any. And if the one we're waiting for is as strong as I think he is, if he's going *to do* what I think he is, then you're going to need to be at the top of your game."

The burden that was hers to bear alone until her partners returned settled heavy on Cassie's shoulders. Wishing she could open the door and walk out, she took a breath, straightened her back, and forced a grimacing smile. "Tell me what you're thinking."

Chapter 22

Drew woke, his mind was clear and he felt better than he had in a long time. Moving, he felt something gritty on his skin and ran a hand up under his shirt to come away with white granules. A tentative taste revealed it was salt. Leaning forward and shaking his head while he ran his hands through the mess, he heard it hitting the carpet with a light patter and caught the scent of something earthy and strangely spicy that he didn't recognize.

Glancing around, he saw Brandon lying in bed; his shoulders were bare above the covers. There were clear rocks that looked a lot like the one from his ring just less green, scattered around him. One lay on the pillow above his head, one beside either hand, a fourth beneath his feet.

His brother's appearance had not changed, though with his eyes closed it was less painful to look at him.

That Cassie's initial reaction to Brandon's return had been compassion and not to immediately arrest him had alleviated the fears that had been creeping up on him. He remained untrusting of her partners, but that he could rely on Cassie to help him untangle his brother from Pritchard, thus giving him an ally, made all the difference for him. He was relieved to be free of the dread that had weighed him down since learning that Veritas was investigating Brandon's relationship with Terry Pritchard. That and the knowledge that he might have to lie to Cassie or even have been forced to hurt her to save his brother. For the first time in his memory his brother was not the only person he cared about, he could no longer deny that. The realization hammered its way into his consciousness with the subtlety of a Jack Russell Terrier.

Voices coming from the front room floated in quietly, rousing Drew from his chair to follow. He wanted to see the source of the one he recognized, curious the identity of the other. When he stood more salt fell from his clothing and he gave his shirt a cursory shake, getting the majority of the stuff off his skin on his way across the room.

As he approached, Drew could see Cassie lying against the arm of the smaller sofa, her knees drawn up and a white blanket thrown over her legs. She had that wrinkle between her brows she got whenever she was upset. Anxious hands wrung his guts and he continued putting one foot in front of the other. The other woman who came into view when he passed through the doorway was reclined, fully stretched out on the longer sofa. Both had cups, his nose said coffee, and he caught sight of the small pot on the counter. There was only a little left, not enough for more than a few swallows.

"Good evening." The woman he assumed was the healer greeted him. There was something in her voice that made him think of his dead mother. It had been so long since he'd thought about her it took him by surprise. The kindness in her tone was the same one he'd heard countless times in his youth when he'd been ill or suffering some scuff or another. Drew hardened himself to the pang the woman's voice elicited.

"Hi." His eyes strayed to Cassie. She was watching him curiously, maybe waiting for him to freak out like before. She was tired along with being worried, he could see the dark circles under her eyes. Drew glanced at his watch. Two o'clock. "Haven't you been to bed yet?"

"We've been waiting for you to wake up," Cassie answered quietly, her voice husky with the sleep calling to her. "Drew Carter, this is Dr. Jones. She's a healer with Veritas."

He gave her a quick wave, waiting quietly for what had to be bad news. He didn't have to wait long.

"Drew, Dr. Jones is one of our top healers. She's been working here in the area on a number of cases that have the organization's attention." Cassie waited to see that he was able to focus, going on only after getting a nod from him. "For months there have been reports of strong paranormal activity, significant raising of energy in pockets from Tampa to Gainesville. Then, two weeks ago there was an incident in Jacksonville."

Drew rethought the coffee, wanting the comfort of holding something warm. Wandering back to the pot he grabbed a glass, the mugs were taken, and poured the last of the pot. Listening, he leaned back on the unoccupied arm of Cassie's sofa. "What kind of reports?"

Deferring, Cassie cast a glance at Dr. Jones who took over. "Reports of a drug. It's being taken by regulars and witches alike with very different results."

He tested the coffee against his lip, it was cooling. Sighing that even this small comfort was not to be, he slugged it down in one disappointing mouthful.

Dr. Jones watched his reactions closely, attempting to determine his state of mind. Cassie had faith in him, that was abundantly clear. Just the same, this was a lot for anyone to take in and this man had thought himself a regular until three days ago. She went on cautiously, ready to stop if he looked overwhelmed. "Witches go into a sort of a frenzy, going after anything that smells of magick. Regulars, on the other hand, see bright halo-like auras surrounding practicing witches. They can see anyone using magick"

"How bad are the attacks on the witches?" Drew wondered if something like that had happened to Brandon.

"Mostly fatal," the doctor said simply, waiting for a sign he was going to have trouble accepting what she was saying before elaborating, yet none was forthcoming so she continued. "Our reports have been limited to random and unexplained violent outbursts involving heavy energy use in different communities. There have been quite a few, too many to be accidental, and who knows how many more there have been that we don't know about." That she wanted to bring an end to the incidents and couldn't was clear. Dr. Jones was visibly agitated. "We have found only one witch left alive thus far and he has little memory of what happened. The only common denominator has been a residual chemical in the victims called Citalopram. It's found in an antidepressant prescribed by thousands of doctors all over the country and on the street to some extent."

Drew swirled the last drop of brown liquid around the bottom of his glass, watching a stray coffee ground get hung up on the glass when the liquid would outrun it. Glancing sideways at Cassie, Drew saw the hint of strain around her eyes and mouth. There was more, she was waiting for it. "At the risk of sounding like an ass, what is it you want from me?"

"Only information." Dr. Jones had seen Drew watching Cassie for cues. His ability to read the young woman was astounding. Especially considering the brevity of their association and the protections the junior agent kept up, as was protocol. She agreed with Cassie's determination of his magickal type. She could see the strength in his ability by the way he read her without physical contact. That was a rare accomplishment for a sentimental witch. When this was over she would recommend the man to the Directors as investigator material. An ability like his would be a boon in the field.

"Your position inside a club affords you a unique insight. We wondered if you'd heard of a new drug being circulated. Something new in the last six months or so. It's most often inhaled, similar to cocaine, although a few appear to have injected it like heroin. Have you noticed unusual levels of excitement, maybe heightened volatility in your patrons?"

"Hmm." He closed his eyes, trying to think. Clubs and recreational drug use tended to go together no matter how much the club owners might try to discourage their use. As far as Carter's went, Drew had been able to keep the dealers out for the most part with only the rare exception. Although, now that he was thinking about it, he'd had more than the usual attempted drug deals in the back alley, and at least a couple of times a week for the past two months he'd turned customers away for being stoned off their asses. There had been concerns of the increase in violence attributed to local gangs. It had affected some other clubs more and he'd worried it would cross over to his. Unhindered by the amulet or ignorance of magick, he was able to put it all together.

With everything he knew now, he couldn't miss the meaning of the occasion two months ago when he'd been rougher than necessary because of a raging headache. It had been after a customer had jumped up on the bar upstairs and was ranting about angels. The guy had been out of his mind on something and they'd thrown him out, not wanting the police in the club. His fingers rubbed his naked finger out of habit while he sifted through his memory, searching for the name he'd heard recently. "Yeah, I think I've seen it in action at our place. It's been making the rounds at the local clubs, it's something called Revelation."

Repeating the name to commit it to memory, Dr. Jones stood, giving them both a polite, if not forced, smile. "I'll call that in and see if we can find more information in the local police files now that we know specifically what we're looking for." She reached the door and turned back. "If you two don't mind, I would like to keep the external stimulation down for Brandon. I'll stay with him but I'm sure you can find other accommodations for the remainder of the night." Opening the door, she made their dismissal clear.

"Yes Doctor." Drew leaned over as he straightened, getting a glimpse of his brother's feet. They hadn't moved nor had the rock by them been disturbed. It was doubtful Brandon was going to miss him if he wasn't there. "Could you call if he wakes up?" He wanted to be there when he needed a familiar face.

Understanding shone in her soft brown eyes. "Of course."

With a visible effort, Cassie threw back her blanket and got up, stretching her arms over her head. "Thank you Doctor." She nodded and touched her forehead in thanks.

In the hall, Cassie and Drew regarded each other awkwardly. It was the middle of the night and although they had a block of four rooms they had been kicked out of one, they didn't have a key to the two belonging to the other agents, and the door adjoining Julia's was locked, leaving Cassie's as the only option if he wanted to stay close to his brother.

She was dead on her feet. The let down from a long night and the drain of helping Dr. Jones with three cleansings was beginning to show itself. With the back of a hand, she stifled a yawn.

Drew could tell she was leaving the decision up to him and held out a palm. "Let me have your key."

Without a peep of protest, Cassie handed it over and followed him in.

"Why don't you lay down and get a few hours while you can. I'm going to take a shower." He threw the key on the table in the front room, a mirror image of the one they'd just left. "Do they have a laundry service here do you think?" He held his shirt out to show her the blood, curious if he looked as gross as he felt.

"Twenty-four hour." She made an effort at levity. "This is one of our hotels, we have all the amenities."

"Really? You guys own hotels?"

Cassie walked through to the bedroom and sank down on the bed where she kicked off her shoes, one after the other. "Veritas has its fingers in just about every industry we touch on a regular basis. It's a necessity really." She shrugged. "Cost saving as well when you think about how much we travel." Her eyes rolled up as she ticked off a few. "Hotels, airplanes, cars, restaurants; like I said, everything." Socks came off and she let them lay where they fell beside her shoes. Naked feet felt good after a long day and she wiggled her toes in celebration.

Drew crossed his arms and leaned a shoulder on the doorjamb. Watching Cassie talk about Veritas and this whole other world, Drew considered a life with them. What he'd done his whole life had been outside of respectable. Working at the club was barely on the other side of the line. A career with an organization that helped people like Brandon and him could feel good for a change. If he learned how to wield his magick as well as Cassie did, maybe he could work with them. She'd said he was talented enough. A lot depended on the next few days and what was going to happen with his brother. If it turned out, he might just have to look into it. He wondered how she would feel about his joining.

"How long do you have to study at the Academy to become an investigator?" Trying to appear only mildly interested, Drew directed his eyes to a tiny crack in the ceiling.

"Depending how quickly you come along it's usually about two years of basics, one year of specialization to be an agent. I could give you a recommendation." Kicking herself for sounding so eager, Cassie forced herself to calm down. Drew was only considering the job change because he didn't know what was going to happen. Even if he went to the Academy, which he should, there was no way he would end up being an investigator or want to see her again. Blaming her and what she stood for was pretty much an inevitability.

Drew noticed the shadow pass over her features and feared for its cause; her usually easy to read expression was mixed and he was confused. He took a breath and told himself it was better this way, he had wanted to know if she was uncomfortable with the idea he might follow her into her world, and now he did. "It's no big deal, I was just curious if you guys went as long as police. Your jobs are about the same."

Stomach knotting at the feeling of his energy tickling on the edge of her protections, Cassie closed her eyes and took another deep breath. Her attempts to center herself were ineffective, she was far too mentally spent. Her defenses were close to coming down and he had none, everything he was projecting both willingly and unknowingly was hitting her and she was feeling the vast majority of it. Frustrated with herself more than anything, she closed her eyes and pushed back, hard. When she opened them again she saw Drew staring wide eyed at the floor. He'd pushed himself away from the wall and stood braced in a wide stance, touching his forehead with both hands.

"I don't think I'm feeling well. I'm going to shower."

Thinking herself a fool for telling him yet knowing she couldn't put it off any longer, it wasn't fair, Cassie stood up off the bed. "Drew, come have a seat."

One hand rubbing over an eye, he raised his gaze to hers and she was able to see the turbulence she'd caused. He blinked. "I don't think that's a good idea. I'm really not feeling like myself."

"That's why you should. I can explain." Hesitantly, he came over and sat. She sank down heavily beside him, their knees less than a foot apart.

Drew's eyes were questioning, the openness she saw there making her wish all over again that the amulet hadn't limited their encounter to being purely physical for him. It hadn't been for her, she could feel it when she looked at him and her resolve to remain emotionally divorced was floundering.

Dr. Jones had seen it, which meant Julia would as well. Cassie cared about Drew and that was why she couldn't let him spend another moment thinking he was doing something wrong and punishing himself for it. Summoning courage she prayed wouldn't fail her, she told herself this was the right move.

"Drew, do you remember when I told you that you were able to get me to tell you things I hadn't told anyone?"

Snorting, he bit back the sarcastic comment that rose to his lips. He couldn't get her to tell him what he wanted to hear, so it was fairly worthless as a skill. "Yeah," he replied tightly.

Cassie hurried to explain, worried he was thinking she'd cornered him into one of "those" talks. "No, listen, that's where your magick comes in. It's what the stone felt in you and amplified." She had his attention and lowered her voice, making herself speak more deliberately, less agitated. "The stone guarded you from feeling anything deep good or bad, right?"

"Yeah." He waited for her to tell him he had been ruined or crippled or something by the ring.

Swallowing, Cassie got ready to tell him, hoping her trust in him was well placed. If she was wrong and he got himself into trouble, she didn't want to be the one to blame for putting temptation in front of him. The truth of it was there was nothing he couldn't persuade people to do for him if he thought big enough. That was an enormous temptation for most people. "Your magick, I figured it out a while back. I didn't tell you because I was hoping we would have you set up with a trainer or at the Academy before you found out," she rambled, off track.

Drew stared, his headache was fading thankfully but Cassie was giving him a new one.

"Your magick is called sentimental because it's tied to emotion. Your charisma Julia asked you about, your gift with women," she flushed, "and your ability to cool down a room, it's all tied together. The ring protected you from negative influences, but it also toned down your natural abilities."

"What does that mean? I can make people like me? You said that before and that's not magick by my definition." He wasn't impressed.

Cassie hadn't explained it right. Puffing up her cheeks, she blew out in a big gush and tried another tack.

"Not just *like* you," she clarified. "You can make people do things for you. It's an incredibly useful tool for manipulating people, and yours is really strong." Cassie watched him carefully. "You could make someone rob a bank for you, kill for you, fall in love with you, anything."

She didn't know why she said the last. She must have been tired. But Cassie saw his misgivings; he was not excited about his magick. In what was becoming a sick cycle, Cassie felt the pleasure and pain associated with her mission. If educated on how to wield his magick, she was sure Drew wouldn't use it to hurt anyone though an ability such as his would have tempted even the morally incorruptible Galahad. "I think you should go to the Academy, Drew. I really think you would be a great investigator and what a fantastic place for a talent like yours." Too anxious to stop talking, Cassie went on. "Julia's that way too. She can get almost anyone to tell her things. Except you, but that was the stone. You should have seen the look on her face when she told us that not only did you block her out, but you were charming her as wel." Cassie guffawed at the memory. "No one has ever fought her off before, but you did. It might have been different if she'd touched you or gotten something of yours, then she might have had you."

He was running his hands through his hair, feeling sticky and gritty at the same time, focusing on the tactile. Preferring it to the less visible things Cassie was going on about. "It was the ring, that's all," he objected weakly, remembering back to his childhood when he'd been able to do no wrong. Teachers loved him, friends' parents and coaches, it was always the same thing. If Drew wanted it, he got it. Luckily his parents had been well grounded and the only ones able to say no. Looking back, he wondered if they hadn't had a little magick of their own to be able to keep him at bay. He wished he could see them one more time, if nothing else than to thank them for keeping him from turning into a monster.

"Only part of it was the ring. It had to get its direction from you." She wouldn't listen to his objections. "If I were wearing it, it would do something different maybe bend the metal in the bar or something." She referred to hers being a physical magick. "But on you it brought out your strengths, getting people to trust you and to like you. It's something you do naturally." Her voice grew more subdued. "You're doing it now, that's why I pushed you out of my head."

Comprehension lit in his eyes. "That was what I felt? You pushing me away?"

"Yes."

"Why didn't it happen like this before? Have I ever 'influenced' you before, you know, made you do something you didn't want to do?" Drew worried for the first time he'd taken advantage of her, of any of the women he'd been with. Here he had been worrying whether he should be with her when it was possible he'd not left her any choice in the matter. That he would only have to snap his fingers to bring her to his bed.

"No, I was able to guard against your influence before." She shook her head.

"Aren't you guarding yourself now?" He asked the question awkwardly, the concept felt strange.

Cassie's sagging frame answered better than words. "I'm tired. It's harder now and I'm slipping." She watched all of this new and heady information sink in. He stared at his hands, running one over the back of the finger where the stone used to sit, not sure whether it was out of habit or if he was thinking back and questioning everything he'd ever done, every friend and woman he'd ever had. Wondering if any of it had been real.

Chancing to touch him, Cassie reached out and let her hand settle gently on his leg, preparing herself for the jolt and making a conscious effort to keep his influence out. "You're a good person, Drew." She spoke from the heart, confessing more than he could comprehend yet. "One of the really good ones. You can't second guess yourself. You have to trust that you would never had taken advantage of someone, it just isn't in you."

"How can you say that? If somebody can't say no to me then how is anything I do not taking advantage?"

"Because even a regular can push back; we all have free will. You would have had to consciously choose to talk someone into doing something. You would know if you had convinced someone to go against their will."

Cassie's shoulders had unconsciously clenched and she felt them relax when she saw his frame do the same. He wasn't guilty. He had never coerced someone to do something they felt opposed to, nothing of any import.

"I'm going to take a shower." His face closed and his thoughts turned inward as he stood and made his way to the bathroom.

Cassie was staring at the one king sized bed and chastised herself for being so juvenile to concern herself with the joint accommodations. They were both adults and there was no reason they couldn't share a bed platonically. Cripes, she'd shared a bed with Quan once. Granted it was only for a couple of hours and it was a totally different situation. But that wasn't the point.

She worked to sound nonchalant. "I'm going to lay down for a little bit and see if I can get some sleep."

Drew looked from her to the bed and then out toward the front room. "I'll sleep out there."

"Don't be silly, you're longer than both couches." Cassie felt the heat creep up her neck and flood her face. It sounded like she was begging him to stay. "I mean, it doesn't make any sense for either of us to get a crappy night's sleep on a tiny couch you can't even roll over on when this bed is plenty big enough for both of us. I trust you to be a gentleman."

He gave her a dubious look.

Cassie rolled her eyes. "I'm not *that* tired. You couldn't make me trust you if I didn't already."

That seemed to settle things for him. He walked around her to the house phone and called for laundry to come pick up his clothes and they promised to have his things back to him in a few hours. They would leave the parcels outside his door so as not to disturb him.

"Could I bother you to put my clothes out while I shower?"

Cassie agreed, intending to put some of her own out as well. She eyed the blood stained pants she was wearing, hoping they were salvageable.

She heard the shower turn on and Drew stepped out of the bathroom in only a towel with his clothes folded and balanced on one palm and she realized one thing that could prove very awkward. He would be sleeping naked and in the same bed as her until morning.

Their eyes met for only a passing second during the uncomfortable handoff. Drew mumbled a thank you and Cassie mumbled something back. She got changed and put hers on top with a note to check for bloodstains, getting the clothes out just in time to see a hotel employee coming to take them. Dressed in a tee and shorts, she settled in to bed where she lay on her side with her eyes closed, figuring that might make things easier.

When Drew came to bed, moving ever so carefully trying not to wake her, she could feel him shifting and tugging his towel with him. Only because she was absolutely beat was Cassie able to fall asleep with the sporadic tingles pinging against her shoddy barricades. Thank goodness for the hardnosed instructor in charge of self-defense at the Academy. She would have to be almost dead to drop them completely.

Drew had his hand on his towel, holding it together even after he heard her drop off to sleep. He thought it would never happen, but sleep finally came for him too.

Chapter 23

Cassie woke up feeling warm and content. The sun shining in through the crack in the curtains was higher than it should have been. She'd thought Dr. Jones would have woken her by now. As she became aware of herself and her surroundings she figured out why she was warm, it was due only in part to the blanket clamped under her arm. The other part being due to the body tucked up behind her and arm thrown loosely over her waist. With an embarrassed flush, she could tell he'd lost his towel some time in the night. Enjoying the closeness, she closed her eyes again and pretended to sleep a little while longer.

Waking sometime in the morning hours, Drew felt Cassie's petite body shift against him and he knew by listening to her breathing that she was awake. He continued to lie touching her, part of him wanted to lean down and kiss the nape of her neck to see what she would do but he didn't want to risk losing what he had.

Feeling her body accept and curl into him, seeing her olive skin against his whiter skin yet untinted by the summer sun brought him back to the last time he'd lain with her. Drew wished he could see her face, it was easier to tell what she was thinking. Although there were times when, even then, she was closed to him. It occurred to him that those were the times when her defenses, as she called them, were up.

When the clock glowed nine forty-seven there was a knock at the door. Cassie jumped up, rushing to open it for the Doctor before she woke Drew. Running a hand over the dark, glossy hair she'd gotten from her father's side, she was grateful for it's thick texture that prevented it from getting too wild, regardless of how she slept.

"May I come in?" Dr. Jones took in Cassie's attire and raised an eyebrow. "Or should I come back?" Both eyes went wide and her focus shifted to somewhere behind Cassie.

Turning she saw that Drew had come to stand in the doorway. His towel was wrapped securely about his waist, arms crossed over his chest. She swallowed and pretended to be unaffected by the sight.

"Here, I found these on your doorstep." The doctor held up a bag. The clear plastic afforded a clear view of Drew's neatly folded clothes within. "Why don't you go put them on?" she ordered flatly and tossed the bag. He caught easily. All amusement had fled her features.

While he was dressing in the bathroom, Cassie took control of the conversation, directing it away from the discomfort her charge's unusual sleeping attire caused. "How's Brandon? Has there been a change?"

Letting the awkward moment pass, Dr. Jones turned her attention back to the young woman in front of her. "Yes, he's growing more agitated." A flash of her disturbance leaked through and Cassie's insides flipped. "The one who's bound him is coming."

Drew stepped out of the bathroom in his jeans, his shirt still in his hands, forgotten in his eagerness to hear her update face to face. "He's moving? Is he talking?"

Dr. Jones' experience did not make these sorts of things any easier. "No, he isn't talking, not clearly. It's mostly tossing and muttering, although I can't make out anything of any importance." She turned back to Cassie. "I've heard from Research. Revelation has been mentioned in three police reports. Cocaine related deaths are up however, and a number of those follow a line from Tampa to Jacksonville all in the last year. We're thinking those are ours as well. Eight of the cases we're investigating involved suspected overdoses and the deaths of three drug dealers." Her gaze flashed up to Drew. "One was not long after the incident two nights ago behind your club. Four ounces of Revelation, measured and marked, were found on the bodies."

"Pritchard is killing drug dealers? Why?" He ran a hand through his hair, it hadn't fared the night as well as Cassie's.

"There's more," the doctor added quietly. "The other dealer was found dead inside his apartment in Gainesville three days ago. His body was set on fire in the bathtub. There was too much damage to tell the cause of death but no smoke in the lungs. He was dead before the fire was set."

"Pritchard wasn't in Gainesville three days ago." Drew shook his head, creases in his forehead. "He was here. He came to the club."

"Yes, but Brandon was in Gainesville three days ago." Dr. Jones extracted a piece of paper from her pocket. "I found this receipt in his pocket. He parked in a ramp a few blocks from the dead man's building. The time on the receipt is less than an hour before 911 got the call about the fire."

Faced with indisputable evidence that his brother was a killer, Drew felt his world collapsing. He had relied on Brandon to take care of him, placing him in this position and allowing Terry Pritchard to get his claws in and put him up to this. Their parents were an accident; he'd convinced himself of that. After the accident that left them orphaned, Brandon had stopped practicing. He'd stopped using magick until Drew had gotten himself in trouble and then he'd used it to turn things around. The timing was right, he knew he was right.

Whatever deal had been struck between Pritchard and his brother had led to this. And it had been Drew who had unknowingly forced his brother to make that deal. He was faced with the cold truth that his brother was a murderer. He was lying nearly dead in the next room, tied by deeds and who knew what else, to a megalomaniacal bastard all because of him. It echoed in his mind until it was all that he could hear. Without a word Drew spun on his heel and walked into the bedroom, emerging a few seconds later with his shoes and a stack of cash.

"Drew where are you going?"

He didn't answer, sliding his shoes on his feet and lacing them hurriedly, jaw firmly set.

223

Cassie was scared stiff. She was supposed to keep an eye on him and Julia had specifically told her to keep him here until they returned. Cassie was still on probation, new magickal stylings or no, she had to toe the line and losing Drew was both personally and professionally out of the question.

"Drew, wait. I'm coming with you." Cassie ran into the bedroom, coming out hopping one-legged while she pulled shoes on, jeans shoved under one arm, and her bra balled up in her fist.

He was nose to nose with the doctor who was guarding the door. Neither looked like they were going to give way. He spoke calmly and quietly to Cassie without breaking off from Dr. Jones. "I have to go alone. It's too dangerous for you."

"That's why I *have* to go. It's dangerous. You're my responsibility, Drew."

That brought his head around. Eyes narrowed, he spat furiously. "When are you going to get that I am not your problem? Look what happened to the last person who tried to save me! I will not let that happen again."

He turned back to the doctor and Cassie could feel it on her skin as he wielded his influence over her, his determination making him formidable. She steeled herself against it.

"Let me go," he commanded.

Dr. Jones wavered. Cassie could see that she was drained from a night of caring for Brandon and not up to a face off. Shadows under her eyes and exhaustion paled skin spoke of a night spent working and using up her reserves caring for her patient. Raw as he was, Drew had the advantage.

"Move Doctor or I will move you." Drew's eye twitched, he was unused to this amount of power running through him. If he wasn't careful he was going to fry himself. It was one of the main reasons Veritas had the Academy for any who showed a strong ability whether they went on to work for the organization or not. To be untrained was dangerous for the individual as well as those around him.

One too many uncontrolled witches had brought on both the Enlightenment as well as the Dark Ages. Veritas had been relentless in their pursuit and education of magickal practitioners the world over since the Inquisition as a matter of self-preservation. And here was Cassie on her first solo assignment, ready to go rogue with an untrained witch capable of massive destruction and an incredible potential for collateral damage.

Seeing it as the only reasonable solution, Cassie stepped up beside Drew and pulled rank on the doctor. Investigators, even juniors like her, could command a healer. The procedure dated back to the days when military might ruled supreme. "Dr. Jones, I order you to stand aside. I am hereby taking responsibility for this man and I alone will answer for his actions."

The doctor watched her for two heartbeats. Drew wisely kept his mouth shut, seeing this as the path of least resistance. Cassie could still see the cording standing out on his arms, fists clenched tight at his sides. With no other option, the doctor stepped aside.

"Cassie please, wait until tonight. Julia and Quan will be here and you will be far more capable of facing this together than alone. Taking an untrained witch against one you know to be dangerous is against protocol." Her brown eyes were troubled, not angry, as she pleaded with Cassie to listen to reason.

The pleading got under her skin and Cassie was wavering when she saw Drew pulling back his shoulders, getting ready for round two. It was her duty to protect him, even if it was from himself. The Directors would not accept ignorance as an excuse for using his magick on a healer. She intervened quickly, holding one hand chest high. "It's an order, Doctor. Stand aside."

Unhappy and unable to do anything about it, Dr. Jones did as she was commanded. "You're being foolish," she told them as they went past her and opened the door. "You're both going to get yourselves killed and who knows how many more, and for what?" The doctor aimed her argument at Drew, knowing that he was the driving force behind their defection. "To get your licks in against someone powerful enough to not only drain but bind a witch without ever having any formal training? This man is strong and he's unpredictable. Please," she held out a hand to Cassie, "please think this through."

Cassie heard Grandmother's warning again, her visions overlapping in her mind. Drew was the man in the mask and she was powerless to control him. Her soul would suffer greatly, she could feel the blackness coming. Bringing her eyes to the doctor's Cassie sighed, feeling old. "This is my path. I have to follow it."

Drew was in the hall, waiting to speak, when she closed the door behind them.

Her blood was still up and she was in no mood to debate the issue. "You take me or you don't go."

The look in her eyes stopped him from protesting further. If push came to shove he wouldn't be able to beat her magick to magick. Grudgingly he had to admit that, with her, he stood a better chance of surviving than without her.

They got in the elevator and Cassie stepped into her shoes, the rest had to wait. "Where did you plan on going first?"

"My place. I need some things."

"Like what? A gun?"

A flicker of doubt glimmered in his eyes and he asked, less sure of himself. "That'll work, won't it?"

She gave him a small smile. "We aren't superheroes. Our bodies are the same as anyone else's." Her brow furrowed. "You just have to be careful about letting him know you have a gun. That's where it can get tricky with a witch."

"How's that?"

The doors opened and Cassie waved him out first.

Cassie shrugged one shoulder. "We still don't know what he can do; chaotics are hard to figure. He might be able to convince you to shoot yourself, or me for that matter." She headed for the front doors to hail a cab. "Maybe he can bend metal and the gun will blow up in your face, who knows." Out went her hand as a yellow car pulled up under the awning.

Drew waited next to her, wondering what the hell he was doing. He almost turned back, ready to wait for Cassie's partners. Then he saw his brother, not as he was upstairs. He saw Brandon on the ice, playing hockey at one of his last games before he'd quit. Brandon had been a god on the ice; he was unstoppable. Every stride, every time he caught a pass and maneuvered it past a guard to take a shot on the net, he was sure of himself. That was the Brandon Drew was fighting for. The Brandon who had disappeared that night fourteen years ago, the one who had lost all of that when he'd been left saddled with a kid brother too scared to face the world. A kid who was too afraid to make decisions for himself. He'd waited for his brother to tell him what to do after that. That kid was gone and so was that self-assured brother. If Drew ever saw Brandon again he wanted it to be as equals. It was time for him to help Brandon for a change.

He shut the door of the cab and gave the driver his address, casting a glance over at Cassie. She nodded at him and sat back. He glimpsed the clock on the dash and eased back into the well-traveled leather seats. There was plenty of time for him to do what he needed to, the question was *would* he when the time came.

Chapter 24

Drew's Z was parked out front waiting for them with two new tires. When he stepped out of the cab, mouth hanging open, Cassie laughed.

"I told you we have people in every industry. Cars can be a great way for police to know someone else is involved." She rolled a shoulder. "We're faster than Triple A at getting a car out of there."

The same way he had for the last two years since he'd moved in, Drew strode up to the building's secured entrance and fished in his pocket for the keys. Cassie put a hand over his.

"Pritchard's disciples have had enough time to find you. Go slow."

He nodded grimly. Drew led the way through the corridor and up the stairs to his floor. They avoided the elevator for the noise that would announce an arrival. When they reached the door Cassie quickly touched his shoulder and held up a hand. She was going in first. He held out his keys pinched in his hand to keep them from rattling, Cassie smiled and winked. Drew was a quick learner. Recalling his rap sheet, Cassie realized he wasn't learning, he was settling into an old lifestyle. Knowing that would help to make him easier to protect, it failed to upset her.

Going rogue had given her a reckless vibe and Cassie was feeling powerful. Mentally she cautioned herself not to get too crazy but it was difficult. This was the first time she'd stepped out of line. Well, second, but both times had been with Drew and now they were on their own without any orders to follow. They hadn't seen anyone since entering the building and it only added to the illusion that they were all alone in the world.

Recovering some amount of sanity with effort, Cassie reached down and pulled power. The Earth couldn't give her what she needed from three floors up, leaving the water in the pipes to eagerly heed her call. Hand filled with energy, she used it to open the door instead of the key, holding an arm out to keep

Drew back. When nothing exploded, they cautiously peeked around the doorframe and slowly walked inside.

Everything was as she remembered it. Drew looked at her and nodded that nothing was amiss. Cassie shut the door and locked it behind them. She hovered in the front room while he went down the hall and gathered what he needed. The clock over the microwave said it wasn't quite noon.

She pulled her phone from her pocket and dialed Julia. Apparently, Dr. Jones had gotten to her first.

"Cassie what in hell are y'all doin'?" Julia's shrill timbre was a new one and her Creole accent made it hard to understand as her words ran together in the unique cadence of the bayou. "Runnin' off with a client on his wild goose chase when I told you to stay put? You're goin' against protocol and puttin' both your lives in danger. You know that. Did he talk you in to this?"

There was finally enough of a pause for Cassie to answer and she did. She'd been working through her rationalization on the cab ride over.

"It's not a wild goose chase, Julia. Drew knows Pritchard. He knows his patterns and his haunts. We're better off on the offensive on this one." She lowered her voice so Drew was less likely to hear. "Didn't Dr. Jones tell you? He's tied Brandon to him. He's probably tracking him right back to us. We're less safe being there than out here."

Julia calmed down, recovering a more genteel tone. Cassie had a point. "The healer said Drew was pretty upset. Is he a danger to himself or to others? What about you? Can you keep his influence from affecting you?"

Cassie considered her questions. Drew was angry but he was thinking rationally and had shown restraint with the doctor. "No, he's not a danger."

"And you, are you thinking clearly? The healer said she thought you were distracted." Julia pressed, the healer had been sure to point out the potential emotional interference in Cassie's judgment. Pritchard was far too dangerous for her to be less than focused on the chase.

Silently, Cassie cursed the doctor and her big mouth. "The thing with Drew is under control. I let it go too far but it was only one time and he only did it because of the amulet. It's behind us now, okay?" She was sharper than she'd intended. It was hard not to be, the subject was a festering sore that just kept getting poked. "I'm going to get a piece of Pritchard for you, for when you come back. That way you can break the binding between them even if he manages to get away again."

"Don't even think about facing off with him alone. I'm serious honey, you're spending too much energy worrying about Drew and his brother to manage if things go bad. Wait for us and we can get what I need to break the binding together." Julia's voice had grown maternal; it was worse than yelling.

"Julia, you haven't seen him." She lowered her voice. "It's bad. If we lose any more time Brandon might be too far gone to break the tie that binds them. If I can find him I can get something to you as soon as you get here." Cassie sniffed, the stress was getting to her and Julia's warmth was pulling her emotions to the surface.

Cassie stuck to her guns, she knew she was right. She'd seen Julia break a psychic connection once before and it was difficult because she wasn't the one who had initiated the binding, but she could do it. All she needed was a piece of Pritchard or something he kept on his person, something that came from him. Hair or a worn article of clothing was usually the easiest to get. And then she would need a sacrifice. Cassie would leave that to Julia, she tended to prefer to choose her own small animals, saying it required a certain something in the animal. Cassie didn't understand but readily accepted Julia's expertise in the matter of all things Vodou.

"Is Drew able to help at all or is he just blindly leading the charge with you following along?"

"I think he's a natural." The doctor must have left out the part where Drew nearly moved her with his influence. "He's been using it for years by instinct and that was with the amulet limiting him. I'm telling you, you don't have to worry about Drew."

There was a long pregnant pause on the other end of the line. Cassie could hear the rustling of her hand over the phone and a rumbling that must have been Quan, though she couldn't make out the words. When Julia did respond, she was slow and deliberate.

"Cassie, you listen to me. I want you to be careful. No matter what you're thinking about Drew and his skills," she was clearly not convinced about them, "you need to keep in mind you are there to shut down Terry Pritchard. No matter what drama is unfolding in the lives of the Carter brothers, you must remember why you are there. We'll help them if we can when our assignment is done. Too many people stand to suffer if we lose our focus over a pretty smile and tight ass."

Bristling at the unnecessary reminder of her duty, Cassie snarled. "Call me when you get in." She started to hang up and thought of one more thing. "Don't forget to bring a chicken."

Julia grumbled an "I know what I'm doing" and the line went silent in Cassie's ear. On the other end, Quan was waiting for the rest of the report, anticipating it was not good. He'd heard most of it. Julia's lips were pressed together grimly; he almost missed her soft "merde."

Back in Tampa, Cassie stared at the phone's dark face. "Please hurry," she pleaded softly, pressing the heel of her hand into her forehead. A headache was coming on, no surprise given the fact that she was potentially throwing away her career and torpedoing her plans to take care of her family without having a clear understanding why. But her gut said Drew was heading in the right direction and she couldn't sit around waiting for her partners and Pritchard wondering who would get there first while she watched Brandon linger near the brink.

She felt a twinge for Dr. Jones but she knew the risks of staying with a patient bound to a sociopath. Healers weren't lightweights; they were trained just as well as the investigators for field work.

Drew had heard Cassie's conversation, even hushed tones carried on the hard bare surfaces of the unit. Guilt stirred in his breast and he attempted to quash it. He could not be held responsible for any sort of repercussions that came her way, he'd told her not to come. It had been her choice to follow him. Except his conscience was not so easily placated as that.

Hearing her espouse her faith in him while under the impression he didn't care about her, he felt something inside him give way. Drew came into view and saw her standing slumped, holding her head and looking lost. He set his bag on the tile with a scrape and she dropped her hand to her side.

He continued into the room, coming up behind her and slid his arms around her waist. For a brief instant he felt her sink into him only to stiffen and push away. "Are you in trouble for coming with me?"

"I came with you because it makes sense." She turned around yet could not bring her eyes to his, nor did she answer his question. "We should get going. We have a witch to catch and I would like to find him before he finds Brandon." Cassie attempted to walk around him. "I hope you got what you came for."

Undeterred, he stuck his hand out and caught her by the arm. "In a minute. Before you go out there and risk your neck for my brother and me, there's something we need to straighten out."

"I've told you it's my job…" He saw fear mixed with something else in her eyes when she glanced up.

That something else was what he'd been hoping for, and before either of them could talk him out of it, he wrapped an arm around her and pulled her close. Drew's mouth cut her off from saying anything else. Everything he wanted to say but couldn't he poured into his kiss. Starting out forcefully, he got her

232

attention, then softened; brushing her lips with his and showing her he wanted more from her, more than just now. He pulled away and waited.

"Why?"

"It wasn't the amulet. I heard what you said to Julia and I wanted you to know it wasn't that the other night."

She blinked and Drew watched her pulse race in her neck. Now that he had seen her true feelings, he wanted to let her know she was mistaken in thinking herself alone in her affections. "I've been trying to ignore what happened except it isn't working for me." Drew ran a hand through his hair, grabbing a clump at the back and clutching it with his head bowed. So open, he wasn't able to face her. "Since that night I've been doing a lot of thinking. About you and me and everything."

Cassie could see how worked up he was, she reached out to touch his arm, letting him know she was listening and was rewarded with a look into his eyes. Soft gray, they were troubled and open all at once. Drew was letting her see into him, frightened at the idea of rejection, willing to try regardless.

"All I've ever had and cared about I've lost. Brandon is the last thing I've got and he's lying comatose in bed, waiting for us to perform some sort of exorcism." He lowered his voice, grown rough with feeling. "Cassie you have a dangerous job and you can get hurt. I don't want to want you because the thought of losing someone else that I care about is something I don't know if I can go through again." He gingerly stroked the scar on her cheek with one hand while the other remained wrapped around her waist, keeping her there with him as if he was afraid she would run. The intimacy of being so close and meeting her eyes was too much and Drew closed his, resting his forehead on hers. "But every time I look at you, I can't stop how you make me feel. You make me want to try. I want to try *with you*."

Drew was asking her to make the decision about taking that next step with him, leaving it to her to choose where her path would take her next. Tears pricked her eyes. She couldn't trust her voice, relying instead on answering him the same way he'd asked. Sliding her hands up, she placed a palm on either side of his face and rose on her tiptoes. When their lips met again, his response was jubilant; kissing her mouth, her cheeks and her eyes, then returning to her lips where, as he kissed her, their passions overflowed.

Cassie made a sound against his mouth, asking for more, and was wrapped up in a tight embrace, his hand sliding up into her hair while the other pressed her body against his. Thoughts of being followed, angry female acolytes and impending magickal battles faded as her fever for him clouded her brain and her body begged to be allowed free rein. She made another little sound, frustrated that even though she knew she needed to walk out of here right now, she couldn't force herself to break from him. Tension built up from years of denial added to the uncertainty of this mission, her future and Drew's role in both culminated in a need for release. For the moment she forgot about tomorrow and the train wreck sure to destroy it all. Her kiss turned desperate.

He felt the change in her, heard the need in that little sound in her throat and with that Drew lost control of himself. There was nothing but her.

***

The hall to his bedroom was littered with their clothing, leading to the two of them lying together in a blissful nest, willing everything else to stay out. Drew brushed Cassie's hair from her cheek where it clung damply. She smiled at him and reached up to kiss him. He shifted his weight on his elbow and leaned down, freezing when they heard a rattling at the front door.

Cassie's eyes went wide and Drew's body stiffened. Rolling off the bed, he moved swiftly out into the hall. Cassie followed, taking a moment to throw his shirt over her head. She couldn't focus to fight if she was standing naked in front of someone, call her vain but it was true.

234

It turned out Drew's primary aim was for the bag he'd dropped in the living room. He had run straight to it and proceeded to dig frantically through it. Cassie reached out again for the familiar feel of water, shocked at the amount of energy that surged up into her receptive flesh. It was more than she'd been able to call before and she wondered if she was growing more proficient now that she'd broken down the barriers to her inner magick.

Her body warmed despite her limited clothing as the organic energy raced excitedly up and down her skin, leaving the entire surface tingling in its wake. One palm flexed open and she pictured a measured amount of energy moving into that one concentrated point, the rest staying with her for a second defense or attack if need be. In her mind's eye she saw the blue ball roiling in her hand and let her eyes rest on the door, ready.

Drew had come up with a gun from his bag in spite of Cassie's prior caution. He held it pointed at the door, not yet ready to count on his magick in a fight and needing to defend his home and lover. He took a few steps sideways to stand next to Cassie, leaving her clear to fight for herself. They exchanged a ready look and waited for the door to swing open.

Chapter 25

The blond waif from the church came through first, her eyes bloodshot over a red rimmed nose. Behind her was someone new, a tall, thin woman, forty-ish with dyed dark brown hair and dull blue eyes. Her face wasn't as red, though Cassie could see the same vacant look in her pink-ringed eyes. Both women were on something and that made them unpredictable.

"Revelation," Drew breathed beside her, echoing her thoughts.

Pritchard was using it on his own people, but why? Did he know what it did? He had to if he had ever seen it in action. Cassie was furious; that was exactly the kind of manipulation that had driven their society to form Veritas. Regulars using them was one thing, but to use each other? It was unconscionable. Cassie's energy surged until her fingers were burning. She had to breath to keep from losing control, telling herself it was not these women's fault they were being used. It helped only barely.

"Demons!" Caroline hissed. "Do you see them, Taryn? Kill the demons and be redeemed in the eyes of God!" Red-streaked eyes rolled, showing too much white to be sane, spittle forming in the corners of her small bow-shaped mouth.

Taryn's sloth was a juxtaposition to Caroline's mania. Cassie was having a hard time imagining what Taryn was going to be able to do to hurt them in her state. Prematurely, she relaxed her guard.

The four stood immobile, none moving until Caroline shrilled her command. "Taryn, now is your time to prove your allegiance. You must prove yourself worthy of God's love."

All eyes were on the woman, Cassie and Drew unable to see the threat as Taryn lurched haltingly without a weapon in her hands. Her staggering advance was zombie-like; Cassie almost felt guilty that she would have to take action if they kept coming.

Then, at the same time as her skin pricked from external energy, Taryn moved her hands in an exaggerated movement that held Cassie rapt. The woman's hand came up and a field of psychic energy blasted out with enough force to push her targets back before wrapping around them in an invisible net.

Instantly the pressure began building inside the net, pressing down on Cassie and Drew from above. From all sides, the electrifying and unrelenting force brought them to their knees. Drew's gun clattered useless to the floor as he clutched his head, threatening to burst from the pressure growing inside as well as out. A thin trickle of blood leaked from his nose. Cassie covered her ears, the energy forcing them to pop as she felt her eardrums straining to explode.

Caroline, giddy at her companion's success, gave a high keening laugh, calling to mind the banshees Cassie's mother had told her about from her childhood.

"Now, crush them, Taryn."

"No, don't. This is wrong, Taryn. We're the same as you." Drew's voice didn't hold the command it had with Dr. Jones however, Cassie recognized the influence running through it.

So did Taryn. Her forehead wrinkled and her hand faltered. The pressure on them eased.

"No!" Caroline whirled on the older woman. "Don't be a fool, he's a demon. He's only trying to trick you. Mr. Terry warned you, Taryn. God has given you a second chance and now you have to pay for your sins. These demons are lost souls. We must do the Lord's work and send them back to Hell to be rewarded."

The let up of pressure on her head let Cassie recover enough to recollect the energy racing through her body back into a controlled ball. Raising her hand, she pointed her palm at Taryn and pushed it.

At once, the pressure on them disappeared and Taryn flew back, sliding to a stop when she collided with the point of the wall. Glancing over, Cassie saw Drew shaking his head, trying to stand, and she turned her attentions to Caroline. She was just in time to catch the woman take three running steps and leap at her.

237

The impetus of her charge knocked Cassie sprawling, her head hit the floor, and Caroline landed on top of her.

Cassie's fuzzy head and the woman's claws flying at her face made it impossible to control the remaining energy still coursing through her, the sheer power exciting her earth nature in the process. Unable to even get herself in a position to send it safely out and back into the pipes and release both, Cassie had a decision to make. She had to send it out now or burn herself up with too much unrestrained energy seeking release.

An image of her grandmother's disapproving face flashed through her mind and she apologized to the ghost of her mother. As Cassie moved her hands from where they had been guarding her face, she managed to get them on Caroline's body. Looking the young woman right in the eye and seeing nothing human, only a wild thing lost to the violent chemical urges flowing through her brain, Cassie grunted, "I'm sorry."

Closing her eyes, she focused, feeling it leap readily to her hands. The hair was standing straight up on her arms as she gathered all the flowing magick from the Water mingling crazily with her other nature into an unstable mass. Urging it into her palms she gave it a push, feeling it burn her fingertips as it jumped from her body and into Caroline's unguarded flesh. She opened her eyes and watched the blonde's youthful body freeze, her eyes going wide. An anticlimactic sigh escaped her open mouth followed by the acrid smell of burning flesh and a puff of ash as Caroline was literally microwaved from the inside out.

Bracing for the inevitable, Cassie felt the impact as Caroline's life force was released into the air, burning strong for a few seconds before dissipating into the ether. The element that had called the woman was Air and it was Air that now reclaimed her. With the body pinning her down, Cassie couldn't see behind her to know if Drew had felt the passing. It would not harm him though he might feel a tremor in the air if he wasn't too distracted by the more tenable physical death in front of him.

Cassie had taken a life and a piece of her soul suffered, never to recover. The shock of what she'd done sunk in and she went numb. Grandmother's teachings came back to her. "Above all else, value life. It is for the Great Mystery alone to take, no man can have that privilege. To defy that is to defy the spirits and put one's own soul at risk."

"I'm sorry, I'm so sorry." Cassie said it again and again, though whether she was apologizing to Caroline or her grandmother or the spirits, she couldn't be sure. The smell of Caroline's cooked body filled the condo while stray pieces of ash fell from her nose and mouth onto Cassie's face. She retched, the dead weight of the smoking corpse too much to bear. Cassie frantically scrambled to wriggle out from underneath it. The scream building in her head came out as her mind and body rebelled against what she'd done. Her arms weakened from the massive energy expulsion, Cassie's will failed her as well.

Drew came over from checking Taryn's body for a pulse, relieved to find she had only been knocked out. He lifted the overly warm body from Cassie, allowing her to scramble out from under it, and eased it back down out of respect for the dead, going against his impulse to throw the stinking thing away from him. The act of touching the dead woman made his skin crawl.

Following her to where she huddled in a ball, Drew knelt at Cassie's side, taking her head in his hands. Forcibly, he broke her stare from the woman she'd killed and put his face in front of hers, filling her vision with his face on purpose. "Cassie, look at me." Dread knotted his gut when he saw her amber eyes so enormous and unfocused. His thumbs stroked her cheeks, too fast to soothe in his own upset. "Cassie, look at me. You had no choice. Do you hear me? You had no choice, she was here to kill us both. You did what you had to do to save us."

Hardening herself, Cassie fell back on protocol to remain functional. Hiding from what she'd done was not an option with so much left looming over them, though she felt the temptation as shock offered to take away the burden of fear and awfulness of what she'd done. Blinking and nodding slowly, Cassie remained ashen. Then, instead of crying or trying to justify what had happened, she spoke dully, "The body; we need to get rid of the body."

Drew could see that she wasn't going to snap out of her shock so easily as with a quick slap to the cheek. Though having seen what she was capable of, he wouldn't be the one to slap her he mused, a little off kilter himself. Sobering, he thought if she had the presence of mind to keep going, so should he.

Drew gave his condo a review, first at the body and then behind him where the other remained unconscious. Years of damage control were what Drew fell back on as his own brain threatened to get tangled up in the possible ramifications of what had just happened.

This was his condo and his girlfriend, never mind he might be a bit presumptuous about that last. Details aside, he would be the first one hauled in for questioning should someone smell Caroline up here and come knocking. Cassie was right, the body had to be disposed of and Taryn would need to be restrained. Having no idea where or how, he set about carrying out Cassie's order.

Giving his stricken lover a parting stroke, he stood and took two deep breaths through his mouth, hoping to avoid the smell of charred human, and readying himself before leaning down and grabbing the body. Drew wrapped one limp arm around his neck and put his other around her waist, giving his pocket a quick pat to confirm his keys were still in there. On his pass by the coat closet next to the front door, he grabbed a light jacket and walked out the door.

Ten minutes later, mind screaming at him that no matter how many times he showered he would never get the smell of her out of his nose, Drew was back and unlocking the door to his unit. The clock was ticking now, even with the jacket thrown over her face, the dead woman's body lying curled up in the backseat of his car might draw attention. It wasn't the full heat of summer, but even leaving someone in a car in the spring like this could draw unwanted attention.

Returning upstairs, he saw that Cassie had been resourceful in his absence. She'd found the duct tape in the kitchen drawer and used it just as she had at the church, binding Taryn's unconscious body at the wrists and ankles, another over her mouth for when she woke. After she'd finished her task, she'd returned to where he'd left her and, terribly pale, she stared unblinking at the spot on the floor where it had happened, her back shoved against the wall.

When he dragged their hostage over to set her on the couch, in his opinion only slightly more comfortable than the tile, Drew had pressed against the woman's hip and felt a familiar shape.

Drew had been planning to get word to Pritchard that he was looking for him, intending to bring the battle to him on Drew's terms. Granted, in his mind he'd wanted Cassie gone by then so she couldn't interfere. In her current state he wasn't sure how that changed things. Was she safer with him or should he send her back to the hotel in a cab? The healer was there, maybe that was their best option.

He could decide that later. Right now, Drew decided to take the gift fortune had offered him and opened Taryn's phone. She had him in her contact list and Drew hit the button. Pritchard answered on the second ring.

"Taryn, have you succeeded?" Pritchard's tone was patriarchal, a father figure to his flock.

Drew struggled to keep a lid on his rage at a man who drugged women and sent them to do his dirty work, calling it a holy endeavor. "This is Drew Carter. I heard you were looking for me?"

If Pritchard was shocked to hear the voice of his target on his assassin's phone, he hid it well. "Carter, I see Caroline found you. Did you get my message?" The weasel couldn't resist the taunt.

"I did. You were very clear," he growled back through clenched teeth, temper ready to explode. He cast another anxious look Cassie's direction. Her lips were moving; he sidled over trying to make out what she was saying.

Drew gave up the one thing he knew would draw Pritchard out. There was no need for tracking or magick or any sort of complicated cat and mouse game. Whatever the reason, Drew knew Pritchard wanted him.

Without fully understanding the reality of how one breaks a binding spell, he could comprehend intuitively that his brother's fate was tied to the man slated for death by Drew's own hand. And before he could do that, Brandon must be released from his bond. Cassie said Julia needed something from Pritchard to work her Vodou. He could get something. He would be pleased to get something, but he was thinking more along the lines of a body part, not just hair or a sock.

"I think it's time we meet."

The man's victorious grin was audible. "Excellent."

Chapter 26

Gretchen sat at her favorite perch next to the big open window. She was absently staring out at the birds hopping around, picking seeds from her meticulously groomed backyard while a squirrel seated on the feeder above chose the best seeds for himself and tossed his rejections to the ground for the rest of the wildlife.

She had lived in this house for seventeen years with her husband Charles until a random violent street crime claimed his life three years ago. Without him she'd been lost; first losing herself in her gardening, then getting addicted to infomercials until a neighbor commented on the daily deliveries, shaming her back to reason. That was when she had met Terry Pritchard, Mr. Terry to his followers.

He had been preaching in the park where she'd taken up walking in the mornings. He wasn't the most handsome of men but neither had been her Charles. Not that that mattered much, she hadn't been interested in love. It was his message that had drawn her in.

"There is evil all around us," he had said in his quiet, unassuming way. "Demons live among us, picking away at our faith day by day. They start out small, giving us small reasons to question. Maybe we see a story on the news about a man hurting his wife or a war in a far away land. Or maybe a holy man stealing from his flock or harming a trusting child." He had looked right at her and Gretchen self-consciously touched the ring she couldn't bring herself to take off, instead moving it to her other hand, marking her as a woman alone. Mr. Terry's intense green eyes had softened and he'd nodded as his thin lips curved into the ghost of a smile. His next words were meant just for her. "They take from us all that we hold dear until we are left with nothing; nothing but loneliness and doubt carving a hole into our very souls that grows with each story, each wrong, until we are filled with darkness. And it is into that dark, empty place that the demons stake their claim making us feel lost and alone, feeling helpless and unable to do anything to fight back."

Mr. Terry had been right. She had become apathetic, letting life happen to her instead of taking control of her sadness. Mr. Terry had shown her that they were at war, war for their very souls, and that Charles had been a victim of that war. His death had not been random, No, it had been demons that had attacked him because they'd seen the strength in Gretchen and sought to weaken her and to make themselves stronger by doing so.

The war took money and resources to spread the word and gather their army of faithful; small bands of them existed all over the world, Mr. Terry said. He was responsible for the faithful in the Southeast. Mr. Terry told her he'd found that women had stronger souls and made better soldiers, which was why he concentrated on them as recruits. Their secret weapon, Revelation, took a lot of money to manufacture as well. Followers were encouraged to give what they could to the cause.

Gretchen had willingly given over the small fortune earned by Charles over a lifetime of honest work building up his pharmacy; she'd sold it to his partner after his death. It had seemed a fitting tribute to use his life's benefit to fight those who had taken it prematurely.

"Gretchen, could you come here please?" Mr. Terry summoned her to where he sat at the table.

He had asked to use her home after the church was broken into and Mary had been assaulted. Gretchen had been glad to help; her home was the largest of any of the followers and could easily house their small flock. All told there were eight full time devotees who lived with Mr. Terry in whichever home he felt suited their needs. He said they needed to keep moving and changing houses to avoid discovery by the demons and they could not go to his home. Demons had been following him for a long time and to go back now would be to face them before they were ready.

She found him sitting in one of her chairs, his dark hair neatly slicked back was still wet from his shower. The clean smell of soap wafted toward her when he waved her to be seated beside him. "Yes Mr. Terry?"

"Gretchen, our time is nearly upon us. Some of the demons have found us." He held out a hand to silence her when she began to argue that they were not yet ready, *she* wasn't ready. "I know that it is sooner than we would like and that our forces are small." He put a hand on her leg, high on her thigh like he did. Her upper lip beaded in a fretful sweat.

She was uncomfortable but he had told her the love he had for her was as a shepherd to his lamb and that he meant no harm in his familiar touches. Once again she told herself not to be so prudish. "We can't hope to fight so soon. Not with Caroline and Taryn gone." He hadn't told them where the women had gone, but they guessed Taryn had taken Revelation to help her see.

Mr. Terry smiled gently at her. "We do not have to fear these demons. They are few and we are strong in our faith. We have all that we need to defeat them." He watched her, his eyes nothing but black pits in the shadow of the evening sun. Rain clouds had brought an ominous gloom with their arrival before the sunset.

Understanding budded in her gaze. "Revelation," she breathed softly.

"Right." He patted her leg, nodding approvingly. "And you know where that is. I trust you can retrieve it for me?"

Nodding obediently, she forced her smile and her stillness. She felt shame for cringing at his touch, forcing herself to let him move his hand higher on her thigh. He did that if he felt resistance, he pushed harder. It was the demons working from within her, he said. They recognized his good and wanted to keep her from it. "How much should I get?"

"Fifty packets."

"Fifty?" Never had they gotten more than one or two at a time. "That's nearly half of our entire supply."

"Don't you trust me?" He tipped his head, calmly awaiting her answer. Mr. Terry never yelled; he didn't have to. All of his followers so craved his approval the slightest hint of displeasure could make them scrape and beg. "It would pain me to think that I have done something to lose your faith. It is a gift that I cherish." Consternation wrinkled his brow and his thin shoulders bowed.

Gretchen was instantly penitent. "No, Mr. Terry. Of course I trust you. I was only surprised, that's all. It's an unusual request and it took me off guard." She offered him a shaky smile and put a hand over his on her leg, a bold move for her. "I'll go now."

"Thank you Gretchen." Gone were all traces of displeasure from his countenance. "And make sure no one sees you."

"Of course Mr. Terry. Should I come back here?" She stood and gathered her purse and keys from the back counter.

"We will be going to them. Meet me at Carter's.

Chapter 27

Drew found it difficult to concentrate on the road. His eyes continued to float to the empty space in the rearview mirror, expecting Caroline to pop up at any second despite the burnt smell that permeated the interior of the car until his eyes watered and his stomach wanted to empty. When he wasn't looking back, he was watching the passenger seat and Cassie who had not spoken since the condo.

The most pressing concern for him now was what to do with Caroline's body in broad daylight. He could not keep her in the car, smell aside someone was bound to notice when they parked. And given the recent increase in smuggling, the water was being patrolled heavily. Dumping a corpse, beyond the clear moral dilemma, presented a problem of logistics and witnesses he had yet to sort out.

While he drove his mind was on a loop, repeating without fail what Cassie had been murmuring when he'd been on the phone with Pritchard. She was going on about a dog and a bird and blackness and a flood. Drew had heard of people being delusional from shock though, never having witnessed it, he found being faced with it unnerving.

"I'm going to make this okay, Cassie," he assured her, sparing a hand to touch her arm. Cold to the touch and unflinching at his caress, Cassie appeared for all intents and purposes to be miles away from here, from her body.

Surprising him, she reanimated enough to turn her anguished eyes toward him and answered flatly. "Nothing can make this okay. I've killed a woman. That can't be undone." With that, she returned her unseeing gaze back to the windshield to stare straight ahead, leaving Drew to sort out on his own how exactly to carry out her orders.

Suffocating on the stench in the car, Drew put his windows partway down, catching sight of a state trooper's light bar in his rearview mirror. Panicked, he took the next exit off of Veteran's Expressway and fortune smiled again. He read the road sign out loud and looked over for a hint of approval. "Big Cat Rescue 4.5 miles." He shut off the part of his brain that rebelled at what he was going to do.

"That'll work," he said to himself.

The road was marked with a blue road sign, Easy Street. Snorting at the irony, Drew fought the mad laugh that burbled in his chest. He was helping his girlfriend to cover up a murder, yet another murder in his life. That made five victims and two murderers; first his brother, now the first woman he'd let into his life. Drew questioned his choice in character, maybe he should stay alone if these were the sorts he was going to go with.

Fortunately the road split, demanding his attention and taking his thoughts from further introspection. The main road that led to the marked entrance was a right and a dirt offshoot veered left, though Drew could see that it jogged back right again, most likely winding around the backside of the sanctuary. It was the dirt offshoot that Drew chose, and it was clear relatively quickly that he had chosen wisely.

The back acreage was uninhabited by humans. A ten foot tall fence, broken by only one entrance was lined with two rows of electric wire, marking it as a boundary. Drew stared at the fence and put the car in park. He hadn't considered this complication. Caroline was too heavy to carry while he climbed the chain link and he didn't have bolt cutters that would have given him access through the chain link door, which was secured by a heavy duty padlock.

He did have another tool available to him and he prayed she was still functional. Looking around at the deserted road, Drew worried they were working against the clock already.

"Cassie." He put his hand on her arm and saw her flinch, unwilling to reconnect with her body. Drew clenched his jaw. "Cassie look at me," he ordered.

The words came from her with nothing behind them. "What do you want from me?"

Unbuckling his seat belt, Drew twisted in his seat to lay both hands on her upper arms, forcing her to face him when he spoke. His touches were firm, hopeful that applying pressure would help to coax her from the place where she hid in her mind.

Cassie felt and heard him but only a small part of her wanted to respond. The rest of her mind had been steadily slipping away without her noticing, leaving only enough to go through the motions needed to handle the details of the assignment. Thoughts of her responsibilities got her mental processes going again and, grudgingly, she came back to see Drew's stress-laden features staring back at her. His eyes scanned her face for signs of comprehension.

"Cassie please, I need you."

It was that last that finally persuaded her to shrug off the warnings within her psyche telling her that she would regret coming back and she felt a surreal moment's disorientation as the rest of her consciousness slid back into place. Eyes refocusing to take in the whole scene while her mind bucked at the return of the burnt smell, Cassie took in Drew's desperate expression.

Drew's face was pale and drawn; the whites of his eyes were showing. He wasn't a regular but had been living as one; this kind of thing was new to him. It was Cassie's job to protect him, and here she'd done the exact opposite. Instead of keeping him away from danger, she had only brought him a new kind.

Disgusted with herself, Cassie cleared her throat and frowned. "What do you need me to do?" She avoided thinking about the body in the back seat as much as she could, even though she could see its legs out of the corner of her eye. It looked like Caroline was napping. Biting her lip, Cassie pushed away her grandmother's voice. Not now, there would be time for mourning and guilt later. For now she had responsibilities and she couldn't keep ignoring them.

Drew stared back at her, examining her features apprehensively, no doubt looking for proof she was really back.

Giving him a quick squeeze on the hand that held her arm, Cassie leveled a calm gaze at him, hoping to project confidence. He licked his lips and gave her a shaky smile.

"What do you need me to do?" she asked him again, being sure to sound stronger this time. Following his eyes as he turned to look at the fence, Cassie saw the pipe outline of a door in the chain link fence held closed by a thick padlock.

Knowing they were going to have to dispose of the body and actually doing it were very different things. Cassie turned green. Casting her eyes back to take in the prone form behind her she felt damnation sink in and although she had never been aware of its presence within her before that moment Cassie felt the Great Mystery abandon her, leaving in its place a painfully empty hole in her being. She could physically feel the loss inside her.

Its abandonment brought Cassie's mind back and made her responsibilities clear. This was her burden, not his. She'd already made him take on far more than he should have. A few deep breaths and she was ready. Without another word, Cassie let herself out of the car and held her palms to the dirt, sucking in the earth's energy that licked and leaped at her fingers from the ground beneath her, entering her body at her call.

A movement off to the right, maybe twenty yards away under some scrub, caught her eye. Cassie inhaled sharply when the tawny cat stood up and stretched, yawning lazily. Its golden eyes never broke from hers.

The sound of car doors behind her told her Drew was out and retrieving the body. A slight breeze brought the smell of cooked meat with it; the large black nose sticking out from the brush wiggled as she scented. Cassie wished she was physically stronger so he didn't have to do this next part but wishes couldn't always come true.

"Drew, we're going to have to move fast," she called out low and mild. "Do you see her? Three o'clock."

"Yeah, I do." He was grunting, struggling under the burden. Dead weight was never as easy as a cooperative passenger.

Risking a peek, Cassie saw that he was holding her out in front of him across his arms, trying in vain not to touch her. Bringing her focus back around, Cassie put her hands down again and pulled harder. The earth responded, a swell of warm organic energy filled her hands and raised her hair. Cassie could smell the damp earth as it shared its bounty with her. The raw power took her by surprise, it was far more energy than she'd ever handled and it took a moment to control it. Fleetingly, she thought of the power she'd mismanaged at the condo and shuddered. Sensing the disturbance, the cat growled and Cassie stopped.

When she did, Cassie felt Drew come up beside her, waiting for her to open the door. Scanning the brush, they could see that the lioness was no longer alone.

One of her professors had said once that animals are drawn to energy, thus explaining the stories of witches' familiars. Cassie saw it with her own eyes as she counted the yellow forms creeping from the shadows where they had been sleeping the sunny day away. She counted four. With a gulp, she realized that was enough to make quick work of the body. Leaving her overburdened conscience behind, Cassie walked forward with one hand held out and opened the lock easily. Lifting the latch it had held in place, Cassie stepped in and moved over to allow Drew to enter.

The cat to their left uttered a low rumble and Cassie gave her a quick appraisal. Not the largest of the pride, the female bore a network of scars across her body and was missing one eye. That she would fight wasn't a question.

"Put her down, Drew," Cassie urged, leveraging the desecration of the body against the fact that their own lives hung in the balance. "I don't think these girls are going to be scared off easily." To prove her point, Cassie kicked a rock at the one eyed leader who barely twitched a muscle. That was the danger of a

251

domestically raised animal born in the wild, no fear and all the instinct making for a deadly combination.

Taking one more step forward, Drew lowered the body gently to the bare sun-scorched ground and backed away. Cassie remained motionless, wordlessly telling him to leave first by allowing him passage through the door. They had barely gotten out when One Eye trotted forward to claim first dibs on the prize. Cassie's hands shook as she latched the door and broke into a jog, heading for the car door, hoping to someday get the sound of tearing meat out of her ears.

They drove back to the condo with the windows down, although no amount of fresh air could wipe the memory of the smell from their brains. Neither spoke till they were pulling up to his clean, modern building, the blonde plaster face speckled with wrought iron railings marking a small balcony for each unit, overlooking the turnaround and central fountain below. Across the street was shopping and small cafes with outdoor tables, most of which were filled with locals taking in the sunshine on a beautiful spring day. A palpable vibrancy emanated from the bustling commons. Wistfully, Cassie watched the people going on about their business fairly confident none of them had just committed murder nor had any just fed a body to a pride of lions.

Drew turned the car off but did not open his door right away, drawing Cassie's interest. When she looked over at him he was rubbing his keys together, watching them. Sensing he needed to talk, she sat back to wait.

"Cassie, what we did. All of it..." his voice trailed off and she waited patiently. "Have you? Is that? What we did was wrong."

"You're right." It pained her to see that lost look in his eyes and know it was because of her and what she represented that he was here. That he'd done what he'd done. She couldn't tell him what he most wanted to hear, that things were going to go back to normal. Nothing would be what he currently considered "normal" ever again.

So to give him what little peace she could, Cassie spoke only to the crime they had just committed. "What we did *was* wrong, but it was unavoidable. Veritas was formed to protect us, all of us who are born as witches in a world that has been removed from magick for so long they no longer understand it. They fear us because we're different. And if we came out now, the same thing that drove us underground in the first place would happen again." Her explanation gained momentum and feeling. Cassie genuinely felt that Veritas was a good thing and what they did, on the whole, was good work. "We would be experimented on, used as weapons in someone else's war, or locked away in some jail somewhere to rot. Caroline died because Pritchard pumped her full of drugs and sent her after us." Cassie's words were meant for her too, bringing with them some amount of comfort and she realized she was speaking not just for Drew's benefit. "Believe me when I tell you that I wish we could have given her to her family for a proper burial, but how would we explain how she died to a medical professional? Electrocution doesn't turn your brain into ash, it never would have been believable. So what we did was wrong, but it was necessary to keep people like us safe." Cassie watched him for signs that this was too much, seeing his hands still working the keys distractedly, an indication of his level of unease. "Everyone like us in the world relies on our keeping secrets. It's what we do as investigators and some times are harder than others." She squeezed his hand. "I owe you thanks for stepping in when I froze." It was hard for her to admit her failing. "It shouldn't have happened. I won't leave you to clean up my messes again. I promise."

His expression locked down, his eyes hardened to steel, and gone was any sign of vulnerability. "We'd better go up. Taryn should be coming down from her high soon and I thought we could ask her some questions."

Chapter 28

Impressed and a little curious that Drew had kept his cool under what would be considered trying circumstances for anybody, especially someone who had seen two other horrific murders in as many days, Cassie followed him upstairs, wishing she wasn't going to have to ruin his life. The clock was ticking now that Julia and Quan were on their way and Brandon was back.

Her personal feelings continually threatened to get in the way of this assignment, as much as she tried to will them otherwise. Drew was a good man and a talented witch with a bright future and, after they had Pritchard, she was to play a big part in his disillusionment. She really should have told him last night after Brandon turned up; she'd had another opportunity this morning, but when he'd opened up to her she had foolishly let herself believe that, by pretending, it wasn't going to end the way it had to.

Wanting to walk out on her job had never appealed to her before that moment. To go home a failure didn't seem all that attractive either; instead she dreamed of running off to some quiet corner of the world, maybe work in a shop or something trivial. Something, anything, where she wasn't required to kill people or lie to someone she cared about.

But that couldn't happen, not yet; not with her partners still gone and in the dark about the pending meeting. Cassie had overheard enough to know Drew had arranged a meeting even if he had yet to mention it to her. Suspicious of his silence, Cassie needed to stay with him until she knew at least enough to send her partners to meet him. That and the fact that, in the end, Cassie couldn't abandon her family or her partners. Call it a point of pride, but she couldn't do it; not and have them think ill of her for leaving with her tail tucked between her legs after a mission gone sour.

They could feasibly wrap this up and be on their way by tomorrow morning. She couldn't wait to be shut of this mission and her first kill, if it weren't for Drew. For his sake, she hoped it dragged out to give him a few more precious hours of ignorance.

When they walked in, the smell that greeted them instantly made her throat tighten. Drew trotted ahead to open his patio door and several windows in an effort to erase the smell. Cassie went straight to Taryn, now both conscious and struggling, where she lay on the stiff couch.

Cassie refrained from touching the woman unless it was absolutely necessary. It was safe to assume Taryn's nerves were raw and her own defenses were more than a little taxed at the moment. She didn't want any sort of energy transference between the two of them. Hunkering down on her heels, Cassie let her arms rest on her knees.

"We aren't going to hurt you." She relaxed her features trying to curry good will. "Taryn, all we want to do is ask you a few questions."

The dull, drug-induced glaze in the woman's eyes had been replaced with hate and a splash of fear as she glared back at Cassie.

"I'd like to take this tape off your mouth but I can't do that unless I know you aren't going to scream."

From the loathing in her eyes, Cassie could anticipate the response. Stuffing the feelings that rose at the idea of what she was going to do behind a false front, Cassie let her expression go dead and she leaned forward until she was nearly nose to nose with Taryn. "You might have noticed your friend isn't here. She isn't coming back." A look of alarm crossed her features and Cassie kept going until her lips nearly brushed the woman's ear, whispering, "Unless you want to find out what happened, you're going to answer a few questions about Terry Pritchard."

Taryn went rigid; her saucer sized eyes exposed each and every blood vessel, already prominent from her recent drug binge. A tear leaked out and ran across the bridge of her nose to drip on the leather cushion beneath her. Once again, stepping around her inner objections and refusing to look back at Drew, certain she'd see the same revulsion she felt for herself mirrored there, Cassie pressed on.

"That's right. All you have to do is tell me about Mr. Pritchard's church and what you know about Revelation." She brought a hand up, letting it stop poised at Taryn's mouth. "Can I trust you not to scream?"

Taryn nodded carefully and, with a rip, her mouth was free. She licked her lips and rubbed them against each other, not having a free hand to pacify the sting or check for blood.

Cassie rocked back on her heels, waiting for her to start.

Taryn cleared her throat and had to start twice before she was able to make a sound. When she did, she croaked the first few words. "Mr. Terry, he leads our congregation at the Ray of Light church down on West Columbus. Mr. Terry is a good man, he sees things others don't see." Her eyes narrowed and bounced from Cassie to Drew standing behind her, belief giving her strength. "Mr. Terry says there is great evil in the world. Demons live among us, corrupting us to do their work on Earth." Her lip curled in disgust at Cassie and her tone shifted to one of malice as her fear was pushed aside in the face of the dogma she clung to. "The demons want to destroy mankind and the Earth itself to prevent man from ever returning."

The blind desperation in her expression smacked of fanaticism, turning Cassie's stomach. Glancing behind her to exchange looks with Drew, she watched him roll his eyes and shake his head. He was no more impressed with the rhetoric than Cassie. The brainwashed woman went on, her voice climbing to reach her intended climactic crescendo.

"The Believers are armed with the one weapon that can flush out the demons, and with it they are revealed to us. Revelation makes it impossible for them to hide among us. We will find them and defeat them, one by one if need be; it will mean salvation for us all."

"And what about you? You're no different from us demons when you take the drug," Drew pointed out.

"I *am* different." Taryn's fiery response exposed her self-doubt. "Mr. Terry says my soul is strong, that's why the demon only comes when I call it. He has offered me a chance at redemption. Only those strong enough to endure Revelation and use it to fight the demons will go to meet God at the Rapture when this world is done. Sacrifices must be made for the cause."

"What about Mr. Terry?" Cassie used Taryn's familiar title for the charlatan. "Isn't he a demon?" She had felt Pritchard's magick; wouldn't using Revelation reveal him to his followers?

Taryn stared at her, horrified at the question. "You demons are fallen, your light is less than Mr. Terry's. It's corrupted. Mr. Terry is filled with God's light. His is a holy light, filled with love for those who recognize him as the prophet and guide that he is for those of us here on Earth. Those who follow him are offered a chance at salvation regardless of our previous sins. It is through our devotions to the cause that our souls are cleansed and prepared for the Resurrection."

Cassie had heard enough. She reaffixed the tape in her hand to the zealot's mouth, cutting off her further arguments on the state of Cassie's soul. That die had already been cast and nothing Pritchard or his lot said was going to change it.

Pritchard's was a rhetoric that had not changed since the beginning of time. Centuries had passed, science and medicine had come out of the Dark Ages, and yet still there were those who would have others believe that God hated humans born with special abilities that manipulate the Earth's energy and magnetic fields, while hypocritically using witches for their purposes against their own.

At the Academy, their professors had explained how those who were born with magickal abilities were no different from anyone else. Some people were overly gifted and excelled while others' skills were a bit more rudimentary. It was similar to athletic ability. Some were the stars of the team while others lent support by being solid players. Hearing Taryn spout such fire and brimstone only served to reinforce what Grandmother had told her when she'd tried to convince Cassie against taking her mother's path instead of using her magick for the good of her father's people.

"Those people will never accept what you are, not completely. Among them you will live in the shadows, kept there until they need you. The Sisahapa will revere you but first you must cast off your mother's people and their ways to embrace the Great Mystery. You cannot live with a foot in each world. You must choose one, and only *this* one will choose you in return."

Sighing, Cassie wondered if she had indeed chosen wrong. Or if her father had, for that matter. He had pushed her to Veritas, maybe even courted her mother with that in mind. Veronica, the beauty who had come from a magickal family with a history with the Academy; her uncle had been an agent. It was because he did not want her to live the life Grandmother wanted for her. He had felt trapped and sought escape for his child through mixing the bloodline, a transgression his mother had never accepted nor forgiven. And with Cassie, the last of her grandmother's line now gone to the "other side," the tribe found itself facing a future without a shaman for the first time in three generations.

Drew walked up and put his hand on her shoulder. A jolt ran through her body. "Why don't we cut her loose?" he suggested mildly. "Without the drugs in her system she's not a threat, you heard her. Without the drugs she can't 'call the demon'."

Patchy as her defenses were, Cassie felt herself swaying. She shrugged off his hand and her own thoughts returned to her. "Would you join me in the other room please?" She rose to her feet, stretching each leg alternately.

Walking down the hall, Cassie heard his shoes on the tile behind her and she waited to close the bedroom door after him. "You are *not* going to meet him."

"Why not?" Drew bristled at her attempt to control him and pushed back. Time was growing short. He needed to leave; Pritchard was going to be expecting him soon.

"You heard her; we're demons. They kill demons." It was bothering her that Taryn couldn't see Pritchard as a demon. Cassie couldn't figure out how that could be. He had been strong enough to kill with Brandon's magick, he had used a man as a scent bag, and she had felt his magick at the club. She knew he was a witch and not solely using others for his power. Yet the question remained, how was he able to hide it from his army of drug addled magick witch hunters? Cassie was obviously missing something and she racked her brain to figure out what.

Closing the distance between them, Drew halted her line of thought by wrapping an arm around her back, pulling her close enough to feel his breath on her cheeks. "Are you telling me I can't go for professional reasons or is it personal?" Half of his mouth twisted up in a teasing smile.

His playful mood was contagious and Cassie found herself smiling back, in spite of her intention of keeping him grounded. Her arms went around his neck and she let him lean in for a kiss. "It's a little bit of both." She replied softly. "You can't go. It's too dangerous."

"I promise I'll be careful." He kissed her again, deeper this time and Cassie felt her body molding to his.

Her concerns about Pritchard's threat grew vague and faded into the background. Drew's influence over her was subtle, creeping up on her by increments. His touch directly on her skin increased its effectiveness significantly until his wants were hard to distinguish from hers.

"I don't think it's wise for you to go alone." Her knees went weak under Drew's lips as they traced their way, inch by inch, down her neck, licking and nibbling a line to her shoulder.

"I have to go alone." Nibble. "I promised." Lick, nibble.

Cassie's breathing was ragged, her body was pushing for her mind to succumb completely, to stop fighting with it for control and to let Drew have whatever he wanted. Cassie recognized her weakness; a tiny spark of her stubbornness that refused to give in was swimming its way up, exploding when it reached the surface of her thoughts and took a breath.

"No!" She put her hands to his chest and pushed. His arm remained locked around her, keeping the contact necessary to undermine her resistance. Cassie struggled to shore up her defenses against his magick. He was getting stronger and she was drained; as long as he was touching her it was useless. "Get your hands off me, Drew!"

His arm tightened. "I have to go. I'm serious. He said I have to come alone." Drew's eyes were hard. He was unshakable. "If I don't go Pritchard said he'll let Brandon die."

"But if you go," she braced her hands against him, pushing to no avail, "you'll die." Cassie was determined to save Drew. His brother's fate was already decided.

Drew steeled himself against the pain he heard in her pleas. His mind was screaming at him to stay right here with her and wait a few more hours. Her partners would be here and they would be able to destroy Pritchard. The problem came down to timing.

The man had threatened to leave if he didn't come today. Pritchard knew Julia and Quan were only hours behind him and he had no intention of being caught. If Pritchard left now, Brandon would be lost for sure. Whatever it was Pritchard wanted with Drew, he would have to risk it. He was banking on the fact that Pritchard didn't know about the strength of his magickal abilities and, if his time with Cassie was any indication, he had a chance.

"I have to go. I'm sorry." He spun them so that he continued his hold on Cassie while bringing himself closer to the door. One hand reached behind him to turn the knob and when his way was clear, he closed his eyes and leaned in for one last kiss. Drew poured his heart into it. He had no way of knowing if this would be their last and he tried to send a final time-buying surge into her, telling her to trust him to handle this himself. He prayed for her to let him go.

Cassie's arms were trapped between their bodies, limiting her physical defenses. She leaned her head back, trying to avoid his lips and beat back his influence in her mind. Her protections rallied for one last tired standoff but when he brought his other hand up to wrap itself in her hair, pressing her face to his, she felt her spark go back under.

Chapter 29

The sound of the steel front door slamming shut broke the final hold of Drew's influence over Cassie and she swayed on her feet, shaking her head. "Damn you, Drew," she cursed, marching out of the bedroom and into the living room where Taryn's eyes tracked her pacing.

A gust of cool air blew in the glass patio door, drawing Cassie's attention outside. Dark clouds were gathering, obscuring the sunset and promising a turbulent spring storm. Shivering and muttering oaths to Drew as well as the weather gods, Cassie trotted around the condo closing up the windows. When she was finished, her thoughts returned to Drew and Taryn and Pritchard. Where in the hell were Julia and Quan? They should have been there by now.

Cassie pulled out her phone and called Dr. Jones for an update on Brandon and to check that Pritchard hadn't snuck up on them. She doubted it, considering Drew's abrupt departure. It was more likely Pritchard was holed up, waiting for Drew. The thought sent a spasm of fear through Cassie and she forced herself to breathe through it, another practice taught in Grounding and Centering 101 at the Academy. No witch can be effective if she is too emotional to draw on her energy source.

The doctor's phone rolled to voicemail. Not bothering to leave a message, Cassie turned to face the couch.

"It must be terrible to know that a demon is heading straight for Mr. Terry and you can't do anything about it," she taunted the woman, feeling a cruel satisfaction when her eyes widened and then narrowed in fury. Pritchard's draw to her was easy to deduce by the quickly manipulated moods of the captive woman, she was naïve and a natural follower.

Cassie went about the condo, attempting to look busy, and ending up in the bedroom, trying repeatedly to call her partners. Both numbers went straight to voicemail. Cassie felt cold and wrapped her arms around herself. It was possible Pritchard had circled back and gotten to them. No one had seen him for days and Quan had been following his scent with no visual. There was no way of knowing if he had been able to evade him long enough to lay a trap. The reality of Cassie being left to handle this on her own was in its own way a relief.

Instead of having to wait for backup she could follow her heart's desire as well as her assignment, both were in the same place. The only problem being she didn't know where that might be. Passing again into the kitchen, she cut a surreptitious glance at the couch and caught Taryn working to loosen her bonds. By the look of the thinning tape she could be loose within the next fifteen minutes or so.

Grabbing Taryn's as well as her own phone, Cassie left the woman with no form of communication. Drew didn't have a landline.

"I have a few things to do and then I'll be back to deal with you," she stated menacingly from the entrance hall, rewarded by Taryn's return glare.

Without a backward glance she walked out and jogged across the street to buy a coffee at the café across the plaza, taking a seat out of the rain the clouds warned was coming down shortly. Several employees from the neighboring stores were hurrying to secure their chairs to the tables with cables and locks.

A white cab pulled up to the curb for a couple leaving the café, the driver waiting patiently at the curb for them to pay their bill. At the same time, movement across the street caught Cassie's eye. Taryn emerged through the front doors of the condo tower. Then, in a complication she hadn't foreseen, Cassie watched helplessly as Taryn jogged across the plaza making a beeline for the cab.

Left to assume Caroline must have had the keys on her, a possibility that could make a second trip to the cat sanctuary necessary, Cassie watched helplessly as the woman leaned forward and gave the driver his destination. When the cab began to pull away, Cassie panicked and frantically looked around for an alternative. Searching the parking lot behind the building would cause her to lose her visual but a motorcycle had been pulled up alongside the building where it would be protected from the weather by the awning. Understandable when she saw how cherry the classic gray Sportster was.

She jumped up from the table and worked to hold down her pace, feeling the anxious bubble in her chest disappearing as the other patrons lost interest in her in favor of the cabless couple drawing ample attention in their dismay at having their cab stolen. Clearing the interior of the building, she automatically put her hands down and began to pull. Her thoughts were scattered, worries about Drew and Julia and Quan had her focus elsewhere and the energy that had been intended to enter her hands instead arced off and struck a table, sending it five feet in the air and somersaulting back down with a metal bending crash on the sidewalk. The employee securing the table next to it jumped sideways, glancing nervously about for the cause.

Cassie took a deep breath and concentrated before she tried again. This time her hands received the energy willingly just as she reached the bike and swung a leg over. The engine purred to life when it felt the current she sent into the ignition and she jammed on the helmet as much for disguise as for safety. Angling the heavy bike out onto the street, she picked up speed just in time to see the white cab round the corner half a block up. After running the light she hung back enough to hide behind a tan SUV swinging out on the other side of the cab to watch safely out of sight.

It became apparent within the first few turns that tailing the maddeningly slow car was not going to be necessary. The cab drove back the same way she and Drew had come this afternoon. Her heart leapt. They were going back to the club, which would be filling up in a hurry this time of night. The storm broke and the first few swollen raindrops hit the visor of her borrowed helmet with a series of splatters followed quickly by the inevitable Florida springtime deluge.

By the time she pulled up to the club, Cassie was drenched and freezing in her short sleeved shirt and jeans, now at least four pounds heavier from the soaking. Pulling around to the side lot,

Cassie saw the silver Z in its customary spot. Once more she wished Quan were here, he could tell her if Pritchard was inside. She couldn't recognize when others were manipulating elements or using any other forms of magick. That was a much more rare talent. All she had was the goosebump warning system that was primitive at best.

And if Julia were here, capturing Pritchard would be a lot safer for those doing the capturing. One piece of the man or anything he'd worn was all it would take and she could make him do anything she wanted. With Vodou Julia could work him like a marionette, and in a public place such as this one, getting that one little hair was as simple as brushing against him in the crowd.

But they weren't here and Cassie was alone. Faced with the very real risks of a solo operation, she was no longer excited by the fact that she didn't have to wait to charge in. However, the welfare of Drew and Jaime and everyone inside that club could depend on her. Not to mention Brandon whose future as a criminal, vegetable or whole, hung in the balance.

Cassie made her way, soaked and chafing, along the building using the small eave jutting out from the roof as minimal protection from the downpour, though the damage had already been done. When she came around the front, her personal pity party was interrupted when something one of the valets said to another caught her ear.

Her eyes flashed up just in time to catch the clear plastic baggie disappearing into the black trousers he wore with his black Carter's tee.

"Where did you get that?" She advanced with purpose, pointing at his pants pocket. At the young Hispanic man's guilty expression for being busted, Cassie frowned sternly and held out her hand like he was a naughty child and she his mother. "Let me see it."

The valet he'd been talking to, the one with his back to her turned around and recognized her. His shiny black brows shot up and he hit his friend with the back of his hand. "Dude, she's with the boss. Do what she says man or you're in trouble."

"I'm in trouble if I do," the other insisted, throwing up his hands in exasperation. "You think she won't bust me for this?" His eyes flicked down toward his pocket.

Tiring rapidly of the game and feeling precious time ticking past, Cassie snapped. "I'm not busting anybody for anything. There's some bad stuff going around and I wanted to make sure you didn't get any of it. Drew doesn't want any of that stuff in the club. It makes people crazy." She wished she had Drew with her, his influence would speed things up.

The valet looked thoughtful, finally ducking his head and fishing in his pants pocket. "What's the stuff called?" His thick fingers were shockingly dexterous for being so short, twisting and spinning the small plastic bag roughly the size of a wallet photograph while he waited for her response.

Cassie's blood went cold as the purple writing spun to face her. "Revelation," she half read, half answered him. "It's called Revelation."

"Shit man, I knew there had to be a catch. People don't just give this stuff away for no good reason." He threw it away in the trash bin below the valet stand.

Curiosity peaked, Cassie read his nametag. "Victor, please tell me where you got that. It's important."

"Sure, no need to cover for the guy now, right?" He was crestfallen to have lost what surely would have made him the life of the party after he clocked out tonight. "There was a guy giving it away in the bathroom."

"What did he look like?"

Victor shrugged and started to step away to take the keys from a young black woman dressed to the nines for a night of clubbing and doing a poor job of hiding her satisfaction at the effect her physique was having on the nearby male populace.

Cassie interposed herself between Victor and his objective. She didn't have the luxury of time to wait for them to roll their tongues back in. Her professional side stepped in. "Seriously Victor."

Sighing, Victor watched his coworker take the keys from the striking woman's long finger and giving an extra grumble when she answered the valet's smile with a coy wink. Cassie's throat clearing brought an angry flash from the young man; already at his limit with her interrogation, by now it had it cost him free drugs and a chance to flirt with a sexy woman.

Not to be outdone, Cassie glowered back. Far less intimidating coming from atop her delicate frame. It was possible young Victor was a sensitive given his response when she challenged him. Feeling the energy leaping to her fingertips, she began to gather the energy to drop him to his knees. Almost simultaneously Victor broke, making any further pushing unnecessary.

"Dude was a normal guy, a little weasely maybe with the slick hair and pointy face, but mostly just looked like anybody." He managed to recover some of his swagger. "Are we done now, Officer?" He said the last with a sneer.

His snide title assignment caught her by surprise and she froze for only a split second. Forcing a small laugh she waved a hand. "I'm only looking out for Drew's interests, that's all. No reason to get mad at me." Then, before she could waste any more time on the young man's anger at thwarted good times, she stalked inside the front door only to be swept up by a passing arm wrapping through hers.

"What the..." she spluttered and dug in her heels, shifting her weight into her hips and pulling back, breaking her would-be kidnapper's hold. Cassie's hands popped up into a guard position in front of her face.

"Jeez what's your deal? I was just being friendly," Jaime defended. "No reason to get violent." She was rubbing the inside of her elbow where Cassie's wet skin had stuck and pulled, giving the bartender the beginnings of a welt.

Cassie scrambled to make amends. "Jaime, I'm sorry. I'm just a little jumpy that's all." She thought quickly. "Storms make me nervous."

At that, Jaime looked her up and down. "I hope you don't take this the wrong way but you look terrible." She wagged her head back and forth, finding humor at the sight. "Have you been swimming in puddles?"

Running an experimental hand down her hair hanging in wet ropes, Cassie got a mental picture of how bad it had to be. She must look exactly like a drowned rat. She noticed she was drawing some interested stares. Glancing down, she saw why. Apparently not everyone was embarrassed by her pale shirt choice, far too wet to be decent at this point. Modestly, Cassie crossed her arms and sidestepped into the shadowy perimeter of the overhead light's glow.

"Yeah, the guys around here would never tell you this but we have some spare shirts in back." Jaime raised her voice in mock aggravation. "Come on, I'll get you something dry." Waving her to follow, the lawyer slash bartender led her down the hall in back toward the elevator, stopping just shy. Of course it was too dark for her to see anything so Cassie bumped into her back when she stopped abruptly and the wall moved away from her on the right.

Naturally it wasn't the wall, it was a door Cassie hadn't seen leading into a supply closet that appeared out of nowhere. Jaime flicked on the light and walked inside. It was crammed full on three sides with shiny metal racking overflowing with paper products, cleaning supplies, black linens and at least one black logo tshirt. As a bonus there was a small black pair of running shorts someone had left as well.

Shutting the door and keeping her back to Cassie to guard said door, Jaime gave her some small amount of privacy to change.

"Thanks, that feels a ton better." The shorts were shorter than she normally wore, but they were dry which was all that mattered under the circumstances.

She turned around and smiled. "It looks better too." Jaime winked. "Although that might not be the popular opinion around here."

The small comfort of dry clothing brought with it brief respite from the specter of the confrontation she was facing. Unexpectedly, she laughed and pulled at the edges of the shirt. "It is a little tighter than the other one. That might help."

Genuinely amused, Jaime reached a hand out to touch her shoulder and Cassie braced herself just in time to keep their energy transfer minimal. She was mostly successful, Jaime's only indication she'd felt something was a quick retraction and she stared at her fingertips in confusion. It would feel like a static shock to a regular, odd considering Cassie was soaking wet and they were in humid Florida where such things were rare. Typical of a regular, Jaime shrugged it off and her mind let her believe it was nothing more than static.

The levity of the moment was broken and Jaime leaned back on the door, folding her arms and regarding Cassie with interest. "So what's up with Drew tonight?"

"Where is he?" She was back in investigator mode in a flash. "I need to talk to him."

Jaime's eyes narrowed and she raised her chin. "He's a good guy and he's obviously upset. What's going on?"

Forcing herself to be patient and not throw the taller woman aside was almost physically painful. She felt her palms itching to tap into the energy she could feel pulsating beneath her feet. It was funny how in tune she was now to the elements that had denied her for so long. Cassie exercised a level of self-control she had no idea she was capable of and closed her hands. To give her fingers something to do, she ran them through her hair, fluffing it up as she felt it drying with the kinetic energy crackling beneath the surface of her skin. Under the circumstances she didn't care if Jaime noticed the rapid drying.

"There is nothing going on with Drew. I just need to talk to him." She used what she learned from the valet as an excuse. "I was walking in and one of the guys out front mentioned someone in the club was giving out drugs I happen to know are tainted."

At that, Jaime's eyes bugged out and her jaw dropped, concern for her boss temporarily forgotten. "Someone's handing out bad drugs here? We have enough trouble keeping the peace with booze. There's a reason Drew works so hard to keep that stuff out of here."

"Right." Cassie clenched her fists at her sides trying to keep from heeding the call of the swirling energy at her feet and in the air with the breaking storm. Mentally she willed Jaime to get out of her way. "So if you don't mind, I need to let him know his club is about to be full of a bunch of hopped up partiers and things could get ugly if we don't find this guy and shut him down."

The aspiring lawyer caught wind that something else was going on and her suspicion returned. "Is that why he's so freaked out?" She was watching Cassie, specifically the animated twitching of her hands. "When he got here I asked him about Brandon. He didn't look good last time I saw him and some of us were worried." Her brows pinched. "Drew's jumpy, he said he didn't have time to socialize. He was busy." Clearly annoyed, she put the last in air quotes. "Something's up with him. I've known Drew Carter for two years and I've never seen him upset and he has *never* been so rude."

Cassie caught a glimmer of the hurt behind Jaime's affront. She made a small attempt to soothe her, Jaime was a better ally than foe. "I'm sure he's just worried about his brother, Jaime; I wouldn't worry about it too much if I was you. Is he still upstairs?"

Jaime looked uncertain, she didn't seem entirely convinced by the shaky reasoning and was definitely considering putting up a fight.

"If it helps, I'm going up there to check on him and lend a hand to get him out of here a little early to rest."

Cassie's planned rescue effort seemed to satisfy Jaime. Not happy, she at least was willing to give way. Shoulders dropping in defeat, she stood up away from the door and clasped her hands in front of her, agitated. "Yeah, last I saw he was upstairs cooling out some guys on the dance floor. He told me to tell anyone looking for him he was up there."

The words were barely out of her mouth when Cassie whipped past her. She had to warn him if he didn't know already. If he did, she was going to stand by him and do her best to get him out of here alive and keep as many people here breathing as possible.

Pritchard was here and working to amp up the confusion tenfold. That changed things. Drew may think he could handle Terry Pritchard alone but there was no way he could handle the witch and a club full of the temporarily insane. Taking them two at a time, Cassie raced up the stairs.

Chapter 30

The maroon sedan pulled onto the Dale Mabry Highway. The interior was filled with the sounds of the breaking storm as it pelted the windshield and combined with the nervous finger-tapping of its driver's carefully clipped nails against her large square teeth. Getting up to speed, the engine revved higher, overrunning the sounds of both.

"We are no help to them sitting in a police station." Quan pointed out, matter of fact.

Shooting him a dirty look, Julia stopped with the fingertips. Her speed continued and she snapped back. "If you weren't so damned stubborn, we'd be there by now and Cassie wouldn't be facin' off against a chameleon with nothin' but a green witch to help her." She sucked air between her teeth and muttered under her breath. "They could both be dead and him long gone by the time we get there."

Quan sat, maddeningly peaceful, staring out the windshield and Julia wanted to wring his neck. The steering wheel made a sound under her tightening grip. His voice was low and quiet when he spoke again. "Anna says it is time Cassie is tested. You agreed with our orders then; do you question them now?" Quan's expression remained unconcerned and his focus forward, yet he was aware of everything, including Julia's mute head shaking in answer. Giving a slight nod that he'd expected as much, Quan continued, "It is her final test, one we all must take. You should be pleased that she has done so well. She will be a fully instated investigator when we return."

Julia's eyes stung and she had to blink to keep them clear. "Is that what they'll tell her daddy when we bring what's left of her home for her funeral? She passed the test?" Angrily she gritted her teeth. "Cassie may have had all the schoolin' we did and more time in the field than most, but what every one of us is forgettin' is that there's a good reason for that." Her fingers hurt and she shifted her grip. "She has a completely different magick today than she's been workin' with that *whole* time. It's too much to ask for her to have it mastered in a few days. And against a chameleon no less, she has to know how to fight the magick *he* chooses to use, and that can change at a single touch. If I'd known it was gonna come out like this I never would have left her."

"Anna knows what she is doing. Cassie is capable."

Julia's hot Creole temper flared in the face of her partner's impassiveness. Maturity only went so far in governing an uneven temperament and she had no reason to play it cool. There was no one here to set a good example for. "How can you be so sure? You're the one who told Anna last month that Cassie was hopeless. Now that she finally figured out her power the two of you are ready to cut her loose?" She snapped her fingers. "Just like that?"

"Her knowledge is sufficient. The last detail for her to unlock was how to call to her energy. I believe that when she found that the last piece of the puzzle, her training was complete. Cassie is her own witch now. Whether she can bring that together is up to her, how much time we give her is irrelevant."

She knew he was right yet it was hard not to think of their young apprentice as more than just a beginner. Julia had never had children of her own and that time was long past for her. Julia had become increasingly protective of Cassie over the course of their field time together and as Cassie failed time and again to perform.

Secretly, she wondered if that was the real reason Quan had spoken to Anna. Not because Cassie was a problem but because he feared Julia had lost her focus, and in their line of work that was deadly. It was impossible for her to admit out loud that he was right. Still, she should have put up more of a fight before letting them send Cassie out on her own. She would have had she known Pritchard was far more dangerous than they had initially thought. Julia should have stayed with Cassie and made Quan drive his own damned self around, license or no license. Stubbornly, she gritted her teeth. "You'd better be right, Quan."

Julia counted off the mile markers flashing past at nearly eighty miles per hour. They would be there in twenty minutes if traffic was kind. She said a silent prayer and asked her family's spirit guardian, Simbi, to watch over Cassie and Drew until they could reach them.

Chapter 31

Lights strobed, illuminating the faces of the three men locked in a standoff on the dance floor. Drew was determined to keep two patrons from killing each other while they, on the other hand, were determined to commit murder. All three stood facing off in a triangle with one of the three armed and everyone except Drew seemingly higher than a kite, making for an unusually difficult negotiation.

Drew's "special ability" as Cassie had called it wasn't working, God knew he was trying. It actually seemed to make things worse, a detail Drew grasped about the same time he noticed they were high. Although it also might have been due to the fact that the blonde knife-wielding man had managed to get a slice in on Drew's ribs and the pain was causing his concentration to wobble. Regardless, the situation he found himself in was not looking good and the vast majority of the dozens dancing around them seemed to be entirely oblivious to the drama in their midst, so unnaturally frantic were they in their gyrations.

The deliberate obliviousness struck Drew and he squinted against the lights, taking several studious glances at the writhing bodies and their faces. His gaze fell back to the blonde holding him at knifepoint. Bloodshot eyes were a common denominator as well as sluggishness to their strange manner of moving, sometimes fluid and then twitching into a tight spasm. It was like being in a dance scene in a zombie movie. With a sickening plummeting of his heart, Drew realized Pritchard was already here in the same way he knew he wasn't going to be able to get the better of him. Beaten, he pictured Brandon lying near death and muttered a remorseful apology. "Looks like both of us are going to die tonight."

Bringing his eyes back to the dark, island born fellow across from him, Drew grimaced and rushed. At least Cassie is safe, he thought to himself as he brought his shoulder into the larger man's solar plexus, knocking him off balance and winding him.

There was a streak of movement off to his side and Drew felt the knife's tip score his bicep. The blonde had joined the fight again.

His speed was uncanny, far too great to be natural. What else had the drug brought on in the man and how long was it going to last? He had time to ponder only for a second before the islander landed hard on the floor, jarring all three and breaking them apart for a few precious seconds before Drew found himself underneath a large dark man who, with a grunt and soft oath, went limp on top of him, leaving only two.

But no, apparently some sort of blood in the water type alert went out to those on the dance floor under the influence of Revelation. Their disjointed movements ceased for one communal moment while they felt the energy run through their heightened senses like a shockwave, drawing them to the source.

The movements of the blonde working feverishly to drag the prone islander from the man below, drew their attention. His lips moved all the while. Drew couldn't make out what he was saying over the music. Crazed, he seemed to be chanting to himself.

Taking the easy target, the hopped up dancers nearest the altercation moved in and Drew heard the angry barrage of curses streaming forth as five or six of the closest zombies closed in. Their bulk blocked out some of the electronic music, providing a frantic soundtrack to at least one man's senseless death. The curses began to move away as the mass maneuvered the poor lone man into a ring of stoned killers. Drew pushed the dark man's shoulders off of him and sat up, keeping his movements small and slow to avoid detection. Never one to run from a fight, Drew was also not a fool and this was not a fight he could win.
Hands touched his arm from behind and Drew jerked away, cocking his fist as he twisted his torso making ready to fight for his life. Dead weight held his legs pinned to the ground.

"Drew, it's me," Cassie shouted over the music, squeezing his arm. "I have to tell you something."

Lowering his fist, he saw her amber eyes wide with panic inches from his nose and wanted to scream. "No! What are you doing here? Pritchard's here somewhere and he's pumped at least half the crowd full of Revelation." Gone was his peace in knowing she was okay. Then, he felt a swelling of hope in his breast. "Your partners? Are they here?" The three of them could maybe handle this mess. His eyes went past her to the door searching for the cavalry.

Cassie grimaced and she shook her head.

Drew's hope went out of him with a gush. "Then we're done," he stated flatly. The dance music hid most of the screaming epithets coming from the far side of the dance floor; there was a crash by the tables as the blonde's body was thrown into one. It attracted Cassie and Drew's attention in time to see half a dozen men and women reaching out to lay their hands on the man scrambling backward, his knife waving wildly in front of him.

One woman screamed when the blade ran across her hand and something fell on the floor. Cassie shuddered to think what it was as she cradled the injured limb against chest and hung back from the mob, the pain taking precedence over her desire to attack. Cassie and Drew watched the crowd split.

In what was quickly becoming a stampede for the door, the still sane clubbers shoved their way past the mob. At the same time, the others pressed in the opposite direction, *toward* the screams. Even the darkness could not entirely hide what was happening around them and those not high on Revelation wanted no part of the violence. Cassie thought about calling the police. With Pritchard still out there and who knew how many in the middle of a drug frenzy, she couldn't risk more regulars being harmed or witches being outed. The police would have to wait.

Another scream, this one masculine, punctuated the steady drums as a tall dark-haired fellow got his hands around the blonde's neck and crushed his windpipe, cutting it off abruptly. Cassie turned her head just as she felt the last of his energy flash out from the blonde. The reaction from the Revelation zombies was ecstatic; the drug heightened their awareness of the magick around them and the energy of his life force rejoining the cosmos filled them with yet another charge.

Then, curiously, the mass of what was left of the dancers turned on the dark haired killer in a bizarre game of tag. He with the most power was the new target. A small orange haired woman with a nose ring and tattoo running down her neck held her hands high and a green ball of energy burst in the air just over his head. This woman had some knowledge of her magick and was not afraid to use it.

He struck back. His return volley was less controlled. It struck the bar behind her, shattering glass and booze. The shards hit the ground tonelessly in the shadow of the raging club track, drowning out all but the loudest and most piercing of sounds.

Shoving off the last of the dead man's weight from his legs, Drew gained his feet and crouched. Sticking a hand out, he grabbed Cassie's arm to drag her back into the dark hall beyond. They stood when they reached the cover of darkness.

"Come on, Cassie." He continued to pull, nearly dragging her off her feet when she planted them.

She held her ground. "Where do you think you're taking me?"

"The elevator." He glared at her. "You're leaving. Now."

They had gotten as far as the office door when Cassie felt his influence beginning to creep across her mind, softening her resolve before she caught on and shored up her defenses as well as tearing away her arm, breaking his hold on her at once. She was ready this time and refused to let him get the upper hand. He bumped against her consciousness again, still trying, and Cassie shot her hand out to slap him hard across the face. The bumping stopped and his free hand caught her wrist.

Drew's voice was easier to hear in the confines of the hall with the soundproofing effect of the carpeted walls and floor. "You can hit me all you want, but you're still leaving." Rage may flavored his tone, but Cassie heard the anguish behind it too.

"Drew listen to me, you can't use any magick. Out there, their dancing, they were raising energy in what's called sex magick.

It's what Pritchard's been using this place for for months." From the stricken look on his face she saw that he'd seen as much. "Without someone to drain off the energy, it goes into the most receptive ones who then become the focus for the group. The Revelation's got them going after each other one at a time other until there's only one left." Cassie stopped, raising a hand to Drew's chest. She was careful not to touch him.

The combination of her sudden silence and refusal to touch him halted his arguments. He considered what she was saying. It made sense; those nights Pritchard showed up and they'd had to shut down the top floor to anyone not already up there, Brandon giving him an amulet to protect him against Pritchard's magick, sending Drew away on nights Pritchard and his women were scheduled to come into the club, keeping him from being dragged into the orgy on the floor.

"That's his end game." She stared at his outline, stark against the dark confines of their surroundings. It was pointless to try to see more than that. "Pritchard is getting rid of the competition. He's found a way to flush out the other witches. Now he's taking them out one at a time using his mindless little drones to make his operation more efficient, all the while making himself more powerful by absorbing their energy." Working it out as she relayed it, she followed the thread weaving its way through what she knew and could infer from the rules governing magick and energy manipulation. "The drug dealers who won't push his product get taken out and he gives it to someone who will. Eventually he'll expand from Florida out to all the Southeast and from there who knows. Once he gets enough followers helping and floods the market he'll be able to expose every witch from Tampa to Tacoma until he's the last one standing. There won't be anyone left except the witches he can control and keep around him to suck power from."

Another scream punctuated the pause between tracks. Cassie felt the next witch die and the music slowed down to a trance beat.

Drew flinched at the energy pulse. "So what do we do?" Acknowledging the fact that he stood a better chance with Cassie

279

than without, he eased his grip on her arms. "Curl up and hide while we wait out his cannibalistic witch hunt?"

Cassie took a deep breath. "First we have to go downstairs. I need to find my pants."

Chapter 32

Seven miles away in his hotel room, Brandon sat up. His pale, sunken figure was a shadow of his former self yet he moved with all the grace of the athlete he'd once been. He went about the room finding clothing and shoes. To have spoken to him would have been difficult, his mind was elsewhere while his body followed its instincts and instructions being sent from somewhere outside his simplistic mind.

Dr. Jones was getting a soda from the machine in the lobby, facing the other direction when he blindly walked past her. Outside, parked under the canopy in front of the hotel, a cinnamon haired woman waited in the driver's seat of a blue Cadillac.

Brandon was curt. "I was waiting."

"He had to wait until the time was right to call you." Gretchen informed him, taking in the gaunt man's condition in dismay. Mr. Terry had told them the cost would be great, the rewards greater in this war they waged upon the demons. Sitting here, staring at this young man who was literally having the life sucked out of him, she had to wonder if it was worth it. Weren't more being lost now with their forcing of the demons' hands? So many had died already, from both sides. Then she remembered that he was a demon, kept solely as a weapon. Evil and loathsome as he might be, a humanitarian twinge of pity for him made her wish that even *his* tortured soul could be released from the existence that was slowly eating him alive.

"Take me to him," the young demon instructed. His hollow tone held a hint of iron.

Gretchen gave him another appraising look and saw determination in the set of his jaw and straight, tall set of his angular shoulders. Regardless of his condition, Mr. Terry wanted the demon and she had to respect that. It was her duty as one of his soldiers.

"Okay."

***

Julia pulled into the side lot and put the car in park, outside the neon glow from the sign out front. The heavy thudding of rain on metal filled the sudden vacuum left by the lack of engine noise and swishing wipers.

She sat, staring straight ahead. They had done this part more times than they could count over the years. Quan would do his thing and get a picture of what was happening inside, then they would figure out their best plan of attack. It was hard to settle herself. In times past, Cassie hadn't been in there facing off against a formidable witch of a type no one in Veritas' recent history had seen.

Quan put his hands together and brought them slowly away from each other, his palms mere inches apart while he built up power and focused it on his search. The rain would give him an extra boost in energy. Except he was taking longer than usual and Julia glanced over, growing more alarmed at the annoyed pursing of his lips. It was subtle, but in a man who never gave anything away, it was tantamount to yelling. She felt a pain in her chest.

"What's wrong?"

He continued to concentrate a minute more before giving a small shrug. "There is too much magick being used in there. None of it is familiar."

"What does that mean?" Fear gripped her heart. "Do you think we're too late?" Julia couldn't face the thought of burying another partner, there had been several in her long career and now Cassie possibly gone, just when she had finally shown promise. It wasn't right.

"I cannot tell for sure." Quan's eyes were pinched closed.

The dome light went on and the sound of rain got louder as Julia opened her door. Quan looked up in surprise. She gave him a hard stare and stuck a finger out at him. "Y'all can come in or stay here. I can't wait any more. Either she's in there waitin' for us to help or she's gone. Any way you slice it, our partner is in trouble and I'm not leavin' here without her, dead or alive."

With that she slammed the door and stalked off, rounding the corner and coming up short when she encountered a large, frantic group of people rushing from the front door of the club. The employees outside were confused, pointlessly trying to please the nearly hysterical throng. Valets rushed two at a time to retrieve cars and doormen worked to slow the mass exodus and help up those pushed down by the crush behind them.

"What's going on in there?" Julia grabbed the bare arm of a thin black woman in a tight blue dress, the same one who had gotten the interest of the valets less than an hour ago. Now her hair was falling down and her dress was torn. Her Jimmy Choos were somewhere back inside.

The beauty's heavily glittered lashes batted nervously over the frantic eyes, barely pausing on Julia in her distraught state. "I don't know, there's a gang fight going on in there I think. I saw a knife and I left."

Julia waited for the woman to look at her again. When they made eye contact the woman stopped, her frame getting loose. The witch allowed the clubber to take a breath and then she asked for more. "What makes you think it's a gang?"

"Well, I'm not sure." She was upset at her own confusion. "I just kind of guessed that because they all ganged up on this one guy and he had a knife." Her panic returned in a smaller dose and she became agitated again. "The guy with the knife killed somebody. I'm sure I saw a body and then the rest of them just turned on him."

"Thank you." Julia put a hand on the woman's forearm. "You are not in danger. Calmly go home and stay there tonight."

Nodding her understanding, the woman resumed her escape route at a sedate walk, her bare feet slapping the wet pavement. She was the only one. The rest of the evacuees were darting across the street. A few waited for the valets to get their cars while most didn't, opting instead to trot briskly down the street and put as much distance between themselves and the alleged gang altercation as possible before guns came into play or the fight moved outside.

"It would seem our timing is ideal," Quan spoke beside her as he put his hands together and Julia saw the arc.

"Think we should just waltz right in the front door?" She knew that was exactly what the man wanted to do. Having fooled him once, things were not going to go well for the chameleon. Quan was formidable under normal circumstances; angry, he was unstoppable. Julia thought of Cassie in there and a cold smile slowly spread itself across her face. "After you."

Chapter 33

"Put this on, it'll hide you."

"I can help," Drew objected, staring at the ring she held out to him.

"No." She was firm. "This is way too dangerous and you have no training."

Drew chafed at being told what to do. "I'm not leaving you to face him alone. You can't ask me to stay here in a supply closet, sitting on my ass while you go out there against however many Revelation druggies are left and Pritchard who already has my brother. I can't lose you too."

Cassie felt sick. If he knew what was going to happen he would probably be pushing her out the door and serving her up to Pritchard himself. "We can talk about it after this is over." She couldn't let herself get distracted right now. Out of its rubber casing, the amulet's proximity to her was weakening her purpose. Cassie set it on the shelf nearest her and pointed at it. "You need to put that on and I need to get out there before more people get hurt." One more lie didn't seem like such a transgression considering this one would keep him from doing something stupid. Cassie offered him a tight smile. "Julia and Quan are on their way here now. You don't have to worry."

Stepping around him, she reached for the chrome handle on the black door. Before she could turn it, his hand slid over her shoulder and she swallowed. Her brave face was threatening to slip as it was and if he didn't let her go soon she was going to crumble. Knowing him, he would never agree to stay out of sight if he knew how scared she really was. "I need to do this."

"I know," he said quietly, not letting her go.

Drew took another step and she could feel the tension singing through his tightly wound body, although when his hand pulled her around to face him it was gentle. Cassie opened her mouth to argue and stopped when she saw his intention. He wasn't intending to argue, he let his hand slide from her shoulder up to her neck while the other went to her waist gliding around and pulling her into him. Drew's eyes were dark and tortured before they closed and his lips met hers.

For a brief second Cassie thought about refusing him, about insisting that this was wrong, that she wasn't who he thought she was. Yet she stayed. Cassie let herself pretend for this last moment that she could choose the course her life was supposed to take. She let herself believe that she could have something real and something normal. That she could have a life with this man she could see herself loving. She found a bizarre comfort in the hope that if she died tonight her pension would go to her family and maybe Drew would never have to think less of her. He would never know of her deception.

When he broke off, he reached up and brushed away the tear that had spilled out from under her black lashes. Cassie smiled weakly and reached for the doorknob behind her back. "Put on the amulet and stay here." Her voice was rough and she took a quaking breath, slowly exhaling. "Please. For me." She pleaded with the one bit of leverage she had; using it made her feel like a phony. "I need to be able to focus and I can't if I'm worried about you out there."

Wordlessly, he took the ring off the shelf and slid it onto his finger. Within seconds, the emotions clouding his gray eyes cleared, leaving them serene and open. Part of Cassie's heart broke, seeing the man she cared about fade into the one she'd abhorred. With a quick nod she walked out, shutting the door quietly behind her and stepping onto the path she was always meant to take.

With no one left to tend to it, the music upstairs had finally stopped and the downstairs had cleared, leaving the place eerily quiet. Even the staff had cleared out at Drew's quiet urgings, passing the word as they'd exited the elevator during the mad rush, the upstairs staff had been called down right after them. Jaime had been the last to leave, demanding to stay and help with crowd control, but Drew had been unbending in his refusal. There was steel in him that would make him a good agent and a better man. Cassie stopped herself from thinking any more about him. It would only serve to distract her and right now she needed all of her concentration if she had any hope at all of besting Pritchard and releasing Brandon's soul. It would be her parting gift to Drew. His brother would face his fate whole; it was all anyone could hope for in the end.

She approached the bar and threw both hands down, palms out. Taking a deep breath, she closed her eyes and called to the earth below her feet. Without hesitation, it sent her what she needed.

"So it's you."

Cassie opened her eyes and turned to face the source of the muffled voice. He was walking toward her from around the bottom of the stairs. He had been in the restaurant and was calmly eating a chunk of bread as he approached.

Now that the anticipation was over and she was facing the man, Cassie felt her nerves steady. "Yes, it's me."

Canting his head to the side, Pritchard regarded her curiously. "Who are you?"

"Cassie Porter, I'm an investigator for Veritas. I've come to bring you in for an evaluation. You've shown yourself to be quite a talented witch and there are people who would like to talk to you."

Pritchard's green eyes went wide. "I'm a what?"

"A witch. Mine is an organization whose purpose is to find and train witches to help them handle their powers. They've been doing it for over eight hundred years." She watched him closely for signs of alarm or that he might attack. By not telling him right off the bat that he would be put to death, there was a tiny chance he might go with her willingly. Veritas was an ends justifies the means kind of organization.

"Would you say I'm exceptionally talented?" The man's ego was easily stoked.

Cassie walked a fine line between disgust for the man who was a murderer and for herself, a big fat liar. Oh, and a murderer too, now. "You've shown promise but you haven't been trained to control your power. You could harm yourself as well as others without guidance." The hair on her arms rose; someone was raising power. Cassie hadn't seen Pritchard make a move with his hands or given any other sign he was up to anything. Her eyes searched the bar for one of his followers, then a flash of energy surged into her, marking yet another witch's demise.

"I'm not going with you." Pritchard grinned smugly. "I think I've managed just fine on my own so far. I'm going to stick with what I've got, thanks."

She glanced up the stairs and saw the little orange haired woman coming through the door at the top. Her bloodshot eyes were focused on Cassie to the exclusion of everything else. Swinging her head back to Pritchard, Cassie saw that he was watching the woman on the stairs. His thin lips twisted into a predatory smile, his tongue sliding over them in anticipation. All of the energy up there had focused into this one woman and Pritchard was hungry for it. Cassie's lip curled.

"What is Revelation?" Seeing Pritchard had no intention of going with her quietly, Cassie dropped the act. "What is the meaning of the 'Apocalypse'?" It had been scrawled on the sheet she'd found in the copy room garbage alongside a rather large dollar amount and what she was assuming were account numbers. Cassie had left it in her room and hoped that someone with Veritas would find it if things got ugly.

Pritchard's body went rigid and his eyes narrowed, turning back to her. "Found that at my church when you broke in, did you?" he spat. "The Apocalypse is coming and you can't stop it."

Feeling reckless, Cassie smirked, wanting to push him. "I wouldn't call that run down office a church." She watched his nostrils flare as his gigantic male pride took the hit. "So I know the money you are bilking from your patrons isn't going toward office space. Where *is* it going? Drugs? Drugs to bring about your own personal Apocalypse?"

His irritation with her went up a notch.

Smelling blood, Cassie poked harder, wanting to see if her guesses had been correct. One on one he didn't scare her. "That's it then. You're nothing but a drug dealing con man. And this Apocalypse you fill their heads with stories about is the day of your big score. You're going to get them all high as kites and the ones you leave alive are to be your magickal batteries. Are you going to tell them they saw something amazing? Maybe that they're the chosen few?" Splotches of red blossomed on his pale cheeks as Cassie struck gold and kept digging. It felt good to take out her anger on him. "You're no different than a common thief, Pritchard. You prey on vulnerable women and you take something even more valuable than their money, you take their trust. When I bring you in, I'll be happy to watch them carry out your punishment."

"And what's that?" he asked through clenched jaws.

Cassie shook back her hair and drew herself up. "As an investigator for Veritas I sentence you, Terrence Pritchard, for knowingly causing the deaths of regulars and witches alike, to death." And for taking away the man I cared about. She smiled coldly at him, "I'm going to watch you burn."

A clattering on the stairs brought her head around and Cassie watched as the woman righted herself.

With a roar, Pritchard lunged at her and clamped his hands around her throat. Cassie's eyes bulged. She'd let herself get distracted, trusting her body to warn her of a magickal attack and ignoring the signs of a physical one. Pritchard turned her body so that she could no longer see the zombie coming her way and in the process, bent her backwards, forcing her to use all of her concentration just to keep her feet. Her fingers instinctively clutched at his arms to break his hold.

Trapped, Cassie closed her eyes and relaxed her hands on Pritchard's arms. She pushed out the energy she'd been holding in, although this time she didn't apologize for what she was about to do.

As soon as she began to push, Cassie's arms warmed and she felt her insides beginning to boil, worse than her most awful fever as a child. Confused, she stopped and opened her eyes to see Pritchard grinning and she realized her mistake. He had used her magick against her.

At once she pulled back and felt the energy rebel. It fought her, seeking a release. "Why are you doing this?" she croaked her. Her mind was burning.

"Because I can."

The room around Cassie went dark and her legs buckled. Pritchard released her and let her fall, landing hard on her side in time to see him reach out and take hold of the lone survivor of the drug induced massacre. A flash of blue light nearly blinded her. The smell of burning flesh was the last thing she remembered as she faded to black.

Chapter 34

Pacing back and forth in the storeroom at first, Drew gradually found it easier to keep his word and slowed to a halt. The ring itched where it rode tighter than he remembered on his finger, the knowledge of its power and purpose making it feel more like an anchor than amulet. A feeling like he was being cut off from a part of himself had been tweaking him since he'd put it on. He vaguely recalled a similar feeling when Brandon had given it to him initially, although it was less noticeable what with the drug withdrawal and sudden sobriety that had followed.

Then, shortly after Cassie had left him, the pain began to build inside his head. It started as a low ache and he began to pace again, nervous energy growing as quickly as the magick outside his little cupboard. Each time the pain thrummed in his skull he imagined another human being falling upstairs. By simple logic and repetition he'd been able to figure out the jolt he felt was his sensing when a witch died.

The first with Caroline had been a minor shock and he'd been too distracted with Cassie to give it much thought, but then when they'd started to fall here at the club it had been easy to work out. Now, when he felt the twinges, he feared the next one would be Cassie and he would have let her die while he sat in here like an impotent lump, letting it happen.

"Goddamn Pritchard," he growled, grabbing his head. "Pure Goddamn evil."

Cursing the man gave him no reprieve. The pain continued to grow, leaving Drew leaning heavily against the racking, his head on the cool metal and his eyes closed, as he panted through the worst of it. Then suddenly, like walking out of a concert, the source ceased, leaving only a dull pounding in its wake. Drew breathed a deep breath in through his nose and out his mouth.

Just as he pushed himself off the shelving, thinking he was clear to emerge, Drew was leveled by a shooting pain that lanced through his skull, leaving him temporarily blinded. Unable to bite it back entirely, his moan broke the silence of the small room. As unexpectedly as it hit, the pain stopped and Drew staggered, gasping. Thinking of ways he was going to destroy the amulet on his finger, Drew laughed bitterly, but it was cut short by one more blinding flash and he tore the thing from his hand, throwing it away from him. He heard it clatter on the floor somewhere under the shelving. Blissfully, the pain stopped.

Drew was no longer able to keep himself in what amounted to a prison cell and he raised a shaky hand to let himself out. It took two tries and he had to wipe his sweating palm on his pant leg before he succeeded. Stumbling out, he kept himself upright with one hand on the wall as a support.

The club was silent. Not a single sound could be heard from upstairs or down. Even when he and Brandon talked shop at the end of the night there were closers cleaning up or shutting the place down for the night. This kind of quiet was unnatural; Drew was on guard for anything.

Grateful for the soundproofing quality of their carpeting, Drew crept forward, keeping his body tight against the wall. A familiar scent wafted to him and he gagged. Fearing the worst, he broke into a run.

Hitting the mouth of the hall, he got a full whiff of barbequed human and put his hand over his nose to stifle it. There, in the space between the bar and stairs, lay the charred remains of a woman with bright hair. Relieved, then immediately repentant, Drew said a grateful prayer that Cassie was still alive.

That Pritchard was nowhere in sight kept him on high alert. Drew continued to scan the restaurant, even venturing into the kitchen. Pleasantly enough, the smell of food in his nostrils partially covered the smell of the woman. His search revealed what he'd already known; there was no one inside, leaving only the upstairs. Pritchard wouldn't have gone yet; he wanted something from Drew and if he'd thought he'd gotten everyone else out of the way there was no reason for him to run.

Leaning on the podium at the host's station with his palm pressed to his head, Drew tried to figure out how he was going to get up there without being seen. The possibility that Cassie was up there with that monster twisted Drew's insides even more than the smell of the fried woman lying smoking on the floor.

Movement at the front doors caught his eye and Drew dropped into a crouch beside the stand, providing him with partial cover. When he saw their faces, relief washed over him. Cassie's partners had come. He looked past them, feeling his heart seize at the absence of the third. He stood up. "Where is she?"

"Isn't she with you?" Julia's eyes searched the space unbelieving.

Quan held up a hand. "They are here."

"They're upstairs," Drew snapped. Having had the short-lived hope that she was safe taken from him, Drew's frustration mounted.

Julia wrinkled her nose and nodded at the smoking corpse. "Who was that?" The smell was getting stronger.

Drew hurriedly filled them in on what they had learned of Revelation and what had taken place upstairs. He thumbed toward the dead woman. "She must have been the last one because there hasn't been a death in a while and I don't hear anymore fighting." Then, remembering why he'd risked his life to come here and meet with Pritchard, he told Julia, "I didn't get anything from him to give you. You need something so you can break the binding, right?"

Quan stroked his nose thoughtfully.

Julia frowned with a sober nod. "Then it's vital we stop him right here. If we lose him this time, we might not be able to find him again and your brother will lose his soul."

"Wait, what? I thought you could track anybody." He focused on the creepy little man. The concept that Brandon's soul was in jeopardy sent a chill down his spine. He'd thought they were talking about death, not loss of a soul. Not an excessively

293

spiritual man, Drew still found the idea mortifying. He wondered if Cassie had known, surely she would have told him if she had.

Shooting Drew a tight look, Quan snapped back, "No one can be expected to track a chameleon."

"A what?"

Julia intervened to keep the two from wasting their energies on each other instead of focusing on why they were here. "A rare witch can mimic another's magick with only a touch. The scent is masked by the magick of the witch he is using, it changes when he discards the witch."

Drew gulped. "Discards?"

"To use their magick he has to take it and it can't be put back. He eventually takes it all until there's nothin' left." Julia looked disgusted, giving Drew some amount of confidence she at least had some humanity left in her and the southern charm she used to manipulate people wasn't all show. "Now let's not lose sight of why we're here and work together boys," she reminded them with a demure smile.

Drew let her jibe go. She was right; he didn't want to waste any more time squabbling with these two when Cassie was up there with Terry Pritchard. The skin on his neck itched in anticipation of another energy pulse, telling him they were too late.

Quan made a sound and went stiff, closing his eyes and frowning as his attention suddenly shifted inward. The other two went silent and waited.

Before Quan could tell them what he had sensed, Drew got all the information he needed when Cassie's shriek rang out, muffled by the glass and soundproofing. Julia reached out a hand to stop him; her alluring exterior disguised the strength that lay beneath.

"Leave this to us. It isn't safe for you up there."

Drew was ready to blow. "I'm tired of hearing about what's too dangerous for me. This is *my* club and my brother's soul we're talking about. And Cassie. I'm going up there whether you like it or not." He glared at them both, challenging them to disagree. "I have some skills too. I've broken up fights. I've been in them since I was eighteen. I can help." He annunciated his last words concisely to make his point.

Julia and Quan exchanged a look and Quan shrugged before starting up the stairs. Julia regarded him evenly.

"I understand you want to do somethin', but this is more than you're used to. Are you sure this is what you want?" The way she asked it intimated a bigger question, though whether it was about involving himself with Cassie or their world in a more permanent way, he couldn't be sure. Either way, his answer was the same.

"I'm sure."

Nodding soberly, Julia moved to follow Quan up the stairs. Drew hit the handrail, pointing when they turned their heads.

"You'll be walking right into his line of sight and he'll have all the time in the world to get ready if he's paying attention. We've got an elevator back there that comes up at the rear of the hallway. It might give us a better chance of sneaking up."

Chapter 35

Cassie woke up all at once, a strange acidic taste in her mouth mildly reminiscent of orange juice. She was lying on a hard, cool surface. At first she had no idea where she was until the light purple running lights around the floor's perimeter cleared it up. At least they'd stopped strobing. Sitting up, she scanned her surroundings to get her bearings. Bodies lay strewn all around her, and the solidness of something against her leg sent a shiver of revulsion through her as she recognized the feel of a human corpse.

Frantic, she screamed and scrabbled backward, crouching and tripping until her back hit a pillar on the far side of the floor. Cassie continued to push herself against it, her body and mind recoiling from the carnage sprawled around her. There hadn't been more than eight people, one of whom was downstairs, killed with *her* magick though not by her hand. There seemed to be more than that dead up here, though that impression could have been due to the varying ways in which the bodies had been dispatched and laid about, she realized with a shudder.

One lay sprawled with her head turned the wrong way, entirely the wrong way. Her eyes pointed up and her body down. Another was contorted, mouth wide in a final agonized scream, while yet another lay pale and peaceful like he was sleeping except for the pool of blood he was lying in. A young girl who didn't even look old enough to be in here was missing limbs, one of which was on top of a table at the edge of the floor. All had died by different hands, different magicks.

Closing her eyes, Cassie breathed through her nose and fought down the nausea and chills that threatened to send her mind into hiding again. So much death brought with it the memory of the woman she'd killed; the faint aroma of the woman downstairs didn't help, and Cassie struggled to keep her wits. She practiced breathing, giving it far more attention than the act itself required. The sound of Pritchard's nasal voice scraped her ears and at first she thought he was speaking to her. A second later, another voice responded and she looked up to see the man's back to her.

"Did anyone see you?"

The voice that answered was thin and tired, his frame too lean for being so tall. His clothes were baggy, telling of recent weight loss. "No one saw. I had your woman drop me at the back door and the place was empty." He paused. "Of anyone who could talk."

"You didn't see your brother?"

At that, the thin man turned to lean on the bar opposite her affording her a clear view. Pritchard had poured himself a drink, which now dangled from his fingers and the emaciated man standing opposite him, wavering as though he would faint at any minute, was Brandon.

"That's impossible," she muttered to herself, her brain arguing with her eyes over what was an impossibility. Cassie prayed to the spirits that Dr. Jones had not been harmed in his escape. Brandon was most likely in no shape to cause much damage, but whoever helped him get here might.

"Have you brought it?" Pritchard asked, a new hunger in his tone.

"Just like you asked, that's the rest of it." Brandon laid a small purple cloth bag on the bar between them and Pritchard grinned.

"Excellent. Funny what a bank will hold for you if you put it in a bag and tell them it's private." He chuckled at his brilliance. "Then I would say we are ready to begin with our next phase." He downed his drink and clanked his empty glass on the metal bar with a crack before turning to meet Cassie's eyes.

Caught staring, Cassie started and knew it was pointless to look away. He knew she'd been listening. She tried to sound braver than she felt. "What's the next phase?"

Like any good zealot, Pritchard adored attention and was more than willing to take the soapbox Cassie offered. "The next phase, little *witch*," he smirked at his own wit and Cassie wanted to hit him, "is to take Revelation the masses. Tonight was a rousing success and my largest test so far. I'd say we're ready to move up to the big leagues after what I've seen here." His eyes roved the bodies and excitement filled him. "There's an after hours club down in Ybor City that would be perfect. This time I'm going to do things a little differently, more controlled. I'm going to lock the doors and then *everyone* gets a free shot of a new kind of drink called Revelation."

"Isn't it bad enough you're killing your own? What do you stand to gain by hurting the innocent regulars?"

"Regulars?"

"Non-magickal types."

Pritchard chuckled in delight. "Regulars. I love it. Honestly I've never really known what made them different, now I do." He checked his watch and shrugged. "It doesn't matter, more in the mix only helps to weed through the others faster." Pritchard relaxed, apparently he had time for a little monologue. He smoothed his hair back and smiled. "When I first learned I was stronger than everyone else I took it as a sign from God. He wanted me to help him rid the world of those who don't believe. The world has become weak because His message is being carried by the weak. With each person I destroy, God's message becomes stronger, I become stronger. I have been chosen to be his vessel, like Jesus. I will be able to *make* doubters believe. And when they are ready to listen, I will be there with God's message to lead them."

"That ain't happenin' you sick little man." Julia's French infused drawl was pronounced in her anger. "Cassie, you all right?"

Cassie brightened, "I am now." Her head spun to catch sight of Julia in the lead with Quan beside her, emerging from the shadows of the light sucking hall. Then her smile faded as the third face appeared and, heartsick, she spun back to catch Pritchard's broad smile.

Seeing Pritchard's pleasure and singular focus, Cassie realized he'd gotten what he'd wanted all along. Unwilling to let that happen, Cassie jumped to her feet, swaying from the sudden rush of blood to her head. "Drew, get out!" She warned and held herself up against the steel girder. Her eyes went to his hand and noticed he was not wearing the amulet. He was unguarded. "He knows what you are!" Drew's power in Pritchard's hands would make the man unstoppable.

Undaunted by the force in front of him, Pritchard smiled and looked back and forth between his prize and his prisoner. He was genuinely pleased at Cassie's horror, nodding confirmation of her suspicions. "I have been waiting for you for so long. I'd hoped to have you both by my side," he frowned at the dying man swaying by the bar halfway between his master and his brother. "This way works too." Green eyes twinkling, he leered at the two agents who had come closer under cover of Cassie's outburst. He checked his watch again. "In about five minutes you're going to be too busy to worry about me." Turning to Brandon, his smile faded and he gave the order. "Come over here to me."

"No Bran, don't let him put his hands on you," Drew cautioned, not wanting to see his brother forced to kill again.

Brandon didn't answer, he only shuffled toward Pritchard. His appearance was appalling; he'd gotten even worse since last night. A virtual walking skeleton, his musculature had nearly been eaten away from the strain placed on his body by his service to the chameleon. Pritchard was sucking the life from Brandon through the connection he'd forced between them. Drew turned his wrath on Pritchard. "Leave him alone, you're killing him. If he dies, you lose his power."

"You're pretty well informed, Drew. It must be the company you're keeping these days," Pritchard taunted, still smiling that used car salesman smile. His eyes sought out the amulet that had kept him from getting his hands on Drew all these years and he pointed at it's empty finger. "You're missing your bodyguard."

"You've talked long enough," Julia snapped. "Nobody wants to hear you gloat, Pritchard. Your savior fantasy is over." She took another step.

"Stop," he commanded, holding out a hand. Eyes shifted from Julia to Brandon. "Come to me now." Dark power oozed from his words and Brandon's face went slack as his will left him and his feet moved faster. Pritchard's hand clamped down on Brandon's shoulder and turned him forcibly to face the opposition. "Drew, I'm sure you're familiar with what your brother can do?" He nodded, smiling at Drew's ashen pallor. "I wondered if you'd figured out the connection to your parents yet."

Cassie watched Brandon's waxy face remain impassive as his sins were confirmed to his brother and she saw the tear trickle down his blank cheek. He was still in there, unable to stop Pritchard from using him yet aware of everything he was doing. The injustice fanned Cassie's indignation and lit a fire that raged within her hot enough to force a sweat.

In the blink of an eye, Brandon's magick snapped to life and Cassie's focus fixed on him and the waves of energy coming from him as Pritchard tapped into his element, Fire. Each wave struck her, dizzying her and before she could right herself, another would hit. The barrage that was his magick threatening to drown her became entwined with the need to stop Pritchard and their joint destruction. The two men twisted into one in her mind and took the pity she'd felt for Brandon and turned it into a singular seething hatred.

He was a killer. He was as much a murderer as Terry Pritchard; worse, he'd killed before he met the man. And it had been *their* fault she'd been forced to kill. It was his fault she'd lost her soul. Cassie's fingers twitched, hands itching to call to her magick and welcome it into her. She took a stumbling step, her world swaying off kilter around her. Her irrational thoughts continued to twist until they became nothing but a mass of rage. Logic was no longer a part of her process. Her palms turned down and she called the earth.

"Do you see that?" Pritchard's voice was dim, dulled by the roaring in her ears. Nothing he said registered, it ran in and out of her mind without sticking.

Her skin tingled as the power built inside her, begging to be unleashed on the murderer in her sights. Taking another step, she called water.

"You are about to see how Revelation works on a witch with power." He failed to hide his excitement. "Taryn was weak, it was the Revelation that gave her what little oomph she had." He motioned to Julia and Quan. "I don't think you've seen it yet so this should be a treat."

No one spoke, not that Cassie was listening. There was nothing but the need to kill Brandon. Cassie lurched sideways feeling mildly drunk, her skin was on fire with the energy coursing through her. Her eyes remained trained on Brandon who could only stare straight ahead unseeing, only vaguely conscious of a hot breeze racing across her flesh.

It didn't matter, none of it did. Her mind had narrowed its focus until all she could see or think about was the source of the magick filling her head. It was odd, she'd never been able to sense magick before, not like Quan yet here she was, *seeing* the waves rolling off the man and needing to stop them. More important even than breathing, she needed to stop the energy emanating from his lean frame before it drove her mad.

Drew pushed past her partners who tried to stop him, breaking Julia's hold and spinning away from Quan. Years of football with his brother and his friends when they were young paid off. He reached her halfway across the floor, grabbing her arm and turning her to face him. "Cassie, look at me. It's the drug doing this. The drug is doing this to you. You're here to *protect* Brandon, not hurt him."

Quan and Julia could only watch, rooted to the spot as they tried to come up with another line of attack that wouldn't spook Pritchard into using Brandon's chaos magick to liquefy them all or turn Cassie on them. Neither one wanted to have to put down their young partner. They both watched Drew, waiting for a tiny second's distraction when they could strike.

Cassie barely registered Drew's words, instead twisting and dropping like she'd done a thousand times at the Academy when practicing self-defense until her reaction was instinct. Free again, she turned back to Brandon, undeterred in her course. Raising her hands, Cassie prepared to destroy the man who had cursed her soul. The hateful expression on her face was terrifying.

Seeing the pointlessness of reasoning with Cassie, Drew turned to Pritchard. "You want me? I'll go with you if you let Brandon go."

That got Pritchard's attention. Bobbing his head, he was pleased with Drew's acceptance. "Six months ago I might have taken you up on that." His expression grew dark, a physical indicator of the depth of the cruelty that lay within. "You said no. Now I'm going to show you why you don't say no to me."

Livid, Drew's brain was clouding and pushing out any and all remnants of reason. All he could see was the woman he cared for, poised to execute his dying brother, while the man responsible for all of their suffering stood by, encouraging it like a Caesar with his gladiators. Clinging to the last of his ability to form a cohesive thought, Drew turned to Pritchard.

"If you don't stop using him, I'll give her another target and then you won't have either one of us to be your robots." Drew took another step to remain abreast of Cassie's staggered advance, keeping himself in her line of fire to make good his threat. If she lunged, Drew fully intended to intervene no matter the consequences. All it would take was one word and a little influence behind it and she would change course in a heartbeat. Brandon couldn't defend himself as he was, and if that meant Drew had to take the hit then so be it. His brother had done it for him long enough. Drew owed him this.

Pritchard's mouth fell open and Drew felt a small thrill of satisfaction. If he was as strong as Cassie said, it would take time for Pritchard to find a replacement and Brandon wasn't going to last long at the rate he was being used. Pritchard could barely keep himself from drooling. "Then come here and let me get a taste of what you can do. I've only seen glimpses but I know it's worth it, I can feel it." He held out a hand. "The things I'm going to do."

"Do not let him touch you," Quan ordered, repeating the same caution Drew had given his brother. "You will be his if he touches you."

"I know," he said without breaking off from his would be puppeteer.

Smiling, Pritchard waved him forward becoming impatient to claim his new power source. "Come on. We don't have much time."

That was precisely what Drew was hoping for. He had no way of knowing how long the effects would last on Cassie; he could only hope that the more time he bought, the closer she would get to reason or that its effect on her might weaken. There was no more putting it off. Drew was within only a few feet of Pritchard's reach and Brandon beside him, standing slack-jawed and frozen, was about to be under Cassie's hands. As if reading his mind, her hands came up, her palms out. A hint of blue mixing with the color of sand glowed on the surface of her hands.

Brandon did nothing to protect himself; his eyes shifted for a brief second to slide over Cassie and settle on his brother. In that moment, Drew caught a glimpse of his brother in the flat blue eyes regarding him sorrowfully. Despite all that he'd suffered to prevent this, Drew was going to be under Pritchard's thumb after all.

When Brandon's eyes closed in preparation for Cassie's touch, Drew struck. Pivoting on the ball of his foot, he lifted his leg as he spun and sent a side kick into Pritchard's ribs, instantly breaking his hold on Brandon, causing him to grab his side. The sudden removal of Pritchard's draining touch left Brandon to drop in a dead faint and before Cassie could lower herself to reach him, Drew put out both hands and flying tackled her, sending them both sliding along the floor away from Brandon's body.

Once Brandon's magick was no longer a threat, Quan reacted, putting his palms together, where an arc flicked up between them. Hunched over with his hand still on his side, Pritchard stared in horror at Quan, holding up the other hand defensively.

"Please, don't hurt me," he begged, no longer the swaggering would be prophet without his minions.

Quan was not to be swayed. One hand went out and a lash of energy shot forth making the air around it shimmer from its intensity. Pritchard's arms and legs were pulled together as the beam of energy bound him, the shimmer consolidating itself around his form and Quan jerked his hand back, toppling Pritchard onto his back. The man's scream was cut off as Quan's other hand shot out and his open hand closed in the air. The captive's lips, pressed firmly together, allowed no further sound to escape, though he continued to gurgle in his throat.

Julia leapt forward and pulled out a special knife, kept for strictly magickal purposes, from a sheath hidden under her pant leg. Pritchard's eyes bulged and she tsk'd. "Quit your crying, you whiny rat. I'm not going to kill you." The knife struck and Pritchard made a noise though all he had lost was a chunk of hair.

Jumping up to grab his glass from the bar, Julia brought it down and held it under the whimpering man's hand where her knife flicked and a high-pitched squeal resonated in his throat.

"Well, it's going to have to do since I don't have a chicken," she explained to him, catching a precious few drops of blood in the glass. "Drew, keep Cassie steady over there. We don't want any interference while I'm doin' this or we'll end up with someone else bound by accident. Hear?"

Julia proceeded to mutter and weave her spell, breaking the binding between Terry Pritchard and Brandon Carter, while Quan strained to hold Pritchard magickally until someone could find a physical means to bind their prisoner. A strong witch, even Quan, had his limits and holding a chameleon without letting him turn the spell back on him was taking its toll.

Drew had his hands full wrestling with Cassie and trying to keep clear of her hands. "Cassie, listen to me, it's over. Do you hear me? Quan's got Pritchard and Julia's going to break the bond. We did it Cassie." Drew was careful not to use any sort of influence on her for fear it would renew her vigor. Grunting with the effort, he straddled her body, holding her arms up over her head by the wrists, her legs by sliding his down across her thighs while she twisted and writhed, hearing nothing he was saying.

Cassie was on fire. The effects of the drug had melted her ability to think clearly and the energy she'd gathered was enough to level this building. The energy turned and twisted inside her, coiling and unfurling until it felt like it was going to tear through her skin. All she could feel was the assault on her senses that the magick from outside and inside of her was causing. It wasn't enough that Brandon had stopped, now it was coming from behind her and she fought to go after it, to grab it in her hands and burn it down into nothingness. Cassie felt the visceral need to tear her attacker apart until nothing was left. Frustrated that her body was unable to carry out her mind's orders, Cassie screamed.

Chapter 36

Gretchen was getting antsy. She had been in the car since she'd driven Mr. Terry's demon slave to him. Having him in the car had made her feel unclean and she didn't trust him alone with Mr. Terry, certainly not with them about to face off against a bunch of other demons. She'd wanted to argue except she knew it would only backfire on her. So instead she had settled for waiting outside, waiting until she saw Mr. Terry emerge. Thankfully it had stopped raining and gave her a better view of the traffic around the club.

When she'd seen the people all come flooding out and the man and woman question one before going inside, she knew the battle had come and that these two were more demons. She could see it in the way they walked unafraid past everyone else hurrying to escape. Most people would have turned around, terrified of what was inside. Not these two, they knew because they were a part of it. They were soldiers in the war, like her.

Unable to wait, Gretchen got out of the car and remembered to lock it before she got too far down the block. It wouldn't do to come out with Mr. Terry only to find the car gone.

Up ahead a familiar figure stood backlit by a nearby streetlight.

"Taryn?" Gretchen stared up the street, shining in the reflection of the neon blue light spelling out the name of the club on the street.

Taryn stared back at her from the opposite side of the entrance. When she stepped into the light she looked like a drowned cat. She'd been caught in the deluge. "What are you doing here?"

"Mr. Terry is inside." Gretchen and Taryn were two of the more levelheaded women in Mr. Terry's ministry and had forged a friendship of sorts. "He's in there with the demons and I had to bring his *thing* to him."

"That makes sense. He sent me with Caroline to destroy two of the demons. They were waiting for us." Taryn told the story in the way that worked for her conscience. "They killed Caroline and I only managed to get free just now and took a cab here. He dropped me off about a mile back when he found out I didn't have any money. I tried to explain that I was doing the Lord's work, but he was not a Christian man. I've walked this whole way." She glanced guiltily at the entrance. "I hope I'm not too late to warn him."

Gretchen came forward and put a hand on the other woman's shoulder. "It'll be okay, Mr. Terry is ready for them. You've done a good job coming here." She wondered to herself why Taryn had bothered to tell the cabbie anything instead of letting him drive her all the way and worrying about it *after* she got here. That was Taryn, always worried what others would think. She'd spent endless amounts of time convincing people to agree with her, which made her one of Mr. Terry's favorites. Gretchen caught herself thinking negative thoughts again and chastised herself; that was how the demons got in. She would have to get better about that or she would not be welcomed into Heaven at the Resurrection after the Apocalypse.

"I've been waiting out here and I can't anymore." Gretchen turned to go inside. "Do you think you could manage sneaking inside? We can peek in just to see that things are going all right and then we can both wait in the car for Mr. Terry." Maybe his creature will die here, she hoped. It would suit her just fine not to have to look at the evil thing again. It wasn't a bad thought if it was about ridding the world of evil, she decided.

"How will we get in without being seen?" Taryn's eyes went wide.

Gretchen caught the bloodshot remnants of Revelation in her friend's eyes and gave her a reassuring squeeze. Even though Mr. Terry told them it was an honor to be chosen to take the drug and fight, Gretchen hadn't quite gotten used to the idea just yet of taking drugs. She'd been raised to believe they were wrong, but this was God's work and sacrifices had to be made. When the time came, she would do her part without complaint, no more being weak. Gretchen was going to make Mr. Terry proud. "Come on, Taryn. Follow me."

Together they went inside and smelled meat. Turning her head, Gretchen saw the body first and put a hand out to muffle Taryn's scream. She was the more emotional of the two and predictable that way. Taryn gave her friend an apologetic grimace and nodded understanding at Gretchen's signal to stay behind her.

They must have looked terribly silly, two grown women climbing the steps of a nightclub on their hands and knees single file but that's exactly what they did, staying low until they reached the top of the stairs and the door to where Mr. Terry had to be.

Figures were visible through the frosted glass and though they could hear some sound, they couldn't make out the words or how the battle was going. It sounded relatively calm though. Gretchen had just turned and was starting to signal Taryn to go back down when they heard Mr. Terry's voice and more talking, then a woman's scream.

Taryn clutched Gretchen's arm and Gretchen shushed her, her own heart hammering in her chest. In that moment, with Taryn looking to her for guidance, Gretchen blanked. It was just like the day the police came to tell her Charles had been hurt and she had to come to the hospital.

For four days he'd hung on, too far gone from the blows to his head to answer any of the questions she was being asked about insurances or their finances. Their family lawyer had helped with what he knew and together they'd guessed the rest. The terror of not knowing what to do had been what crippled her after Charles' death. It hadn't let up until she'd found Mr. Terry and the girls. All of them seemed to be lost like her, united in their belief in Mr. Terry's teachings.

Recognizing the same old fear rising up inside her, she struggled to be brave for Taryn, and to show Mr. Terry that she was a good soldier. He could count on her. Holding up a hand, she warned her to be silent and crept forward, setting a hand on the door and pushing. Taryn scooted over on the catwalk in front of the glass so that she too could see inside once the door was open.

Slowly, the door opened and the sounds of muffled struggles could be heard. Gretchen craned her neck around the glass, expecting at any moment to be discovered, only once she saw inside she could see why no one noticed her, there were demons everywhere, all of them doing awful things.

Nearest her, there was a man and woman engaged in a sexual act. She was no prude but the way he was moving on top of her was indecent. The woman was fighting him and at first Gretchen felt sympathy until her eyes turned toward her and she saw the red eyes of a demon brought out by Revelation. Gretchen made the sign of the cross over herself. Holding her breath she watched the two continue to struggle, only breathing again when she saw that the woman had not actually seen her and wouldn't raise the alarm. Turning her head, she saw her worst fears realized.

Mr. Terry lay with his arms and legs against him, wriggling like a butterfly struggling its way out of a cocoon. She could see no bonds on him. The demon slave lay next to Mr. Terry, unmoving and white. Good riddance, she thought to herself.

And kneeling over Mr. Terry, bleeding him into a cup with a knife in her hand was the female demon she'd seen outside. The Asian held his hands out aimed at Mr. Terry and Gretchen figured out it was his evil that held Mr. Terry, soon to be drunk dry by the demons, even the two fornicating on the floor. The scene was straight out of the fearful art she'd seen as a child in Mass. Demons having their pleasure at the destruction of man.

Easing herself back out and closing the door noiselessly, Gretchen crawled back down a few steps and sat staring out over the bar below, and into the empty street beyond.

Taryn sidled up to her, whispering, "Those two on the floor were the ones who killed Caroline."

Gretchen took in her friend's large white ringed eyes, waiting for direction. "What would Mr. Terry do?" she whispered back.

Both of them sat, struggling with the decision, until another scream rent the air. The female demon's screams decided her.

"We must destroy them." She said certainly though she did not entirely believe she was saying it aloud.

"How?"

"We will burn their earthly bodies and send them back to Hell where they belong."

"How will we save Mr. Terry?"

Gretchen swallowed, her throat felt tight. "We won't."

Taryn's hand flew to her mouth. "You want to burn Mr. Terry with them? That's murder."

Laying a hand on her friend's arm, Gretchen let the tears in her eyes flow unchecked down her aging cheeks, feeling older than she had in years. "He would willingly make this sacrifice if he was asked. We are helping him do the Lord's work and take the demons with him." She stopped, holding the back of a hand to her nose, overcome for the moment. Recovering herself, she sniffed. "We will tell the rest of the followers about his sacrifice and we'll all spread his word together. We can keep his fight alive."

Gretchen smiled sadly, thinking Mr. Terry would like knowing that his followers were committed to him even after death. Though she didn't think anyone would argue when she told them she thought they could fight on without the drugs. They had always frightened most of the women. Only Caroline had been different, declaring they made her feel powerful. Gretchen had always thought it was a ploy for Mr. Terry's attention.

The blonde woman and some of the other younger ones had often gone into a back room to have long "discussions" with Mr. Terry about their ideas. Sometimes they'd all gone out for the night, coming back reeking, tired, and rumpled. It wasn't hard to figure out what they'd been doing. Gretchen hadn't blamed Mr. Terry for taking what was offered; after all, he was human. Thought it did confuse the message, she felt.

Taryn smiled weakly back and nodded through her tears.

Patting her hand, Gretchen descended the stairs in a crouch until she reached the bottom, feeling Taryn following along behind her. With the decline of public smoking, there were no matchbooks on the bar though a quick jog behind it revealed a brandy snifter full of them, all emblazoned with the club's name. Gretchen grabbed the entire thing and trotted back to Taryn, still wiping at her eyes.

Gretchen was strong for her friend, putting on a brave face and tucking her doubts far away where Taryn couldn't see. She held out the glass. "Take a bunch. We'll light the books and throw them around. Find things that will burn."

Obediently Taryn did as she was told, dipping her hand in and taking enough she had to cup the overflowing matchbooks in her other hand. Following Gretchen's direction, she started lighting the first book and threw it down toward the back of the hallway. The synthetic material caught at once.

The women threw another book behind the bar, pouring a bottle of high proof alcohol out first to give it something to burn. They followed with one up the stairs and two at the bottom, sealing in the demons. Taking only long enough to say a quick prayer for their martyred leader, they ran from the building, coughing from the smoke already growing thick inside.

Chapter 37

The incessant drumming assault on her senses, having driven her to the brink of insanity, had finally begun to subside. Her struggles gradually lessened until at last, exhausted, they stopped altogether. Gradually, Cassie's mind returned to her.

First, the roaring died away to let her hear Julia's quiet incantations and the haze that had nearly blinded her lifted so that she could see the lighted squares of the flooring under her cheek. Blinking, Cassie turned her head and looked up to see what she was stuck under.

When the dark form above her took shape, Cassie was mortified. Drew, sweating and panting hovered over her staring down, a red angry spot rising on his cheek. Cassie tried to talk, surprised to hear how hoarse her voice was. "Did I do that?"

Drew nodded, not sure if she was really back from the worst drug trip he'd ever witnessed until he saw the shamefaced expression spread over her features. Exhausted, he rolled off and collapsed with his hands on his chest.

Cassie wanted to get a better view of what her partners were doing and tried to sit up. Drew saw her struggling and put a hand behind her back to help, giving a tiny nod at her mumbled gratitude. Pritchard was sitting with his feet out in front of him while Quan bound his legs, being careful not to touch him. His hands were already secured behind him. He'd used strips of a white bar towel as restraints.

Catching sight of her change in position, Quan glanced over at her. "We are pleased you have returned to us."

Julia smiled faintly. Her face showed signs of strain as she held out her hands, palms up, in supplication to thank her Loa, or family spirit, and her ritual was finished.

Uncertain what she'd missed, Cassie turned to Drew. "What happened?" Her hand rubbed at her aching head.

"Are you feeling okay? You don't remember any of it?"

Cassie saw the signs of tension around his eyes matched by the wariness in his tone as she shook her head. Drew was not just concerned for her well being, he also wasn't taking any chances in assuming the drugs were completely out of her system. "Drew, I'm fine. Don't worry about me." Cassie pushed herself to her feet and, as dizzy as it made her, she managed to keep from wobbling in front of him as she made her way to her partners.

Absolved of his guard duty, Drew made his way directly to his brother's side.

Julia gave her a tight smile. "Can you call the pilot? We're going to need to get him out of here before anyone comes looking."

The mention of taking Pritchard back for his trial brought with it the reality she'd feared all along. She nodded at the man lying in a rumpled heap, his brother working to straighten him out and checking for signs of life. "And him?"

Finished with tying Pritchard's feet in a homespun version of hobbles that would allow him to walk and not run, Quan sat back on his haunches and considered Brandon, saying exactly what Cassie figured he would. "He must answer for what he's done." His black eyes met Cassie's, taking in her bloodshot eyes and shadows underneath, then glanced back at Brandon, seeing a human who had, by all evidence, made an ignorant mistake and then been used up nearly to termination. Kindly, he added, "The Directors will consider all that he has been through. He will not be faulted for that which he did not willingly do."

Drew had paused in his fussing, glancing up at hearing them discussing his brother. "Are you saying he might be in trouble for this? It wasn't his fault; he was under a spell. You saw it yourself."

Cassie could hardly bear the despair riddling his face and knew that her duplicity would be revealed soon. As much as it pained her to do so, she chose to tell him herself as opposed to having

313

him find out later. It would only get worse with time and she could bear to see the evidence of her betrayal only once.

Clearing her throat, Cassie came clean. "Drew, we came here for Pritchard and we found Brandon. He's been a part of this and he has to answer for what he's done just like anybody else." She reached out, feeling a pang when he pulled away. "They'll take his binding into account." Cassie's voice died away, seeing him unmoved by her tiny offering of hope.

"Does anyone else smell smoke?" Julia stood.

To answer her query, alarms whooped and red lights flashed, making any further conversation a competition of decibels and a few seconds later the sprinklers gave Cassie her second drenching of the night.

The fact that his club was burning down seemed of no concern to Drew. Pushing himself up off the floor, he made his way to the door and pulled it open to see that the entire downstairs was engulfed in flames. Smoke followed him back inside the glass barricade and his worries were immediately for his brother.

Brandon still hadn't moved and the fire escape would be tricky one-handed. He was already working out in his head how he was going to get Brandon down. "It's bad," he alerted the three. "The sprinklers aren't going to kill it in time. We're going to have to go down the fire escape," he shouted his report, pointing back toward the hall. For the second time in as many days he considered grabbing Brandon and running.

Cassie and Julia made no move, nor did they appear concerned; both merely looked to Quan who gave a little nod, stood, and put his hands together. Drew watched first in frustration, then in absolute fascination as the man closed his eyes and his lips moved. For a few seconds nothing happened and Drew almost wished he had the ring to gauge how much magick the man was raising. Amazed, Drew watched as a form took shape, breaking the water above Quan as it fell down around him. The form was one Drew had seen in books when he was a kid talking about Chinese legends. This thing was a dragon with a fish's tail. Clear in color, it wouldn't have been visible but for the hard outline where the water was diverted around it like a man in a shower. He wanted to push it off as a figment of his imagination or a product of fatigue except after what he'd seen that week, he couldn't.

In seconds, the pipes above their heads stopped spewing water and then began to groan as the water in the pipes backed up. Groaning gave way to the screeching of metal as the pipes below reached their capacity and finally blew open in the ceiling beneath them to rain down a formidable deluge on the flames below. The pipes went silent, as did the alarms leaving the quartet in an uncomfortable vacuum, at least for two of them.

"I hope you have insurance," Quan quipped as he walked past Pritchard to the bar, hung over the edge for a minute and came back up with a full bottle of vodka, his drink of choice and less a full bottle of rum. Without warning, he swung the bottle of rum down onto the man's head knocking him out cold. "I am very tired. Please carry him to the car."

Drew watched in stunned silence as Quan walked through the glass door and Julia crouched beside Brandon who was stirring, roused by the cold water. She put a comforting arm around his shoulders and stroked his arm. Brandon sat up blinking, taking in the bodies and Pritchard lying beside him, cringing before Julia explained he had not done any of this and that his will had been returned to him.

Seeing Brandon walking off with a woman he knew wouldn't hesitate to put him in jail, and giving his brother only a vague wave of acknowledgement, Drew could hardly keep his temper in check. Gaping in disbelief as they disappeared down the hall to the elevator, he waited until they had left to turn back to his charge. He was staring down at a glass of blood sitting on the floor beside Pritchard, who was slumped against the bar, deciding how to best handle the dead weight, when his thoughts were interrupted.

"We'd better get him in the car before he wakes up."

Drew didn't turn his head, preferring to keep his eyes on the enemy he'd known all along instead of the one who had blindsided him. He didn't raise his voice when he accused her. "You're going to bring him in and he's going to be tried for murder just like Pritchard. You've known you were going to do it all along."

She could have argued or pointed out how she had told him from the start that there might be consequences, but in the end he was right. She had pretended not to know after it had become clear. She had let him believe there was some other way out for Brandon and it had been a lie. "Yes, it's my job."

"Your job sucks." He bent down and, with some grunting and shifting, got Pritchard turned around so that he could prop the man against the side of the bar. Laying him over his shoulder, he walked out, brushing right past Cassie and leaving her alone among the carnage.

She grabbed the bag of Revelation packets and marched out, hoping no one would bother to look at her because she knew her broken heart was written plainly all over her face.

Chapter 38

The plane ride back to Veritas' regional headquarters in Chicago, was awful. Julia had a book, Quan had his iPod, Brandon still looked half dead and could hardly keep his eyes open and Pritchard had woken from the blow to his head only to be given a heavy dose of lithium to dull his power and keep him asleep for the duration.

From the second they boarded, Drew made his position clear. He took the aisle seat across from his brother giving him both seats on his side for room to sprawl and effectively claiming the back four seats as theirs. The isolation was no surprise although seeing it still hurt. Sitting in the window seat in the row next to Julia, Cassie fidgeted with her seatbelt and flipped through one of Julia's gardening magazines Julia had shared. Being part earth witch, Cassie kept up on Herbology and Botany. And now that she was able, she could use that knowledge for some more complicated spell work. Using raw power was okay but she could make things like amulets and protection charms if she learned how to feed the energy into an object and make it stay. By the same token, she would need to study up on the differences between salt, fresh, and tap water for mineral content and conductivity.

"You might as well get some rest," Julia suggested, noticing her fidgeting, her magazine lying on her lap. "There will be time to work things through later when everyone's had a chance to think." She nodded toward the last of the seven rows of seats. "It's been a nightmare of a week for him. Leave him some time to process it."

Cassie nodded, giving Julia a sad smile. "You're right." She felt her chin quiver and ducked her head, crying was an embarrassment and not something she'd been raised to do openly.

There was a sound of metal sliding on metal and the seat beside Cassie shifted. Julia's arm slid around the young woman and gently offered her a shoulder. For a second, Cassie thought about refusing but whether it was exhaustion or relief or the fact that right now she missed her mom, she didn't know. Cassie let herself be soothed and, before she knew it, her cheeks were wet and she was weeping softly into Julia's shirt.

Drew had seen Julia go to Cassie and had guessed at what was happening by the time he heard a sniffle or two above the engines. She deserved to be upset, he told himself. How she could live with herself lying like that to people just to get her man was unbelievable. Thinking back to the first night they'd met when she had thrown herself at him, Drew wondered if that had been her plan all along; that her tender heart had been an act, that she had manipulated him from the start and none of it had been real. Underneath his anger and hurt he felt an inkling of guilt for such vindictiveness and shied away from it, preferring anger to the agony of betrayal.

To distract himself, he made a quick call to Jaime to ask her to handle the insurance and the police. That the authorities would link the arson with the gang fight inside was a blessing. Insurance would most likely cover the damages, although rebuilding was the farthest thing from his mind at the moment, leaving him again with nothing to take his mind from the woman who had betrayed his trust and fears for his brother's future.

Glancing over to see his brother sleeping peacefully, Drew managed a smile. If nothing else, Brandon had himself back. Jail or no, he had his soul and that counted for a lot.

Drew stared out the window, concentrating on the patterns made by the lights from the towns below and tried to figure out where they were. Eventually his eyes grew tired and he shut off his light, sleep taking him when he figured they were somewhere over Atlanta.

Chapter 39

They all piled into a dark SUV for a thankfully short and uncomfortably quiet ride from the airport, a pall cast over all of its occupants. Brandon and Drew rode in back with Drew positioned protectively between his brother and Quan. They had spread Pritchard out unconscious across the rear bench seat. Cassie took some small delight in hearing Pritchard's body strike the back of the seat in front of him every time she stopped suddenly and hearing him roll back into his seat when she accelerated. As a result, it was a jerky ride and no one complained. Several times Cassie caught Julia giggling behind her hand.

Veritas' headquarters was in a typical office building in a suburb of Chicago, looking no different than a bank or insurance company's main offices. The exterior could even do with a facelift, Cassie thought. Nine stories of smooth white cement were broken by three dark-tinted windows running the length of the building in front and in back, ending at the top in arches over the vertical bank of windows. No external signage marked the identity of its single tenant.

When they pulled into the underground ramp and paused at the glass booth, Cassie nodded toward the back. "We've got an unconscious prisoner in custody." The attendant nodded and picked up a phone.

Their arrival at the downstairs entrance was attended by a regular employee standing outside the dark metal door wearing a black suit and pushing a wheelchair. Regulars were employed as assistants for situations such as these. They could handle prisoners the witches could not touch. It was actually more common than one might think, what with the mixing of elements and such: a water witch couldn't be expected to physically escort a fire witch without one being at a disadvantage.

"Hello Marcus," Julia greeted the six foot four muscle man with a friendly wave.

Marcus waved back with a hand as big as Cassie's head. "How was your trip, Ms. Decartes?"

Shrugging, Julia smiled at him. "They just keep getting longer, Marcus."

Chuckling, Marcus peeked inside the truck and opened the back to reach in and wrestle out the limp body to put him in the wheelchair. He stuck his head back in, jutting a square jaw at the thin man next to Quan. He knew they weren't agents; Marcus knew everybody. "Anybody else need help?" He was studying the sickly man's state. He didn't look like he could walk.

"We're fine," Drew growled.

Marcus shrugged and withdrew his head to shut the door and waited for their party to unload. Drew helped Brandon out of the truck and Cassie watched Brandon put an arm around his little brother's neck. She braced herself for what was in store and trailed several steps behind.

They rode down, not up, and Cassie realized they were going to meet with the Directors. Surprised, she flashed her wide eyes up at Marcus. "We're going *now*? What about our debriefing?"

"They have a meeting in Barcelona tomorrow afternoon and wanted this handled first," Marcus explained. "They heard he's a bad dude."

No one said a word. Risking a sideways glance, she could see Drew's jaw was clenched tight. He was preparing himself for what was to come. Cassie's throat constricted and she swallowed hard, wishing there was something she could do to change Brandon's fate.

The shiny metal doors opened to reveal a stark minimalist lobby with bland cream-colored tile and paint, casting the illusion of being in a doctor's office instead of a bunker.

The older brunette receptionist for the lower unit, Veritas' Crime and Punishment section, glanced up at the sound of their approach and smiled politely. "They're waiting for you in room two." She spoke with a Slavic accent and pointed to the equally sparse hallway behind her.

Marcus took the lead with the Cassie bringing up the rear. Pressing a button beside a shiny metal door, Marcus leaned on the handles of the wheelchair in front of him and waited calmly.

"Enter," a crisp male voice called over the intercom.

Again Marcus led the way while Julia stood aside to wave everyone inside. Drew couldn't help but feel a new empathy for cows being led to slaughter and surveyed the room as they entered, waiting for the poleax to fall. His arm tightened around his big brother's side. Brandon gave him a wan smile.

"Don't worry about me, Drew." Stopping, Brandon turned to face him. He hadn't said ten words since they'd left the club. His sudden speech halted his brother immediately. Though still lined and drawn, Brandon looked more himself than he had in a long time. "I'm serious, Drew. What I've done carries penalties and I'm ready to face them."

The ball in Drew's stomach was turning cold and heavy. "How can you say that? They're going to try you with that maniac. You two are totally different." Drew pointed to the chair, already passed them. "You didn't do what you did on purpose."

Years of hiding the guilt and shame from the accident that had changed them both forever had added years to Brandon. It had not only been his servitude to Pritchard that had worn him down. Brandon never imagined discussing that night with Drew and mention of it now brought the events back as vivid as the morning after, when he'd helped tuck his brother into the cab to go back to Tampa with their aunt and an uncertain future. He ducked his head when his voice broke. "Do you know the worst part about what I did back then?" His eyes were pink and glassy and infinitely older when they again met the dark greys of the man he'd raised as much out of obligation as out of love. "Seeing that look on your face when you figured out what'd happened. You never said anything, you probably never even admitted it to yourself, but I saw it when you stepped into the squad car that night. You were crushed, but you wanted to be so brave to impress me. It killed me to know I did that to you and I swore I would never do it again." He put his hand on his little brother's shoulder; it was bigger than his. When had he grown up? "You have the same look right now."

"That was different." Drew defended his brother against his self-recrimination. "That was an accident. You never *tried* to hurt anybody. He used you to kill those people." Angrily, he wiped at his cheek, choosing to glare at the damp fingers that came away versus seeing the serenity in his brother's eyes as he readied himself for a reckoning that had been coming for fourteen years.

"I still killed people, Drew; it's time I faced that." Brandon turned his head toward the interior of the room and spoke. "It kind of feels good to come clean after all this time. I'm ready for whatever their verdict might be." He turned back to Drew, a hint of pride in his voice. "You grew up good. Mom and Dad would have been proud." Tightening his arm around his brother's neck Brandon embraced him, separating with a squeeze of the arm and a nod before he stood straight and ran a hand over his short dark hair, sprinkled with a lot more salt than he'd had a year ago.

Left alone, Drew put his hands on his hips and breathed hard to keep himself together. The same funny feeling he'd gotten after his parents had died was creeping in from his periphery. It wasn't an earth shattering loss on the first day; it had come at odd times like when Drew was in high school and had been proud to be chosen for the speech team, he'd wanted to tell his father, and when he had to learn how to dance and wanted his mother to teach him. Both times he'd tracked around the house not sure what was missing. And both times it had been Brandon who had cheered him on and had let him step on his feet. Drew understood the need for his brother to face the charges and he even understood there had to be a penalty. Except his brother wasn't the killer Pritchard was; he shouldn't stand trial with him. Drew tried to follow Brandon in to stand beside him in support but when he tried to lift his foot, Drew couldn't move; he was stuck.

Julia came out from where she stood on the other side of the doorway and spoke softly to him, "It's time."

Embarrassed at his inability to face the inevitable, he ducked his head, keeping his eyes from coming all the way up and found his feet, moving quickly past her.

Taking a moment to settle her nerves, Julia closed her eyes and held out her hands, calling upon her family Loa once again. The deity her family prayed to was close, she could feel it. Lips moving rapidly, she said her piece and opened her eyes when her prayer was done. It was time.

Chapter 40

The room bore an uncanny resemblance to a racquetball court. Drew's head swiveled around to take it in, a feat that took little time given the small space and minimal décor.

The gray concrete cube they found themselves in had at least a fifteen foot ceiling to match the width and depth. Nothing hung on the walls and there was no furniture. Drew fought down a shudder for why that would be.

Only a white circle painted in the middle of the floor, measuring no more than three feet across, marred the unbroken smooth gray expanse. Pritchard's chair was wheeled to the edge of the circle where he was removed and Marcus propped him up one-handed. The rest of their party formed a loose line behind him, waiting.

The three Directors stood with their hands behind their backs, all three in very normal looking and exceedingly well-tailored dark suits. All three were men, one looked Italian or French maybe; his skin was olive reminding Drew of Cassie. Irritated, he pushed the parallel away. The other two also had a European look about them though their coloring was lighter and less defining.

The Italian spoke first, his accent pinpointing his origin. "Welcome back Investigators and congratulations on a job well done." He turned his eyes to the newcomers, stopping on each in turn. "Some of us have not yet met in person. My name is Alessandro, I am a Director for Veritas. My partners," he indicated them with a well-manicured, elegant hand, "Franz and Carlo have asked me to preside over the hearings today." Drew caught sight of a large ring and checked to see that each man wore one in place of wedding bands.

Remaining polite and keeping a relatively bland expression given the serious nature of his position, Alessandro turned his attentions to Pritchard who was very close to falling over at any second. "Purgo," his voice rang out in the small space, echoing off the walls.

Pritchard shook his head and rolled his shoulders, the effects of the magick and drugs being pumped into him gone with Alessandro's command. Marcus, no longer necessary, returned his hands to his sides and backed up to join the rest of the observers.

"Terrence Pritchard, you are a chameleon. It is a rare gift and one we have not seen among our ranks in over a century." He gave an approving nod.

Drew could only see the side of his face. He watched his lips curved into a smug smile. He was proud; Drew felt no pity for the man.

"Do you know what you are? Why you have these powers?"

Pritchard twisted first one way, then the other before locating where Cassie stood on the opposite end of the line from Drew. He pointed. "The girl told me I'm a witch?"

Alessandro nodded, slow and deep. Franz and Carlo remained mute, watching with interest as if they were taking mental notes, and not just of Pritchard, but of all parties present. Drew swallowed; he hadn't realized he too would be on trial.

"Indeed you are. But before Ms. Porter told you of your true nature were you aware of your powers?"

Pritchard nodded eagerly, licking his lips.

"And you used those powers for your personal gain, damaging and even taking the lives of other witches. Is that correct?"

Face going blank, Pritchard finally sensed the trap. His tongue ran slowly over his bottom lip as he carefully considered his answer. Finally he found his voice. "The glory was not for me, it was for God. I am merely a humble messenger." Alessandro fluttered his eyes and turned to the witnesses; he didn't believe a word of Pritchard's defense.

"Quan Long, I trust you have evidence for us?"

325

Bowing deeply Quan stepped up, being careful to avoid the circle on the floor. "My interaction with the subject was limited. Julia and I followed his trail to find that he had used another person to mislead us. That party was dead when we reached the end of the trail. Cassie remained behind and handled the majority of the investigation." That Quan glossed over his embarrassment at being duped gave Cassie a minor point of amusement to distract her for a second.

Alessandro's brows shot up and he turned to Cassie cutting her levity short. "Is this true, Ms. Porter? Did you take point on this mission?"

"Yes, sir."

"And what have you to report about this witch and his actions?"

Clearing her throat, Cassie stepped forward on the other side of the circle and Quan backed up. "Um, well, in my investigation I learned that Terry Pritchard preyed upon vulnerable and impressionable women to use their money and their lives for his own purposes."

"She's lying!" Pritchard interrupted, glancing from Cassie to his judges in a panic. "It was Carter's idea, not mine!"

Instantly, Drew moved and Marcus laid a hand on his arm, giving him a slow warning shake of the head when he glared at him. Drew settled back to watch the rest, unable to feel his legs. Brandon didn't flinch.

Mild mannered Alessandro showed a hint of the power that had earned him his place in the Directorship as he angrily cut the accused off with a roar, the air around them hummed with power. "You will have your chance to speak, Mr. Pritchard. Until then I would appreciate you not speaking or I will make it so that you cannot." It was brief and he had his demeanor back to bland in seconds. Turning to Cassie he prompted, "Please continue."

Fortunately Cassie had been through a hearing before and was familiar with the process. Although she had never been called upon to give testimony and found herself unnerved.

Gulping again, she continued. "He used the women by giving them a drug called Revelation." She held out the small purple bag that she'd been carting around since leaving the club. "He's laced a pharmaceutical called Citalopram with unknown chemicals designed to make witches and regulars have hallucinations and behave violently. He's been using the drug in conjunction with certain magickal practices to draw and focus the energy of those around him without regard for others. I've informed him that the sentence for his infractions is death."

The countenance of all three Directors had become increasingly dark during Cassie's testimony and when Alessandro turned his eyes to Pritchard, now fidgeting worriedly in his circle, there was no doubting his fate. "And are you familiar with his associate, Mr. Carter?" His tone was pinched with controlled fury.

"Yes, sir." Cassie wasn't confused about her moral predicament any longer. In one of those strange moments of clarity she knew what she was going to do. The life she'd been living wasn't hers. It had been constructed and steered by others with little interference from her for its entirety. The job, being an investigator, was as good as any other to her new way of thinking. Being an investigator was a fine job, helping witches to control their powers and live good lives, taking out those who threatened innocents.

Except it was all meaningless if it meant she would let someone she cared about be destroyed in the process. What about helping him? Her decision made, Cassie took a deep breath and, hoping it would be enough, answered the Director.

"I want to clarify that Brandon Carter was not Terry Pritchard's associate." She pointed to Brandon, catching sight of Drew's eyes pointed forward, refusing to look at her. Determined, she pressed on unable to look at him again. "Pritchard discovered Brandon's power and bound him to himself so that he could use him against his will in at least three murders. Pritchard also

327

attempted to use me to execute Brandon by giving me his drug. It would have worked if it weren't for Brandon's brother, Drew Carter. He both disabled Pritchard *and* restrained me without regard for his own safety. Drew's actions enabled my partners to capture Terry Pritchard."

Drew squirmed under the scrutiny he felt directed at him, keeping his eyes forward out of nervousness. Cassie's attempt to ingratiate herself with him by throwing him a compliment could not undo the damage she'd done to his brother, calling him a murderer and tying him to Pritchard as an accomplice.

Her voice yanked him from his thoughts when he heard her change of direction. "If I may sirs, I would like to add something I feel should be considered in the case of Brandon Carter."

Their gazes returned to her and Drew held his breath. Brandon's face was unreadable although his chest moved faster as his breathing accelerated. Drew squeezed Brandon's shoulder in a quick display of support. Brandon twitched his lips in thanks without turning from his judges.

"You may." Alessandro watched her closely.

"As you know from our reports Brandon Carter is another type of rare witch, he has a talent for chaos magick." She could see from the lack of surprise that they had been keeping up on their reports. "When I was sent in to learn what I could about Brandon and how he was associated with Pritchard I didn't meet him right away, I met his brother, Drew. It was through his brother that I learned the most about Brandon. As I said, I'm not sure how Terry Pritchard learned of Brandon's magickal ability, but Brandon went to great lengths to protect his brother from Pritchard's influence. When I finally did meet Brandon I found a man unable to stop himself from doing as he was compelled. Pritchard forced him to use the same magick that was responsible for his parents' deaths on the men behind the club." She pointed to a file in Franz's hand. "You've seen the details in the report I'm sure."

All three nodded. The Directors had been paying this one close attention.

"I'm convinced the death of their parents was an accident and one he has been trying to make up for since by protecting his brother from the same dangers of uncontrolled magick and manipulation by the man who would use it for his own purposes. Brandon Carter could not possibly have been in control of his own actions until now because the binding Terry Pritchard had conducted completely undermined his will. Brandon Carter's involvement in Terry Pritchard's operations has been under duress and he cannot be held responsible for the crimes committed with *his* magick under Pritchard's command."

When Cassie finished, the room was quiet. Pritchard was too frightened to move, his face even whiter than his normal pastiness. His tongue resembled a reptile, so quickly did it move in and out of his mouth. She couldn't face Drew, her skin itched where she could imagine his eyes burning into her, certainly glaring for talking about his brother's mistake. Feeling foolish for having spoken so freely, she mumbled a "thank you" and took a step backward.

"Ms. Porter," Franz called her back. His accent was strange, she'd heard once he was from Austria but it sounded mixed. "You have been very thorough in your knowledge of this assignment. I must ask, what is the nature of your relationship with Mr. Carter?"

"I only met him earlier today, sir. It has been very limited."

Franz cut her off with a wave. "Not that one, the other. The grasp you have on the subject is quite thorough and your delivery passionate." His blue eyes were severe. "In my experience, in order to gain such intimate knowledge of one's subject, one must cross certain lines." He lifted an eyebrow and his blue eyes bored into her, his suspicions clear. "I have to wonder if you have compromised your ability to remain impartial."

"Please sir," Julia came forward to stand beside Cassie. "This was her first mission acting on her own and Cassie was tested

329

personally as well as in her magickal abilities. As you are aware, her mixed nature has proven challenging and Ms. Saraferas had placed a tremendous amount of importance on this mission for her." She glanced over at the young woman who was staring straight ahead, trying not to look scared. "It was her final test and her career with Veritas was on the line. It is impossible to believe that she could have performed any better. Not only did she and Mr. Carter succeed in isolating and holding Terry Pritchard until Quan and I could assist in his capture but she also uncovered the existence of another witch in Drew Carter. It was through her personal interest in Mr. Carter that she was able to establish the nature of his power. Given what I have heard about his strengths as a witch, it would appear Cassie's diligence has intervened in time to spare us another disaster like his brother's. I stand by Cassie's performance and find no fault with it."

"Ms. Porter am I to understand that you behaved inappropriately with a person of interest during an assignment?" Alessandro resumed control of the trial, his expression stern.

Drew watched the Directors turn on Cassie and in spite of his anger, felt an urge to speak up. He'd had no idea their relationship would have jeopardized her career, she'd told him it was her choice. He remembered the last time they'd been together when he'd come on so strong and felt guilty for having brought her to this. Worse yet was the sinking feeling that she was sacrificing herself for him, not Brandon. He wasn't on trial and she didn't need to do that for him.

"Please sirs." Drew stepped up to the other side of Pritchard, carefully avoiding the circle as had the others. "If we want to place blame anywhere, I'm due my share." He rushed on, forcing his eyes to meet each of theirs, intimidating as they were. He could feel the power coming from each man, consciously avoiding the urge to layer his words with his influence. "It's my fault Brandon went to Terry Pritchard in the first place and I crossed the line with Cassie, not the other way around."

"It wasn't your fault, Drew." Brandon joined in.

Needing to give his brother the absolution he wouldn't accept, Drew continued explaining himself to the Directors ignoring his brother's interference. "I went to the police and I found the report on our parents' death when I was eighteen. I thought I could handle it but I couldn't. Brandon knew it and tried to convince me not to; I did it anyway. That was when I went off the rails."

"How can you be at fault for being upset at finding out that your brother killed your parents?" Brandon interrupted again, joining his brother in his agitation. "I was too busy working angles to be there for you. I did what I had to do to get you back before I lost you for good."

Drew faced his brother. "At what cost, Bran? You made a deal with the devil because I was chicken shit. You can't take the blame for everything I've ever done wrong because of one mistake."

A throat cleared behind him spinning Drew back around to face an irritated Alessandro and company.

Alessandro addressed the group as a whole. "We are prepared to carry out the sentence on Mr. Pritchard immediately. As for Mr. Brandon Carter, we will request that you remain in Veritas custody while we consider your case." There was a minor break in his mild expression when he spoke to the young agent. "Cassandra Porter, you are suspended until further notice. You are excused. Marcus, if you would call for a crew we will be done here in a moment."

"Yes, sirs," were mumbled and the investigators ushered Drew and Brandon from the room with Marcus standing guard at the door while Pritchard remained behind, trapped by invisible bonds. He was powerless to step outside the circle, so strong was the magick that had been used to draw it. Julia led their troop back to the elevator while Quan hung back with Cassie.

"You have done well, Cassie." He afforded her a rare compliment. "It took great courage to do what you did for Brandon. You have given him a chance to be spared."

She snorted. "We'll see. I think all I did was throw myself under the bus."

"Is your conscience clear?"

Stopping to regard her partner, Cassie pondered the question. He hit it on the head. If she hadn't given the Directors the additional testimony she would have always wondered if she could have saved Brandon and wished she could have explained herself to Drew. She had done both. "Yes, it is."

He gave a satisfied grunt and began walking again, Cassie trailing a few feet behind for some much needed privacy.

The elevator brought them back up past the parking ramp into the lobby. With the dark marble floors and slip mats it could have been any business, not one of the only four such places in the world owned by Veritas and responsible for the policing and educating of witches worldwide.

"Is this where the Academy is too?" Drew asked of no one in particular.

"No, but it isn't far from here," Julia replied cryptically. "Only those who are invited get to know its exact location."

"It did not used to be that way," Quan added. "Not until several generations ago when a mixed blood, angry that he had been denied, attacked leaving many dead and the Academy closed for years until it could be rebuilt and sufficient protection spells put in place."

Drew waited, wondering what would happen next. His eyes ignored his refusal to look at Cassie; they seemed to be drawn to her, finding her every time he would force himself to look away.

Julia and Cassie were standing off to the side, he could see that she was pale and the lines around her eyes had grown more pronounced giving away the exhaustion hidden by her straight shoulders. He'd seen her like that before and knew she was putting on an act. The knife in his heart twisted and as much as he wanted to, he couldn't consider thanking her for doing what she had for Brandon until he knew that his brother was safe.

A final hug from Julia, a wave to Quan, and a guarded glance at himself, and Cassie walked out the front doors to a parking lot. Minutes later, he saw a small yellow Volkswagen pull out and drive away, not that he was looking.

"Well," Julia said from right beside him; he hadn't seen her approach. "I sure hope that's not the last we see of young Miss Cassie Porter. It'd be a damned shame to lose somebody that special." She sighed. "Quan, could you stay?" She indicated the Carters with a long finger wagging between the two. "I'll get started on the paperwork."

Quan nodded that he would and Julia dabbed at an eye as she waited for the elevator to take her up to her office.

The wait was short. Only a few minutes had passed when an average sort of woman dressed in a gray suit stepped out of the elevator and asked them to come with her. At the curb, a white Suburban waited with a bald driver in a dark suit.

Their drive was brief, taking them to an adjoining suburban neighborhood where they pulled into an attached garage and entered the two story red Colonial with black shutters and white pillars out front. The interior was clean and lightly furnished. Their escort's heels clattered hollowly on the shining hardwood. Sunlight poured in through the ample windows and gauzy draperies, the heavier tan curtains pulled back for the daylight. Drew did not miss the shadows from the bars on the windows he assumed were there for reasons other than theft prevention.

"Can I get you anything?" their female escort, or guard depending how you wanted to look at it, asked them.

Brandon waved them off. "I think I'd just like to lay down."

The woman stepped back, allowing her male counterpart to escort Brandon upstairs.

"I'd like to do the same." Drew didn't want to have to talk to anyone while his brain was running off in a million different directions.

"Right, follow me." She walked past him and led him up the white painted staircase, pointing to the left at a closed door. When they reached the top, the bald man walked past them to retreat downstairs. "We have clothing in various sizes in the closet if you'd like to freshen up." Walking ahead, she swung the door open and pointed toward another door at the far end. "Each room is a self-contained suite with a private bath; you should have everything you need. Feel free to call if you need something to eat."

Unspoken meaning: you don't need to leave here for anything.

Glancing down, he saw the soot on his clothes and guessed he didn't smell any better than he looked. "Thank you."

Without responding, she backed out of the room and closed the door, leaving Drew to his thoughts.

Chapter 41

Cassie went home and slept for fifteen hours, a personal record. When she woke up she took a hot shower and sat down to the first real meal she'd had since the Indian food at Drew's. Thinking of him hurt but it was a welcome pain. Their time together had been good, even if it had been tainted by her deceit. In the end, as with her blocked magick, the fault had been hers alone. Cassie swore to herself she would be more forthcoming in the future.

Somewhere between her shower and grilled cheese and soup, Cassie thought of Grandmother's vision and sat back, crossing her arms with a "huh." Grandmother had been prophetic as usual, from Drew and Cassie as a dog and sparrow to the flood of events that had confused things. Pritchard was the man, not Drew, blinding her with drugs. She smiled to herself, realizing that it had been the dog, or Drew rather she thought with a smirk, who had pulled her from the man's pocket. They had nearly come out of it all right, but in the end the flood had proved to be too much. Pushing away her meal, which had suddenly lost its flavor, Cassie went to visit the only friend she had left who would listen without judging.

Bunny had been happy to see her, squealing and popcorning all over her cage demanding to be picked up and snuggled. They sat down to share some carrots and watch a documentary on sea life neither one was interested in when a knock at her front door made her jump. Living in a secured entry apartment building limited how many people came to her door, as did her secluded lifestyle. It had to be the neighbor girl, Janelle, she was due to stop by and pick up a check for taking care of Bunny while Cassie was gone.

Guinea pig in hand, she opened the door smiling. "Hey Jan..." The greeting died on her lips as did the smile.

"Hi Cassie." Drew stood at her door. "I thought it might be best if I surprised you." He held up a white bag with the green outline of the Taj Mahal on it. "I brought Indian." Bunny's excited squeak from Cassie's surprised squeeze drew an interested glance from him.

Not knowing what else to do, Cassie stepped back to let Drew in. He stopped just inside the door and let her take the bag, following her inside where she set it on the table.

In the awkward silence Cassie walked around the table and put Bunny back in her cage, which she objected to loudly. "How did you get in here?" She avoided his eyes.

He replied with a self-conscious shrug, "I talked my way in."

A nervous giggle escaped her lips before she caught it. "Be careful, now that you know you can do that you're going to be held accountable." Her smile wavered when she met his eyes and mistook his stormy expression. "Oh Gods, Drew I'm so sorry. I tried to sway them, I did. They take death, even accidental ones, very seriously."

Her sincerity broke the hold Drew's uncertainty had over him and he closed the distance, covering the ground in two long strides. Hesitant, he took hold of her hand. "No, Cassie you did help. The Directors gave him a probationary enrollment at the Academy. He's okay for now."

Impulsively Cassie threw her arms around him and hugged him tight. Drew returned the embrace, running a hand over her shining black hair. Closing his eyes he inhaled, taking in the scent of her.

Pulling away awkwardly, Cassie blinked up at him. "He's on probation?"

Drew's arms fell to his sides. "They said he'd shown an ability to restrain himself when he wasn't being controlled. An education on how to protect himself from letting it happen again will give them a chance to watch him over time and make a better judgment based on character."

Cassie sniffed. "Oh, well that's great." Taking a few steps back she put a more comfortable distance between them, it was hard being so close. "Thanks for coming to tell me, it was nice of you."

"I wanted to thank you in person for what you did." He fidgeted with the zipper on the black running jacket he'd borrowed from the safe house. Chicago was much colder than Florida in March and he'd wanted more than the lightweight garment. Unfortunately, it was all they had and a delay to stop at a store had been out of the question. As soon as Brandon had gotten the call from Julia and they had been released from custody, Drew had hopped in a cab and come straight here in the borrowed sweatpants and tshirt. At least he'd left Florida in his black trainers so he didn't look like a complete goob.

She waved off his undeserved gratitude. "I had to tell them about what kind of person Brandon is, they couldn't make a fair decision without knowing that."

"You took my word for what kind of person he is, Cassie. You risked everything for me." His assumption was confirmed when her head came up at that. "I know you had to be honest about the case to the Directors because it was your job, just like you couldn't tell me anything or I would have taken Brandon and run." He swallowed. "I know now that if I had, he would have died." Drew cleared his throat. "You went beyond what you had to do and I know that was for me." Drew took a tentative step. "I'm here to see if there's a chance things aren't too messed up between us."

Cassie studied Drew, the despair she saw in his dark gray eyes revealing not grief for his brother, but for her. She put her hand to her mouth and felt her eyes getting ready to go again; she'd been an emotional wreck since she'd left Florida and felt her face grow hot at her failure to keep her emotions in check in front of him. "How can we when neither of us has a job? I don't even know where I'm going to live." She motioned to the room around her. "Even my apartment belongs to the company."

337

Grinning that her concerns were material, Drew put his hands in his pockets to keep from reaching for her. The next move had to be hers or she wouldn't know if it was her choice or him behind it. "Dr. Jones reported in last night and she had my bag. Between that and the insurance from the club I can get us by until we figure things out."

"That's kind of you but I can't be beholden to you, Drew." Cassie put her hands in her pockets, worried that if she touched him now she would never let go.

"Fine, then pay me back when you're back on your feet," Drew argued stubbornly. He felt her slipping and had to hold on.

Cassie felt his influence tickle up her arm, raising gooseflesh in its wake, and she was tempted to let it draw her in. However, as she was preparing to push him out of her head, she felt him withdraw. He wanted her response to be honest and not his doing.

"What about your training?" She chose a subject less personal. "You're getting better but there's a lot to learn and not just about your magick. There's a whole other reality out there."

Shifting awkwardly and running a hand through his hair at being caught, Drew ducked his head. "I've earned myself a place at the Academy as well. Apparently Quan offered to take me under his wing when I'm done."

"Quan?" Cassie made no effort to hide her shock. "He never offers to take *anybody*. They had to practically ram me down his throat."

He shrugged. "I guess his last experience changed his mind about new recruits."

Cassie flushed again. Her phone buzzed on the table; it was Anna. Holding up a finger, she answered, "Hello Anna."

"Cassie, glad I caught you. I've just gotten out of a meeting with the Directors, it seems you made quite an impression on them."

Heart in her throat, she swallowed and heard the word come out choked. "Great."

"You've been reinstated, effective immediately." Anna went on, ignoring Cassie's broken response. "We will expect you Monday morning, starting with a thorough run through of your duties as a fully licensed investigator. I would assume that is enough time to get your things in order and return ready to work?"

"Yes ma'am."

Cassie hung up and set the phone back on the table. Studying the face of the man she'd fallen for, she felt her insides knotting up. "Does your offer extend to an investigator or would that be a problem?" Cassie worried he wouldn't want her if she wasn't fired, he'd said before he wasn't big on women who worked at dangerous jobs. "It's a lot of travel but there's usually a week or at least a few days in between assignments when I'm home, and not everyone we go after is as bad as Pritchard."

Drew didn't care to listen to the rest, he didn't need to. When he saw the sparkle back in her eyes he knew she'd gotten back her livelihood and with it, her pride. His mouth on hers cut off any further attempts by her to argue him out of wanting to be with her.

When finally he let her breath again, Drew stroked the side of her face. "It looks like I'm moving to Chicago."

Unable to keep from smiling like a fool, Cassie ran a hand down his chest and teased, "You're going to need a better jacket."

End

Watch for the further adventures of Veritas agents in the next installment of The Veritas Chronicles *due out* **Summer 2013**

www.ingramcontent.com/pod-product-compliance
Lightning Source LLC
Chambersburg PA
CBHW021444240626
47153CB00001B/290